Forever

THE TRELAWNEYS OF WILLIAMSBURG

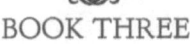

BOOK THREE

ANNE MEREDITH

For Judy Motley

And, as always …
with love …
for Joshua

Notes from the Author

This novel is the third in *The Trelawneys of Williamsburg* series. There is a complex revenge murder mystery that crosses three centuries and all of the books, and it is not recommended this book be read independently. Consider first reading *Tender* and *Immortal* before beginning *Forever*. Each book contains plot developments that put in motion events of the next book, as well as revealing events that occurred in previous books. Reading the books out of order will not be the optimum reading experience.

Those who do not remember the past are condemned to repeat it. — George Santayana

We have to do with the past only as we can make it useful to the future. — Frederick Douglass

Prologue

"Did you know I was born free? Grew up like any other little girl in Saint-Domingue, the child of a freedman and woman. *Affranchi*, they called us. Not a nice name. I remember those island breezes, mangoes as big as my head. And then I was taken as a girl by one of my own and sold to a slave trader. We got on a big ship with guns. I never saw my family again.

"I fought tooth and nail against that seaman trying to manage me. I think it was that fight that Gideon first loved about me. He couldn't understand the Creole I spoke. Another man had to take over—Gideon told the captain he couldn't hurt me. The journey to Virginia had barely begun before he rescued me. Told the captain he'd pay a fair price for my freedom. He always said, best bargain he ever made."

She smiled at the memory.

"I know what slavery feels like. And I know what redemption feels like. My Gideon showed me firsthand, centuries ago. He saved me and gave me a new life."

Now, she lay dying.

A much younger woman sat on the edge of the nursing home bed, holding her thin, gnarled hand and trying not to look at the clock on the wall. Her own time here drew short.

But she had imagined this woman many times over her life, and she was loathe to leave her now. She had heard so much about her—and yet not nearly enough.

The most beautiful woman I'd ever known.

Like a goddess.

Well, she looked like you, my dear.

The last description, that of Papa, was her favorite. For even at this woman's advanced age, the memory of the serene beauty of her youth shone clearly in the face that reflected her indomitable spirit. Sarita Juste Miller was at peace, ready to go home to her Gideon.

The young woman looked at the next bed. Her grandfather, Gideon, lay there—his upturned hand outstretched toward Sarita's, his eyes gazing sightless toward her.

Sarita lay on her worn, flat pillow in the small room, and Juliana considered idly how many events and choices she would have to change, to allow her grandparents to die with dignity. Two narrow hospital beds, two vinyl chairs for visitors, a rickety lamp table between the beds—the lamp dark now—and an old photograph in a frame. No other reminders of who these people had been, or how they'd lived their lives, lingered in the room. Only the stale smell.

In the end, she could do nothing to change it.

"Don't look at me that way, child. I am here at my own choosing. Gideon!" Sarita's eyes widened suddenly, and she reached out for her husband's hand with a surge of strength. She rested her hand on his, understanding. "He's gone ahead. He always had to open the door for me."

Her grandparents had lived a life, and would die a death, that in fact men and women dreamed of—sharing a love that made them one, without ever having to bear losing each other.

"My darling," she said, a smile lighting her face, "you must take care, as Ruth did. You are in danger."

Juliana patted her hand.

"There are men—evil men—trying to hurt our family. They've tried to hurt us for so long. Just for pure hatred."

2

Along with love and laughter, Sarita Juste Miller had known hatred and had been its target. A native of Saint-Domingue and the daughter of former slaves from West Africa, she had dared to marry a white man. She had escaped the slavery of the 18th century only to land in the Jim Crow era of 1953 with all its baggage of three centuries.

The woman's breath grew shallow, and Juliana buzzed for the nurse. The nurse arrived, noticing Gideon Miller. She patted his shoulder lightly as she checked for a pulse, then ran her palm down over his eyes, closing them.

After checking Sarita's pulse, she shook her head gently and whispered in Juliana's ear. "Stay as long as you like, but you'll want to say your goodbyes now."

"But ..."

With another shake of the head, the nurse left.

"Grandmother—"

"No, dear. Listen to me. Leave this time. Ask Ruth Freeman. They'll try to kill you, too. Hug your father close when you see him—and please don't forget to tell him how I loved him. And ... so proud of him. You can't begin to guess the adventures he's had in his young life, the good he's done."

Ruth *Freeman*. She almost missed the rest of her words. Sarita spoke of the matron who lived at Rosalie.

And she went on, then: "The men ... wanted to kill your father. Even when he was only a small boy."

She struggled for breath, as if to say more. And then her breath left her. She stared over Juliana's shoulder as a half smile came to her face, and the girl cried out for the nurse.

This time, after the nurse tended to her patient, she asked Juliana to leave. "We'll be in touch with the family."

Tears closed her throat at the finality of it. She had hoped with this journey—her last trip through the labyrinth, she swore to herself—that she would gain wisdom to guide her in her rudderless existence, her voyage through time.

She had learned nothing. She'd already known beforehand that her grandparents shared a deathless, timeless love. They

3

had died within minutes of one another, bound by that love. Again her gaze moved to Gideon, and then caught on the photograph on the lamp table.

She reached out to grasp the photograph, drawing it near. Only then did she see its subject was three couples: her grandparents a few years back, not quite so frail, stood on the left. A younger couple, perhaps in their thirties, stood on the right; and, between the two couples, another young couple. The young women of each couple—both striking beauties—stood beside each other, with their men on the outside.

Gideon wore Navy Full Dress Whites, contemporary to this era. Beside him stood Sarita in a dark golden gown.

The young man on the other end also wore a uniform – that of a police captain. He seemed awfully young to wear the gold bars. Something about him made her smile. He had an easy, relaxed grin, and laughter lurked in his light brown eyes.

The woman beside him, a tall, stunning beauty, held a tiny baby in her arms, sleeping happily in a pink blanket. Just above the baby, on the woman's dress, she spotted a stick-on nametag: *Helen*.

In the center of the photograph stood the other young couple, the woman also holding an infant in a pink blanket; the man, also in Dress Whites. Looking closely, she thought he might be a few years older than his wife and the other couple.

Body language told her that the two young couples were close friends. Each couple turned instinctively toward the other. The women, in the middle, bent their heads toward one another and looped their free arms around each other's waists. The babies between them, their tiny booties touching, formed an almost perfect heart—half white, half black.

The police captain and his wife were black; their friends, white. Gideon and Sarita, on the left side of the photograph, a striking harmony of the two.

The couple in the middle wore no nametags, no clues at all to their identity. He might be a few years older than his wife. Did the woman have a small mole near the corner of her eye?

Then she noticed a subtle detail, almost obscured by the dramatic photograph of the white and black women who clearly loved each other.

Sarita, standing to the right of the young Naval officer, had her arm twisted possessively around his free arm, and he laid a reassuring hand on her arm, even as he rested his other hand on his wife's waist, just behind the baby.

Only one woman would dare to cling so possessively to a man while he held another woman: his mother.

Her heartbeat tripled. Could this man be Robert Miller—a Naval officer, and her own father? The man who had deserted her, left her as an orphan in the eighteenth century, was a man defending freedom?

Disturbing emotions warred within her: anger, yearning, fear, and, as always, confusion. *Why?* It always came back to that. Why had her parents deserted her in another time?

Faint suspicion came to her. What if it weren't true?

Two attendants interrupted her thoughts, arriving with a stretcher at the door to the room. She slipped the framed photograph into her carpetbag and left the room. She had no assurance the photograph would make the return trip safely— in fact, each time she'd tried to carry back contraband before, it had remained behind. Through experimentation, she'd learned that the artifact would be returned to its rightful place in time.

But she had to try.

Thoughts of her grandmother filled Juliana's mind, even as she tried to focus. She had to get back to the labyrinth—now.

She hadn't said goodbye to her, hadn't told her of the many times she'd thought of her over her lifetime. She hadn't thanked her for enduring the cruelty, the indignity, she had endured, even as an old woman, that Juliana might be born into freedom. Worse, she hadn't asked her what she knew of the labyrinth—of traveling across time.

As she walked down the long hall toward the exit, she noticed a disheveled man shuffling along toward her, cradling a paper bag worn soft with overuse. He stared at a fixed spot in front of him as if something were there that only he could see, mumbling angrily under his breath at the invisible foe. His wild black hair and beard were unkempt, his eyes dark and feral.

Juliana saw underneath his raw ferocity a rugged handsomeness, but she felt only pity. He was likely a homeless man who'd wandered into the facility seeking shelter. Even an inmate of this place would surely not suffer such filth.

One hand was tucked inside the bag, guarding his pathetic treasures, and her compassion was stirred.

Then his eyes narrowed, focusing on her face—on her cheekbone, and the small, crescent shaped scar there. She grew wary at his interest.

"You look like her," he said, suddenly lucid, his voice low—as if he rarely spoke except to himself.

She was perplexed—like who? Sarita, perhaps; but how did he know her? Then she looked closer—on his cheekbone, in the same place as the scar on her own cheek, he bore the tattoo of a crescent moon.

In a sure motion, he withdrew his hand from the bag and raised a pistol toward her.

She stood frozen in shock, and a sudden, loud crack rang out—a gunshot, shattering the clock on the wall behind her.

The shards of glass and metal falling about her galvanized her, and she removed her flintlock pistol from her carpetbag and raised it at him.

Another man entered the hall—slender and calm, his dark hair graying at the temples, his eyes an icy blue. He held up his arm and spoke in a low drawl. "Please don't shoot him. He's my brother, and he's off his meds. Jack, give me the gun."

Juliana was a crack shot, and ready to defend herself. Who were these men? The face of the second, elegant man gave away nothing, but the desperation in his voice moved her.

He loved this lunatic.

"Leave me alone, Shep." The man—Jack—slowly raised his trembling hand, pointing the pistol at his own head. "So tired of all the noise, all the drugs."

In a moment, she lifted her arm and fired. The ball landed where she'd aimed, knocking the handgun out of his grasp. She kicked it away, toward the other man, who stooped to grab it.

For only a brief moment, she was given pause at what she'd done, letting this troubled man live. Could she have changed anything of importance in the future? It was the first time she'd done anything that might leave footprints. At first, it was instinctive—saving a person's life *had* to be good, didn't it?

Just behind the other man, Shep, a security guard arrived, his own pistol drawn.

"Put the gun down!" he shouted at her. "Get on the floor."

"I'm afraid I can't do that," she said, her voice low, soothing, as she backed toward the door. "I only stopped him from hurting himself."

The security guard—no older than Juliana—waited, at a loss, puzzled by her antique firearm. She wondered if he understood that it required a laborious reloading, and when she placed it in her carpetbag, he leapt at her.

She landed a well-placed kick, knocking him to the floor, then wrenched herself free and pushed through the emergency exit. The door swung open, sounding an alarm.

She raced into the night. The guard recovered and chased after her, close behind. She had but ten minutes to get back— and a quarter-hour walk.

She easily outdistanced the guard, crossing a busy street in front of a bus. By the time the bus had passed, she had disappeared into the crowd in the shopping center parking lot.

She hurried through the shopping center and out the other side, and then into the woods that surrounded Stonefield. Running as she hadn't since she was a child, she soon emerged into a clearing near the James River. The night air grew cooler.

She climbed the hill, and in the glow of the full moon over the land, she saw that the home was still deserted—its inhabitants not yet returned. She hesitated, her heart swelling with yearning for her family. She wondered who would live in this house now, two centuries after she grew up there, virtually alone. She simply could not spare a moment to investigate, even were she so tempted to disregard the rules of this particular road.

"Juliana?!"

Before she thought to do otherwise, she stopped, gasping for breath, and looked toward the men. Two men, one with blond hair, the other salt-and-pepper, and yet strikingly similar. She didn't know them—she couldn't have, in this time, could she?—but they didn't seem to be a threat. He'd said her name in disbelief—as if he thought her presence here impossible. And they had no idea the pistol she retrieved from her bag was no longer loaded.

The blond looked at his companion. "I told you 'twas her. 'Nay! She's but one of our own descendants!' Dolt."

The older man sent the other a glowering gaze.

The blond spoke with the inflection of her own time, but wore the same jeans and shirt as any other man of *this* era.

Raising the pistol, she called, "Who are you?"

Both men raised their hands, and the older man spoke. "We mean you no harm. We've met, when we visited with Marley, nearly six years ago. Well, no, that's not right. You two met the day of your grandmother's confession, and—"

"My grandmother just died in this very place. And I don't know any Marley."

"No, your other grandmother—"

The blond shoved him. "It hasn't happened yet, in her life."

Again, the men exchanged a look of realization, and the blond went on. "She's here in the twentieth century from a different point in time, a ... er, traveler herself."

Suspicion filled her at his pinpointing the truth. "I've never met my other grandmother. She lives in another land. If you'll excuse me. I cannot tarry."

"No. Please. Perhaps we can help one another. We're looking for two men who may live in this neighborhood."

She simply didn't have the time. Her heartbeat would soon be echoing in the labyrinth.

Without further apology, she rushed into the house. Inside the darkened, silent home, she stopped, her gaze taking it all in for only a moment or two. Were the people here descendants of hers? She couldn't imagine how she would even meet a husband, living alone as she continued to do. She so longed to walk through the house, lingering over photographs of people she would never know, knickknacks soon to be forgotten for all time, learning about whoever lived there.

She dared not.

In twenty years she had not, nor would she now. She had tested the limits of her guardians' patience, but here she was filled with enough healthy fear to resist the temptation. Curiosity here could mean her own doom.

No impact whatsoever. The creed of her life, learned at her uncle's knee. At times it made for an empty existence. The shadow of grief awakened within her, and she walked to the aged, worn window seat, closed the drape, pressed the latch to lift the seat, and climbed down into the narrow stairwell below.

Only then did she think again of the men she'd met just now. They knew her, but she didn't know them. At last she understood. They had first met at a different plot point on their intersecting timelines. But they both had worn modern clothing, so how could they have met her later in life?

She's here in the twentieth century—a traveler herself.

They were time travelers.

Juliana was a time traveler of great expanse and sophistication. With the labyrinth, she had access to an endless resource for such idle tourism—as all people would, still farther into the future. In the eighteenth century, it would live only in the labyrinth.

Her having met these men on a trip to the future would have explained it. Although she was widely traveled, she still vividly remembered all the people she'd ever met during her many journeys. Those men, she simply did not know.

At that moment she heard the back door open—the door she'd entered through.

Someone had followed her into her home—and in either case, she had no time to spare for dealing with them.

She closed and latched the window seat and skipped down the long, winding staircase. How she'd marveled, the first time she'd seen the vast labyrinth that lay deep beneath Stonefield— another world, its narrow stone paths stretching forward and backward endlessly into eternity. She'd been a child of only eight then, overwhelmed with wonder. It had seemed an infinite cavern. Indeed, once, when she ventured down a few years later, she counted the steps that wound endlessly down.

There were nearly seven hundred steps on the staircase.

She had learned so early in life to race down these shallow steps, taking up to half a dozen in a single, light-footed leap, that now she could descend in just a couple of minutes.

When she emerged from the staircase into the labyrinth, she looked up, into the dark, celestial expanse above, as inky blue-black as a moonless night, at any hour of the day. She was well underground now, and yet looking up at the labyrinth sky was as dramatic as looking into the night sky in the darkest desert. It was always night in the labyrinth. But now, she had traveled into that other dimension, a changing platform that would take her to any time throughout history.

She was astonished as always at the stars winking in the underground night sky of the labyrinth. An endless place that, no matter how far she walked into it, never ceased, each bright spot representing galaxies, representing stars.

Representing human lives, she understood now. Lives, clustered together into families, communities, countries, eras, worlds, universes, and beyond.

Footsteps thundered overhead, scattering her thoughts. She could still hear Stonefield of the twentieth century—she was still in danger of being lost for all time. She would visit this place again, but for now, she hurried. Even though it was unlikely anyone would think to open the window seat, it wasn't impossible. After all, she had done so herself as an inquisitive eight year old.

Yet she stopped, as she always did, to find the cluster of stars she knew so well in the labyrinth sky—those stars representing her family.

Turmoil radiated in the dull bronze cast of the stars, unlike the jeweled, diamantine shine in other stars. Here and there another community showed similar gray or bronze dullness—reflecting unrest, disruption in the family. The longer she looked, the more trouble she saw; so many families suffering.

Her visit to her grandparents' deathbed had changed nothing. It was her directive and her lot in life; in the end, the labyrinth sky was but a reminder of that.

The cluster shone brightly white—all suffering gone. Excitement thrilled her. Had she—and the stars returned to their dull gray, and her shoulders sank as she reached the booth where she'd stowed her clothing. Nothing had changed.

She pressed the obsidian stone and a hollow opened, a small chamber lit with a pale blue, glowing light. There hung her clothing, and she quickly removed the jeans and button-down blue shirt she'd worn to the year 1992, hanging them in their enclosure. She placed the talisman that had hung around her neck in its jeweled case and locked it away, closing the stone enclosure that concealed it.

She hastily donned her own clothing, then noticed the thatched red blots marring the other clothing—warning her that her own body had left its humanity behind. Not blood, merely a spiritual marker visible only in the labyrinth. But indeed it still required blotting out.

She pressed the button on the wall beside the clothing and drew back her hand. A nearly silent buzz, and a single moment later, her DNA had been cleansed from the clothing, washing away all traces of the year 1775, restoring it to its proper place in time. It was as if she'd never arrived there—except for the memories she'd taken with her.

A successful time travel.

She closed the cavity where the jeans and blouse hung and checked again to make sure everything was in its place. This step was the most critical in the time-travel process. An oversight could cause havoc in her future—or in that of another who might someday use an artifact she had used.

She removed her pistol to her own roomy pocket. She had learned that the period clothing didn't in fact matter for the short trips—but it certainly helped calm down strangers to arrive clothed. Although the clothing changes always took a few minutes, they simplified everything, avoided distractions, and in the end saved time. Occasionally, she'd realized to her dismay, anachronistic clothing did not migrate smoothly. It was unbecoming to arrive naked at one's destination.

She looked again at the inventory list of the small enclosure. *Women's clothing, men's clothing, 1990s. Necklace belonging to Sarita Juste Miller, mother of Robert Miller, expiring May 7, 1992.*

And she noticed the link to the labyrinth's central nervous system, her drifting gaze catching an occasional event in the countless moments scrolling there. *On this day in history ... Gideon and Sarita Miller die (1992) ... Brezhnev becomes president of the USSR (1960) ... Germany surrenders to the Allies (1945) ... Grant leaves the Wilderness for Spotsylvania (1864) ... Robert Browning is born (1812) ... George Washington attends his inaugural ball (1789) ... Rashall Adams falls in love with Juliana Miller ...*

She gasped at the sight of her own name there, for the first time in her life. She quickly turned off the display, hiding the mysteries of *This Day in History*. She was allowed to learn nothing about her own future.

She trembled in fear as she hastily twisted up her hair and pinned it at the back of her head. She had hoped to visit a moment in her father's life. When scanning the index of time artifacts earlier, she'd been in a hurry to get back before her guardians returned from their trip to Richmond, and had only noticed the date and *Robert Miller.*

Not for a second had she intended to see any details of her own life. Confusion filled her. She knew no one named Rashall Adams—how could he fall in love with her? Ah—perhaps another Juliana Miller.

"Quite sloppy indeed."

"I'm so very disappointed."

Dread stole down her spine at the voices of her guardians, standing behind her, and she turned. They must have come in through the root cellar.

The old man and woman who had raised her gazed at her without expression. How many times they had warned her to take care in her travels, never to encounter those of her own family in other times.

"Do you want to become like us, frozen in time at the most painful part of your life?"

It wasn't the first time they had warned her of the worst fate possible for those who persisted in dabbling in their own past: the fate that they themselves had suffered. She dared not ask them who Rashall Adams was. They weren't scolding her about noticing the display—they were angry about her visiting Sarita Miller. They knew nothing about how much she had wished to change their deaths, to give them a bit more dignity—nor that she never would have tried. It had taken her only a moment to understand that the circumstances of their deaths were very likely exactly what they would have chosen. It was never wise to guess the motives of another without knowing their circumstances.

She turned away from them and stored the carpetbag, that neutralizing talisman that had both allowed her antique pistol in the trip to 1992 and that returned her to this time.

She recalled her beloved guardian's slack-jawed gape the first time he had realized she'd discovered his secret of time travel. Uncle Malcolm, the softer-hearted of the two, had stared at her speechlessly when he saw her there. So long ago, now—and how many astounding sights she had seen since then, days gone by, days yet to come.

And yet, her only interest had been in learning more about her own father and mother, and why they had loved her so little they'd left her on her guardians' doorstep.

It had taken her all these years to learn very little indeed.

"Had you ever told me more about my parents than their names, perhaps I would have known the times to avoid. Perhaps my curiosity may have been sated instead," she muttered. "Robert and Cassie Miller—names as common as a head cold. I only want to meet them. To ask them *why*."

For years, during those rare times when she'd left Stonefield to visit Papa Hastings, the merry old man she loved at Rosalie, she asked everyone she met if they knew anyone named Miller. No one ever had—at least, not her parents. They had utterly forsaken her, vanished as if into thin air.

She had learned so much since she first began traveling in time, but not about her family.

She had learned of Grey Trelawney, for whom Papa had once worked. The slave-trader had died so many years ago in a terrible fire, no doubt a retribution for a soul beyond redemption. And she had visited him on his ship, the *Swallow*, and watched him only a few minutes as he tossed sleepless in his bed. She had traveled to find out what made him do what he did, but she soon saw that he had no regard for his trading—or himself.

Grey Trelawney.

A shiver of fear went over her as she recalled the salt-and-pepper haired man she'd met a few minutes ago. She hadn't recognized him at first, dressed in modern clothing as he'd been. *He* was Grey Trelawney. What had he been doing in the future—250 years after he'd died?

Now it was the practical Aunt Mary who spoke, her face filled with uncharacteristic passion. "Let me warn you, child— it will be no more pleasurable to be frozen in your youth and beauty than it would to be frozen in your dotage and weakness, as we were. Continue as you have done today, and you will be removed from time entirely, living out the rest of eternity and watching those you love most living. Loving. There are worse things than growing old and dying, Juliana."

Her merry uncle's face, normally animated with joviality, sagged with the weight of centuries of time he'd known as he spoke. "Trust us. We know firsthand. You cannot change the past. Why do you think we warn you so? *We both tried.*"

"I only want to know why!" she screamed. "Why did they leave me? I was but a babe, abandoned and bereft and alone."

Malcolm stared at her, compassion lighting his eyes. At length, he said, "You were not alone, my darling."

"No, Malcolm."

"She deserves to know the truth."

"And she will, soon enough. She must learn to live her true life, rather than continue this glamourous lifestyle, jet-setting about eternity. It is not our place to tell her."

"Was it our place to conceal it from her?" Malcolm retorted.

Aunt Mary ignored that. "Juliana, you think traveling about in time has no consequence because you return to the exact moment you left—but that isn't true. Each hour you spend traveling is exacted from your real life. Consider how much you've traveled over your life, and your life is shortened by that amount of time."

She was brought up short at that.

"But worse than that—the man you spared today. Can you begin to guess who he was?"

She shook her head mutely.

"You shall learn today. Remember the name Jack Manning, for that's who you saved. Now go. Leave here, now."

She turned away from her guardians with a sigh, weary of their stoic refusal to tell her anything about her childhood. Yet another trip to yet another time with yet another failure, with no more understanding of her parents. When she glanced back, both old people—no older now than her first memory of them—were gone. As always. Jet-setting, themselves, about eternity.

For a moment, she recalled her aunt's warning—had she cut her own natural life here short, spending it in times that weren't her own? And yet, had any of it mattered? She'd come not a moment closer to learning anything about her parents.

She forced the reminder of her many failures out of her mind and set the carpetbag in its storage place. This carpetbag had been woven and sewn in this time, and finished on this day, Sunday, November 26, 1775.

But just as she reached for the button to cleanse the bag of any remnants of 1992, she recalled the purloined photograph. She wrenched open the door, withdrew the bag, and pulled out the photograph.

Quickly she thrust it into her pocket, shoved the carpetbag back into its enclosure, then pressed the button to cleanse it. Her breath caught. How close she'd come to eradicating this small piece of her past—so far in the future. How tempted she was, now, to run the artifact through the system to learn the origin of any DNA on the photograph—perhaps it had been a gift to her grandparents. Her fingertips nervously brushed the corner of the artifact as she moved toward the reader.

And she heard the warning of the labyrinth clock.

She flew up the winding stairs, racing against the loud tick-tick-tick, pounding in the cavern like the heartbeat of God, reminding her she was in her last minute to leave the labyrinth.

She reached into her pocket as she ran, finding with joy the photograph and pressing it against her to keep it from falling out. *Dear God*, she prayed, considering long and hard as she made the request, *if only you'll let me keep this small bit of my past, I promise I'll not travel in time for pleasure again. Only if you show me I must.*

She stopped, for just a moment—dear God, how she would miss the labyrinth and its mysterious pleasures.

She reached the top of the stairs. Catching her breath, she pushed up the window seat over her head as she climbed out into the alcove enclosed by heavy curtains, relieved at the sunny afternoon light on the other side of the curtains. No matter how many trips she'd made, how much excitement she felt over visiting faraway places and times, she was always relieved to get back to her own life. She lowered the window seat back into place, pressing it closed and fastening the clasp.

She was back in 1775. She slipped her hand into her pocket.

The hair on the back of her neck stood up as she withdrew the photograph. There it was. It had survived the journey—only without the frame. She flipped it over.

> *"Gideon —thanks for so much. Swear I'll keep that*
> *promise. – Cam. Semper Fortis, S8."*

In a different handwriting, the words "December 1988" were written neatly in the upper corner.

And as her eyes closed, she pulled the photograph close to her heart and opened her eyes once more. In the bright sunlight filtering through the curtains, she saw again the smiling young woman beside the Naval officer—a stunning beauty. Her face was marred by the tiniest birthmark at her cheekbone. Reflexively, Juliana's fingertips covered the scar at her own, both of them shaped like a perfect crescent moon.

Abruptly, she heard footsteps again in the living room just outside. Then, a beloved, familiar voice: "My dear, you have a visitor. A young lady."

Papa! Her great-grandfather.

Her heart still hammering from the trip up the stairs, she slipped the photograph back in her pocket, then grabbed the book that lay there as she sat in the window seat—as if she had been interrupted from reading Aristotle.

She slowly drew back the heavy drapery, setting her book aside. She still held the pistol in her skirts, by old habit. That, she also set aside with the book. Where had Will gone off to now? He was nowhere to be seen.

As much as she loved her great-grandfather, her gaze focused instead on the woman standing beside him, staring back at her, watching Juliana.

The woman's hair was as curly as her own, but lighter, with a tinge of the sunset—like Sarita Miller's. She gazed at Juliana curiously, her attention lingering on the pistol she held against her skirt.

"Dear, this is Merrilea. I've told you about her."

And she remembered the words of Grey Trelawney, only minutes before—and centuries from now: *You two met the day of your grandmother's confession.*

Having just left the deathbed of her father's parents, she knew she was soon to meet her other grandmother.

"Merrilea," Papa said, "This young lady is Juliana Miller—your sister."

Chapter One

Virginia, 1781

Nothing was what it seemed.

On the outskirts of Richmond, a Carnival celebration went on in a grand plantation mansion. Young British Army officers danced and flirted with gaily costumed maidens over selections from Bach and Haydn. The lord of the manor observed the festivities silently from his wingchair near the fireplace. The rector of an Anglican church sat across from him in another wingchair, sipping warm French brandy.

A kitchen servant bent to offer guests a tray of mulled cider. A white-wigged matron surveyed the selection as if she thought all the silver cups but one were poisoned.

While she dithered, the servant's dark eyes cast about the room until she saw him, standing behind the master. Like everyone else except for the master, he wore a masque. In his case, the ornate white Harlequin masque, checkered with red and black, covered his entire head with cutouts for his eyes, nose, and mouth. His clothing, gloves, and shoes were white as well; the stock tied at his throat, blood-red. All this had been provided by his employer and dear friend, the young French marquis. Not an inch of his skin showed.

It was the whitest he'd been in all his thirty-four years, he mused.

He didn't mind the charade; at least he was warm—far warmer than the troops spread throughout the countryside. And his disguise enabled his presence, serving as the master's manservant who tonight enjoyed a rare evening off.

Odd, that the thought of his mother would enter his mind now—but his clothing reminded him. When he was a young boy, she'd dressed him in a white suit for church, musing how much he brought her own father to mind in his "dress whites."

As with many of his mother's peculiar sayings, he'd never heard the phrase from anyone but her.

"His name was Cameron," she'd said.

Rashall glanced down at the master of Black Oak. An eccentric sort, he celebrated the trappings of religion without concern for the whole point of the institution. During a visit to New Orleans a decade or so ago, Mardi Gras had made its impression on the old man, and he'd brought the celebration back home with him the next year. He found it invigorating to watch the debauchery without participating himself. And so he supplied his guests with overflowing cups and plates on this Tuesday evening while troops starved, living on roots and wild greens and whatever squirrels they might get their hands on. Salt pork and cornmeal or flour when they had it.

His own commander had been straightforward when he gave him the disguise. "Look for a man in a bone breastplate."

No one wore such a disguise, and he was beginning to grow anxious. The gathering would soon come to a close.

He caught the eye of the servant distributing the cider, and she nodded. Outside, the drums began, a slow, steady call.

He bent to Grimewood. "The festivities are ready, sir."

"Aye."

The old man came to his feet and tapped his walking stick against the oak floor. Twice was all it took. The boisterous crowd fell silent and the guests turned to their host.

"If you'll follow me to the gardens, an unforgettable treasure awaits us."

He closely followed the old man as he crossed the short distance to the great oak doors that led to the grounds, and as the footmen threw back the doors, a gust of winter cold blew in. Rashall glanced into the stormy sky then bent from the waist, extending his hand in welcome to the crowd as he led the way.

Gentlemen hastily grabbed their ladies' cloaks and the guests hurried after their host as he strode down toward the wide, brown lawn. Mothers whose husbands were fighting in the wilderness held their children close and officers reassured their ladies as they followed his direction into the cold.

Their path was lined with cressets burning heart pine, lighting the way and warming the cold, moonless night. At the end of the lawn lay a pile of wood a dozen feet across and nearly as high.

The drummers, a group of grim-faced men of all ages enslaved by Grimewood, perched on stumps around another cresset illuminating them. One man's flexed hands danced against the skins; the other men waited, still, their hands poised over the skins.

Rashall followed just behind the master, stopping at the end of the path and swinging his own walking stick with a dramatic flourish in a wide circle that ended at the ground as he led the group toward the gigantic wood stack. He drew an invisible line six feet from the stack and slowly gestured with his other hand for the crowd to come forward. The smell of pine fatwood and oil-soaked cloth filled his nostrils, and he opened both hands, invisibly pushing the crowd back farther from the wood.

When they were assembled, Rashall gestured toward the drummers, and the crowd fell silent. Other drummers abruptly joined in with a relaxing, Caribbean cadence, and the beat began to build as, one by one, dancers appeared from the darkness behind the wood, moving to the rhythm. Shirtless in the winter cold, they wore homespun trousers rolled up to their knees as they danced into the light, entertaining the master's pampered guests.

Rashall looked on dispassionately. No silken comedy masques here.

One of the men reached from behind the wood stack and withdrew a stick, handing it to the next man who danced past, then the next, until each man had a stick. They clicked their sticks with each other's, adding to the song of the drums. As they danced around the stack, each pair of dancers spun, then clicked their sticks together as if fencing.

Rashall's attention moved between the dancers and Grimewood's guests, many of whose faces were alight with fascination and faint fear as the primitive pace quickened.

Grimewood himself tapped his walking stick against the dry grass in silent time, the rhythm infecting him. There were rumors about his own parentage—born to a wealthy South Carolina landowner with a lascivious wife.

Rashall noticed the guests as some responded despite their impeccable breeding—a slow nod here, a slyly tapped silken toe there. He turned to the crowd, thrust his walking stick into the ground and raised his arms over his head, bringing them together in a clap.

They were a repressed throng, though, and a good ten seconds passed before they caught on, led by a lady near the back. Other ladies joined in, followed by their dutiful escorts. In the dreary winter night where far-off lightning drew a gasp from the crowd, where countless troops lay unsheltered awaiting their next battle, those who remained loyal to the Crown were entertained.

A new dancer emerged, also shirtless, his face painted white and black, a bone breastplate across his chest, and the audience's clapping grew even louder. This man carried a lit torch. Rashall almost smiled at the marquis' joke as he recognized the man.

The dancing circle of men drew past, stopping in unison as they traded sticks for unlit torches, each with a tightly coiled rag bound to either end. Their sticks were tossed atop the wood pile. This continued until the entire line of men had a torch.

The pulse of the drums quickened and rolled into a rhythmic call as the lead dancer passed his fire to one dancer. That man passed his torch to the next, and the progression of fire continued until each man now held a torch with both ends lit. The lighting of the torches kept time with the building rhythm. The thin, high peal of a flute joined in with the drums, its mysterious melody both plaintive and insistent, filled with the promise of the primitive unknowable.

The drumbeat grew faster even as another, heavy drum joined in. The clapping fell away as they could no longer keep time with the fierce joy of the music.

The lead dancer, in the breastplate and war paint, ran straight toward the crowd with a loud cry, and the guests shrank away several feet. Rashall noted with silent amusement the indignation evident among several officers. *How dare this savage approach civilized men so!*

Never had he been so glad for a masque.

All at once the dancer ran to the fire stack, swirling his torch over its surface with sensual interest, as if he were stroking a woman's body. Within a few seconds the wood exploded into a huge fireball, and the crowd gasped in awe and delight at the bonfire warming the night.

The lead dancer added another torch to his first and lit it, passing it to the next man, who caught it and passed it down the line as the lead continued adding more torches. The procession of new torches went around until each man held two double-ended torches.

Rashall pressed the crowd back farther, and they gave a great gasp as the fire dancers formed a circle a few feet away, in the clearing between the bonfire and the drummers, dancing and juggling their torches between two, then three dancers. Then the entire troupe juggled the torches as if a single entity.

He scrutinized Grimewood, wondering if he knew that the lead fire dancer was not one of his own slaves, but a man from Rosalie, a few miles farther down the river. He pressed his lips together at the amusing thought—of course not. He'd have been strung up straightaway.

He admired the on-point precision of the dancers. These men would never be compensated for their art. They would never perform in the great theatres of the land, nor would their endless hours of practice—in the little free time they had—be adequately acknowledged.

But dear God, the sheer joy!

Despite their seemingly hopeless lot in life, the fire dancers at Black Oak were well known along the river for their skill and grace. They wore the same clothing in which they worked the fields, but in the firelight the homespun blended with the darkness of their skin and became an ancient golden costume, celebrating the freedom to respond to darkness with joy. The louder the beat of the drums, the softer and rounder the peal of the flute, the higher their torches flew.

Their skin shone with sweat in the firelight as they threw countless designs in the night sky—and Rashall smiled for the first time that night. No one in the crowd, not even Grimewood, could recognize the designs they drew in the darkness, save someone far above. And perhaps it was to Him they offered their dance, their joy.

With a slow inhale and exhale, he allowed his gaze to subtly rove over the crowd. The eyes of the women were round with the scandalous attire of the dancers, with their raw, sexual appeal. The men watched alertly as if expecting them to revolt at any moment. Grimewood watched in smug satisfaction at the performance as he might observe a hound fetching a duck.

None of them could even begin to process what they witnessed tonight.

Only as his attention moved over the crowd did he notice the woman who had first joined in with his clapping. She was the only one in the crowd who continued to move in excitement with the dancers.

Tall, with thick, black hair tamed into a chignon, she wore a glittering black masque that caught the firelight as she moved. A slow, dull ache went through him for the first time in many months—and it surprised him, how much he welcomed that pain. He thought he'd stopped feeling anything.

She looked so much like *her*.

He caught a deep breath and moved surreptitiously out of the fire's spotlight and into the shadows. His time here was short, but he had to speak with her, whoever she was. This was the first time any woman had ever drawn him as Juliana had.

He slipped through the crowd to the steps leading to the double doors, where she stood, nodding in time to the fire dancers. She spoke in quiet tones to an older couple who stood there, and he strained to hear her over the drums. She was looking toward the woman and he drew nearer, afire at the sound of her voice.

It was Juliana. It was her.

"But I understand spies are here tonight," the other woman whispered.

And she laughed, that rich, soft laughter he had perhaps first loved about her.

"Nonsense," she said. "They're quite easy to recognize."

At that, she turned her head, focusing on him through the masque. And if he were any longer capable of blushing, it would have shone through his own masque.

"Are they?" he asked.

Her polite smile slowly fell away as she stared at him, growing again into a bold explosion of happiness. For a moment he feared she would hug him, and he would be lost.

But she didn't. In the next moment she reined in her happiness—as if remembering.

And only then, when he was fully within his own fantasy— after all, only seconds had passed since he'd first seen her—did he remember the news waiting at his mother's, when he'd stopped in Boston a year past.

She's married, son.

His own father had delivered the black tidings, having heard it from one of the Trelawneys who'd escaped war-torn Virginia for war-torn Boston.

Married a Loyalist.

"Of course not," she said, her voice husky. "Only patriotic Englishmen here tonight."

"Ah, yes," he said. And because his eyes and mouth were all she could see, he allowed his eyes to drift boldly over her lush, comely form.

Dressed primly in a black gown that matched the somber mood of the times, she had covered the deep décolletage with a lace that—despite her best intentions—only enhanced her appeal. Were she outfitted in sewn-together flour sacks, his body would've responded the same.

I love you, he said silently, willing her to hear his thoughts. *I fear I always shall.*

"The dancers are quite exotic and beautiful," she said, without ever taking her eyes from him.

"Yes. I think they've quite frightened some."

"Only those who don't recognize joy when they see it."

His flirtations fell away as she spoke to his very heart.

The drums built to a crescendo; his time here grew short. Abruptly, he caught her left hand in his and raised to his lips the gloved fingertips, kissing the ringed third finger that forbade him more. "Goodnight, madame. Enjoy the fire dancers."

"But—please ..."

Even as her voice echoed in his mind, he strode through the empty house to the library, where a fire blazed in the hearth. An unremarkable traitor stood there, sipping tea. Rashall was mildly surprised; Loyalists, he had expected tonight, but not this man.

"Close the door, Jim."

His mind still reeling with the thought of Juliana, he obeyed, trying to corral his wild thoughts.

"My compliments on the disguise."

After a moment he nodded. "Lafayette believes me to be an amusing but faithful servant. I merely wear the uniform."

"Take off the masque. I distrust it."

As well you should, you pompous ass. No one as treacherous as Benedict Arnold should trust his own shadow.

"I cannot. It will destroy it and I cannot finish my work here."

"Then convince me. Tell me something only you and I would know."

"That you're much better at whist than I."

The brigadier general laughed, and Rashall pretended to join him in his egotistical pleasure.

"I doubt that's a great secret, but I'll accept it. What news do you have for me?"

"The Continental Army in the South is suffering from widespread starvation and frequent desertion. They are northern troops, and fear a hellish summer campaign and the fevers that would come with that." That much was true. "But they continue to volunteer and Lafayette's troops now stand at perhaps five thousand."

That was believable but untrue. Of course, he needn't tell him that Lafayette's real hope lay in the French Navy.

"I see. Please send along to him this letter you discovered." He extended a letter complete with Arnold's seal.

Rashall accepted the letter, no doubt stuffed full of Arnold's inflations. It would be an amusing contrast to the other intelligence. Now, he thought to push for perhaps a bit more by exploiting Arnold's well-established ego.

"He is after you, sir. Take care. I understand the militia in these parts are angry as well."

"I am neither surprised, nor worried. Phillips is on his way to meet me."

"William Phillips?"

Arnold glanced at him. "Do you know him?"

"I met him when I was visiting kinfolk at Monticello last year. While he was a—er, *guest* of the governor."

Not even this was true. Except that Major-General Phillips had indeed visited Jefferson—as a prisoner of war.

"My men and I continue our journey to Portsmouth after the festivities conclude. You're welcome to remain."

"Portsmouth?"

After only a moment's hesitation, Arnold said, "I am to establish a naval base there. I expect reinforcements. I am vulnerable until then."

Or until you escape the country entirely. He'd just gotten through telling him that Phillips was on his way to reinforce him.

Perhaps ironically, Rashall's skills at deception had been honed as a vicar. He was expected to react with love at the most heinous confessions.

In the end, the Church had been right—although it hadn't known why. He lacked the skills to serve as a priest.

Now, he watched the general without expression. Presently, he looked up from the fire to meet his gaze. "Will you stay the night? I'll ensure you're adequately entertained."

His meaning was clear. Rashall envisioned a night spent with a strange woman, imagining her to be Juliana.

"No," he said, more forcefully than he liked, adding, "Thank you. I'd like to try to visit my family when I've conveyed your message. Safe travels, sir. There's a storm coming in from the coast."

"Well, I'll leave that for Phillips to concern himself with." The general gave him a quizzical look. "You seem to have family all over Virginia. Have you not?"

"You don't know the half of it."

He left the major-general musing before the fire, soon emerging at the door near the dining room. There, he noticed the silver service of coffee left over from after dinner. He stopped long enough to gulp down two cups—he'd need it for the long ride ahead.

So if Phillips was headed upriver, who was he planning to reinforce? More than ever, he was certain Arnold's plan was to escape. Not so much from instinct, but from his mother's unwitting reference to the deserter in a bedtime adventure story when Rashall was but a child.

"And after destroying all the beautiful homes that our people worked so hard to build up and down the James River, that rascal sailed away and lived out his life in merry old England."

That was the beauty of his mother. She had occasionally given him glimpses of the future, but never any hard facts. She spoke of the end of this war as any fervent patriot of the time, certain the rebellious colonies would prevail. Rashall couldn't yet fit the pieces together, so for now he focused on the task before him.

He set aside his coffee cup, passing the kitchen as he headed to the servants' quarters. He entered the last cabin, depressed at the shabby place—nearly as cold inside as out. It only reminded him of the tidy village the Trelawneys had built up at Rosalie that was so far superior to anything other servants had ever known. Drafty and unlit, the dwelling was little more than a shack.

He remembered that day so long ago now when his sister had said as much to their mother—and his father's amused upbraiding, when he dismissed her as a snob. The memory was bittersweet. Helen, his beloved younger sister, had been gone a year now, lost to the grippe—what they were beginning to call the flu. Not a day passed that he didn't miss her. He loved to remember her as she was—always just a little bit better than those around her.

The drums on the other side of the estate went silent, followed by enthusiastic applause. He found his pack and slipped the letter into the hidden partition in the seam, then quickly disrobed. He shook out and folded the costume and carefully packed the masque in its protective form, stowing it. He dressed and shouldered his pack, then glanced out at the door. The dancers were returning to the cabins, talking and laughing under their breath.

He glanced about, and even as he searched, the man soon emerged not from the group, but from the house. That was curious. What cause had he found to be inside the mansion? Suspicion rose in Rashall.

The man removed his bone breastplate and wiped at his war paint with a wet cloth. Under his arm he carried an unlit torch. Just one end was wrapped with cloth.

Only a moment passed as they looked at each other, while the newcomer finished removing the war paint. Then a wide grin lit his face as he grabbed Rashall and hugged him hard.

When he drew back, he held out the unlit torch to Rashall—a man he'd known since their mother had ransomed him from this very plantation with the beloved son she'd lost, Martin. Rashall had no memories of a life before Martin had been a part of it; in truth, he could not distinguish him from the blood brother he'd lost to smallpox. He only remembered crying when they left this new brother behind, with Ruth, at Rosalie. He hadn't understood why they couldn't keep him— after all, he was going to be named Martin, too. His mother had to explain to him that his brother had died, but that his death enabled Martin of Black Oak, born a slave, to become Martin Trelawney, a free man.

His brother's death was his first step in understanding redemption. His brother had died that another might live.

"What in the world were you doing inside the house?"

"Looking for someone. News of that man's death would cheer me."

"Don't risk your cover for something you can't change."

"Everybody in the county hates that man for his despicable lasciviousness."

"How is our mother?" Rashall asked, changing the subject.

"You tell me. You've seen her since I have."

"Ah. Well, it's been a year since I left Rhode Island—I thought perhaps Ruth might have heard from her."

"Mail is unreliable these days unless you're instructing the torching of plantations, and since Bronson came home—"

"Hawk's back from Rhode Island?"

"I thought you knew."

"I left Rhode Island to join the Marquis. Is he well?"

Martin reached for a shirt and slipped it on, buttoning it. "Well?"

"No. He was on the *Jersey* for six months."

He couldn't have heard him right. "Not the prison ship."

"The same." He found his shoes and socks and slipped them on. "He's not himself."

"What do you mean?"

And even as he asked the question, they heard Grimewood, making his way to the cabins. "Where's my pretty lass?" he called.

Rashall's jaw hardened. Normally the reminder of Grimewood's nightly rapes would have upset him, but his attention was focused on the news about Hawk's captivity on the notorious prison ship.

"Was he injured?" he pressed.

"Not physically. But for now, we both need to get out of here."

"Come with me. I can take you down to Rosalie."

"I have a mount downriver." Martin took the unlit torch and slipped it into the pack. "Break it over a log. The letter's inside. If you're found out, light it all."

"Of course. But when—"

"Only God knows." He clapped his brother on the shoulder and slipped out into the night.

The storm began as he found the horse where he'd left her in the woods, and he started down the narrow river road.

Two days, two exchanges of horses at friendly farms, and he finally made the camp. He dismounted and gave the horse to a boy to care for, then found the general's tent. He stood just outside, shaving with heated spring water, feeling his way without the aid of a mirror.

"I see you can take the aristocrat out of Versailles, but you can't take Versailles out of the aristocrat."

Elegant even in the wilderness, he gave a dramatic sigh when he saw Rashall. "Ah! There you are. Do you have it?"

"Yes."

Rashall opened the pack and carefully withdrew the costume with a flourish. "None the worse for wear, I promise. I know how you love your *haute couture*."

Lafayette lifted his chin with a sniff, his eyes dancing with amusement. "You know I mean the correspondence."

"Oh! That, too."

The two men slipped into the tent. Rashall closed the flaps of the tent and slipped the letter out of his bag and handed it to him. He placed the costume on a stand inside the general's tent. "That's the fraud from Arnold. But this," he went on, removing the slender wooden cylinder, "may interest you."

The half-shaved Frenchman smirked. "Shall we have a fire dance?"

"Did you know your other contact is my kinsman? Sir Bone Breastplate?"

"I did not know. A rider had given me the intelligence."

Rashall tapped the center of the torch against the frame of Lafayette's cot, and in the crack that appeared, they saw the cream-colored stationery rolled into the hollow tube.

Lafayette broke the seal and opened the letter Arnold had given him while Rashall removed the scroll and gently flattened it, scanning its contents. It was an ordinary letter from a soldier to his sweetheart.

Rashall lit a candle while Lafayette began to read. "Well, it seems that Cornwallis has lost a thousand men," he remarked in mock alarm. "Where *did* they go? What about you?"

"Dear Susan, As I lie in the open field at night with mud in my ears, I pine for Thee. Thy generous bosoms—"

"Silence!"

Rashall laughed as he warmed the letter over the flame. In this cold, it was a trick to warm the invisible ink without setting fire to the whole letter. A lesson you learn but once.

"I do have other news that I believe is genuine, but I'd rather you put away the razor first."

"As you wish."

The general quickly whisked away the rest of his stubble, then rinsed and put away the blade.

"Phillips is en route to join Arnold."

"Phillips. William Phillips, you mean."

Rashall nodded.

In truth, he had only known the name because Lafayette loathed him. Major-General William Phillips was the man who'd killed the Frenchman's father on another continent nearly two decades before at the Battle of Minden, during the Seven Years' War.

The young major-general frowned into the candle for a good minute. "Thank you for making me put away the blade. I might have injured us in my—um, excitedness."

"We do what we can. Now then." Faint scrawls began to emerge between the lines of the letter. Numbers. He sighed in deep aggravation. "It's in cipher. Well. Give me a few minutes."

He set to deciphering the letter, while the general went out into the camp.

By the time he looked up an hour later, Lafayette had returned with two plates of food. Fried salted pork and hoe cakes.

"Sure sign we're both starving," Rashall said. "That truly smells delicious to me."

"It is indeed *délicieux*. I called for my family's chef from Auvergne. He is now outside, setting a soufflé in the oven."

"No need to mock." He broke off a bit of cornbread, still hot from the fire. "This isn't bad. Whoever did this cooking needs to be relieved of combat and allowed to stick with this, for all our sakes."

"And the letter?"

"From none other than Great Britain's Commander-in-chief. Clinton is sending troops to reinforce Phillips. And he doesn't approve of Cornwallis's plans to leave the Carolinas for Virginia."

"Ah. So … everyone is coming."

Rashall nodded.

Lafayette daintily sliced off a piece of hoe cake, made an hors d'oeuvre of sorts with a bit of pork, and brought it to his mouth with his knife, chewing thoughtfully. At last, he spoke.

"This is fearsome, friend. Our only hope lay on the sea."

"Isn't that a laugh. How many years did my friend Hawk and I terrorize the sea – French ships included – without accomplishing much of meaning? And now, we find ourselves entirely without a ship when we could use one."

"Piracy's loss, my gain," Lafayette said. "But I do hope Rochambeau has a plan—and that they employ it, soon."

"Rochambeau? Don't you mean Washington?"

The younger man favored him with the sort of look his own mother gave him when he asked stupid questions. "You know better than anyone that my loyalty lies with our Commander-in-chief. But Comte de Rochambeau will have to rely heavily on the French Navy in this battle if we are to win."

He couldn't deny that. Rochambeau commanded more troops than Washington himself.

"Ah. I will write my dear commander now. Did you know, by the way, that none other than Patrick 'Give me Liberty' Henry wished to declare Washington a dictator? Oh, a temporary measure to be sure. But what is the thinking? If you like, take a nap there in my cot. It is not luxurious, but it has no rocks and is out of the wind."

Rashall gladly accepted the offer. He left the tent long enough to find a stream to wash his hands and face and brush his teeth.

When he re-entered the tent, he glanced at Lafayette's letter and shook his head. "How many times do I have to tell you?"

"What now?"

"You *don't* need all those capitals. It makes your letter look like a lunatic wrote it."

Without stopping the quick scratching of the quill, the hasty jabbing into the inkwell, he murmured, "And this matters why? The Commander-in-chief knows I am not."

"You think we might win this thing?"

"I know we shall." He looked up, startled, his mouth ajar. "Ah. You think others may read these someday ... and think me insane?"

Taken by surprise at his expression of earnest concern, Rashall gave a low chortle. "Finds out he's going to be famous someday, and *then* he gets concerned about grammar."

After a long, thoughtful look at the paper, he waved his quill at him. "Go to sleep, you nosybody."

Again Rashall fell into a fit of giggles as he slid gratefully into the Frenchman's cot and pulled the blanket around him. "Busybody. Don't let me sleep too long."

And his last thought, as he fell into a deep sleep, was as always of the woman who held his heart—and who belonged to another man.

Chapter Two

Was this truly her life now?

Juliana blinked as she looked around the dark carriage, awakened abruptly when the wheels lurched to a halt. Deep in the night, they reached Stonefield. She was awakened not by the tender whisper of her husband, nor by a gentle nudge, but by the abrupt tap of a cane against the closed leather window.

"Missus, we're here."

Not even her husband's voice, but that of the coachman.

She shook her head, trying to rid it of the memories of Rashall. Before the party at Black Oak, it had been five years since she'd seen him, and yet it was as if no time had passed. Behind his masque, she had seen the spark in his pale brown eyes and hear the laughter in his voice. It was his voice, after all, that she'd first recognized at the party.

She sighed. What kind of man hosted a soiree during a war, when his own kinsmen were dying throughout the land?

What kind of person had she married, who had insisted on their attending such a crass event?

As if to answer her question, the carriage door opened wide, revealing Enoch Morgan. He simply waited, staring at the stone beneath the carriage wheels.

And, worst of all, what kind of woman was she—unable to keep Rashall from her mind?

She pushed away the lap blanket, folded it and set it aside, then alighted into the icy night. The wind whipped at her cloak as she walked along the stones to the door. Enoch reached the door just before her and opened it.

"Good night," he said, bowing stiffly.

"Will you not—stay the night?"

Be my companion, the helpmate you promised in times of trouble? At least look at me as you reject me?

"I must rejoin my men on the battlefield."

With that, he shut himself back into the carriage—even as she found herself relieved at the news. Why again had she married him?

She whistled for Will and heard his answering bark, far in the distance. Only Will paid that much attention to her—not that she was complaining. Most days, Will was all she needed.

The coachman looked down at her uncertainly. In a stage whisper, he asked, "You need some help getting in, missus? Building a fire? Looks dark in there."

She shook her head and gave him a smile in reassurance. "Don't worry, Caleb. I'll be fine."

The sudden thunder of Enoch's stick against the roof of the carriage startled them both, and he nodded toward the door, appealing for her to at least go inside.

She hurried inside, closing and barring the door. The clop of the horses' hooves faded into the night. The slow tick of the grandfather clock oriented her in the darkness and welcomed her home, its pendulum reminding her she'd been away nearly a week this time.

She found her way in the dark, felt for the key on the mantel, inserted it into each side of the clock, in turn, and wound it. The action steadied and gave order to her own world, and she moved about the darkness, finding the tinder box and lighting the logs she kept at the ready in the hearth.

In twenty-eight years of rising in darkness to tend to her duties, she had learned every bump and ridge of the room.

Although she wasn't without her share of fears, fear of the dark wasn't among them. In minutes, she'd set a blaze burning in the hearth, and the kettle of water heating.

She found a quilt in the cedar chest and brought it with her to the rocking chair before the hearth. There she stopped, studying the doll that sat there, happy in her cotton-head oblivion. Well loved, her mobcap askew and her ruby-red silken lips faded, the doll had been her first foray into sewing beyond simple embroidery, nearly twenty years ago. Aunt Mary had praised her efforts; Uncle Malcolm's austerity had softened for the first time into merriment when he saw the doll she'd made, and even he had beamed with pleasure at the delicate creation.

Miss Betsy, she called her.

Once, the doll had vanished, and she scoured the house and the grounds looking for her. She'd never found her, until that day.

The truth was, she had always suspected where she'd lost the doll, but her guardians' displeasure when they learned where she'd been had kept her from visiting again.

Until that day.

And for the first time in ages, she remembered that curious day when she'd gone looking for Will, who was out roaming in the woods. Only a few months before her twelfth birthday. By the time she'd made it home, Will had already beat her back. She heard him barking with ferocious threat—not the sort of bark he used with her, but that he used in warning an intruder.

She had arrived home to find Will locked inside the house and Uncle Malcolm holding out the doll to her sternly. *"Now where did you leave this, lass?"*

He must have found it on the stairs, but she didn't care. Happiness had filled every inch of her as she rushed to take the doll—until she'd seen the man beside the house, walking away. Had he retrieved her doll from that forbidden place? She could not see his face, but something about his broad, straight shoulders, and the way he carried himself—tall, strong, sure— stirred her, filling the emptiness that had plagued her, her entire life—at least until the day she'd met her sister.

Why had they abandoned her?

She brushed away the old, nagging familiar. She had no use for its accusation. At last she knew the answer, now. They had not abandoned her; her grandmother Hannah had.

A sudden scratching at the door startled her, and she opened it to admit the muddy mess that was Will. The black mutt yelped and whined at her in excited conversation, and she laughed, stroking him, her fingers sinking into his wet fur and massaging his skin.

"Ah, you filthy mess. Kitchen."

He trudged down the hall, panting, knowing the drill. Over their years together, he'd come to welcome what he'd once loathed.

She drug the steaming kettle into the kitchen and emptied it into the large tub. The dog delicately stepped over its side and sank into the warm water. He dipped his face into the water and lifted his snout, shaking his head and sending water everywhere.

A few minutes later, she sat under the quilt before the fire, stroking Will with a towel as he grew warm and dry. A sharp gust of wind in the chimney made the flames dance, and embers flew up in counterpoint.

Will whimpered at the sound of the storm, and she pushed at his snout. "You colossal fraud. You were just out there playing in it."

He fell onto his back, his mouth falling open in something resembling laughter, and he writhed playfully, offering his white belly up to her.

She scratched his stomach, then rose to stoke the fire for the night. Crossing to the nearest bedroom—her own—she opened the door to let the warmth seep in. The wide, four-poster bed taunted her with its emptiness.

Christmas a year ago, she had married Enoch Morgan. He had been courting her since she was a young girl. A wealthy nobleman with properties throughout Richmond as well as the Tidewater, he had married as a young man but lost his wife soon after. Not until he spied Juliana, visiting Williamsburg with her grandfather, had he been attracted to another. He never stopped courting her—until, finally, they'd married. Then, as if he'd learned a despicable secret about her, he'd abruptly lost interest.

She herself had learned the truth when the maternal grandmother she'd never known visited five years before—the same day she'd met her own sister—and Rashall. Hannah Hastings had spoken of the same travels that Juliana had known—but Hannah had known nothing of the labyrinth.

Hannah had, however, known the young boy, born in 1742 to a freed slave and her white husband, disappearing for a time before returning to the 1760s, a time of turbulence and unrest, for his bride—her own daughter.

Juliana's parents.

In all the time since then, she'd stayed away from the eerie place that lay far beneath the earth. That eerie, magnificent door to everywhere. Any time.

At least she understood why her parents had never come for her.

They could still avoid that fate; if anyone could, they could.

She was pierced with the reminder of the truth. Just one time had she left footprints—and that was in the act of saving the lunatic who had meant to kill himself. And in that single act, she had doomed her own parents.

As she always did, she reminded herself that anyone would try to save a life. That she hadn't known. But, in the end, what she knew was that she had learned as a tot the creed of her life: *Leave no footprints.* And she had rejected it that night.

She washed and dressed for bed and knelt on the cold oak floor by her bed to say her prayers. Each night, as now, she prayed only for peace; peace in her heart, peace in her life, peace in her country. Peace in this lost world.

As she rose to sit on the side of the bed, she noted the pocket watch she had given Enoch as a wedding gift, alongside the handkerchief he'd placed there beside it when he had undressed that night of their wedding.

When she had joined him in the bed, he lay unmoving, his chest rising and falling in a shallow rhythm. At last the sound had relaxed her to sleep, and when she awakened at the chime of the clock striking two, he was gone. No note, no explanation. Only later would she learn from Uncle Malcolm that he had joined the fight—as a Loyalist. Not until then had she known his politics, but it had likely spared Stonefield from the destruction all the homes of the James River had suffered.

She climbed under the covers and patted Enoch's side of the bed, and Will joined her. He sniffed the pillows, turned in a circle three times, and plopped down, placing his head on his paws to watch her.

She stared back at him in the light coming from the fire in the other room. She closed her eyes, willing herself to sleep. She ought to be tired—she hadn't slept in a bed since she'd left Stonefield for Black Oak, Grimewood's plantation.

That awful man. He made her Enoch look like a pious saint, using his servants as a harem of concubines to increase his wealth in human beings. She forced her mind away from the thoughts of him.

Whatsoever things are pure, whatsoever things are lovely ... if there be any virtue, and if there be any praise, think on these things.

In her mind she saw again the men dancing in the firelight for the entertainment of Grimewood's guests. Perhaps only she and Rashall understood why they danced, and it was certainly not for Grimewood. On this, she pondered.

And inevitably her thoughts returned to Rashall.

The pulse of the drums pounded with her own in her memory as she'd watched him in the moonless night, his muscled strength taut as he drew the guests forward toward the fire and then a moment later pushed them away to safety.

What had he been doing there at Black Oak? He was no Loyalist. When the old woman standing beside her on the steps had prattled about spies there at the gathering, she found the notion amusing. And then, there was Rashall.

He looked more like his mother than his father. She'd first met Camisha Adams the same day she met her son, and she'd noticed the resemblance then. He stood as tall as Bronson and as broad-shouldered as his own father, Ashanti. But he had his mother's eyes—tilted up at the corners, light brown until they darkened in anger, when they would glitter in warning.

Excitement coursed through her, and she threw back the covers, sliding her feet into her slippers and rising. She pulled the thick robe around her and tied it at her waist, and grabbed her pillow.

Again she noted her wedding gift to her husband, lying abandoned and untouched on the nightstand. With sudden, hot anger, she grabbed the watch and chain and handkerchief and stalked into the other room, dashing it all into the fire.

A moment later, the crystal cracked and dissolved into the flames, and she gasped at her destruction, at the anger that possessed her. Why did he hate her so, after pursuing her for so many years? It was as if he married her simply to prevent anyone else from having her.

She couldn't take it anymore. She had to get out of here, out of this unending tedium, and there was simply nowhere to go.

She glanced toward the window seat. She had not descended those stairs since the day Rashall had arrived in her life. Since she heard her grandmother's awful cautionary tale.

God forgive me.

She dropped the pillow to the chesterfield and walked toward the window seat.

Will bounded toward her, barking in forceful warning, as if she were walking straight into the fire itself.

"Down. Stay."

She pointed to his rug at the hearth, and he obeyed her with a whimper.

Leaning over to find the catch that she'd first discovered as a child, she opened the seat and climbed into the stairwell. As she closed the seat above her head, Will jumped onto it, barking angrily at her betrayal. Never again would she risk losing him; such travel wasn't meant for children or dogs, she had learned the hard way.

She hadn't bothered with a candle, and the darkness was complete. She flew down the winding stairs, her feet light with carefree anticipation. Holding her nightgown above her ankles, she felt the liberation of each step.

She reached the narrow stone passageway that led to the labyrinth—that place she'd explored with endless curiosity as a child. She inhaled with pleasure and gazed into the celestial sky at the asterism of her family—still the same troubled colors.

Leave no footprints.

She placed her hand against the reader. "Good evening, Juliana. Present your artifact."

"I do not have an artifact and humbly request one."

"What is your desired destination?"

"Stonefield, near Henricus, in August of 1994—"

"This destination is inaccessible to you."

The historic village was just down the road in that century—she would be able to arrive back at Stonefield in little time. "I wish to visit Henricus in August of 1994—"

The month of her birth—and her parents' deaths.

"That destination is inaccessible to you."

"I wish to visit the Richmond police station in August—"

"That destination is inaccessible to you."

The machine had never interrupted her, nor so persistently denied her petitions.

But then, never had she so blatantly ignored the basic rules of travel—for she wanted to leave indelible, living evidence behind. Something to try to make up for the evil she'd enabled.

She sank to the ground.

What event should she like to see? She had not yet seen everything—so much in the world still left to see. She cast about in her memory for something she would enjoy. She loved a good comedy, but nothing came to mind.

She rose. "Christmas Day, 1775. I wish only to observe unseen."

"Trenton? Perhaps 1776?"

The machine's system spoke as an obsequious server recommending a bottle of Bordeaux. An upgrade must have been installed; it had never made suggestions before. This, of the famous night George Washington crossed the Delaware River, was both meaningful and dramatic.

For some minutes, Juliana stood there in her nightgown, considering what she hadn't seen yet.

And then she remembered her promise never to travel in time frivolously again.

"No. Never mind."

A thought came to her. Before she knew it, this dull, ordinary day, this sleepless night, would be a moment she could only look back on.

The sights she'd visited over her life were indescribable. She had watched a madman invade a continent and destroy six million innocents two centuries hence—and she had seen a babe born in a manger, nearly two millennia past. On one particularly snowy week of her life, she'd visited thousands of places and periods of history, one 24-hour period at a time. She left her time in one minute and came back in the next—yet lived an entire day in that other time.

She had tasted the foods of a future she would never otherwise know; she had inhaled the pure, sweet air of an unrecorded time before history. All of it, she remembered in lavish detail.

She'd seen far more historic events than anyone would ever see—except perhaps a person like George Washington or Martin Luther King Jr.—yet she'd glimpsed nowhere near all of mankind's mysteries.

And yet she had made no impression whatsoever in any of the worlds she'd visited, or on any of the countless people she'd known.

As she arrived back in the labyrinth, she stopped.

Leave no footprints.

It was her byword in her travels, a term of service as well as a warning from her uncle's voice of experience: *Change nothing, or live to regret it forever.*

Malcolm had never explained his regret, or its cause, but she took it to heart. Tonight, as she yearned for Rashall and wanted nothing more than to have an ordinary life with him, she swore that—one way or another—she would live a life of her own.

She had plenty of time to get out of the labyrinth, but she'd taken the stairs anxious to find her own life, whatever it was. So when she reached the top step and pushed at the window seat, she was unsurprised to find she couldn't open it.

A grudging bark greeted her. *Stay down there and think about what you did, young lady,* the dog seemed to say.

"Down, boy," she called. She heard him jump to the floor, and she climbed back into her ordinary life. The trip up the 674 stairs had exhausted her, and she returned to bed, her dog beside her.

As she fell asleep, she thought of her sister, whom she hadn't seen in months. Marley couldn't begin to understand her. She couldn't have ever told her older sister how she'd lived her life, all the things she'd seen, all the people she'd known, all the customs she'd learned, and all the miraculous advances of the distant future.

Nor all the people of the past who, with all their mysterious motives, were just the same as modern people were, no more, no less. Trying to do the best they could, with their limited knowledge. What *is* modern, anyway? Other than tomorrow's antiquated, barbaric ways? If only Marley knew what the people of the year 2276 thought of her own generation.

Then again, her sister had once lived in the future before she returned to the time where she belonged. If Juliana herself was lonely without her family, perhaps her family was lonely without her. If she couldn't tell Marley all about her life—at least perhaps she could learn more about Marley's. And perhaps, along the way, learn how to be a better sister.

Chapter Three

"Dear God, I miss the music so."

Marley whispered the words as she looked out the window at her husband, splitting wood in the gathering twilight.

She didn't often miss the things of her time. She had, once—mostly after Bronson had first joined the Continental Army, and she was left to raise a toddler and a newborn on her own. She'd missed soaking in the bathtub, and the frosty luxury of stepping into a cool home, free of mosquitoes, on a muggy summer afternoon. But at last, she even got used to living without those luxuries.

What she'd never gotten used to was the absence of music—good music that was everywhere in the twenty-first century. Whether it was an endless supply of any genre she wanted to listen to on her headphones or a commercial jingle on the car radio, music had been everywhere in her old world.

As much as she loved the sounds of life in the Tidewater, she missed the sounds of gospel music; of classical and country; reggae and rock; bluegrass and blues; Motown and modern folk. So many kinds of folk—and blues! She missed it all, there at the touch of a button, to make the workday more pleasant. In the end, that was all she missed from her old life.

Even as she spoke, watching her husband work outside, she revised her prayer to one of gratitude for the sight.

He worked methodically, grimly, as if attempting to hatchet out the nightmares of the past three years of his life.

He swung the maul, split the log, and stepped away for Abigail to gather one of the logs up in her arms. He tossed the others past her toward the woodpile. He wasn't fond of his daughter engaging in such menial labor, but his wife had persuaded him that it was healthy for her to learn the satisfaction of work. Someday, she promised him, their daughter would thank him for preparing her for life by making her self-sufficient.

And in the world as it was now, they had no reason to believe that the child would grow up better off than either of her parents had been.

Marley smiled as the child straightened the tiny kid leather gloves her father had made for her and hugged the log as she scurried to the woodpile. She hefted the log into place and patted it as if it were a pillow, then bent to retrieve the others in turn for the same delicate treatment.

Bronson checked the head of his maul for the fifth time, as if worried it might fly off and strike the child. Undoubtedly, her helping slowed him down—but that's what parenting was all about.

He glanced up, directly into the window where she watched him. The direct stare he gave her made her blush as she hadn't in years, and as he looked, she raised her chin and gave a small smile of encouragement.

He looked away.

It surprised her, how much that hurt. So much that she had to tell herself he hadn't actually caught her eavesdropping on his private moments with their daughter. He had only been glancing toward, perhaps, a bird he spotted near the window. She almost would have convinced herself, except that it happened each time they drew near to one another. Across seventy-five feet, she felt his heat each time she looked at him.

But he no longer seemed to feel her as once he had.

"Look, Mama! Look, Mama!"

Sam pulled at her skirts, distracting her from her musings.

She rinsed the last dish and reached for the towel as she turned to her small son. She'd busied him with a piece of chalk and a slate board on the floor.

He grinned, his blue eyes flashing fire as he displayed his handiwork. Only three, but he'd scrawled out his name in three-inch tall letters across the oak floor.

She sighed, taking the chalk from him and writing his name on the slate. "Not on the floor, Sam. On the chalkboard. See?"

Confused at her unhappiness, he looked from the floor to the slate. She wiped down the floor with the dishcloth, then the slate, then handed him the chalk. She gently directed his small hand to the slate. "We write on our slate."

He shaped the letters with painstaking slowness, and she gasped in delight when he finished. "Good work, Sam!" She hugged him close. "Now, what does this say?"

"Sam!"

"There you go," she said, patting him as she turned to wipe down their supper table.

When she turned again, he'd scrawled the letters back across the floor. "This say Sam!" he said, pointing at the word.

"No!"

She took the chalk away and placed it on the table. He scrambled to his feet, climbing onto a chair to reach for it.

"Sam, no. No more writing until you learn to write on the slate."

He began to whimper, and she shook her head. "No. You know that won't work with me."

The back door slammed, and she glanced up. Abigail walked in, her face long. The opposite of Sam, she bottled up her emotions and focused them in trying to please her parents.

"I thought you were helping Papa."

"He told me it was nearly bedtime and you needed my help," she said, untying her cloak and cap and placing them on the peg, hastily slipping on the small woolen shawl there. Her gloves, she'd placed in a pocket.

Bedtime! It was barely six o'clock. But it was indeed dark outside. And heaven knows they were all tired.

She tried to steady her own overwhelming emotions, a powder keg of longing and loneliness and anger at Bronson. She had held down the house for three years now, and she needed his help. She needed him.

What she needed was a good—

Sam let out a long, loud wail.

"What's wrong with *him*?" Abigail asked.

All at once, Marley's building emotions left her in a fit of weary laughter. Abigail watched her brother with disdain, her arms folded across her chest, but his wailing pierced the veneer of disinterest, and worry entered her eyes.

Abigail had a servant's heart—Marley had never had to instill in her the traits she naturally exuded. When other children might have thrown a competing tantrum, she sought to alleviate his pain.

"He wants to write everywhere but the slate, so I took the chalk away."

Abigail patted her brother even as the back door slammed again. A moment later, Bronson stood there. "What's wrong?"

His genuine alarm surprised everyone. Sam's cry caught on a dry hiccup.

"What do you mean?"

"I heard the boy cry."

Only then did she notice his faint trembling, his breathlessness.

"He's all right," she reassured him, reaching out to touch his arm. Her heart swelled—he had grown so lean in these years, and his continued lack of appetite troubled her.

"I thought—never mind." With that, he returned to the wood yard.

Marley's hand, still poised in midair, fell to her side. She turned and smiled at the children. "It's all right. He has some things on his mind."

Abigail led her brother into the downstairs nursery and soon had him laughing and playing on his rocking horse. The rhythmic sounds of the maul against the chopping block, the fall of the split logs, gave the evening its own comforting song in counterpoint to the children's play.

Marley swept and mopped the floor, then removed her apron, placing it on the hook. She sat at the table, reading *Tom Jones*. She exhaled, feeling a semblance of peace she hadn't known all day.

This house really needs a proper window seat, she thought in dismay. How again had it gotten built without any at all? She smiled at the memory of Bronson scolding Silas and Hasty for their omission. He'd mentioned it to them more than once.

The children returned and she glanced up. "Will you read to us, Mama?"

"Of course, Abby, but you know how to read all of your books."

"But I want to hear one of yours. Like that one, about the foundling."

"Yes, Mama, the fongling," Sam added.

She smiled; it wasn't a matter of the novel being over their heads. She'd never made it through the first paragraph before they were both asleep.

Their small faces lifted to her in interest, and fierce love for her babes warmed her. She gathered them both near. "Oh, my darlings. We'll read a chapter. You both know it's time for bed."

Even as she spoke, the clock in the main room chimed seven. She left the lamp burning so her husband could see his way in. She hoisted the heavy pot of water from the hearth and replaced it with another to heat. She lugged the hot water with the hallway lamp ahead of them upstairs to the nursery.

Abigail laid out their nightclothes as she prepared their bath water in the basin, mixing the hot water with the cold water in the pitcher. Two quick sponge baths later, they hurried into their warm nightgowns and into the small beds they were already outgrowing.

How much she wanted another child—and how glad she was for these two.

She perched on the stool between their beds and began to read. After they drifted off, she quickly brushed their clothes and placed them on the chairs at the foot of their beds. Miracle of miracles, that the clothes could be worn again. She carried the lamp down the hall to her bedroom.

Oh, the years it had been since she had considered this *their* bedroom. How could three years seem like a lifetime?

She performed her evening toilette and changed into a nightgown and robe, heading for the kitchen with her book. As she'd passed the nursery, she heard their giggling—already they were back awake. She tapped on the door.

"Go to sleep."

In the kitchen, she looked out into the night for her husband. She was surprised to find the yard empty, the wood split and his tools put away.

She found him in the main room, seated in a rocker, staring into the fire. "The children are in bed?"

"Yes. I was just going to read a while. Would you like for me to read aloud?" She lowered herself to the chair across from him.

"I'm going to bed myself soon."

"I'll join you, then."

The look he gave her brought her up short—one of dismay. She pressed her lips together, attempting to steady herself.

"If you would only talk to me, it might help us both."

"What would you like to hear?"

"I only want to help you."

"Merrilea, I'm fine. I wish you'd stop worrying about me."

Merrilea. She couldn't remember the last time he'd called her his Marley.

"If you're fine, then—" She bit her lip, stopping the impetuous flow of words.

"Go on."

After a long moment, she did. "You were trembling tonight when you thought Sam was hurt."

He gave a long, ragged sigh. "Truth to tell, I barely know the poor child. I didn't know what might have happened."

And then, emboldened by his admission, she brought up *that* night.

"Do you remember that night—the last night with Rashall? When you turned thirty?"

"What about it?"

"Grey."

At last, he turned to look at her—as if she were insane. "Grey? My brother, you mean? What about him?"

"His visit that night. We were expecting him back so soon, but he hasn't been back. Do you think something might have happened?"

He only stared at her.

"What is it?"

"I've truly no idea what you mean."

And his face said the same. He wouldn't—or couldn't—remember the night they'd visited with his brother Grey, dropping in from the twenty-first century for a casual chitchat. They'd talked about the persistent threat of James Manning's sons. They'd talked about Bronson and Rashall helping him. And then—nothing.

"You and I talked about it several times afterward. And then, before much time at all had passed, you headed to New England. And here we are today."

His lean jaw went hard as he came to his feet. "Madame, I would have you occupy yourself with the concerns of ladies."

"And I would remind you that as my husband, you are my concern. And that for the past three years, except for an occasional letter with few details, I never knew whether you were alive or dead. In all that time, I was both mother and father to our children—especially the little boy you don't even know."

She saw it, then, for only a moment—pain and fear, entirely unshuttered, deep in his eyes, as she'd never seen it in their life together. Then it was gone, as if she'd imagined it.

"I'll sleep in the guest room tonight," he said. At the door he stopped, his hand gripping the doorframe. "Marley, I beg your patience."

She reached out to touch his shoulder in support, but he was gone, disappearing into the spare bedroom, leaving her alone.

He'd called her Marley—her first glimpse of the man she'd married since he'd left three years before.

She placed the metal screen around the hearth and silently climbed the stairs, hearing the children in the darkness. Were they singing?

They were—their voices soft, growing softer by the line, until the last few words dwindled into sleepy silence as they sang themselves to sleep.

> *"... I'm gonna let it shine*
> *Don't you try to whoosh it out, I'm gonna let it shine*
> *Don't you try to whoosh it out, I'm gonna let it shine*
> *Let it shine, all the time, let it shine ..."*

Tears of dark joy dampened her eyes. Yes, tonight she had much to be thankful for.

Chapter Four

Williamsburg, Virginia … a wintry morning in the year 2051
<u>Once and Future Carpenter</u>

Rachel heard the song from her husband's study as she finished a teleconference. The Avett Brothers, a folk music group her old-fashioned husband adored, had recorded the song decades ago. What she heard wasn't the Avett Brothers, though; it was her eldest granddaughter, several years before, singing a duet with her father. Her young, soulful contralto voice led the melody, while Tate played the guitar and sang harmony, modulating his powerful tenor not to overpower her. The sound of Tate, teaching his daughter what he loved and letting her take the lead, nearly broke her heart.

The recording had been a Christmas gift that year for Grey.

As if summoned by a thought, a chime sounded and she saw the faint form of that beloved girl, sitting in her room, wiping away her tears as the simulator waited for Rachel to answer. Today's Caller ID. She knew it was physically impossible, but the child resembled Camisha so much, with her large, upturned dark eyes and her wide, generous smile and ready laughter. She looked nothing like Emily; she favored Tate. At the moment, she was a bit of a wreck.

Rachel pressed her thumb against the chip on her wrist and smiled in anticipation of talking with her granddaughter. The hologram opened beside her easy chair, and she set aside her computer.

"Good morning, sweetheart," she said, holding out her arm. She didn't care for the feeling of the simulator, but Cammie had grown up with it, and at times she didn't know whether the child could tell the difference between a sim-call and reality.

Cammie waved away her offered embrace. "I can't, right now. I just wanted to talk with you a few minutes. Wait—what's that I hear?"

"Oh—your grandfather's listening to the video you made him for Christmas, that year."

Her face crumpled into sobs, and she shook her head. "Mute me. I don't want to upset Papa. And I don't want to hear Daddy singing right now."

Rachel pressed her lips together, muting her own tears as she ran her first two fingertips along the barely visible outline of the simulator as if performing a benediction, protecting her granddaughter's image so only she could see her, then tapped her earpiece to confine the sound to her ear. "Better?"

She nodded, blowing her nose. "I don't suppose there's any way you could come back up, could you?"

Four months had passed since Tate's death. After they'd flown up for the funeral in Manhattan, she'd stayed on for another three months to help their transition. She'd only gotten back home a few days ago.

"Tell me why you'd like me there, darling."

"I just miss him so. And Mom's acting so weird, hanging around all the time, I can't even think straight. And I miss you. And I'm so tired of people staring when we go out anywhere."

Rachel listened as she unburdened herself of it all—her constant reawakening to the pain of her father's death; her mother's emotional distance even while she attempted to comfort her; her own frustration at being unable to help her younger sisters understand where their father had gone.

And Tate's earlier life as a popular singer had put the small family under an international spotlight that no eleven-year-old could be expected to shrug off—even if it was all she'd ever known.

She thought she understood part of Emily's odd behavior, although they'd spoken of it only obliquely in the Sotherns' Harlem home, overlooking Central Park North. All three of her children bore the same rare DNA marker that had ultimately killed their young father.

Peculiar, that with all the advances of their time, men still died randomly of disease the medical community still couldn't prevent. Each time an old disease was eradicated, a new one was identified.

That Tate had been black had been only incidental in their lives; his most obviously differentiating feature was his wealth and fame. In an interesting turn, all of his children had been born looking like their mother, and had each slowly grown into the exotic good looks that had come from their father's side of the family. Idiotic fashion magazines hinted at the eleven-year-old Cammie being perfect for a career in modeling. As if the world at large were her parents, deciding her future for her.

Some things never changed, she thought.

"Are you still going to your dance classes?"

The child glanced at the floor. "I didn't go yesterday. I was going to cancel tomorrow's."

"You know, your body responds to the signals you send it."

"Yes, I remember. I just ..."

Rachel waited, suspecting the truth.

"Daddy loved watching me dance."

As she gathered her thoughts into a single truth, Rachel thought of the child's eponym, the woman she'd seen just once—and even then, impossibly—since she returned to this time. And both she and Emily had been too stunned to explain to her the honor Emily had bestowed on her eldest daughter with her name.

After all, it had been Camisha, as a young girl, who'd told Rachel what she was about to say. She'd told her this about her parents, adding, "Now I don't know where they are, but I'm pretty sure they're in heaven. Otherwise, they wouldn't have ever let you go live with somebody like Mr. Sheppard."

Rachel hadn't known at the time that Camisha had already seen the newspaper article that held the truth, and she knew that both her parents were dead.

"Sweetie, I think that in heaven, where there's no pain, people we've lost can't see their loved ones on earth suffering. Now they might feel in their hearts that we need help and put in a good word for us. But when we're doing the things that make us happy, then they can look down on us and see that. That's the kind of happiness they have in heaven, the kind not even angels get to have. Cammie, when you're dancing, you can bet Daddy's dancing right along with you."

The child's eyes brimmed with tears as she smiled at Rachel. "Do you really think so?"

She nodded, reaching for a tissue to wipe her own eyes. *God, I miss her so much.* Both Cammie and the woman she was named for.

Without warning, Cammie reached through the muted simulator and hugged her, and with the virtual sensation of her touch, the pain of missing her granddaughter filled her.

That, in the end, was what she disliked about the simulator; it reminded her what she was missing. This young woman, growing up, in real life. No matter how sophisticated the electronics, they were never as good as the real thing.

"Don't worry, honey, we'll come up. I'll talk to Papa and bring him with me. He misses his work here when he's away, but I know how happy he'll be to see all of you again."

With that, Cammie sniffed and brightened, again blowing her nose. "All right. I can't wait to see you again. And I'll try harder—I'll practice my dancing this afternoon."

When she disconnected the call, she could hear the song again from the other room; Grey was on an auto-repeat. Such times nearly drove her insane.

She rose and walked to his study. Standing by the window, he looked out on Duke of Gloucester Street at the sparse

January visitors. When they'd received approval to finance the reconstruction of a modest colonial home that had stood not far from Bruton Parish Church, Grey had involved everyone imaginable in its creation. He had turned it into an educational program, from the archeological dig through its eventual construction—as he did everything he touched, as if still attempting to atone for sins from forty years before. From three centuries before.

This room was merely a smaller version of the gorgeous library in his own Rosalie, richly paneled and filled to the ceiling with books.

Love for her tortured husband blossomed within her.

This was the slowest tourist season of the year, and the best time for the two of them to get out of Williamsburg. He grew restless when he wasn't able to impact as many visitors. He was surprised when his program became one of the most popular there, since it was such a somber topic. The living history medium continued to struggle with how to present slavery without further injuring black actors, and the appearance of a genuinely repentant trader finding redemption hit a resonant note.

He disliked it when she commercialized what he felt was sacred work: educating the next generation about the atrocities of the past, lest these atrocities be committed again. Viewing anything in terms of its marketability had been drilled into her since childhood, though, and it was hard to wash out.

No matter how she looked at it, she couldn't help but admire Grey's work.

Today he wore his interpreter's garb, which she loved—it brought to mind the man she'd come to love, more than three decades ago. At his age, his hair heavily silvered, he was still magnificent. More so. Every line on his face made him sexier to her.

Through the window, off farther in the distance, she saw the bare limbs of the catalpa trees that guarded Palace Green. *My granny called them Indian cigar trees. There were forty-five of them when I was a kid.*

Camisha's voice in her memory came to her from that last day she would see her in the twenty-first century—now thirty-five years ago. Would a day ever pass that she didn't miss her? Would she ever get over the urge to discover her fate? And—her sisters? More than once, she had done Internet searches for her sisters. She'd found nothing about either of them, and five years before, she'd learned why, at least for Merri, when she saw her in the ruins at Rosalie. She'd never learned anything about Juliana—and eventually, she let it go.

The only thing that ever soothed her curiosity was the knowledge that in time, Camisha and Merri were dear friends.

And that, she told herself for the thousandth time, would have to be enough. She would not go back to that place where—beyond any stretch of logic—she'd seen Camisha, at her own age now. While they were out visiting old Rosalie, little Cammie had seen a little boy in the ruins. And then—

"Cammie called?" he asked over his shoulder, startling her.

"She didn't want to upset you."

He turned the music off, returning his attention to the few people in the rain-slick street.

"Why don't we spend a couple of weeks with them?"

"You just spent four months with them."

She walked forward and touched his back, her fingers threading into his hair. It was loose today; how she loved the silky feel of it. "A change of scenery would do you good. We can visit Cortland, see their latest programs."

He turned away, walking to his desk. "I'll miss my programs here."

His none-too-subtle rejection didn't deter her.

"You know they have someone who can do that work in your absence—and very capable indeed. Frederick Douglass."

"Next month is Black History month. He'll be busy then."

"Why don't you want to see your grandchildren? And Emily?"

He raised his head. The last time she'd seen that expression on him was forever ago—back at Rosalie, when she'd confronted him with his work, trading in human lives.

"You know me better than that, wife."

Any other woman would have told him to drop the colonial shtick, but she knew better. You can take the gentleman out of the eighteenth century, but ... He was still the man she'd met in 1746. And she loved him for it.

Abruptly, he rose and left the room. She heard him in the attic presently, then saw him pass by with his suitcase on his way to their bedroom.

She went right along after him.

"Do you want me to book a couple of flights?"

"Thank you, no. I'm driving up there."

"Still captaining your own ship."

He gave a noncommittal harrumph at her quip.

"Grey ..." She hesitated, uncertain how to say it.

"I haven't had any rum," he answered her unspoken question without resentment, embarrassing her.

"I didn't think you had. Only ..." That he well might change that, along the drive. Quickly, she went on, "Only that the weather isn't good."

"It's just rain."

She gave a half smile. "It was only rain, that night I first got to Rosalie, when you were nearly struck by lightning."

He'd told her the story of finding her naked and asleep in the rear entryway of the house, so long ago. The half-memory came to her now as she watched him pack without responding. It might have been easier had he not been wearing his gentry finery, but he'd given a talk that morning, and he had yet to change. The silk and satin were a reminder of that elegant world he'd once known—the seductively charming gentleman he still was.

It had been so long since he'd held her tenderly.

"If you fly up, you can get there in just a couple of hours. It would be such a wonderful surprise, for the children and Em."

"Rachel, I need time to myself. You know how much Tate meant to me."

"And to me."

He glanced up at her, giving an expressionless nod. "Aye."

"Grey, you don't—somehow blame yourself for his death, do you?"

"Leave me be!" he burst, bracing his fists on the bed.

After a long, tense moment, she said, "It *wasn't your fault.*"

He snapped the case closed. "How do you know? I see the headlines daily, laying blame at the feet of men like me for all the troubles in this country. Perhaps this very defect of his heart was born centuries ago."

"That's insane."

He grew cold. "You cannot perceive this, Rachel. Let me go."

"We made a promise to each other," she said, trying to clear her throat of impending tears. She forced herself on. "You cannot leave this way. I'll let you go alone if you must, but if I have to walk all the way to Manhattan, *I will not let you leave angry.*"

He looked at her for a long moment, then exhaled and shook his head. "Very well. I would not have you anxious. Here."

He retrieved her case from the corner—she'd not yet even placed it back in the attic—and opened it on the bed, matter-of-factly opening her drawers and beginning to pack for her. He abandoned the task, uncertain what to put there. Instead, he reached into the closet for slacks and a sweater.

"I'll change and get the car."

He walked into the hall bathroom as withdrawn as before. She stood for some minutes, trying to pull herself together long enough to pack.

I miss you, Grey.

In another hour, the car was warm and packed. Like the courtly, colonial gentleman the twenty-first century couldn't seem to destroy, he unfolded a plaid throw over her lap. Never mind that their automobile had individual climate control matched to her metabolism, or that she was quite capable of grabbing the throw out of the back seat. This was the man she had loved from the first, and the noise of modern naysayers about chivalrous ways like his left him unmoved.

"Did you check your court schedule?" she asked.

"Of course. Nothing this month. Montgomery can take care of anything that arises while we're gone."

There weren't many men who would go to law school at the age of thirty-five to become a public defender, but he had—to fill the void Camisha had left when she'd remained in the eighteenth century. The consulting business Rachel had established had enabled her to be free to advise the foundation here, and for him to do whatever he liked.

He wedged a small pillow in her headrest, as he knew she liked it, and closed the door quietly. Soon they were headed west on I-64. Grey chose Vivaldi for the drive, and she relaxed into the pillow, soon drifting to sleep.

When she awakened, the first sensation she knew was Grey's hand over hers, his thumb stroking it lightly as he drove. She turned her hand up to meet his, but it was as if she'd startled a bird. His hand returned to the steering wheel.

"I didn't mean to awaken you."

"It's all right. How long have I been asleep?"

"Not even an hour."

"Where are we?"

Then she saw the street sign as they exited the highway: *Visit Old Henricus Historical Park.*

"Just outside Richmond." He cast her a reserved glance.

"Grey ..." She froze in dread, watching the car eat up the miles of narrow, two-lane highway winding toward the James. "I don't want to go there. You know that."

"Go where? I bought a property some time ago and wanted to show it to you before we drive on."

"You didn't."

But even as she denied the suggestion, he turned off the rural road where she saw the sixty-year-old metal sign: *Harriman Road.*

Instantly she heard the voice from so long ago: *"Wellness check, Fourteen Harriman Road. I can hear what sounds like a little girl crying. We'll have someone there soon, honey. Can you tell me your name?"*

The unforgettable sound of the police dispatcher, when Rachel had called for help for her parents. She hadn't understood her call would instead report their murder.

She had awakened from the nightmare of reliving that night countless times when she and Grey had first returned to her time. He had attempted, again and again, to take her back to the place so she could make peace with her past, but she had refused.

"Why are you doing this?"

He didn't reply. Finally, he drifted to a stop by the familiar mailbox. He lifted his arm over the back of the seat as he turned to her. "We both have our demons, Rachel. I face mine every day in my work so that people won't ever make the same foolish mistakes I made. I bought your childhood home years ago so that someday, when you were ready, you could face yours as well."

She said nothing—staring blankly at the mailbox. The very same old rural mailbox they'd had when she was a child.

"I will not go in."

"You will, if I have to carry you."

"My parents died there. Why would you force me to look at it all again?"

"Because I love you. Because you forced me to face reality. Because if not for you, our daughter and I would have died lost souls. And because I know there's a reason for you to visit this place again. Can you not trust me after all this time?"

She looked into his eyes. *With my very life.*

He opened the car door, climbed out, and walked around to help her out into the cold, rainy morning. She stepped onto the stone path for the first time since she'd left in the night with her sisters, nearly sixty years before.

Chapter Five

Stonefield—April, 1781

Juliana stood at the edge of the clearing, the bitter wind whipping at her cloak. She felt none of it. She stared at the rector who stood before the small assembly gathered under an ancient oak.

"I know that my Redeemer liveth, and that he shall stand at the latter day upon the earth; and though this body be destroyed, yet shall I see God; whom I shall …"

Her mind drifted yet again. She couldn't follow the service. Her gaze lowered to the earth at her feet, where her husband had been buried two weeks ago. In all this time, she hadn't shed a tear for him. What worried her most, unfortunately, was how others might perceive her lack of grief. She felt empty.

He was a mean, small man and I'm grateful to be free of him.

Her young nephew began to whine, and she glanced past her sister at him. On Merrilea's other side, George reached to take the small child from her, silently distracting him with a game of peek-a-boo. All this, Juliana saw before her gaze returned to the cold earth covering her husband's coffin.

She folded her gloved hands together, lest her sister attempt to take her hand to comfort her. She couldn't bear her kindness—not today.

God help her, she did not want to be here. She wanted nothing to do with the crowd of well-meaning friends offering their last respects to a man they thought she never should have married—miserly, cold, and a Loyalist to boot.

Of course, they'd all been right.

But all the better she was here, enduring their undeserved concern, for the penance it offered. The week after the visit to Black Oak, while she had been obsessed with the memory of Rashall Adams, a man of God, her husband had lain dying outside Richmond, overcome with smoke when caught in one of the plantations the British had torched.

And because Enoch had been such a generous benefactor to their cause, his commanding officer had ensured he was returned to his widow's home for burial. The thought of that man's kindness to her should have been enough to distract her, but only one memory filled her mind, her spirit—her body.

Rashall.

Her eyes closed with the overpowering memory of him. She clamped her teeth together to prevent the sound of his name from escaping her, as it often did when she was alone. It stormed over her, the sound of his name a rush of passion and living that he had always been in her life.

No one knew how often she had traveled in time to that moment when he had first entered her life and looked at her with naked desire, despite his shy, awkward manner. It had been the single most pleasurable moment in her life, ever—and she a married woman.

No, a widow now.

Traveled in time.

For most daydreamers, that was only a figure of speech. For Juliana, she had sought out the labyrinth, that place where she'd spent far too many hours of her growing years, retrieving the Final Artifacts of various strangers' lives to visit corresponding moments in time.

Go outside and play, Aunt Mary would say, when she heard the slide of the drapery around the window seat, knowing where she was headed. *That girl's wasting her life, in other worlds.*

She didn't quite understand the cosmic formula that made time travel possible, but she didn't need to. The system made it simple for almost anyone to travel throughout time.

She heard it, then, rescuing her from her distant reverie. The sound of a woman's voice trilling over the syllables of a single word for no less than ten seconds, followed by another, at last, singing the hymn as a spiritual. In the silence of the woods, the acapella notes echoed with painfully clear purity. On the next verse, George Adams took two steps away from the congregation to join the woman, singing in harmony. He had his father's voice, his father's passion.

Ruth's song had begun with a solemn whisper that, with George's youthful counterbalance, soon blossomed into enraptured worship. Juliana watched her, captured by the passion, the mercy, the somber gravity, that moved through the woman as she sang the story of the slave trader John Newton once had been. No professional arrangement could have more perfectly captured the essence of the song.

"*'Twas grace that taught my heart to fear—and grace my fears relieved—*"

Juliana had experienced countless versions of this song during her travels: raucous blue-grass sessions by Mumford & Sons and organ-backed classics by Shirley Caesar; tear-filled anthems by Aretha Franklin. And in one rare accident of time, she had heard the song sung as a plaintive prayer on a fire escape at a Harlem bordello by a young girl named Eleonora Fagan—who would go on to become Billie Holiday.

And never had her soul been pierced more deeply than this simple version, accompanied by nothing more than the tenderness of the singers.

Marley had taught Ruth the song last year when she accidentally discovered what a powerful gift the older woman had for singing. *"Her voice reminds me of Mahalia Jackson. I still remember the old videos of her; such a singer."*

At the time, Marley had felt obliged to explain to her what videos were—since she had no way of knowing that Juliana had traveled to watch the actual sights occur. The way people in the twenty-first century spent hours they could never recapture browsing articles about pointless celebrities and trivialities of the day, linking from one to the next, Juliana had spent traveling through time, an hour or day at a time.

Marley slipped two fingers into her sleeve and withdrew a lacy handkerchief, passing it to her. She dabbed at the tears, feeling as if she'd been caught trying to get away with something. It wasn't as if she were crying over Enoch. Truth to tell, she didn't know why the silent tears slid down her cheeks.

The song concluded, and Ruth and George rejoined them.

"Mrs. Morgan."

She raised her head, facing the expectant vicar, who held out his hand toward the path.

She glanced at her sister as she turned away from the grave, and she noticed the alert concern on Marley's face. Even now, no judgment from anyone. Enoch's funeral service had ended, and she remembered nothing from it except the hymn—and the memory of Rashall.

Perhaps—just perhaps—if her husband had kissed her just once—had found the least interest in her after their wedding— she might have had something, anything, to remember him for. But today she stood the same virgin bride she'd been over a year ago when they wed—now a virgin widow.

The next hours passed in a rush, while the mourners from nearby farms, from Richmond, and from far-off Rosalie, down by Williamsburg, ate dinner crowded into and around her home. No alcohol was served, though—not even Ruth's beloved blackberry wine. Enoch had forbidden it in his will.

She wasn't too surprised when guests began to drift back to their homes afterward. A sober funeral was a short funeral.

She pulled her tapestried shawl more tightly around her from her place in the rocking chair by the crackling fire, still shivering as she glanced around the warm room. Those closest to her were there. Across from her, on the other side of the fire, sat her great-grandfather Godfrey—Papa—chatting amiably with Dan, Ruth's husband. Ruth sat nearby, listening to her youngest grandson tell a tale.

Marley sat on the chesterfield to her right, feeding little Sam and herself. Her young daughter sat beside her, softening bits of carrot pudding in sauce and sharing it with the brother she doted on. "More, Abby!"

Next to Abigail sat George, and here Juliana's gaze stopped. Rashall's son carried none of his father's genetic material, but he had his mannerisms, his expressions. His studious alertness, always looking for places where he might help; his ready laughter, always seeking to lighten the heart of another; and his loyalty, always caring for those he loved. How he must worship his father.

His gaze was focused on a Trelawney daughter, adopted into freedom from a plantation along the James. This adoption had struck close to home. Years ago, Ruth Trelawney's own daughter, Leah, had died giving birth to a stillborn daughter—a double blow for Ruth. Tutored in Camisha's redemption of children from other plantations, Ruth had quickly found a possible match at Shirley Plantation. They had journeyed through the thick woods in the night to the place. Soon, a young woman owned by the family gave birth to her daughter. This young girl, named Susan according to the wishes of the birth mother, gave Ruth comfort. Leah had wanted to name her child Susan after her own sister, known as Sukey.

Leah's stillborn daughter had taken Susan's place in the grave of the slave child on the distant plantation.

Juliana leaned toward Marley. "What made you take up Camisha's habit of ... um, the night-time ... ?" She struggled for an ordinary way to describe it, certain her no-nonsense sister wouldn't approve of the phrase *baby-swapping.*

Marley cast a discreet glance toward her children. She wouldn't have attempted to explain such affairs to them.

In a lowered whisper, she said, "I had no choice. I had to. We live in a risky time; why not make those risks count for something?"

Abigail peered at Marley to discern her words.

Juliana nodded. "I see." She then glanced toward Susan and murmured, "Young George seems quite taken with her."

Sam had finished his meal, and Abby led her brother to the window seat to entertain him with a book.

"What does your husband think of your midnight midwifery?"

"He believes in it, he simply doesn't want *me* doing it. If a member of the other household happened to arrive in the middle of the switch ... I shudder to think what might happen."

"To a white woman?" Juliana asked with a smirk. "All you'd have to do is make up whatever you'd like, and you'd be believed."

"Likely, you're right. That doesn't stop him from worrying, or from resenting me for doing it."

"Despite our own grandmother having been a slave."

Marley exhaled at her sister's needling. "As if your own Enoch wanted you anywhere near the likes of me or Bronson."

Juliana lowered her head, surprised at how the jibe pricked. She herself had said the same thing many times over. With Enoch's Loyalist politics, it was a wonder anyone had shown up today. The only friend he'd had in the neighborhood— Gerald Grimewood—had skipped the service entirely.

And yet, as she sat there staring at her hands, letting her sister's casual remark pierce her, she realized what she felt wasn't nearly so much pain as it was guilt—for feeling so little toward Enoch.

"Forgive me, Julie." Marley held her sister's hands. "What a vile, thoughtless thing to say, on today of all days."

"It's no more than I've said myself. He was a stiff-necked, awful man. My only mistake was in ever marrying him."

Now it was Marley's turn for awkwardness. For it had been she who had suggested she marry the relentless suitor, if for no other reason than protection during the devastation of war. Oddly, though, she brought it up in the context of Rashall, as if he had anything to do with her marrying Enoch Morgan. Juliana had never figured that out.

Marley sighed, as if she'd explained this dozens of times. "I was trying to make you notice Ray."

"By pushing me toward Enoch?"

"I was being sarcastic." The last word, she nearly whispered, wearily.

"Why not just tell me?"

"I thought you knew!"

This made even less sense. "If you thought I knew, why say anything at all?"

Marley looked back at her. "I'm sorry. Rashall is a good man. I suppose you know that by now. I was trying to say how worried I was about you, being up here all by yourself."

"You said, 'Why not just marry Enoch Morgan? He's persistent enough.'"

"And I'm not used to people taking me that seriously!"

Juliana nodded, letting it go.

Her guardians *were* away from Stonefield as often as they were there, tending to matters throughout time. Marriage to Enoch Morgan, she had thought, would perhaps ensure her safety from the threats of the wilderness such as the native tribes and any wandering ne'er-do-wells. A practical solution for a woman who had no interest in ever marrying.

Before, that is, Rashall's unexpected return to the Tidewater.

A sudden loud rap on the front door arrested the quiet murmur of conversation in the room. Hasty, one of Ruth's sons, rose and crossed to the door.

Juliana stopped at the window seat to quickly place the children outside it and closed the heavy drapery around it. She'd not been much older than Abby when she'd accidentally discovered the concealed switch that opened into the labyrinth.

Hasty opened the door before she arrived. Martin, George, and other men rose, ready to come to their aid.

"Good afternoon, sir," Hasty said.

Grimewood stood there in a triple cape overcoat and tricorn hat, all black, his walking stick held out as if to knock again. His gray hair hung loose around his shoulders, and daylight intensified his ugliness. He looked like the homeliest of bullfrogs. Pockets of flesh hung under his bulbous, watery blue eyes as he cast his glance about the room in contempt. He stopped on the slender figure of Susan Trelawney with an interest that revolted Juliana. Then he drew his attention back to Hasty.

"Is Hastings in attendance?"

"I'm Hastings," Hasty said.

He might have thrown water in Grimewood's face. "You're not. You're a ... a negro."

Hasty looked around in deadpan shock. As Juliana arrived beside him, he asked her, "Is that so, Juliana? Am I truly a negro? Because sometimes that mirror plays tricks on me."

"Go sit down," she murmured under her breath, pushing him away even as she faced Grimewood. "What business could you have that's so important it couldn't wait until another day? As you clearly know, he and all my visitors are here to pay their respects to my husband. You remember Enoch, do you not?"

He cocked his head at her angry defiance.

"My condolences, madame. I assure you I did not know. *Is* Mr. Hastings in attendance?"

"I'm right here," Hastings called out in annoyance from his chair near the fire. The men between them stepped aside so he could be seen. "Might we meet next week at Rosalie?"

"No. I have journeyed to Rosalie in search of you once already, and to Williamsburg. They sent me here."

His outlandish lies disgusted her. He lived on the next plantation up the river—an hour's journey at most.

Hastings gave an indelicate snort. "Fortunate indeed for you if your plantation still stands, after Mr. Arnold's most recent treachery. What is your business, sir?"

"The business of illegal records."

The silence was pierced by only the steady fall of rain outside—and, finally, Juliana's voice.

"What illegal records could you mean? My family will not be bullied by groundless accusations."

"Records that do not account for the presence of more than 500 free blacks, living at Rosalie, long after they should have quit this colony."

Hastings exploded with a mocking laugh. "Pah! Our records are pristine. Has the treasury not been promptly paid all taxes for all those living at Rosalie?

"Taxes are not my interest, sir. I am aware that you manage Mr. Thomas Trelawney's accounts as well as those of the former slaves who now own a good portion of Rosalie. Most of whom have been educated as well under your mismanagement."

This last transgression clearly bothered him more than the rest.

Every adult in the room was focused on the man, masking their dislike. Juliana, however, was distracted by the sudden fiery appearance of Ruth coming to her feet, as silent and powerful as a flame rising from a torch.

"And what of it?" Hastings asked, still treating the man as if he were a pesky mosquito.

"You know it is illegal."

"What is?"

"All of it. Their very existence in Virginia is a mockery of the law."

Juliana, out of patience, moved to slam the door in his face. Grimewood swung his walking stick, wedging it between the door and the frame.

"I will not be trifled with, madame."

"State what you want, then, and be on your way. You are trespassing on Miller land and no longer welcome," she said.

The man's face melted into an almost grandfatherly smile. "As I understand it, the land belonged to Brigadier General Enoch Morgan, a loyal servant of the King. I will tell all of you—especially you," he said with a raised brow, roving over every black member of the family gathered in the room, "that the law mandates that you leave Virginia after being declared free. I have documentation indicating you were freed in July of 1746. You have flouted the law for nearly thirty-five years."

"Then let me tell *you*, sir."

The frog went silent as he faced Ruth, who instinctively glided in front of the grandchildren clinging to her black skirts.

71

His mouth fell open; this affront to his dignity was more than he could take. His face, pink from the bitter wind and his own anger, went deeply ruddy at her tone. He was simply too shocked to respond.

"Rosalie Plantation's been my home nigh on 45 years, since I came here as a girl from South Carolina, bought, redeemed, and educated by Mr. Grey Trelawney. I've tended her tobacco, I've cooked and served her masters' meals. I've sewn and mended her sons' clothing and that of her grandsons and granddaughters. I've dried their tears when they learn what an unwholesome world they've been born into. I've loved every one of these children, Mr. Trelawney's, Mr. Grey's, Mr. Bronson's, just as if they were my own. I reckon they love me, too. And let me tell you, I *will not leave them*. This is our land.

"I've worked, sir. I've worked hard and my brothers and sisters and sons and daughters have worked hard. We rightly have our freedom according to the law, and we aren't going *anywhere*. This is our land, I tell you.

"Your kind took my mama from her home, took my daddy from his, and took me from my mama, and me just a young girl, not much more than a child.

"I will not stand for it again, you hear me? This is my home. This town, this colony, this country, this *land*. It's my home, and my family is fighting for its freedom against men like you, same as Mr. Hastings fought for ours. You will not take me from my home again. Mark my words, sir. This is our land."

The room fell silent as she leaned toward him, her fists on her hips, and Juliana felt a fearsome uneasiness as the bright red in his face drained away, leaving him pale and expressionless.

He didn't have to slam the door as he turned to leave. Ruth slammed it for him.

Chapter Six

When he heard the news of the death of faithful Loyalist Enoch Morgan, Rashall rode hard through a thunderstorm to reach Stonefield to pay his respects at the funeral. He was late. For this he thanked God.

He was dead tired, every muscle in his body aching from the long ride. He'd stopped at the stable to brush down his horse and feed her. Now, as he watched from just inside the barn, he heard the old man call Ruth by a foul name before turning away and hobbling down the small path to his carriage.

Grimewood knew him, and he couldn't afford to be exposed. Juliana's husband had been an infamous Loyalist, but he'd bet money not another person here today could say as much. He'd heard Ruth giving him what-for as he'd arrived.

The carriage rolled away toward the setting sun, and he started to step out of the stable. He stopped short as someone walked around the house from the back exit, carrying a lamp.

Juliana.

Before he could reach her—or even think to call out—she'd descended into a root cellar. Not too far beyond the house, he noticed the small clearing with a mound of black dirt marked by a simple wooden cross. The grave of Morgan.

He crossed to the cellar and lifted the heavy doors. A path of uneven stones led steeply down, and he descended far enough to close the doors behind him. There, he left his heavy pack.

"Who's there?"

The sound of her voice—how often he'd dreamed of this moment.

"Juliana, it's Rashall."

He rushed down the stairs to find her at the back of the small cellar, near a passageway of some sort. She set a lamp down on a shelf nearby, unwittingly illuminating herself to his hungry stare.

Odd, that the passion he felt for her was tempered in a moment into compassion. She had lost weight in the weeks since last he'd seen her. The same black gown she'd worn the night of the costume ball now hung loose on her. She'd gathered a black wool shawl close about her. She seemed like a lost child, her face drawn with grief and worry over whatever loathsome tidings Grimewood had brought.

And he could not stop himself from moving toward her.

Neither did she stop him.

He brought her into his arms, holding her close—dear God, she was so cold! Most women were so small he'd felt awkward at moments like this. Not so with Juliana—she just filled his empty arms. As he slid his arm around her, she buried her face in the hollow of his shoulder near his heart. His other hand slid into her hair, unintentionally removing the clip holding it in place, and it tumbled down her back.

Despite himself, he sighed in pleasure as he drew her even closer. At last he was *home*.

She was weeping against his chest, and he grew aware that he was speaking. "I'm so sorry, my darling. It's all right."

He had comforted countless parishioners during his time at the church in Bermuda. He had bitterly mourned being away from the island when he heard of the Great Hurricane that had all but destroyed it last fall—he should have been there with them.

And he had comforted his mother when she lost her own Helen a year ago, while he himself was overcome with grief.

But never had he felt anyone's grief as he felt hers now.

He moved his cheek with sensual awareness against the top of her head, stroking her hair as he murmured reassurances.

"It isn't what you think."

Reluctantly, he raised his head. "Then tell me about it."

She shook her head, looking up at him in the lamplight. Her full lips, upturned to him, were only a few inches from his. "Just hold me."

That, he could do. He ignored his body's response and held her closer, his large hand spanning her lower back to support her. He knew that she, a widow, must surely understand the effect she was having on him.

Her hand, resting at his throat, slipped underneath his coat and shirt, her fingers spreading across his bare chest. His breath caught.

"Perhaps we should rejoin the others," he said.

"No."

Her voice was thick with tears even as she ignited fire within him, unbuttoning his coat and pulling herself against him. "You're so warm."

Warm didn't begin to describe it.

"Juliana." The word was a strangled plea.

"I've been so cold for so long."

He enclosed her in the coat, against his warmth, and she sighed in pleasure as her hands rested near the small of his back. Then he felt her lips, open on his throat.

He kissed her temple, stroking her hair. "I'm sorry I was too late for the funeral. I know how you must miss him."

"No," she said sharply. "You don't. Rashall, I never—he never ..."

He saw the raw grief in her tear-stained face—but for what, he no longer knew. She spoke with contempt and hatred.

And he thought he understood at last. Morgan had married this woman not out of love, but for some less noble goal. What had he done to her?

"Did he hurt you?"

She turned away from him for the first time, hugging herself. He removed his coat, placing it over her shoulders.

"He never touched me."

To distract them both, he asked, with genuine curiosity, "How did he die?"

"Ah. In a hell of his own making. Suffocated by the smoke of a fire in one of the plantations he was destroying."

Her bitterness hung in the air between them, and she lowered her head, turning back to him. "Tell me why you never answered the letters I sent to you at St. George's?"

It shouldn't have surprised him, that no one there had bothered to write her. "I never received them. I was with the First Rhode Island Regiment—with Hawk."

"You left the church?"

He sought an explanation that satisfied him. "George didn't explain it to you?"

"I rarely see anyone. This is the most festive occasion I've known in years. No disrespect to my husband."

"But—why didn't you go live with your sister? You knew Hawk was fighting, did you not?" The accusation in his tone embarrassed him, and he quickly added, "I simply thought they would have sent someone for you."

"Perhaps they thought I was not home when they came." Distance entered her eyes, even as she looked away entirely— was she lying to him? Then, noticing how deftly he'd changed the subject, she faced him again. "No. He didn't explain it. What happened?"

"I was asked to leave. A new archbishop informed me that the bishop who ordained me years ago lacked the authority to do so, for a person of my *background*. I took that to mean the background readily apparent on my skin."

"That can't be."

He smiled gently. "You sweet, daft idiot."

She laughed.

"I know you live in seclusion, but there's a vile world beyond this cozy cottage. A world I must return to soon."

Her disappointment might have pleased a vainer man—but it only reminded him of his inability to be the man she needed.

She looked away, as if in hopelessness, and her voice was shallow. "Please don't leave me again."

"I will not. No more than I could five years ago. My heart remains here, and when I lie awake hundreds or thousands of miles away, it finds its pleasure in you. And when your heart breaks, I feel that pain."

She gave his coat back to him. "I need *you* with me. Speak plainly if you—care for me."

"If I care for you," he whispered, his hand rising to her face. "I would have you live free in a country where you and I can love freely. I would have our children living free—in a world where such a feat isn't the small miracle that it is here."

"I can take you to such a world; you would find it of little comfort. This is our world. This is my life and yours. Please stay here with me."

He fought it with every shred of decency in him. And he lost.

In the cool darkness, his mouth found hers and he kissed her as he'd dreamed for the past five years. And she held him fiercely, bringing him even closer into her with an eagerness that startled and enflamed him.

He drew away, his lips resting in her hair. "Your husband lies yonder, dead not yet a month. You must take the time to mourn him before I can honorably even speak with you. This is our world, yes. But a world riddled with war. Every man over the age of 16 is out there fighting and dying, and I must rejoin them. And I'd like to visit my son before I go back."

"George? He's right upstairs."

"Then Hawk is here as well?"

The look she gave him troubled him. "George has been apprenticing with Martin. Since Bronson got home, he hasn't been himself."

Apprenticing with Martin? What in the world?

"Yes, I've heard that. But why wouldn't George live with Marley and help take care of her?"

"That I don't know." She looked away.

"All right. What is it, between you and Marley?"

"I don't understand."

"You don't get along with her?"

"The truth is, I don't know her. I live far away from her, and I haven't found out whether we get along."

"You are within a few hours of one another by river. And her husband, as I recall, is a sailor."

"But I am not, and he's been away these past three years. And if I'm honest, I don't understand her. If you lived in a world where life was as easy as it is in the time she came from, why would you choose this life, filled with hardship and disease?"

"Then you believe it? The time travel?"

"I know it's true."

"How?"

She hesitated. "Do you think she's lying?"

"Not exactly. It just defies—"

"Logic."

They turned at the sound of a new voice behind them. At the inner recess of the cellar lay a dark passageway that he hadn't noticed before. And there stood an elderly couple who were vaguely familiar—yes. He'd first seen them that day he met Juliana. The man had spoken just now—the merry fellow he remembered as Malcolm.

"Rashall Adams, at your service. You're the couple who raised Juliana, are you not?"

"We are not a *couple*." The woman cast Malcolm an exasperated glance—as if irritated at being featured with him in the same breath. "But yes, we are Juliana's guardians. You're Camisha's eldest, aren't you?"

"What an excellent memory you have. A pleasure to see you both again."

She gave a polite nod. "Juliana, you're in mourning, dear. You should be upstairs comforting the other mourners."

"We were visited by that cowardly Grimewood. And Rashall is my guest."

"And again I offer my condolences, madame," he said, turning away from the newcomers, with a warm gaze just for her. "I, too, will join the others."

With that, he escaped the cellar. When neither Juliana nor the others followed, he quietly closed the doors behind him. Dusk had fallen, and he made his way inside.

His heart lightened when he found George, laughing with Martin and Susan, one of Ruth's grandchildren, near the fire. He mightily wanted to hug his son, but he couldn't miss the young man's interest in the girl, so he merely nodded at him.

"Father!" The boy rushed to him and threw his arms around him, and Rashall pressed his lips together as he hugged him "You just missed Juliana. I think she went down to find more candles. Or oil. Or something. I've forgotten."

The boy had grown six inches. If this damned war didn't end soon, he, too, would be joining those boys on the battlefield, unsure which end of a musket was the business end.

"I saw her as I was coming in. I've brought you something. Whenever you've finished your conversation, let me know."

"Rashall! Get your handsome self over here." Marley was across the room, and he made his way to her. "You cut off all your hair!" She threw her arms about his neck.

How he'd missed her—and, of course, her husband.

He laughed at her shocked exclamation. It had been five years since he'd worn his hair long.

"Look at you! Still as beautiful as you were when Hawk fished you out of the sea. And this must be little Abigail?"

She introduced her children to Ray.

"Well, this young fella looks just like his papa—except for his grandfather's black hair." He bent over and lifted Sam in his arms, and the boy's blue eyes widened as he observed his beaming grin.

When he fretted, Rashall placed him back beside Abby, who curtsied for him. He bowed and kissed her hand, and she giggled prettily. "Where's your father, child? I can't believe he'd let you wander about the countryside without him to protect you from knaves like myself."

She smiled uncertainly, tugging her mother's skirt, and Rashall straightened, smiling down at her.

Marley sent the children off to play with some of the other young children. "You do my heart good, Ray. Are you well?"

"All things considered, very well. I'm doing courier work for Lafayette." True enough; the less she knew, the better. "And my old friend, I take it he isn't here. How is he?"

He saw the emotion in her eyes. "All things considered, I suppose, very well. He could have come home missing an arm. Missing a leg. Or just a letter from a grateful nation—"

She cut herself off, pressing her fingertips to her lips.

"Instead, he came home missing himself?"

She nodded, turning toward him. He drew her against him, letting her cry silently against his chest.

He couldn't imagine the man with whom he'd once roamed the seven seas allowing his wife or those sweet children out of his sight—let alone traveling all the way to Stonefield without him.

"Give him time, Marley."

"Can you come home with us?"

"Sure. Why don't we take Juliana along, too?"

Her tears caught on laughter. "Might've known you'd suggest that."

"I'm serious. She's out here in the middle of nowhere. I would've thought she'd come to live with you and Hawk."

"I've asked her so many times. In fact—no, never mind."

"What?"

Marley was no liar, so he recognized the signs of evasiveness in a moment.

"Just tell me. I'm real close to being a priest, soon as I get this skin problem cleared up."

She laughed and slapped his arm. "Oh, Ray, you'll hate me. I told her the same thing. I mean, that she shouldn't be out there all alone. I *thought* I was pushing her toward you. Instead, she married that old creep Morgan."

He leaned back, staring upward in realization. "So I have you to thank."

"She knew all she had to do was write you in Bermuda."

"She did that very thing. By then I was with the Rhode Island First."

After a long moment, she asked, "Why, Rashall? Why not the Navy? I've asked myself that question for years now."

"Then you don't know me as well as you thought." She still waited, and he shook his head. "You have the smallest state in this country, in the whitest part of this country, fighting with more blacks than any other. Fighting for the freedom of those who would keep them enslaved. I don't know a more selfless cause."

"Ray, many more of this country oppose slavery. You appreciate that, don't you?"

He turned over the philosophies he'd debated to death in his mind over the past few years. "I appreciate the unwholesome truth that the longer this institution exists in this country, the worse blacks are treated. We came to this country as indentured servants, just as poor whites did. Somewhere along the line, a misguided George Whitefield began to preach a gospel of slavery. Many were converted to his perverse theology. Still others began believing the dehumanizing lie of race to justify their cruelty. This will continue for how long, Marley? You're the time traveler. You tell me. For how long will we allow a person to define what is or isn't a human being based on their own personal circumstances?"

"You did the right thing, Ray." She watched her children playing with Ruth's great-grandchildren. Then she raised a haunted gaze to him. "I only miss my husband."

"Then let's go begin the search."

"Wait—tonight?"

"I cannot tarry. I'm due back in camp soon. How did you get here?"

"We walked with the rest of the Trelawneys. Not everyone could come, though."

He sighed. "All those years on a ship, wanting to be on dry land. And now it's a three-day hike when a ship could be there in three hours. Very well. Go get your sister."

She looked around the room in confusion. "The rest aren't leaving yet. And they're her guests."

"She'll come if you ask her, though."

"Did you not believe me when I told you I've asked before? Ray, she wouldn't leave this place if you were mad King George."

"Surely that's her guardians' handiwork, protecting her."

"She's a grown woman of twenty-eight. She knows her own mind. Truth to tell, she's the most confident woman I've ever known. She's like a warrior."

"Yes." Pride stirred within him. "Exactly. You've put into words what I sensed in her the first time I saw her that day. As courageous as you are, I see a fearlessness in her almost to a fault."

"Well, I can at least try again. Have you seen her?"

"She was down in the root cellar, a few minutes ago."

He stepped into the kitchen for a quick bite while he waited. The place was packed with more from that extended family he'd come to love during visits from Boston as a child.

"Look what we have here—don't tell me you deserted your post, son."

Across the room from him stood Hasty, Ruth's youngest natural-born son, Rashall's own age. On his shoulders was perched one of his children. The last time they'd seen each other, he and his wife already had five—all boys.

He clapped him on the back. "How many does this little guy make, Hasty?"

"Seven, altogether. Mary just had a little girl."

"Where is everyone? Your brothers—your father?"

"Little Dan, Big Joe—even Daniel, my nephew—they're all off with the militia. Father's back home, holding the place down. There's no way everyone could have come today. I'm headed back out myself next week."

"How's your father?"

"Getting older, you know. Little tired."

"I'm headed out to see him now."

"Ray?"

He heard Marley's call, and turned. She nodded toward the door. He made his farewells to Hasty and joined her.

"Did you get anything to eat?"

"Not yet."

"Well, if you'd like to do that, I'm ready to go."

"What about Juliana?"

"I can't find her. I looked all over the grounds, in the root cellar, in the barn—everywhere. She does this disappearing act every time I'm around. I can't begin to imagine where she hides."

"All right. Let me go collect Martin and George, and we'll head out. Juliana has a mare—surprised to see it hasn't been impressed."

"Really? Are they doing that?"

"*We* aren't. The British take everything they come across and destroy what they don't want. Lafayette's pushing for it—a rate of twenty-five percent. If you have four horses, the Continental Army could take one."

She curled her lip. "I can do the math."

"Yes, well. When the Royal Army raids a plantation, guess how many they take?"

Her mouth dropped.

"All right, then. You and the children can ride. My horse has to rest, he's been going hard all night."

"I'll pack food for the trip."

He, too, looked for Juliana while George saddled the mare. In the root cellar, he found a wardrobe blocking off a path down deeper underground, paved with stone. How he wished he had time to explore. But this was going to be a long trip, on top of another long trip. He couldn't afford the time.

He found George in the barn, just finishing up.

"Almost forgot," he said, lowering his heavy pack to the ground. He reached inside and withdrew the new flintlock long rifle, planting its butt in the ground next to his son. "Stand there beside it, will you?"

Understanding the ritual, George grasped the barrel of the firearm and stood up straight and proud. The muzzle almost evenly lined up with his chin. The sight of his young son standing so close to the instrument made Rashall's heart heavy.

"How tall are you, son?"

"Tall enough to understand what a long rifle can do, wise enough to know when to use it—and when not to."

Rashall cleared his throat. "Looks like you've finally grown into it, then. Thought it was high time you were properly outfitted to protect yourself and your loved ones. What's the most important rule?"

"Don't ever point it at anything I don't want to destroy. A long rifle is for killing."

"Now tell me, just in your own words, what you've learned in the last few years about arms."

George was a serious boy; he'd developed a fine sense of humor since he'd adopted him, but he'd a had a tough young life, and he didn't have a frivolous bone in his body.

"Well, I guess what I've seen in the last year, is that the British troops going through the countryside here have one goal, and that's to destroy our way to defend ourselves. They go after every foundry and iron works they know of. Quickest way to beat your enemy, I figure, is to take their arms. Martin says if they ever do that, we'll be at their mercy."

Rashall couldn't express the pride he felt for his young son. He said simply, "Well done. We can practice your shooting when we get to Rosalie."

The young man—for boy, he no longer was—couldn't contain his excitement. He was speechless as he inspected the rifle in the light coming from a full moon. "She's beautiful, sir. I'll put her in my own pack."

Soon, they were gone, headed down alongside the river road. Martin, most familiar with the backwoods, led the way. Although the children started out animated, they soon fell asleep with the easy rhythm of the mare. The others fell into a companionable silence for the long walk downstream. They were lucky to have a clear night with a full moon.

Rashall walked beside the mare, occasionally glancing at Marley as she grew sleepy. No matter how many times he asked her, she swore she didn't need to stop. He'd forgotten how tough she was—on board the *Adventurer*, she'd fallen asleep sitting up, after working from sunup till long after sundown.

"Well, I'm not sure about you," he called out to Martin, "but I'm getting sleepy. What do you think about making camp here? Or do you know a better place not too far ahead?"

"What, maybe in that pile of leaves over there? Man, have you lost your—" Martin caught himself, looking back at the others. He saw Marley, smiling serenely in the saddle.

Rashall noticed that her arms seemed frozen in arrangement around her sleeping children. "Why don't I carry Sam for a while, give you a break?"

"If he wakes up, that would be no break. We're fine. Let's just keep going. Perhaps we can stop for an hour or so when the sun rises?"

He nodded. "Of course. Do you think my talking would awaken them?"

She shook her head.

"Because I've been thinking about what I'm going to do when this war is over. Now if you ask me, from what I've seen, things aren't going to be too promising for someone like me in this commonwealth. So I'm thinking about going back to sea."

"No!" Marley's drowsiness seemed to leave her in a moment with that. "Why? We wouldn't see you for years."

"The only place I've seen on this earth where men are equal is the seven seas. I miss it."

"Not me," said Martin. "I got seasick going to Boston last year."

"You get used to that, I promise."

"Afraid not. I'm headed west, to the frontier. Where my people are."

"The frontier? Boy, your people are from the Carolinas."

"I'm not talking about *them*," Martin said, dismissing Rashall's reference to Black Oak—built by a family originally from South Carolina. "I mean my father's people. The Sioux. I already know a lot of Lakota."

"Not this again."

"I don't care what you say. You come around every couple of years, dust up trouble and run off in another direction. I grew up here. I see the looks we get when we sell a better grade of tobacco cheaper—without slaves—because we don't waste our money on silver tea services and Arabian and Andalusian horses. We buy books. Why do you think Grimewood was out there today? His tobacco is competing against ours. And ours always wins. Ours drives down his prices, and him not paying a halfpenny for his labor. He hates our guts *not* because we're black, but because we're smarter than he is."

"What do you think, George? When you reach manhood, what are you going to do?"

"I'm going to marry Miss Susan Trelawney and have eight fat little babies."

The entire group laughed at that.

"And are you going to support her fondness for purple ruffles with your clever jokes?"

He giggled at his father's teasing.

"You have to finish your education first. I hear Martin's been apprenticing you. Can you speak Lakota, too?"

"I'm going to thrash you," Martin called pleasantly.

"I've been learning carpentry. I already know accounting."

"He's a quick study, Ray."

"Good," Marley put in. "Maybe he can build the window seat that Hasty forgot."

"He didn't forget. Miss Juliana said you didn't want one."

"She *what?*" Marley sat up in the saddle, then quickly soothed the children as they roused in their sleep.

Martin stopped in his tracks, shocked at her reaction, and George nearly tripped over him.

"I'm sure she didn't mean that," Rashall said, trying to close the chasm between the sisters. "What are your favorite lessons in school, George?"

"I like it all. The only thing I don't like is Miss Marley's Current Affairs."

"Current Affairs? What's that?"

She said, "We just discuss the political climate. We're in the most exciting time of our country's history, Rashall."

"Yes, I only heard that about six thousand times from Mother when I was growing up. It always brings to mind the old Chinese curse: 'May you live in interesting times.'"

"I could do with a little dullness for a while," Martin said.

George spoke up, silencing the rest. "It's just the war I don't want to hear anything more about. And that's all there is. War, war, war. Battle of this and siege of that and why aren't the militia armed better? I am plumb tired of studying *war*."

This brought the conversation to a halt. And then he recalled the one thing that always cheered up his family and his congregation. Back when he had a congregation, anyway.

"Hey, you remember that song your grandmother sings, whenever she gets down?"

"About the river?"

Rashall grinned at his son. "Yes. The one about the river. I'm gonna lay down my sword and shield, down by the riverside. Where?"

"Down by the riverside ... down by the riverside. ... gonna lay down my sword and shield, down by the riverside, and study war no more."

His son and his cousin effortlessly went into a three-part harmony, and before long, Marley joined in, resting her hands lightly over her children's ears.

They sang softly, the way his mother had taught him and Martin, and they'd taught George. And they were so immersed in the song, they didn't hear riders approaching until they were upon them.

In a moment, they fell silent.

Two Army officers on horseback looked from Marley to her escorts. "Halt. Good evening, madame. May I ask who you are?"

"Merrilea Trelawney. And you?"

"Lieutenants Sedbury and Wolfington, from Massachusetts. And you men. May I see your papers?"

Rashall schooled his features into a pleasant mask. "This is Martin Trelawney, a free man of Rosalie. I am Rashall Adams, originally from your own state. And this is my son, George."

"And I presume you have permission to be traveling?"

"Free men don't need permission to travel, sir." His mask was slipping.

Both men, perhaps his age or just younger, exchanged looks. The man who hadn't spoken moved his hand to his sword. "We request proof of your claim to be free men."

"And if we don't have it?"

This from Martin, who could stand to keep his mouth shut once in a while. This was one of those whiles.

"Then you'll join us for a march to our camp upriver."

"You'd leave this lady and her babies unescorted in the wilderness?"

While Martin was running his mouth, Rashall noticed the older man of the two moving his hand to rest on the hilt of his sword.

Rashall raised his hand. "Please. Silence." He pushed off his right shoe and slipped a finger into the hidden compartment, retrieving his pass. He held it out to the man who'd first spoken. "Lieutenant Sedbury, is it?"

Sedbury glanced at the paper dubiously, then accepted and opened it. He held the note closer, reading it in the moonlight—his eyes growing wide. Without speaking, he passed it to the other man. They exchanged a stricken look. Wolfington murmured—thinking he was unheard—"Erm … d'you know his signature?"

Sedbury silently nodded and returned the paper to Rashall. He straightened in his saddle, his face grim as he snapped his hand to his brow. Wolfington repeated the salute.

Rashall returned his gesture. "At your ease."

"We had no idea, sir."

"You couldn't have. Be on your way."

"No, sir. We'll safeguard you to your destination. You can ride my horse, and your son, Wolfington's."

"Be on your way, men," Rashall repeated.

After a tense moment, the men lowered their heads and rode on.

Rashall and Marley broke out laughing.

George looked on in awe at his father.

"Courier, my foot," Marley said with a grin. "Who exactly are you, good sir?"

"Just an ordinary patriot, fighting for his country. I was more surprised they didn't impress these two into service."

Martin looked at him in seeming ignorance, asking, just as if he didn't already know, "Exactly whose signature's on that paper you showed them?"

His younger brother was clearly better at spy work than he, asking questions to which he already knew the answer. He held it out, and he and George inspected the document, reaching the signature.

"Oh, my!"

G. Washington

George passed it to Marley, who looked on, still holding her children. "Looks like he finally came around for you."

"I'd much rather be on a ship."

"Well. Good thing it wasn't a Loyalist patrol, instead. I don't think they'd be too impressed with Washington's signature."

"That's okay—I've got one for that, too."

"The hell you do." Martin met his eyes with a grin.

"Watch your language, son. And no, I'm not going to show you my Benedict Arnold signature. That's going to be an heirloom item for my great-grandchildren."

"Well. Soon as this is over, I'm headed for Ohio Country."

Rashall gave him a sober stare. "You'd best focus on the task at hand. If England wins this war, no man on God's green earth will ever breathe free air."

Chapter Seven

He stood under a leafy old oak on a verdant lawn that spread out into the rolling hill below him. Endless columns and rows of domed tablet headstones, identical in shape and size, marched out as far as he could see.

Others approached in a funeral procession, and he watched, standing apart from them.

The rhythmic clip-clop of the horses drawing the caisson broke the otherwise peaceful morning silence. He hadn't expected to make the old general's funeral—he'd sent his wife on ahead with the others—but it seemed he'd gotten there after all.

In the next moment, uniformed men bore the coffin toward him. He looked down and saw the freshly dug grave at his feet, and he darted out of the way. When he looked back, the coffin had been settled beside the grave on a black-draped stand.

Then he heard music—the simple peal of three notes on a bugle. A young man joined in, singing. He knew the young man, but he couldn't remember him. He'd never heard the song.

Day is done, gone the sun,
From the lake, from the hills, from the sky
All is well, safely rest
God is nigh.

People on either side looked toward him expectantly, waiting for him to pay his respects, and he walked toward the coffin. Although he stood in the light of day, he realized the lid of the coffin was oddly in two parts, the top part opened to reveal the departed down to the waist. A flag draped the lower half of the coffin. An American flag, but with many, many more stars than the flag he knew.

Dread filled him as he walked forward; after all, Enoch had died weeks ago. Hadn't he already been buried? Why was his coffin open? When he drew close enough to see, he realized that the man who lay there was not Enoch Morgan. He wore an unusual military uniform of whitest white. A row of gold buttons ran down the middle of the jacket, and decorations lay pinned on his left breast pocket. His collar lay in a high, stiff circle around his neck.

He let all these details distract him from looking at the man's face, for he feared the truth. Finally, he looked.

Rashall.

He went cold and dizzy, as always, and he tried to take a steadying breath. He looked again.

No—the man was not Ray, but he resembled him. Fear overcame him and he turned away from the coffin in dread.

The mourners surrounding him had metamorphosed into the other prisoners on the *Jersey*, lying chained, dying, dead. He tried to run away but there he was again in that hellish existence, chained to the boy who had died two nights before.

But it wasn't the *Jersey*. It was the *Adventurer*, his old ship—and those around him were his crew. Old Padraig and all the rest, bound in the same chains that held him. The boy chained to him was young Jem.

His breath caught in his chest, his voice in his throat. He could not cry out—could not move. Could not breathe. Only felt the tears of anger, of horror, of utter helplessness, stinging his eyes as he prayed. For what, he no longer knew.

Then, deep in his subconscious, the one shadow of a sane self left within him strengthened him: 'twas but a dream.

He bolted upright on the chesterfield. He'd sweated through the wool blanket in the cold room. He gasped for breath as he stared at the cold hearth. A full moon was reflected on the melting snow outside, and through the unshuttered window facing the street.

How tired he was of the snow. It was April already. Would this winter never end? He longed for the sun—and balmy island aromas. He knew of any number of remote island Edens, free of the acrimony and discord of this place. But he'd found himself unable to walk away from the fight of his countrymen. As if his wife would have allowed it for a moment.

The thought of Marley ran through him like a flash fire. How he yearned for her—and how he wished to be the man he once was, who had in a moment known that he was hers, and she his. Who had found restful sleep for the first time in his life, in her arms. How could he face her now with the nightmares that had attended him since he'd escaped from the *Jersey*? Waking up gasping for breath, even sobbing, soaking her with his sweat? Never.

The night terrors had started on the long walk back to Rosalie after his escape. He'd made camp alone—and woken up trembling uncontrollably, and as often as not screaming.

He had yet to sleep in his own bed in the three weeks since he'd arrived home. Mostly, he'd slept in the stables.

He noticed the trembling of his hand and pressed it against the sofa. He quickly tried to pull himself together, listening for other sounds in the house. No one stirred—neither his father nor Hannah, the lunatic he'd married a few years before.

Right now, he was about the last person to be throwing stones when it came to mental fevers.

He rose and raked out the hearth. His hands trembled again and he forced himself through the act. No one was there to cast pitying glances at his infirmity, and he grew calmer as he built a fresh fire. He started a fire in the kitchen stove, then put water on to boil. Taking pails outside, he filled them with fresh snow from the rain barrel and returned to the house.

Simple tasks that he could conquer—those were his salvation. If not for need of wood and fire and water, he'd find little purpose in his existence right now.

Only then did he think to look at the clock. It was a little after 3 a.m., and he sighed. He found an Edmund Burke pamphlet in his father's study, took it to the fireplace, lit a lamp, and tried to read. Once, it had been the sort of place he could count on to lose himself within minutes: *A Philosophical Enquiry into the Origin of Our Ideas of the Sublime and Beautiful.*

He had first read the piece as an assignment from his professor at William & Mary. The memory of that man worsened his anxiety. It wasn't that he was an ogre; far from it. He forced himself past his anxiety, embracing the notion of the impossible. Had he, as a boy—*could* he possibly have—met the man who was to one day be his own father-in-law? A man from the future?

He pushed the thought away and started reading again.

"THE FIRST and the simplest emotion which we discover in the human mind, is Curiosity. By curiosity, I mean whatever desire we have for, or whatever pleasure we take in, novelty. We see children perpetually running from place to place ..."

His poor, neglected children. Abigail barely a toddler when he left, little Sam just born. Yet now he could scarcely tolerate their presence, for fear of harming them somehow with his uncontrollable moods.

And Marley—his Marley. Oh, how the thought of her set him afire. But since he'd been home, his unpredictability had stamped fear and worry on her face.

He couldn't focus. He set the book on the side table then brought the lamp with him as he silently climbed the stairs. Passing his father and stepmother's room, he headed for the empty bedroom at the end of the hall, walking inside and closing the door behind him.

Two portraits stood on the inner wall, and he placed his lamp on the table, illuminating them. He stood before a woman dressed in the fashion of a more peaceful era, sitting in the garden behind this home—the very garden where she now lay buried, with a statue of two angels at her headstone.

It was said he had her eyes. He couldn't tell. All he could see was a very beautiful woman who he suspected was a bit tougher than most imagined. The artist had her staring off somewhere over his shoulder, in the general direction of the Governor's Palace, with a corner of the house in the background of the portrait. Her pale, delicate hands—in lacy mitts, her fingers bare—lay crossed on her lap. He looked more closely. Her nails were cut short, and the fingertips of her right hand curled up casually underneath her left. Those fingertips were pinkened, accustomed to hard work.

No surprise there; his own wife still worked twice as hard as his men had on the *Adventurer.*

"I've never known a more beautiful woman. Nor kinder."

The voice behind him was soft and gruff. He looked back to see his father in a dressing gown and nightcap, peering at the portrait in abiding love.

"I'm so sorry I woke you."

"I should have brought you here more often when you were a boy. In Bermuda I was almost able to forget. But each time I came back … I lost her all over again. She will always be my tender darling."

"What was she like?"

Perhaps odd, that he'd never asked the question. But his father's grief was never lost on Bronson. As a small boy, he'd not wanted to hurt him, and all the servants whispered how much he'd loved the young missus.

Thomas quietly closed the door behind him and walked forward to join him, never taking his eyes off the portrait.

"Words failed me when I wanted to explain. Son, she was everything to me. Why do you think this room's closed up now? Hannah can see it in my face when I'm in here—where you were born."

He had parsed it effortlessly—no longer was the room the place of her death, but a place of joy and second chances.

"She was stronger than any woman I'd ever met, wiser than some women twice her age. If it weren't for her—and young Rachel, so headstrong—I'd never have made peace with Grey. And my dear little Emily."

He moved a foot away, gazing at the laughing little girl who, gossiping townsfolk said, looked like her father. She was as blonde and blue-eyed as Jennie.

"Father, what did Grey look like?"

Thomas pressed his lips together, controlling his emotions.

"He looked like me. And he looked like you. Hair black as night, eyes silver as a storm. He bore the weight of the world on his shoulders."

"But Emily—"

"She was his daughter. He couldn't have loved that child more if he'd formed her out of clay himself. And she was my dear granddaughter."

He spoke pleasantly, a reminder that fathers were made of stronger stuff than mere eye color.

"Father, what if I told you I met him once?"

He sobered as he turned to look at him. "Grey, you mean?"

"Yes."

Thomas took a deep breath, then clapped his son on the back. "I'd say I married a stranger story than that."

Bronson laughed. The emotion caught in his chest on something like a sob—he couldn't remember the last time he'd laughed. Remembering Hannah asleep down the hall, he bit his lip, hard, to try to steady the tumult within him.

His father—still taller than him by an inch, even in his old age—easily turned him into his arms, hugging his son close. Bronson didn't dare move, for fear of dissolving into sobs.

"But it can't be, can it? Am I insane, to recall such things? To dream the dreams I do?"

Thomas gently pushed him back, gripping his shoulders and meeting his son's fearful gaze with a calm stare. "You're a Trelawney. You spent two years in brutal combat. Another on a prison ship. You *escaped* from that ship and got home without any help. Son, you lived nightmares. A man's mind gets tired when he sees such things, day after day. 'Tis no more than a weary mind, a troubled soul. You'd be insane if it didn't bother you."

"I just wish the nightmares would stop."

"What do you dream?"

He hesitated, unwilling to put such a nameless phantom into words. "It starts out differently each time. But it always ends back on the prison ship, except the prison ship is my old ship, the *Adventurer.*"

"Not *Immortal.*"

"No."

"I'd say you're worried about a duty you feel you've left undone. And the different ways the dream starts out points to your answer."

"Tonight it began with a funeral."

"For whom?"

"I didn't know him—though he brought Ray to mind. He wore a uniform, perhaps that of a Naval officer. I saw an anchor in a metal insignia. But the uniform ..."

"Yes?"

"Well, the cap rested on the flag. The uniform was a style I'd never seen in any Navy." He hesitated, and then his next words rushed out. "As if it were from a different time."

This gave Thomas pause. "You've said Ray was disappointed when the Commander-in-chief passed him over for a Naval appointment, did you not?"

He nodded.

"Perhaps it's more about your concern for Ray—or someone close to him. His boy, perhaps."

"I've not even looked in on George since I got home," he admitted. "I've been so unreliable in the simplest of matters. I miss Ray more than you could ever imagine. The last I heard from him was when he left Rhode Island to work with Lafayette."

"Why were you asking about Grey?"

He hesitated, looking back at the laughing little girl. Emily was somewhere between Sam and Abby's age when the portrait had been painted.

"I do truly believe I met him a few years ago. Just before we left Rashall at St. George's and returned to build our home." When he glanced at his father and only saw him watching with interest, he went on. "It was aboard the *Immortal.* He showed up out of the middle of nowhere. This truly happened. Marley recognized him—she claimed to have seen him the year before in the ruins at Rosalie, when we were there for Thanksgiving."

"You can't mean a ghost."

"Absolutely not. He was as physical as you and I are now. He looked to be in his sixties. Do you think it possible?"

"To travel about in time? Ancient Eastern mystics have spoken of it for millennia—as long as they've been speaking of a round earth. Look how long it took for us to accept that. Who's to say what isn't possible?" He hesitated, then added in a low whisper: "I can tell you this: no bodies were ever found in the ruins of Rosalie. I never heard anyone cry out, as they would certainly have done."

Again, he touched his shoulder, as if to encourage him. "My son, I believe the portal there is real. It brought me peace, to know they all had found a happy home elsewhere."

Without warning, he crossed the room to open the door, finding Hannah scurrying away. She hurried inside their bedroom and closed the door behind her.

He sighed, walked back, and hugged him. "She is a pitiable old woman. When I am gone, be kind to her."

"Father, please don't speak of such things."

"I am perfectly sound and feel fine. I expect to outlive her, as fragile and tormented as she is. But it's just a favor I ask, just in case. And now you know why I whisper."

He leaned back and smiled. "It's odd. Before you were born, your mother made me promise to love you. She knew how much I loved her—how lost I would be without her love. But you, my son. You made it easy to keep that promise."

Bronson watched his father return to his room and he left the larger bedroom empty on his way downstairs. It was nearly morning. He was so tired—and yet sleep offered no comfort. If only he could sleep peacefully for just an hour. Dear God, how he missed his wife.

He walked outside on the path and looked down the quiet street. He noticed the Courthouse on Market Square and remembered Camisha telling him and Marley about the spectacle at the Capitol: the trial of Grey Trelawney for the murder of his wife. He couldn't imagine such a thing—let alone a woman, a black woman, arguing for his defense.

And he recalled that night—not so long ago, but now it seemed like forever since his brother had visited to ask his help. Why had he never returned?

Grey, where are you?

Chapter Eight

"I bought the place for a song," Grey said lightly, attempting to put his wife at ease as they walked along the stone path toward the home. "Back then, no one cared about this little parcel of land out in the middle of nowhere. Of course now, developers have built out this far and farther. It's a priceless few acres of waterfront real estate with original wild land along the James River."

"Well. If you got a good deal, that's what matters." She shot him a look, then went silent. Finally, curiosity overcame her, and she asked, "Who lived here before you bought it?"

"Your sister and your grandmother."

Her face lost its color. "What? I thought she—I *saw* her that day with Camisha, at Rosalie. She's in the eighteenth century."

"Yes. And apparently she already was, by the time I looked up Stonefield. It was up for auction by the bank. There was a ne'er-do-well squatting here at the time—name of Jim Bainbridge, as I recall. Jimmy, he called himself. He cleared out fast enough when I asked him what had happened to Merrilea and her grandmother."

"Why didn't you tell me you found her? I looked for her for all those years, never realizing she went by an entirely different name."

"I didn't find her. I had the same problem. I did find evidence that a Marley Hastings had disappeared. I first heard about it at work. That Bainbridge fellow said they went on vacation to Florida, to an old hotel built out of a shipwreck. I found the hotel he meant. I truly believed they were just strangers. Hastings is a common enough name."

She shook her head with a sigh. "It doesn't matter anymore. I'm so tired of trying to piece the mysteries together. I just want us to live our lives."

"That's how I felt. At least I did, until I found her car."

"What?"

"The hotel in Florida had it. The small craft that they took out to Mayaguana went missing. When they finally found the crippled boat, neither your grandmother nor your sister were among the survivors. I still wasn't sure that she was your relative, but by then I suspected they were very poor people, and I settled her hotel bill just the same. I had a kinship with her since she worked for the Foundation. The hotel gave me her car key—the car was still in the garage. And if you look near the front entrance, you'll find it."

"Really?"

He jingled his keychain as he looked for the key, then he stopped, looking at her.

"I tried to interest you in it so many times, over the years. I had no idea it was related to Marley. We'll go take a look, in a bit."

He inserted the key into the lock and watched his wife's face as he unlocked the door.

"You know," he said, "you're as tough as any I've known in this time or my own. *You* protected *me*, allowed me to come back here and get back to work, to grieve over Tate. You stayed with Emily and her children as they grieved him. And for all that, when I look at you now, I see only the little girl in that newspaper photograph from six decades ago. Still trying to take care of everyone but yourself."

She looked away, into the woods behind Stonefield, as if seeking the neighboring farmhouse she knew was just a bit off beyond those woods. The farmhouse where she'd hidden with her sisters, waiting for their parents to come for them. She'd told him all about it, in those first days after she regained her memory.

"But for all you know about this house, everything you fear, there's a lot you don't know. No matter what, I won't leave you as you face it."

With that, he opened the door.

He'd last been to the home a month ago, while she was still in Manhattan with Emily. Long ago, he'd tidied everything and placed what he thought might be Marley's belongings in boxes in the smaller of the bedrooms. Everything else had been deep-cleaned many times through the years. He'd visited while she was off on a work conference here or there—and joyfully prepared for the hope of her arrival, only to be stubbornly refused yet again.

"Let me turn on the heat," he said. "Stay here."

He walked down the hall and turned on the old style thermostat, and he heard the furnace ignite. Warmth soon came through the vent, along with the smell of burning dust that always accompanied these old heaters. As he returned to the kitchen, he chuckled to himself. Once he had marveled at the concept of instant heat. What blessings modern human beings had, without ever taking notice of them, let alone giving thanks.

His wife stood planted in the same location. He had no idea what this house had looked like when she had grown up here. But he saw her chin lift, her eyes widen almost imperceptibly as she took it in, and he knew she remembered.

The gas stove and electric refrigerator both worked fine now, more than a hundred years after they'd been built.

"I don't know when it was wired for electricity, but I think perhaps the 1940s, when it was modernized to include indoor plumbing," he said. "I've had all the appliances inspected."

"Daddy never changed anything about the house. He repaired things, but he was careful to keep it as it was when he and Mama bought the place."

"He was a historian. He would've honored that aspect of its history. The man I've researched—"

The look she gave him shut him up. "You know about my father?"

"You've told me almost as much as I learned. But he was a professor at the college—at least three different times over two hundred years. He left a legacy of reverence for all the best aspects of history."

"But how—why didn't you tell me?"

His shoulders slumped, and he closed the back door with a sigh. "How many times have I asked you to come here? It wasn't something I could blurt out over tea. You were quite clear that you didn't want to hear any more about those days."

"Can you blame me? Do you remember how many years I had that nightmare of finding them …? You know the one."

"Yes. Every year when I asked you to come here, until I gave up. Look, there's something I have to tell you about him, as well."

The wariness in her eyes pained him, and he pushed on. "Max and Jack Sheppard were James Manning's sons."

This disarmed her. "James Manning—the overseer at Rosalie?"

"Manning learned about how to use the portal at Rosalie from your grandmother. He sent his sons into the future to kill us and Camisha. At least, so he thought."

"So Jack Sheppard wasn't even supposed to be in the actual *world* we live in."

He shook his head. "No. Rachel, what happened to you was unspeakable. But your fear of that memory empowers it. Max and his brother died long ago. The past is gone. And you're not meant to live your life in fear."

"The past is gone. Some message, coming from you."

"Don't try to twist my meaning. Living in the now is what life's all about. But if we know our past—if we face our past and all its hate-filled symbols, no matter how ugly, how painful, how awful … perhaps then, we can remember what mankind is capable of. And we can make a better *now*. Rachel, it's what I

FOREVER

teach every day of my life. How do you think your suffering makes me feel?"

"I wasn't afraid of the past; I was afraid of losing you. Emily completely forgot her old life at Rosalie eventually because we never talked about it. She named Cammie after someone she remembered as being a schoolteacher of hers. She even forgot having seen her when we visited the old Rosalie ruins a few years ago. Well, I can't forget that it was all real. I was afraid that all of this had something to do with you being with me, in the twenty-first century."

"There's more to it, and I think you know that. Malcolm was very clear on that point. It was the only way the people of Rosalie could be freed."

She looked around the room once more, noticing the old-fashioned hand-crank ice cream maker on the floor beside the counter. She gave a half smile. "I'd forgotten. We used to make ice cream in the summer. Merri added bananas and peanut butter one time—Daddy called it Elvis Delight." Her laughter spilled out. "Please don't make me explain who Elvis was."

"I am quite well aware. Very picky about the blue suede shoes, as I recall."

Her smile mellowed as she looked at him. He took her hand, kissing her knuckles. "Ready to go on?"

He felt the squeeze of her fingers as she released him and turned toward the hall. As she passed the chrome-edged dinette with its faded yellow vinyl chairs, she looked on, as if watching her father saying grace.

And as he had so many times over the past four decades, he remembered the young boy who'd been born on his ship to one of his finest sailors and his beautiful island girl wife.

"Your grandparents were the finest of people. They lived here in the 18th century, with Hastings' son and his wife—your other grandmother. 'Twas this very house where your parents would have met as children."

"Did you find out anything about them in your research?"

"No, not from my research." For the time, he withheld what he had learned about them.

She tilted her head at him.

He leaned to brush his lips against her forehead. "One thing at a time, darling."

How he missed touching her so. He felt her breath quicken, and he hugged her lightly, inhaling the womanly scent of her. "Let's go on."

She walked through the hallway to the first open door—the largest bedroom. He watched her react to the room with wonder, pleasant memories alight in her eyes.

"Oh, Grey, it's actually just the same as it was when we lived here. Even the same quilt, there across the bottom of the bed."

"I didn't expect to hear that. The room had been decorated with rather cheap, modern items when I found it. I discarded those and replaced the mattress with this one, and made the bed with items I found stored in that cedar chest."

She covered her mouth with her fingertips.

"I think your sister and your grandmother possibly had a difficult life. That Jimmy person—who I found living here—was not an honorable man."

She didn't seem to hear him. She moved forward to the headboard and picked up the framed photograph from the ancient bedside table.

"I had completely forgotten this! These were my grandparents. I mean, the mixed couple. And this couple ..."

With her other hand, she withdrew her reading glasses from her pocket and put them on. Grey followed suit. He'd found the photo only recently; though he thought he recognized Gideon and Sarita, he was uncertain and had hoped she would know.

"Then you did know them? Your grandparents?"

She shook her head, her hand now covering her mouth.

He walked to her, placing his hands on her shoulders, then sliding one arm around her and hugging her, even as she continued to peer at the photograph.

"These two are my parents, here in the middle. And the baby was me. They were all at ... I can't remember. Some military function, I think. Daddy told us about it when we were little. He said this man over here was his best friend in the Navy. The woman—his wife, I guess—looks so familiar."

"And the man, too, to me. Of course! He looks like Rashall—" He stopped speaking, not nearly soon enough.

She gaped at him in disbelief. "Rashall? How would you know what Rashall looked like? Did he grow up to be someone important?"

Actually, I've met him. This, of course, remained unconfessed.

"Look, darling," he said, distracting her with the woman's nametag. One of those quaint, handwritten, peel-off things they'd loved at the turn of the century, before technology grew invasive and allowed people to learn about strangers indiscriminately as they approached them.

Helen.

After a long moment, she laughed in excitement. "Do you suppose that baby's Camisha?"

"Since Helen and Cameron had no other children, I'd say she would have to be."

This much, at least, they'd both learned from Helen.

"She would love this. Do you think we could take it to her? And don't think I've forgotten that comment about Rashall."

"Certainly we can take it to her. Let's go on, for now."

She slipped the photograph into her pocket and they walked to the next room—the room the girls had shared, nearly as large as their parents' room. He had found the twin beds and Juliana's crib in the attic, tossed in willy-nilly—no doubt by the unremarkable Jimmy.

Grey had repaired the beds and replaced them in what seemed logical locations after repainting the room the creamy white he saw beneath the garish pink that someone had painted it.

Rachel gave a wordless sound of pure joy. When he had bought the house, he suspected this had been the room where her younger sister had grown up. He couldn't imagine the historian that Marley had been, selecting such an awful pink—perhaps her dotty grandmother.

"Did you do this?"

He nodded. "I had to guess where the beds might've been."

"It's exactly the same. Oh, Grey!"

Unexpectedly, she turned to him and threw her arms tight around his neck, kissing his earlobe. "Thank you so much."

He held her close, kissing her hair, and then he chuckled. "Probably not the wisest thing, to do what I'd like to do, in this place."

She smiled at him in that way he knew well, then walked to the window seat, inspecting the draperies. "It's all the same."

She walked around the room, arriving without warning at the closet. She gave a small cry and stopped. He'd replaced the light bulb and left it on for this moment. She stared into the closet where she and her sisters had hidden that night. "I remember it being huge, perhaps even a walk-in closet. It's just an ordinary small closet."

She looked away. "Poor little Merrilea. Having to face this every day. Why in the world wouldn't our grandmother have put her in the next room?"

"If the woman wasn't the wisest, perhaps she at least knew it was better for the child to face her phantoms early and render them powerless."

"The light bulb, though. She was still afraid of the dark."

"There's that old saying—sunshine being the best disinfectant."

They left the room, stopping at the unfurnished third bedroom. "I wasn't sure how your family used this room, so I've left it empty. The boxes contain Marley's belongings, except the books. Those I left in the shelves in the main room."

"Do you mind if we look at her things later?"

"Of course not. I think it will bring you pleasure. Come."

He led her out of the hall and into the main room of the house—the room whose memory had tormented her for sixty years.

The huge hearth that once had been used for cooking was clean, with seasoned logs stacked on the grate. In a corner near the window stood a spinning wheel. A sofa faced the hearth, which was flanked by two easy chairs.

Behind the sofa was a long, low bookshelf filled with the children's books he'd found packed away in the attic. Another seating area lay there, with an early American rocker, two more wingchairs, and two small children's chairs, near the bookshelves. All that was arranged exactly as he'd found it.

And in this room, she took command. She made herself at home, and he allowed her to lose herself in the place without his intrusion.

She walked to the bookshelf and perused its contents, her arms wrapped around her waist. She withdrew one book, opened it to a page, laughed softly, then closed it and put it away.

She crouched beside one of the children's chairs and looked around the room, as if traveling back to a memory where she was small enough to fit in that chair.

She noticed the window seat. He had painstakingly preserved the drapes that were now drawn back, revealing the place where their parents had played with them, taught them to read, and spun romantic tales of days of yore.

But she showed no curiosity about the seat itself, where the hidden release catch lay that opened the seat into the stairwell below. The stairwell that led from the transformative world of books down into a portal to any world since the beginning of time.

She did not know about the labyrinth. If she had, she could not have resisted opening that seat now.

And at last, inevitably, she turned to the front door of her home. She looked down at her own feet as if in prayer, then took a deep breath and crossed the room. She stood just on the other side of a large, new rug he'd recently placed at the entryway—a hand-hooked rug from his workplace, styled in the colors of the time.

She stared at the rug, unmoving, for a while. Her father had been killed just inside that door. Her mother, only a few feet beyond that.

And she seemed to ignore it completely. Or perhaps it was suddenly too much for her.

Abruptly, she opened the door and walked out onto the porch. She looked to her left, and he knew what she saw. Another bittersweet keepsake he'd found tossed roughly into the attic. He'd read the police report, and he knew that on the night the girls were found in the deserted farmhouse a mile away, the police had also come upon their red wagon. The wagon where Rachel had packed their sad little collection of provisions which had run out long before, and where she had kept a makeshift crib for her baby sister.

He took a deep breath and followed her outside. She simply stared at the red wagon. He found the set of old keys in his jacket and unlocked the old sedan.

Presently she walked down the steps, approaching the car. "This junk heap was Merri's?"

He chuckled. "I told you. I don't think they had two shillings to rub together. What little they had, Bainbridge likely drank away. Just a wastrel and blackguard."

She smiled. "I love you so much. Wastrel and blackguard. And it's two nickels to rub together. Only in ye oldie timey days did this place have shillings. What's in the trunk?"

"You know, I don't think I ever opened it. When I paid to have it driven back, I'm not really sure I knew at the time it was a place for storing belongings. As time passed, I forgot about it."

"Well, let's have a look."

He unlocked it and glanced inside. There was very little there, aside from a heavy bag of trash. He lifted it out to discard.

"Well. There we have it. Your sister was a neat freak. No long lost family secrets here."

They returned to the porch. He stopped at the steps and looked over the wagon. *Radio Flyer*, it said. He remembered her description of that night, and he imagined it piled high with groceries, and her infant sister somehow balanced in the middle of it all. He imagined a child of six pulling that wagon over a gravel path to that deserted farmhouse, and finding sustenance for her sisters and herself in the wilderness.

What a singular person he had married.

She wordlessly turned away from the river and they walked back to the house. Climbing the stairs to the porch, she glanced once again at the red wagon. "Shall we take it with us? Perhaps give it to the children?"

"No, but I'm going to bring it inside."

She pulled it along, dragging it over the threshold. One of its wheels caught on the rug, pulling it back. She froze at what she saw.

And before he could guess her intention, she pushed the wagon aside, then knelt and threw back the rug.

When he had first taken possession of the house, this room had been carpeted. He'd ripped out the carpet and underneath the dust and grime he found two large bloodstains, perhaps ten feet apart.

He had scrubbed the stains numerous times, but he couldn't bring himself to replace or refinish the entire floor, for this very reason.

Her pale fingers traced over the old stains there that couldn't be scrubbed away—the reminder of that awful night. She crawled the few feet to the other stain, and he saw a teardrop fall to the floor. And then another.

She hid her face in her hands, sobbing silently, and he dropped to his knees and caught her in his arms. He soothed her, allowing her tears.

"How did this happen? He was a military man! Jack Sheppard, from all we knew, was insane and drugged out on top of it. My father had been out of the military for a while, but he almost always carried a gun. How could this have happened?"

He stroked her hair, but she wriggled away from him. "No! There has to be a logical explanation. My father was a Navy vet with a dresser drawer stuffed full of ribbons and medals for bravery in combat. He carried a pistol everywhere he went. How could someone like that have been killed by a meth head with a damned kitchen knife?" Her eyes went wide as she faced him. "Oh, my God! What do you know?"

How well she knew him. He sighed, rubbing the back of his neck. "The police report included toxicology reports—he'd had a few drinks. Your mother had the car keys in her pocket, so she was likely driving. His pistol was still on him when the police arrived. Jack Sheppard may have been a meth head, but he knew to attack Rob first, and ... You don't truly want to walk through the crime the way they recreated it, do you?"

She looked away from him. "So that's it? A few drinks?"

"Rachel, he was impaired badly enough that he knew he couldn't drive home. The place where they had dinner was only ten minutes away, so he was still impaired when he got home."

"But he *never* drank! I can remember the number of beers I ever saw him drink on one hand."

"That ... probably made it worse, you know—if he wasn't a drinker."

She swallowed hard, blinking. "Then it was all his fault."

"Are you mad? He and your mother—your entire family— were the victims."

"He could have stopped it."

He watched her silently for a long time. "What would you tell Cammie if she were saying such a thing to you?"

"She's said as much, in the past four months." She bit her lip. "I would tell her that her father loved her very much. And that he would want her to stop whining and go on with what's left of her pathetic life."

He smiled. "Well, I don't think you or your father would be quite so harsh. In the first place, your father *would* ask your forgiveness. The sooner you forgive someone you think has wronged you, the sooner you can go on with ... well, what's left of our pathetic lives. "

She bent down to put the carpet back in place. "One thing I do know now. They weren't supposed to be here at all, Grey. Thirty-five years ago, we thought the time anomaly was me being back in the eighteenth century, but it wasn't. It was my parents being *here*. My father was supposed to grow up as a contemporary of Thomas Jefferson and George Washington. The son of a former slave, who knows how he might have changed this country. Instead, he grew up in this century, and by the time he returned, he was far older than they were."

"And he impressed upon Jefferson the ideals he had."

"So what was the point of him being in the twentieth century? Just to get older? When you look at the photograph of him and my mother, remember that he was only born four years before her. People don't seem to realize that time still goes on when you're in the other time. By the time he met my mother, he would've been much older than she was."

"Then perhaps while he was here, he understood firsthand the urgency of American ideals, in the people around him."

"You know better than anyone that people back then understood it as well as we do. No doubt better. They didn't belong here, Grey. And neither do we."

"And what of Emily? And her children?"

She shook her head silently.

"Well. Speaking of which, I suppose we should get going," he said, taking hold of the decrepit garbage bag again. "We'll drop this in the dumpster on our way out."

They arrived back in the kitchen, and she gave the place a long look, then walked outside.

"How much the world has changed—but this place never seems to," he remarked. "I brought Gideon and Sarita here when he left my employ. When you mentioned a stone house, back at Rosalie, it occurred to me it might be the same place."

They arrived at the dumpster near the corner of the highway, and just as he was about to toss it into the container, the bag split and a heavy box fell to the ground.

"What in the world?" he asked, lifting the box from the ground—an ancient, dusty box covered in leather. He turned it over and gasped, brushing away the wet leaves on its face.

Dirt had found its way into the trash bag over the past four decades, and he lightly blew at the dust on its front, then with a finger cleared away enough to see.

THE TRELAWNEYS OF WILLIAMSBURG.

"What is it?" Rachel asked.

Hastily, he glanced inside the trash bag for anything else of value, but it was empty. He tossed it into the dumpster.

In the center of the leather cover was a small painting of Ruth Freeman—but much older than when he'd known her. The image was surrounded by other women and men, painted at different points in time, all black.

He opened the leather cover, where there lay countless ledgers. Without removing it from the box, he opened the first cover.

This is the diary of Ruth Freeman Trelawney of the events beginning July 4, 1746.

"Dear God," he whispered, emotion filling him. "Rachel, this is a journal. A collection of journals. It goes from the days when we last lived in the eighteenth century, until … " He looked to the back. "My God! It continues on up to the Civil Rights era! I've never seen such a find in all my life. There's nothing else like it in any public collection."

"Let's go home," she said. "I'll drive, and you can read."

He held out the keys to her without objection, and walked toward their car, uncertain whether he should even be reading this outside a controlled environment. For the first time in months, he felt alive. There was a reason for him to have bought this place. If he accomplished nothing else in his life, this alone would be worth it all.

Chapter Nine

The weary group of travelers arrived at Rosalie at midday on Sunday, and they heard the hardy throng of worshippers singing as they drew into the village. *'I am bound for the promised land ... "*

Martin and George climbed the steps of the meetinghouse, leaving Rashall to escort Marley and the children the rest of the way. The children were hungry and fussy, and when she found the house deserted and dark, he saw her own weariness.

"No Hawk? Where do you suppose he wandered off to?"

She shrugged. "He might have gone to visit his father."

"Maybe he's at the meetinghouse. What can I do, then?"

"Don't worry about us. I'll be fine. If you want to build a fire, that would help. But you need to get on to church, too."

He built the fire and brought in fresh water, but quickly realized he was underfoot. She'd been alone so long, she was used to doing the job of two. He hugged her quickly at the door. "I'll check in on you before I head back to camp. If you see him before I do, tell him I'm looking for him."

Ten or twelve paces off, he looked back to see her standing in the doorway, watching him. Little Sam was balanced on one hip, and Abby stood in front of her mother, eyeing him closely. Dark circles under Marley's eyes made her look older than she was.

"Please come with me."

"I'll try to catch up with you if they're in decent spirits. I just can't bear for them to cry because they're tired. I'd probably cry, too. Ask Dan to please understand."

He nodded and was off.

He slipped into the crowded meetinghouse quietly, standing near the back with George and Martin. Dan was finishing up his sermon. *Matthew 21:28-31* was written in chalk on the small slate near his pulpit. The parable of the two sons.

"Then the question we need to ask ourselves is, will we fall away—or will we be faithful? Will we be like the son who told his father that yes, he would work in the vineyards—and then disregarded that promise? Or will we remember our father's call to the harvest and do as he asked us?"

He went on as Rashall's mind wandered to the last sermon he'd heard—on his way out of the northeast, in the Methodist church his mother attended now. When he'd been defrocked, she'd sworn never to set foot inside another Anglican church as long as she lived.

That sermon had been at a fairly plain church in Boston. Inevitably, he recalled St. Peter's, back in Bermuda. And he let the thought pass. Once it had been too painful; then, the affront too great. Now, he mainly felt sorry for those forgotten souls in St. George's.

Did you ever consider that perhaps God wanted to spare you? That he wanted to refine you for a higher purpose? That you would have perished in that Great Hurricane, if not for being sent away?

He sighed, recognizing that Voice.

He noticed the many women who were there without their husbands. All of the Trelawney men who could be spared were serving with the militia. Given how things were even a few years ago, it was a bit of a miracle—the Commander-in-Chief still wasn't fond of blacks serving. Even Congress saw a moral inconsistency in allowing a race that wasn't afforded freedom in this country, to fight for the freedom of those who enslaved them. Benedict Arnold had turned everything on its head, destroying plantations along the James, liberating slaves that had belonged to those plantations ... and so Washington had allowed blacks to serve. And free blacks and enslaved alike joined militias on both sides throughout the land.

And then, who should enter his mind but the famous George Whitefield—an Anglican as well as the most well-known evangelist of the century. He was said to have taken the gospel to more people than any other man throughout history. Phillis Wheatley herself had written an ode to the "happy saint" on his passing.

Rashall wasn't inclined to pass judgment on dead men of God. After all, Whitefield had preached to enslaved people, something few white preachers would stoop to do. He had strongly admonished plantation owners of the South for their treatment of their slaves—though he had no qualms with the institution itself.

And yet, it was his preaching that had conditioned people to accept slavery as God's will. He used the Bible to justify it, something that turned moral unbelievers away from God.

There were solid reasons for accepting flawed people who did the sort of good that Whitefield had done in his life. He just wasn't sure that advocating greed that reduced human beings to the worth of farm animals—as long as you properly fed those farm animals, mind you—was what one would call a flaw so much as it was a lie of Satan.

When Dan prepared to close the service, he opened the Book of Common Prayer that Rashall had given him years ago. The same book he'd used to perform Hawk and Marley's wedding. The sight gave him comfort.

As he finished, the choir rose at the front of the room. They sang _There is a Balm in Gilead_, and he wished again that Marley had come with him. She was frazzled within an inch of her life. They lived far enough outside the town proper that a woman whose husband had just returned from war could be spared at church that morning without punishment. But this song—it was a replenishment to his soul, for so many reasons.

Like many of the hymns and other songs they sang in church, his mother had taught it to Dan's wife, Ruth, as well as her own children. Hearing it now made him feel closer to his mother—and in the next heartbeat, a world apart. For all his travels and adventures for the past two decades, he loved home more than anywhere else. And he missed his family.

As he had held Juliana a few nights ago—he knew he was home. *She* was his home. The thought of her burned within his heart.

When the service ended, he passed the time in small talk with the others until the usual crowd around Dan began to clear. He reminded him so much of his Uncle Jeremiah, back in Boston—although he seemed to see Dan more often.

At last, he faced the big man, who broke into a wide grin, then reached out to hug him hard. When he pushed him away, he gestured down a hallway. "You hungry?"

"I'm always hungry these days."

They laughed and walked into the other room. "Would you look at this," Rashall said. "When did you add this on?"

"New fellowship hall. Just a few months ago. Have a seat. Sukey'll take care of us."

They sat in a quiet corner. This was the first time he'd seen Dan since they'd left for Boston, over five years before.

"You getting enough sleep? You look tired."

"Speak for yourself, boy. You look my age."

"I haven't slept a normal night through in a year. So no wonder I look a hundred and ten."

"Now, now. You watch yourself."

Presently, Sukey arrived with two plates and the promise of drinks. She bent down to hug Rashall. "You handsome fellow. Where have you been hiding yourself?"

"I've been running all over the countryside. I'm just on a short leave. I'll need to go back soon."

After she'd brought mugs of cider and left again to help others, Dan remarked, "We lost Sukey's husband Matthew last year. That's been hard for her. He doted on her so."

"She's still a beautiful woman. She'll find someone."

They ate in companionable silence for a few minutes. Rashall knew he had no time to waste; before long, the crowds would be flocking around Dan again. It went with the territory of pastoring a large church.

"Dan, have you thought any more about leaving Rosalie?"

"Leave Rosalie? It's everything I've worked for my whole life. Did you take a look around the village?"

"I tell you, we just got in. But I was afraid you'd say that. Right after Morgan's funeral, I heard Ruth kick old Grimewood off the property. Told him she wasn't going anywhere."

"And that's the truth."

"But there are so many opportunities farther out west."

The older man laughed softly, a wheeze infecting his laughter. "You think old Granny and Granddaddy Freeman-Trelawney ought to head out by wagon with Martin?"

Rashall didn't smile. "I'm serious. Grimewood is trouble."

"Don't say that around Ruth. She already has a log in her eye over him."

"George and Martin told me what he said. I think you ought to consider heading to a place where freedom isn't such a shaky proposition for a black man."

"Tell me where that is, son, in this day and time. Back in Africa, where the abolitionists would have us go? Where they're still selling their brothers and sisters into bondage? It's up to us to work for the good."

Rashall was silent. It was exactly what his mother would have said.

"You get up and come with me."

Rashall followed the big man as they made their way outside and toward the other houses. The village was deserted, with everyone back in the fellowship hall—or off fighting.

On one side, they passed the schoolhouse. "Ruth has trained two dozen teachers who share the duties with her now. That way there isn't too much stress on anyone. Let's take a quick look inside."

What once had been a simple schoolroom had also been added onto, and there were at least four separate large classrooms to support a broad range of students. "They break the children into levels, and each teacher has a specialty. Sometimes we have someone come in and teach their trade, or profession, to the older students. Depending on the student, of course. Not everybody's Cicero or Copernicus, but everybody's got their strokes of genius."

A simple building, painted white, stood beside the school. "This is the library. Reckon we have almost as many books as Master Grey had once upon a time in that fine mansion of his. Matter of fact, we salvaged quite a few from the Rosalie fire. Every time we can beg, borrow, or steal any kind of book, in it goes. I want to show you something."

A small breezeway connected the two buildings. There was very little they hadn't considered, here.

In the library, Dan led him to a remote shelf and plucked out a volume. *The Book of Life.*

"Ruth's listed every child we've ransomed from slavery. And she's listed every descendant of those children."

Rashall scanned the names there, beside each of which was the child who'd taken their place in the grave. His brother's was the first listed. *Martin Obadiah Freeman-Trelawney … Martin Jeremiah Adams.*

"You'd better bury this under the church. If somebody like Grimewood got a hold of it, nobody here would be safe."

They walked the full length of the village. He looked out over the modest but comfortable homes for the upwards of eight hundred inhabitants of the town. No slave cabins here; instead, homey cottages with neatly tended gardens.

The entire area smelled of fresh lumber. On the far end of town was a carpenter's yard, a blacksmith, and a tanner. A well-tended section of acreage waited spring planting of vegetables. The acres where tobacco had grown the previous year lay fallow this season. And of course, beyond that, the tobacco acreage, where seedlings were beginning to sprout through the pine boughs protecting them from late frost.

"We'll be hilling next week, getting ready to transplant the seedlings. With so many of the men gone, everybody's working, even little ones. We're also thinking about ways to get fresh water into town, maybe even each house. Besides the human back, you know. Big Joe has some thoughts on that. He says it involves physics."

Rashall looked on the place with the eye of an outsider. It was enough to impress anyone. And Martin was right. If Grimewood had gotten wind of this place, no wonder he hated the Trelawneys.

"The good Lord's blessed us. This village is twice as productive and profitable as Rosalie ever was. Now do you see why we can't go?"

"I can sure see why you wouldn't want to."

Dan gave him a sly look. "Now I know, much as you hop around, you think everybody ought to live their life that way."

"What's that supposed to—"

"You know good and well what that means. God practically has a fish swallow you and drop you down in the middle of this place, and instead of obeying, you ship out for an island off in the middle of the ocean."

"I thought I *was* obey—"

"Things get a little shaky there, you run back home to Mama."

"I didn't run back home to Mama! I joined the Rhode Island—"

"Then you get a wild hair to go off with that Lafayette fella, and where do you suppose God sends Lafayette? Right back to Stonefield. So what do you do? Run off here, telling us to run away, too. What are you running away from now, boy, and where you gonna run off to next?"

Rashall stopped protesting. He looked at the old man before him—the most faithful man he'd ever known. He turned to look back at the meetinghouse, remembering the cathedrals he'd known around the world with their stained glass, gold-leaf icons, and carved woodwork. Dan's meetinghouse stood, understated and plain, marked only by a roughhewn, weathered cross.

"And that young lady? You'd better marry her now, son, before somebody else beats you to it again."

Rashall sent him a sharp look. "She's in mourning, sir."

"You think this is a tea party we're living in? This is life, Ray. You only have one of them, and the wisest man ever lived said for us to eat our food with gladness, and drink our wine with a joyful heart, for God has already approved what we do. Enjoy life with your wife, whom you love, all the days of this otherwise meaningless life that God has given you. Whatever your hand finds to do, do it with all your might. And when you think there's more in life than you can bear, you look to God, and you'll find he's been bearing you up all along."

Chapter Ten

Juliana watched the last of the visitors leave with oddly mixed feelings. Ruth Freeman-Trelawney was well past her prime at fifty-five, but she had the vigor and energy of a woman half her age. She and Hasty led the wagons back toward Rosalie, and Juliana wanted to beg her to stay.

While she'd been here, Ruth and Sukey had helped her do things she disliked doing—like refreshing the stuffing in her mattresses and the feathers in her pillows. On the third day after the funeral, the sun had come out and warmed the land, and Ruth threw open all the windows and doors and announced to the children that it was time to let the sunshine in.

Everyone had gone to work replenishing the cottage. The women scrubbed and waxed the place from top to bottom, and the men cleared half an acre of land for the spring garden.

Ruth herself took on the task of inspecting the foodstuffs in the root cellar. She put the youngest children to work transplanting the dormant plants that lined one side of the cellar floor, and they sprang to the task as if it were the most gladsome game. Half the garden was soon filled. Her herbs, she kept back, not yet confident the threat of frost was past.

Juliana eagerly assisted Ruth in the cellar, if for no other reason than to keep her wandering past the wardrobe Uncle

Malcolm had placed to keep trespassers from accidentally discovering the labyrinth's alternate passageway. This was the route that her guardians preferred into the magical realm.

She had grown up appreciating solitude, but no more. Now, she waved back at Ruth as the wagons headed south toward Rosalie in the early morning sunlight, wanting to go with them. Marley had left early, and she missed her. This time, she'd wanted to go back with her sister. She could see her weariness. She wasn't sure what was troubling Bronson, but something was undoubtedly wrong with him, or he would never have allowed her to cross the countryside without him—Ruth or no Ruth.

She walked down the long, sloping path toward the river with Will, then followed the river, grateful the days were growing longer and warmer. By the time they got home, she was glad it had been a long walk. The place was spotless. They'd left her with nothing to do but gather wool—something she'd spent far too much of her life doing.

Without expecting to find any joy at all in it, she took a short trip to the past—and she resisted the most pleasurable memory presented to her, the night she'd last seen Rashall, when he'd kissed her. She didn't have to travel in time to relive that. Neither did she select a noteworthy historic moment. Instead, she revisited the moments with her sister just a few days ago. Now she noticed Marley's exhaustion as she hadn't before.

She returned from the trip quickly. *Was it worth it?* she asked herself, as the headache descended. A time travel headache could last for days.

Her old doll sat on the ledge around the window, and she sank into the window seat, bringing the doll close, stroking Will. She closed her eyes and remembered the day she'd lost the doll. It was the winter after she'd turned eight.

Aunt Mary had gone out visiting sick neighbors, she said, and left Uncle Malcolm in charge of her. Malcolm had told her he had to run out to the barn, and she had climbed into the window seat with a book. The book slipped behind the cushion, and when she reached to get it, she accidentally pushed the metal catch that opened the window seat.

When she realized the window seat could be opened, curiosity overcame her. She climbed off the seat, pulled it back, and saw the stairs. She stepped into the dark stairs below, fascinated that they went on and on. Soon she made the trip down into a game, skipping or jumping as if the stairs were built on a scotch-hoppers pattern.

"One for sorrow, two for mirth, three for a funeral, and four for birth," she had called, reciting the magpie nursery rhyme as she hopped down the stairs.

She smiled at the memory, astonished at the child she'd been. What a marvel, that she'd made it down all those steps without becoming afraid and racing back up. But even more surprising was how welcoming the labyrinth had been to her. Even now, she interpreted that to mean she was supposed to travel. A child could not have navigated such a complex system unless she were meant to.

The voice in the heavens had spoken to her as a wise grandfather, asking her where she should like to travel. And since it was a week before Christmas, she told him the most wonderful place she could imagine. The first Christmas.

She had witnessed shepherds arriving, a heavenly host singing, a baby's young mother guarding her precious bundle as if she were the most seasoned matron on the planet—all around a lowly manger.

While she joined in the singing, she noticed a puppy at the manger, craning his neck inside to nuzzle the Christ child's toes. The baby jerked his chubby foot and gave a laugh at the puppy's kiss and Juliana watched in wonder as a golden glow spread from the child to the puppy. She sat at the foot of the manger, pulling the naughty puppy into her lap.

When she'd returned to the labyrinth, she took the puppy with her, her heart pounding in excitement. She'd seen the Baby Jesus—and gotten a puppy, to boot!

The puppy had hurried her up the stairs as time drew short, his urgent yelps driving her on as she heard her heartbeat echoing in the stairwell. She didn't yet understand the constraints of time—nor of time travel. Nor did she yet know Will's character, always protecting her. But she was worried the puppy would fall, so she'd raced up the stairs after him.

When they emerged from the window seat, she remembered she'd left her doll down below, and she'd turned to go back down once more.

"Oh, no you don't, young lady."

She'd frozen. Uncle Malcolm.

"And what have you been doing down there?"

"I went to see the Baby Jesus's birth. Was that bad? I saw the shepherds and the angels."

And she then very likely became the first child ever to need to have ordinary time explained to her as something that people in her time couldn't generally navigate. She had come by the activity so honestly, she couldn't grasp the so-called laws of science that so many believed forbade such activity. She had traveled in time as easily as any child making a mud pie.

Malcolm had made it very clear, though. He had also first spoken that mysterious saying of his—*Time is never free.* Years would pass before she fully understood what he explained. Time travel was such that one traveled to another time in one moment and returned in the next. It felt as if none of the time spent in other worlds was real. But in fact, each moment spent in that other time was subtracted from your life.

She didn't yet understand whether it meant she would age sooner, or die earlier due to some invisible hourglass running out. Maybe it was as simple as missing out on one's own life cut short that experience. But now, as she considered how many thousands of hours she'd spent in other times, she knew it had shortened her life somehow.

She understood now why she'd stopped time traveling when she met Rashall—because she didn't want to waste another moment of time in any world without him, no matter how wonderful or interesting.

Again, another truth Malcolm had taught her came to her: *"Time is not an endless resource ... wasting it in trivial endeavors robs us of those moments for which we later wish just a few hours more. Juliana, in this life, we see through the glass darkly."*

Would she gladly have given back time she'd spent in the early Roman Empire ... in outer space ... for a few days—weeks—more with Rashall? She recalled her grandparents, dying within minutes of one another. There was no comparison. She would gladly trade all of the thousands of hours she'd spent in the most exciting moments throughout time—for a peaceful, quiet home with Rashall.

Herb tea did nothing to help her headache. She walked to her bedroom and lay down on the bed, hoping for sleep that at least might blunt the pain. Only as she lay down did she realize she still held her doll.

&

He'd seen the storm move in from the Chesapeake Bay, darkening a cloudless late afternoon sky. But he still had an hour's ride before he reached Stonefield, and he rode through the storm, undeterred.

Still exhausted, now wet through and cold in the cooling early evening, he mounted the steps. He knocked softly at the door.

No one answered, but presently he heard whining and scratching on the other side of the door, setting off an alarm within him. He quickly opened the door and stepped in, closing and barring it behind him.

Before the hearth, Juliana sat in a tub—just partially submerged. She watched him expectantly, and in a moment his hungry gaze took in her beauty. Never had he reacted more immediately to a woman, and he had to turn away to speak.

"Are you all right? The dog was whining."

How insipid all that sounded—while his eyes closed and he saw her again in his mind. He forced his attention to the dog instead, scratching him behind the ears.

"Will you help me out?"

"Juliana, I'm only a man."

"Very well."

He waited, listening to the splash of the water as she rose and drew a towel about her.

"Handsome dog. What's his name?"

"Will. As in, will you have a bath?"

She touched his back, and he turned. She wore a dressing gown with layer after layer of silk. Still it displayed the generous curves of her woman's body. With a steel will, he brought his attention to her face. Droplets of water slipped from her hair and clung to her temple. Unable to stop himself, he pulled her against him, kissing her temple.

"My darling, you're so cold. Please—get in the bath and relax. Will was likely begging you to save him from that fate."

Her voice was soft and husky, her hands light on his chest. She gently loosed herself from his arms and removed his oilskin coat, hanging it on a peg. She knelt at his feet, making as if to remove his muddy boots. Her servitude was too much for him to tolerate.

"No. I'll do it."

He removed the boots and set them aside on the mat. Her fingers returned to his buttons, flying over them. Her palms rested on his bare chest, her fingertips sliding upward. He saw her breath come more quickly, her eyes brighten as she pushed the shirt off his shoulders, then off his arms.

"Juliana, no."

He drew her close, stilling her feverish movements. The smell of her fresh-washed hair, the feel of her warm skin underneath the silk, the soft curve of her breasts pressing into his bare chest was almost his undoing.

Instead, he held her until she stilled, rubbing his cheek against her hair. "My love," he said softly, still wanting her mightily. She pressed her hips almost imperceptibly against him, and he gave a soft sigh of pleasure at the incendiary contact.

"Yes," he said, struggling to find a safe change of subject. "I'll accept that bath. Do I smell something delectable over the hearth?"

Her lips opened against his chest, and he allowed his hands to slip lower on her waist as if to press her closer—then he gently set her away. He balanced on one foot to remove one sock, then another, then thought it safe to look at her again.

Her gaze was drifting over his body, settling in the place where she could clearly see his need for her.

He walked toward the room that he had learned before belonged to her uncle. "Do you suppose your uncle might loan me a set of clothing until mine dries?"

That made her laugh. "You know you would never fit into Uncle Malcolm's clothes. My husband, though, was larger. It's probably too large, but at least till your clothes dry."

He'd been so aroused by even the partial sight of Juliana naked that now he was ashamed to notice the pain on her face.

"Will, come." He trotted after her as she disappeared into the bedroom she'd shared with her husband. He pulled the heavy tub to one side of the hearth, then placed the fireplace screen around it, at least offering him some privacy. He slipped out of his trousers and hastily climbed into the tub.

Juliana left Will in the bedroom and returned with an armful of clothing. Unable to see the tub behind the screen, she paused, her eyebrow raising. "What's this?" she asked, unsmiling.

He laughed at her pique, standing still as she took in the sight of him. He was well aware that few women in this world were so guileless about their admiration of their man.

Thank God she couldn't see how that admiration affected him this moment.

"Well," she said pleasantly. "I'll just put these *right here* so you can come and get them when you're ready for them."

She set the clothing on a chair across the room from him.

He laughed as he lowered himself into the water and quickly scrubbed.

"You asked about food, as I recall."

"Something does smell good."

She walked past him to the hearth, pretending to glance over the screen. Grabbing a pothook, she set the Dutch oven to one side. She opened it and used potholders to remove what looked to be a pie of some sort.

His stomach rumbled loudly, and he laughed in embarrassment. "All right, perhaps I'm a wee bit hungry."

She smiled as she placed the pie on a trivet to rest. "Just a simple pie from some of the leftover pork. With some apples and onions and perhaps a potato."

"I don't suppose you'd like to wait in the other room?" he said.

"My heavens, no," she said, giving him a flirty smile that excited him to the soles of his feet. He'd never known anyone like her.

She sat on the chesterfield, leaning forward, her elbows on her knees, her chin in one hand as she watched him. The fireplace screen had a decorative pastoral design punched into it, and he got the feeling that she could see every detail of his body through the occasional hole—a ludicrous thought. But the way she looked at him as she evenly shook her head made him wonder.

So there would be no opportunity to find relief from this unholy hunger eating at his midsection.

And then, again, beyond her teasing stare, he noticed a tension in her.

"What's wrong? The dog whined when I arrived. Are you not feeling well?"

All artifice fell away from her, and she took a deep breath. "I have an awful headache. I get them occasionally. I was trying to chase it away with more pleasant diversions."

"Ahh. Maybe I can help there."

Her eyebrows rose as she smiled in anticipation.

He fought a smile. "You are a naughty, naughty young girl."

She laughed. "Then you know one of old Hattie's herb remedies?"

"No. Different approach."

He finished the bath and rose again in the water, reaching for the towel he'd spotted earlier. He met her eyes unashamedly as he toweled himself dry, and he saw the shyness enter her eyes once more—as if she were still a maiden rather than a widow.

He climbed out of the tub and drew the towel around his waist, then bent over to drop his clothing into the water to soak. Crossing the room quickly, he took the clothing into another room and put it on. Morgan had been a portly man, but it was warm and dry and it was better than nothing.

"Decidedly *not* an improvement."

Her dry complaint made him laugh as he set the fireplace screen away without ever looking away from her. He tugged the tub into a far corner and fed the fire with several logs, stirring it into a roaring warmth. Thunder rumbled more loudly, and the rain poured outside the window.

"Every time I think the winter's over, it proves me wrong."

As he bent over the huge hearth, a realization came to him: He loved everything about this home—and this woman. It held little evidence of Morgan ever having lived here, and he wondered if Lafayette's suggestion about the man—marrying her as a ruse to mask his disinterest in women—were true.

He turned to face her. She was watching him, and she waited.

In the five long years that had passed, from the moment he had first seen her to the moment she sat there, looking at him almost brokenly, she had somehow not changed. The deep stirring within him was the same as that he'd known in that first moment.

Except one important detail.

Those luminous green eyes gave him pause. In the root cellar he hadn't seen it. Her expression was still as placid, but—did he imagine the dark sadness, as of wisdom, in her eyes? That was different. When he'd met her in the root cellar, the darkness had obscured the details of her face. Earlier, she'd disguised this part of herself with desire. Now, her pain was clear.

She cast him a hesitant smile. "Forgive me. I'm plagued by these occasional headaches, and this one arrived just before you."

"Why don't you just go on to bed? You don't need to entertain me."

"Do you not understand yet? I've missed you. If anyone were capable of dispelling such pain, it'd be you. Let's sit a while. Perhaps your magic will cure it." She gestured toward the sofa, and he responded with the same gesture.

"Would you care for a glass of wine? I haven't had any for the longest time—such a luxury right now—but we do have several bottles from Rosalie."

He gave her one of his old smiles, finding a nearly lost part of him restored. "Not Ruth's famous blackberry wine."

"Do you like it?"

In truth, Rashall hated the stuff. He had a fondness for good wine, but this was too sweet for his liking. But when he spoke, it was for the affection he had for all that this wine symbolized in his life. Happy times visiting the Trelawneys with his mother; Thanksgivings sweetened by its berry; and the memory of the last time he'd drunk it, in this very home.

"A connoisseur might dismiss it. I associate it with the happiest days of my life. Even more so now."

Again it blossomed in her eyes and over her lips—that smile he remembered but now, again, tinged with a shadow he couldn't define. It alarmed him. What awful leavings of war had she seen since they'd parted?

"Go warm your feet by the fire. I'll pour the wine and bring you some dinner."

And for the first time in years, he allowed himself to be ministered to. He sank to the homespun rug, letting the warmth of her home move through him.

When she returned, he was relaxing on the rug before the fire, leaning against the base of an armchair. She lowered a breakfast tray to him, and he placed it on the rug between them. She fetched the wine, pouring it into glasses and handing him one.

He swirled the wine in the glass, inhaling its wild, fermented berry aroma as she knelt beside him, resting against the other armchair. Never again would he think of his mother or the

Trelawney Thanksgivings when he smelled this wine. It was now intertwined with this woman's memory—forever.

He cut off a bit of pie and held it out to her, and she shook her head.

"You just made a pie. You have to be hungry."

"I started it baking earlier—before my headache. Please, eat. It makes me happy to know you're having a good meal."

This brought a smile to his face. "Truly?"

"Of course. I worry about you."

She folded her silken skirts underneath her, and as she sat he allowed himself the secret pleasure of casting his hungry gaze over her golden curves. He had known so many stunning beauties in his life, beauties of every variety known to the earth—but none her match. Simply sitting beside her gave him a deeper pleasure than the most unspeakable carnal acts he'd engaged in while sailing the seven seas.

She had an otherworldly sophistication about her, in her bearing, her poise, that belied her identity as a simple girl raised in the Virginia countryside. She seemed the offspring of a Persian prince and a faerie—or perhaps a courtesan.

A dozen years ago, he and Bronson had sat at the tables of pashas in faraway, exotic countries, and had known their women as companions. He had learned to speak several languages during their travels—and been schooled in debauchery.

No woman had ever stirred his excitement as this simple Virginia lass, and he didn't understand it. Something in her eyes spoke of a sadness—even more pronounced today than it had been when they'd first met, more than five years before. Even beyond what might have resulted from marriage to a man like Enoch Morgan. She seemed to carry the weight of an era and beyond on her conscience.

As she settled comfortably near him, her dressing gown brushing his feet, he lifted his glass to hers. "To old friends."

With a placid nod, she lifted her glass and they tasted the wine. For a time, they enjoyed the quiet of the room, the sublime pleasure of each other's closeness.

"Do you think the war will end soon, Ray?" she asked at last, her gaze directed at the fire. One hand held her glass; the other was concealed in the folds of her gown. The warmth of the fire caressed the inviting swell of her breasts, and he cleared his throat, steadying his unruly passion.

Instead, he focused on her question. "I hope so. What about you?"

She shook her head with startling finality. "No."

"What makes you say so?"

She raised her gaze to his, noticing his frank enjoyment of her. The color on her cheeks deepened becomingly, and with every good instinct within him, he fought the overwhelming instinct to take her in his arms there before the fire. Neither did he look away from her—as well he should.

"You know Benedict Arnold is in the region, do you not? Along with Cornwallis and Phillips. And Lafayette."

She nodded. "Yes. I have also heard the French navy is on the way. At least, that's the hope of the militia. And likely the Continental Army."

"So many boys and men—without even a decent pair of shoes. Such a waste, it seems at times."

Companionable silence again. Finally: "This will sound selfish, but I wish I had absconded with you all those years ago and taken you to a remote island to live out our lives."

She laughed aloud, and the sight made him smile.

At last she sobered. "I wish you had, too."

"All right, let's go to bed."

"Rashall!" she exclaimed with girlish laughter.

Her prim rebuff to his unintentionally risqué remark warmed him. How he loved the sound of his proper name on that husky voice.

"To rid you of your headache. An innocent cure, I promise."

He rose, setting their glasses on a table and replacing the fireplace screen. He took a tea towel that lay beside the wine bottle and walked to the porch, plunging it into the freezing rainwater in the barrel. He squeezed out the water and when he returned to the firelit room, he found her standing in the middle of the room, now looking very much the innocent, all sophistication gone.

Grasping the small lamp on the table, he murmured, "Come."

She led him into her bedroom, and despite his promise the action aroused him all over again. Immediately inside the room, however, he remembered that she'd shared this bed with Morgan. But when she turned and looked up at him, they were once more alone.

He placed the lamp on the bed stand. He turned back the covers and held out his hand, inviting her into its cool quiet.

Instead, she silently drew away her dressing gown and placed it on a nearby chair.

He felt his blood pulsing in arousal; he could not have drawn his gaze away had Gabriel himself commanded him to do so.

She might as well have been naked, for all the thin nightgown did to conceal her, instead faintly displaying her curves for his pleasure. He thanked God for the dimness of the room.

She slipped into the bedclothes and he saw the surprise cross her face as he pulled the quilt over her. "You won't …"

He gave her a simmering smile. "That would cure my ache, but not yours."

He sat on the edge of the bed and folded the tea towel, placing it over her forehead. Then, gently, he leaned down and stroked her temples.

"How long have you had these headaches?"

"All my life." She gave a small smile. "One night when I was very young, I went to bed and said my prayers, and then the Lord's prayer, and as I lay in bed I started thinking of the notion of *forever*. Eternity. No beginning, no end. Forever. My mind attempted to imagine that time without end. It terrified me so, I couldn't sleep for hours—and I had my first headache, pondering forever. The next day, Uncle Malcolm explained to me that human beings can't understand the infinite, because we live in finite bodies. We see through the glass darkly. Someday, he said, we'll all understand."

He gently drew the tea towel down her forehead, placing it over her eyes.

"How old were you?"

"Maybe five, six."

"Such a mysterious creature you are. A thought few adults encounter, coming over a winsome little child."

She didn't respond.

"Yet still you have the headaches?"

She sighed slowly, relaxing. "Well ... after certain activities."

"Such as?"

"Er ... well, after I spend too much time in the window seat."

"My mother used to scold me for reading too much, as well."

She laughed softly, and he felt, again, that odd distance enter her. He ignored it, lightly stroking her temples until he felt sure she slept. Then, in a low, lulling voice—almost a whisper—he sang a song he remembered from his childhood.

Always

As he finished the song, he lowered his head, aching to kiss her goodnight. She pushed the towel away, her eyes wide in puzzlement. "How do you know that song?"

He smiled, knowing she saw his affection for her in his gaze. "'Tis a song my mother sang to me when I was a child, feeling poorly."

"But she couldn't have known—oh, of course. Camisha."

As he rose to leave, she caught his hand. "Please, Rashall. Stay with me. Sleep with me. I know you're tired. When's the last time you had a decent night's sleep?"

He couldn't remember.

She threw back the covers beside her, and he agreed, praying for the strength to withstand the temptation she presented. She turned over, leaving room for him, and he lay behind her, inhaling deeply of her aroma without drawing closer.

She moved easily backward into his arms, and he gave a deep sound of pleasure at the sensation. His lips brushed the back of her neck as his hand slipped around her waist. His other hand slipped underneath her, and she wriggled against him, her firm, round bottom cradling him.

He flattened his hand against her waist, stilling her. "Juliana."

She still held his hand, and she placed her own hand between her breasts.

He laughed softly, stroking her arm instead. "Are you sure you have a headache?"

"Almost gone. Will you sing again? Just to help me fall asleep?"

And he did, softly, sing them both to sleep.

In the night he awakened, and it might have been a dream, except the pleasure was too real. Juliana was touching him, her open mouth kissing his chest, running over his nipples. He opened his eyes—the lamp was still burning.

She lifted her head, gazing at him in the lamplight, and he cupped her neck and brought her down to kiss him, welcoming her open mouth, his hands racing down her back and to her full hips, his fingers spreading over them. Her gown had slipped up in the night and lay high on her thighs. He flipped it aside, afire at the touch of her skin, clutching her close to him.

"Juliana, do you know how often I've dreamed of this?"

And it had never been nearly as enjoyable.

He stopped to notice the sight of her rising over him in the bed, her knees straddling his hips. In another moment, he would be inside her. She lifted her breasts to his mouth and he accepted her generous offering, pleasuring her. Surprised at her stricken cry, he drew back.

"Did I hurt you? My teeth, perhaps—"

"Dear heavens, no," she gasped, placing her nipple back within his reach. "I've just never felt anything so wonderful. No one has ever—"

He drew away. "You mean to tell me …"

"I told you before," she said, attempting to draw his mouth back to her body. "Please, my darling. Make love to me. I have been in torment for you. Please end it."

He gently brought her down to him, holding her against his chest until she quietened some. But he noticed the quick rise and fall of her chest, and he turned in the bed, placing her head back on her own pillow and kissing her tenderly. When she reached for him, shyly, he took her hand and placed it at her side. The other followed suit.

"Just relax," he said.

Easily, he lifted her nightgown up and over her head and tossed it aside. The pleasure he allowed himself was this—gazing on her lovely body, far more beautiful than even he had imagined.

He slipped his hands under her thighs, lifting and parting them, and he poised between them. When he saw the anticipation glitter in her eyes, he shook his head silently. Instead, he took her hands and intertwined her fingers in his as he lowered his mouth to her supple breasts, pleasuring her until she began whispering his name.

"Cry out all you like, my love. No one is within miles to hear."

Still holding her hands in his, his thumbs caressing her palms and wrists, he lowered his mouth between her thighs, kissing her inner thigh, then the other. He teased her mercilessly, increasing rather than ending her torment. This woman—this woman who would be his wife, and soon—was everything to him, and he had never been gladder that he knew how to pleasure a woman, and well.

"Please, Rashall," she whimpered. "Please do it."

He lowered his mouth over her, tasting her, her need for him, and as he hummed with pleasure deep in his throat, her hands broke away and rested at the nape of his neck, shyly encouraging him with a whispered *yes*.

"Yes what?" he asked softly, teasing her.

"Kiss me there—more."

"Where?"

She pressed herself up against him. "There. Please. More. It's something I've never felt before, Rashall. My darling Rashall. *Please*."

It was all he could do not to thrust within her, but he settled his mouth, his tongue, over the swollen flesh and suckled gently, then harder and still harder. She pulled him closer and cried out as her pleasure rolled over her. He slowed the flick of his tongue, drawing slightly away but continuing the delicious soothing until she had recovered and he felt her flesh throbbing for more. The taste of her intoxicated him—as sweet as any wine. He continued the rhythm of pleasuring her, then letting her almost roll away, then bringing her back again, perhaps half a dozen times. Each time, the sound of his name echoed throughout the woods. By the time she begged him to stop for fear she would die, he was drunk with the headiness of her.

She collapsed—slowly, numbly—into the bed. He laughed softly as he drew himself up beside her, turning her over again so that he could sleep against her. Fully erect, he drew close to her, relishing the feeling of her velvety skin against him.

"Heaven help me, I only want you more now. The taste of you will be another memory of you to drive me mad with hunger. I want to taste you again already."

"I want you inside me," she said frankly. Again she would have rocked herself into his touch, but he held her in place against him. She reached back, her cool fingertips grasping him. He stopped her. He did not want that to be his first time with her—and he was far too close as it was.

"Where will we find a place where we can live honestly and love each other?" he asked, kissing her temple, caressing her breast lightly, then carefully placing his hand on her thigh. "Took me a while to realize that some in this society do see my people as inferior."

She lifted a hand to stroke his cheek. "You forget. Your people *are* my people. I grew up thinking my parents had deserted me until Hannah's story that day."

"Juliana. Surely you don't think—"

"I told you. I *know* it's true."

He went silent. Then: "Why did you ask about the song?"

"You truly want to know?"

"It's why I asked."

"The song won't be written for another hundred and fifty years. You know it because your mother sang it to you. I wouldn't be surprised if your grandfather sang it to her."

"But how?"

She gave a long sigh. "Not tonight. Tomorrow I'll take you. But prepare yourself, for you'll soon have the same headache I did."

Chapter Eleven

Juliana awakened from the best night of sleep she'd ever known. Cozy in the quilts, she reached back for Rashall.

He was gone.

Her heart fell in disappointment and surprise.

"Want some breakfast?"

She sat up. He entered the room with a tray, and before she could stop herself, she gave a great sigh of relief.

"Don't tell me you thought I'd run off?"

"There is a precedent."

He laughed. "I'm done running, baby. I'm ready for you to show me that promised land where people can marry whoever they please."

"Oh, and here I was happy just to smell good coffee for a change."

"All right. Nota bene: the girl can't make coffee. I can deal with that."

She giggled, unaccountably moved at the simple pleasure of his teasing her. She sniffed and wiped her eyes as he placed the tray on the nightstand.

He bent to kiss her forehead. "Morning, Miss Juliana," he murmured. "What are you upset about now?"

She shook her head with a smile and swallowed. "Look at this! How did you do all this?"

"I may be a mere man, but I get by."

"Why don't we eat at the table?"

"Don't trust yourself in here, do you?"

She cocked her head, a hint of a smile about her lips. "Do *you* trust me?"

After a long moment, he nodded toward the door. "Out."

At the table, she noticed two small, well-worn sheets of parchment that had been unfolded on the table to dry. Without commenting, she noted the signatures at the bottom of each page. The humble *G. Washington*. And then, the ostentatious *B. Arnold, MGenl.*

The signatures matched the men.

She nibbled at breakfast as she watched him make himself a plate. "I can't believe you can make crumpets."

"Here's a funny story for you. I made one for your sister the morning after she arrived onboard our ship, and she thought it was hardtack." He shook his head. "Bless her heart."

A slow smile went over her face. "You know, you have a lot of expressions in your speech that the average colonial American doesn't. Haven't you ever noticed—or wondered why?"

He grew serious as he joined her at the table. Easily, he took her hand and spoke a simple prayer over their breakfast.

What an unusual man he was. As passionate as the next man—or perhaps more so. He seemed to become aroused any time he was near her. And yet he spoke of God—and to God—as if he were a close family member.

"I used to think it was a regional thing. My mother grew up around here. Ruth and Dan have some of her expressions as well. But I think they got them from her. And when I met Marley, who talks *just* like her—well, I started listening to others when I was in Williamsburg, and I knew Marley and Mother had to've gotten it from somewhere else."

She nodded once.

"And you're saying that somewhere else is more of a some*where* else," he went on.

"Yes."

The morning fire had been going for a while, and he'd placed his boots on a spare andiron in the hearth, beside the fire, to dry. At last she realized that when she looked at Rashall, she was observing a lifetime of discipline. Either from his upbringing, his life as a privateer, his training as a priest, or his military training.

"So what's this?" she asked casually, gesturing toward his papers.

"Just what they look like." He reached out and handed them to her, his pale brown eyes clear in the early morning light. "I have no secrets from you, Juliana."

She set the papers aside, unread, and lay her hand alongside his cheek. "You've already shaved. What time do you usually get up?"

He turned his face to kiss her palm. "I hardly ever get to sleep. Last night was a luxury I haven't had since I left St. Peter's. And I have to get back to camp soon."

"Not yet, please."

"Not until I have my proof about this nirvana where people can marry who they like."

"That is definitely *not* what I said. What I said was that I could take you to a time where you can marry who you like. It's no kind of a nirvana."

They quickly scrubbed up the breakfast dishes and put them away, and she led him to the window seat. "If you ever visit and I'm not home, I'm almost always down here."

"Down here?"

She unlatched the window seat, and he looked over the edge. She watched the surprise and curiosity move over his face as he looked into the winding stone stairwell.

Almost immediately, Will began whining. He barked once, as if an intruder threatened. For Will, the window seat was the worst of intruders.

"He doesn't like the window seat?"

"I lost him once. He might remember that. Also … " Even as she started the tale, she decided against telling him how she'd owned this dog for twenty years, yet he never got old.

His black hair never turned white; his joints never ached; his eyesight never dimmed, his sharp sense of smell never failed.

"What?"

"I don't want to go into it right now."

"Well, I hereby withdraw my 'no secrets' offer." He raised an eyebrow at her.

"It isn't that. It's just ... not right now. Basic time travel is a big enough hurdle for you for now."

She closed the seat and climbed onto the narrow ledge surrounding the cushion. "You kind of have to balance here, then open it. You press this catch, and it opens, like that. Just follow me down, and be sure to close the window seat behind you."

She moved down into the darkness. "You might want to bring a lamp, if the darkness bothers you, " she called.

"Wait for me!"

She paused on the stairs, closing her eyes and asking for wisdom and patience. If he were of a certain mind, he might reject this entirely.

The thought came to her in a moment: Would she risk losing a man like Rashall over this?

She quickly hurried back up the stairs to the opening into her supernatural world—a world she'd never thought to share with anyone.

"Are you sure you want to do this?"

As she spoke, he jerked his foot back up onto the frame with a nervous squeak. "What are you doing? I nearly stepped on your head!"

"I'm just worried about ... what you might think of it. It isn't a spiritual or unspiritual experience. It's outside of it, as much so as any technological creation is. Like the wheel."

"Get back down there," he said with a sigh. "Technology like the *wheel?* Dost thee think'st thou shalt affright me, with thy magical fire? What kind of a dunderhead do you think I am?"

She skipped back down the stairs, stung at his retort. "It's a little more than fire. The only reason I'm so comfortable with it is that I started when I was old enough to be curious about the world around me. I didn't yet understand the concepts of history, to tell you the truth. Don't forget to—"

"It's closed!" he said, reading her mind. The stairwell was lit only by the light of his lamp.

She went silent, rushing down the stairwell so as not to impede his process. As the light from his lamp faded, she called, "Are you all right?"

"How far do these stairs go?"

"There are six hundred and seventy four of them. I should've told you. I think it goes down about a quarter of a mile."

She waited for him to catch up, then let him move down ahead of her to pace their progress. In the cramped space, their bodies fit intimately. He held her to keep her safe as he edged down the stairs around her, and she drew close to him, lifting her mouth to his.

He smiled and met her gaze. "Is this how you want me to go? Because I have no sense at all when I'm around you, and I'm on the falling side."

She gave him a coy smile and slipped away up the stairs, allowing him to pass.

"Because I think I'd have been fine with that. Not a bad way to go."

She reached out and gently pushed at his face, and they continued down the stairs.

"How old were you when you first came down here?"

"Eight."

He paused, looking back up at her in amazement. "What kind of child were you?" he asked rhetorically.

"A very lonely one. A very weird one. I pondered *forever*. I walked down these stairs thinking I was walking into the center of the earth. It was pitch black, and I just sang all the way down."

He laughed.

At last they arrived at the bottom, and as they stepped onto the stone floor, he looked carefully around the place.

"Put your lamp there. We might be in a hurry coming back, and you'll probably want to be able to see."

"Doesn't the dark frighten you at all?"

"I know this place by touch, I've been here so often. My feet know each dip in the stones on that staircase; my body knows each worn curve of that wall."

"This is what you were blocking off from me, when we were in the root cellar?"

"Yes."

"What happened between then and now to make you want to share it with me?"

She had to consider that. "Your persistent belief that there's a better time somewhere for you and me. *This* is our time, Rashall. We have no other time. I have less than your average person, through my own foolishness."

"What do you mean?"

"Not right now."

He sighed. "Of course not. Someday I'll graduate time-travel college, and then I'll be tough enough to hear. All right. What next?"

"Well, you have to agree to some conditions. First of all, I have to know if you want to remember everything or not."

"You mean I might not even remember going?"

"If you go merely as an observer, you won't remember. You remember going, but nothing about what you saw. No one sees you while you're there. It's just to pass the time. But it's also safer, that way."

"Why would a person even want to do that?"

"It's just entertainment. It's kind of like watching television."

She realized her gaffe too late. "Let's see. It's like reading a book, or watching a play, except you learn nothing from it."

She saw the tension on his face—he believed her. "And if I go that way, I won't remember anything about it?"

"No."

He shook his head. "No, I don't want to do that. I want to remember every moment of my time with you, of course."

He said this off-handedly, and his matter-of-factness surprisingly moved her.

"There are rules you must follow. I've never taken anyone with me, but Aunt Mary took me somewhere once to make a point. So you have to stay with me so you can make the return trip. While we're there, don't change *anything*. I don't care what you see. If you see a man walking down the street naked, reciting Shakespeare and laughing, let him be."

"So it's kind of like visiting Paris," he quipped.

"Oh, you don't know the half of Paris. Anyway, there are some nuances to changes you can and can't make, but just play it safe and don't change anything. Keep your head down. The biggest rule of all—don't tell anyone you're from another time. There are other rules, but the terms of service will be planted into your subconscious."

"The *what?*"

She looked up at him and smiled. "Don't worry. I won't let you get hurt."

"Ah! Reassuring for a man to hear."

She walked ahead of him through the passageway to the labyrinth, and as he arrived at the end of the passageway, she saw his slow gaze of wonder as he took in the place.

"Another very important part of it is to be sure you're at the time portal in plenty of time."

"What time portal? I remember your grandmother talking about that, but I thought she said it was at Rosalie."

"You'll find out. They're all over, we just don't notice them. Just try to stay with me. If we get separated, go to the time portal immediately so you'll get back in time. We're only going for a short trip. Twenty-four hours might be too much for you. Remember—hold on and never let go."

"That's—why is that familiar to me?"

"It's what my father said to my mother, when they were traveling back to the twentieth century. My grandmother told us about it that day."

"Yeah, but that's a pretty obscure reference for me to remember."

She stepped forward into the labyrinth and led him to the identity reader, but the system didn't greet her as it usually did, in its almost human terms. And then she realized it was regulating its responses to Rashall's presence.

But he was captured by the infinite sky soaring high above the labyrinth. "That can't be the sky—what is it?"

"It *is* a sky of sorts, where every human ever created is represented in a family, as we all are. Those in the purest diamond clarity, still and brilliant, are families that have gone on to their reward in heaven. You see how some seem to beat slowly, as if by the power of a human pulse?"

He nodded, awestruck at the human heavens.

"They *are* human pulses. Each star represents a person. Those groupings that are darker are families in turmoil."

"Explaining why most are."

"It's the lot of humanity."

He nodded slowly, glancing at her.

"That's my family, up there, she said, pointing. Of course, he couldn't tell which of the many groupings she indicated. "Never mind. You'll see when we identify ourselves."

"When we—?"

"Hello, Mr. Adams."

The voice startled him, and he looked around, increasingly stricken that no one else was there except Juliana.

"Hello?"

"Good morning, Mr. Adams. Verify your identity."

Juliana gestured toward the reader, and he lifted his hand and placed it against the purple hand that appeared briefly in the pale blue.

"DNA match. Rashall Ashanti Adams. Born in Boston, Massachusetts in 1747. Insert your artifact, Mr. Adams."

Juliana gasped at the sight in the labyrinth sky. When Rashall had placed his palm against the reader, his star had beat steady and true—brightest white. In his family of stars, she saw an array of varying colors. And to each of these stars, countless spears of fiery light flew between stars throughout the heavens.

"What does that mean?" he asked.

"It's relationships your family has to other families. See how some are dark, some are light? A few are blood-red, bronze, even rust—all of these indicate turmoil."

"I wonder if it's all the ransomed children."

"Well those are more associated to your mother, I would think. Or maybe Ruth. Maybe it's the people you're spiritually connected to. Your parishioners?"

"Insert your artifact, Mr. Adams."

"We are traveling together and do not have an artifact," Juliana said, taking Rashall's hand and intertwining their fingers. "We humbly request an artifact."

"Verify your identity."

She placed her hand in the reader.

"DNA match. Juliana Juste Miller. Born in Richmond, Virginia in 1994. What is your desired destination?"

"I ask you to read my heart privately." Without being asked, she placed her palm against the reader.

Rashall raised an eyebrow. "Starting to think we have trust issues."

"Your return must be arranged at the portal in the corner telephone booth."

Juliana sighed. "Are you joking? Why not a police box?"

"The police box is an anomaly at your destination."

"And the telephone booth isn't?"

"I don't understand," Rashall said. "Any of this."

"You be quiet. I'll explain to you when we get back. Until then, you just think about whether thou wanst to make fun of me next time I try to help prepare you for something."

"Please agree to terms of service."

In the pale blue reader, a silhouette of two hands appeared. Without being asked, Rashall raised his hand along with her.

While the terms downloaded to Rashall's subconscious, he gasped and attempted to draw his hand away, unsuccessfully.

A moment later, the second cylinder descended, a few feet away. His face was ashen.

She touched his cheek. "Look at me. Everything's fine. Just stay with me. I'll explain it all—in time."

He nodded. "What if I'm ... not strong enough for this?"

"I would not have brought you here if you weren't."

The clothing chamber opened, and she withdrew the men's clothing and handed it to him so he wouldn't see the date of their destination. She understood the potential of this trip to discourage him.

He walked into a separate corridor and changed, then returned carrying his boots, with his own clothing folded over his arm. He wore a pair of snug jeans, a button-down shirt that emphasized his lean, muscular build, and leather boots.

She was similarly dressed, and they eyed each other approvingly. "Is this how they dress in the future?"

"Present the artifact to comply with terms of service."

She gave him a small pirouette, and when she saw his face again, she saw shock there. "I can see your entire body. Your long legs, your delicious bottom. You cannot go out in public this way, can you?"

She kissed him. "Where we're going, no one will give this bottom a second glance."

"Ah. All the men have died, then, I see."

"Present the artifact to comply with terms of service."

"What's this?" Rashall asked.

He held up a cell phone, and she explained it. "Wait till we get there—it won't work here. I have one, too."

She belatedly wished she'd brought her pistol, but it was too late for that. They placed their belongings into the chamber and closed it, and she glanced at the artifact she'd been given—the key to a bodega in the area they were visiting.

She clasped his hand and drew him near.

"Present the artifact to comply with terms of service."

She lifted and pressed the artifact into the reader. A flash later, the pain pressed in around her head, and she tried with everything in her to remain conscious.

She failed.

Chapter Twelve

Juliana awakened abruptly.

Included in her costume was a modern watch—time was her first thought as she became conscious in their destination. When she glanced at it, she saw a tiny timer inset in the face—they'd already lost four minutes.

Rashall lay collapsed beside her. She shook him vigorously. "Ray—wake up. We're here. Come on! Let's go."

He stirred lethargically.

"*Hurry.*"

"Where are we?" he asked, completely disoriented. "I can smell the ocean nearby. Or … something like it." His nose wrinkled, and he coughed at the awful smell.

"Look at yourself."

He came to his feet, taking her hand and pulling her up. "Now I remember. Holy—this place stinks like London."

"Look. Right there's the phone booth. Remember where we are. High Street and London. There's no other phone booth, so that has to be the one. If we get separated, come right back here immediately. If I'm not here, it means I've already gone back to our time. So go into the phone booth, clear your mind, and look until you see the portal. You'll know it when you see it. Then just walk through it, back into the labyrinth at Stonefield."

"What is this thing again?" He'd figured out how to turn on the cell phone, and was fascinated with it.

"It's a way people communicate when they're apart. It also has access to a great deal of the world's knowledge—within a very limited spectrum. For instance, if you wanted to learn about someone's family, you can do a search. But please, don't let it distract you. People miss half their lives with their noses stuck in those things."

"What did you want to show me, then?"

"Let's take a walk down there. Just keep your head down."

As they turned a corner, they saw a car in front of an old house that once had been a beautiful Georgian home. Now it was riddled with graffiti, its windows broken out and boarded up. An automobile drifted slowly down the street.

Loud bass boomed from the car, where four young men sat. She and Rashall were still in the shadows, and she pulled him back around the corner.

"Is that supposed to be music?" he asked.

"Let's go back. I don't feel good about this."

They returned to the corner where they'd started, ready to walk into the phone booth and end the trip. A group of young people walked down the street, laughing and talking. Juliana smoothly pulled Rashall into the shadows, hiding behind the edge of a bus shed.

One of the young boys in the crowd stopped to kiss a girl, his hands roving over her with casual intimacy despite his audience. The others in the crowd hooted and made lewd remarks, and she saw Rashall's jaw tighten at the spectacle. She pressed her fingertips to his lips.

Suddenly lights flashed and an engine revved in the street, and the young people stopped, turning. They walked back up the street to the corner across from the bodega. A patrol car pulled up to the bodega with a screech of brakes.

An officer jumped out of the car just as a young man—no more than perhaps sixteen years old, if that old—emerged from the bodega carrying a paper bag close to his body, his other hand hidden under the bag.

"Stop! Show me your hands! Hands!"

The teenager stood still as the officer raised his firearm.

"Put down the bag, son. Show me your hands. It's going to be okay. No! Don't—"

Abruptly, the teenager pulled the bag closer and raised his other arm at the officer, revealing a handgun. He fired several times—wild shots, but he hit the officer more than once. He turned to run down the street.

At that moment, the loud car Juliana had noticed on the next street pulled up alongside the teenager. Someone in the car fired once, killing him instantly. They leapt out, grabbed the paper bag from under the robber, and jumped back in the car as it sped away.

It was over.

Two in the crowd of teenagers had pulled out their cell phones to record the exchange between the officer and the robber, but they barely had time to press RECORD before the officer lay dead. They exclaimed in shock as they ran down to see what had happened to the robber.

No one on the street paid them any attention.

"I've been here before. Not this exact location, but the time. I find no sense in the place. They have luxuries beyond anyone's wildest dreams. All the clean water they want, anytime, delivered to them through a pipe inside their home. All the comforts anyone can imagine. Ease and a good life. Many work only eight hours a day, and they have two entire days every week to do whatever they wish. Technological marvels to boggle the mind."

He was stricken, pale. "These people live like animals. That boy. That degenerate, acting the fool with that young lady. He was younger than George. Who raised him? And who lets those young ladies walk the street like strumpets? They're still children!"

"Their parents grew up just like them. Rashall, your parents settled in Beacon Hill. In the year we're in at the moment, Beacon Hill is one of the most expensive places to live in Boston, which is one of the most expensive cities in the country. It's considered an exclusive neighborhood. And it *began* as a black neighborhood. Nobody even remembers that now."

He shook his head. He looked as if he might be sick. "Are we such animals? You and I aren't. What happened?"

"It certainly isn't just black people. I could take you to places where there are as many whites, just as poor, acting just as foolish, for just the same reasons. And yet they still cling to the myth of race. A myth that was created in the moral darkness of slavery to give wicked men power over black people.

"They do it still, in this time, even as science has shown them that there's no such thing as race, except in social constructs that become self-fulfilling. Look at this. Things like this happen every day. Thousands every year. There's the bodega owner. He's black. The police officer was black. The robber was black. Those gang members are black."

"What year is this?"

She hesitated. "Twenty-fifteen."

"Dear God in heaven." After a long moment, he shook his head. "Will our people never find a place of honor and leadership in this country?"

She hesitated, unsure how much to tell him. "Many blacks *are* leaders. Many are men and women in Congress, professors of colleges, pastors of churches, scientists in research. We work in every type of profession in the world. And yet so many boys of all races continue without fathers in this time. In this world, anyone can get married to anyone else. But so many don't. They have 'baby mamas' and 'baby daddies' who still go out and dishonor one another. On those streets is an area of housing for poor people. The state pays for their housing."

"Sounds like, even in this time, that the military is the only place on dry land where men are considered equal, regardless of race."

"Oh? I could take you to that officer's funeral, where you will see hundreds of men arrive from all over the country. Men of all races, who will weep over him as a brother."

"Well, I would imagine they are quite like the military in that way. But who leads this country, that he tolerates such conditions as this?"

"Oh, Ray," she said sadly. "You don't want to know. This is a system that's been built up over decades. He can't fix all that. It's going to take people everywhere making better choices for another fifty years."

He glanced at her in impatient disbelief as she made excuses for the man.

"All right. Look it up on your phone. I showed you how."

And he did.

They sat on a concrete border that lined the sidewalk. People had emerged from their homes and now hurried past on their way to the scene of the two killings. The dead men lay perhaps only fifty feet apart.

"Figure out who's leading the country?" she asked gently.

Several moments passed before he looked at her. "Juliana," he whispered.

"I know. The president can only do so much."

He shook his head. "No. Look."

He held out the phone to her. The man who smiled in the photograph looked enough like Rashall to have been his father.

Beloved police captain stabbed to death; Cameron Carlyle found dead.

Or perhaps his grandfather.

"He dies in the spring of 1994 'outside Richmond, in a remote area near Henricus.' Sound like Stonefield, to you?"

"Or somewhere very nearby."

"It says here he was a police captain and did all kinds of benevolent work—helping young boys, involving businessmen in the community to help, mentoring … what does that mean? I don't understand it in this context. Advising?"

"In that time, a mentor is someone who is an expert in a certain area, and he or she shows a novice the ropes. How to become an expert themselves."

"Ah. As a master would treat an apprentice."

"More or less. In this specific case, an accomplished man usually shows a young man without competent parents the basics of getting started in life. Something as simple as proper grooming habits, or how to tie a tie, or good table manners."

She watched the sadness move over his face. "What's wrong?"

He shook his head. "Just reminds me of my son—how he was when I found him. But he was an escaped slave in the 1700s. It's upsetting that children are so lost, more than two hundred years later, with the benefit of freedom and parents."

She went silent. She had plenty of opinions about it, but no answers—and no encouragement.

They moved through the neighborhood for a long while, taking their time observing how people lived in a Virginia port town in the 21st century. He grew contemplative at the noise, the dirt, the violence and ignorance they saw everywhere— even in the middle of the night.

"Hey. Give me that phone."

Juliana went cold at the young man who appeared behind Rashall. She'd been so involved in conversation, she hadn't even noticed his approach. Rashall stood still, looking down as she turned to see the man, who held a weapon against Rashall's back. A second man stood behind him, holding a knife of his own.

"You, too," he said to Juliana. He held his free hand out to her, gesturing quickly, and she passed it over Rashall's shoulder.

In that moment, Rashall moved so quickly she couldn't have described his movements if she'd had to. In the next, the unknown man was flat on his back, trying to breathe, his knife clattering to the street. A moment later, the blade glittered in the night as Rashall tossed it in the air, lifting his eyebrows in almost jovial invitation to the other man.

The man stepped forward. "Give me the phone, old man."

He glanced at Juliana in bemusement. "Baby doll, he called me old. I think I might cry."

He kicked at the other man's knife; then, almost as if performing in a ballet, turned twice and leveraged the man over his shoulder. He joined his friend, gasping for breath.

Juliana grabbed his hand, and they raced around the corner and down the block to their original location. One of the men had recovered and was chasing them.

Rashall gestured toward the phone booth. "After you, milady."

Juliana ran to the phone booth, opened the door and peered inside. "All right, it's here in the phone. Just focus right here. I won't go through until—"

"I see it. Go."

She grabbed Rashall's hand and stepped through the portal, and he followed just behind her.

"Don't let them follow!" she added belatedly, even as someone almost made his way through the portal. Rashall shoved forcefully at his head, and the man popped back into his own time and, no doubt, a crushing headache from colliding with the telephone full force.

"All right, we're back. If we had traveled directly out of here, we'd have had to make it up those stairs and into our own time within our allotted travel period, or we're trapped. But remote portals deliver you straight into the other time. Like the one at Rosalie. It isn't always this exact, if you're with someone."

"What do you mean?"

"One of you might end up a few miles away, but you're both in the same general destination."

He shook his head. "This is going to sound awful, but I guess I've proven I'm no priest. That knife fight, such as it was, made me miss Hawk more than ever."

"Then let's go see him."

Even as he smiled at her, she saw the pain of the travel headache descend over him, and she gently hugged him, rubbing his temple. She sang softly, "I'll be loving you— always. With a love that's true—always. Days may not be fair—always. That's when I'll be there—always. Not for just an hour, not for just a day. Not for a just a year, but always."

When she drew back and saw his gaze on her, she smiled. "I think I forgot half of it, and sang the rest of it off-key."

She sobered as he dropped to one knee, there in the labyrinth.

"Juliana, I know you're in mourning, but I beg your forgiveness for my part in the years of happiness we've lost already. And I promise you today my love and affection, my charity and protection. Forever and always. I ask now for your hand in marriage, the first moment you're ready."

She framed his face with her hands and kissed his mouth. When she opened her eyes and he took her hand to leave the place, she stopped him, glancing up to the sky.

Overhead, the two stars in their separate familial asterisms shone as diamonds. Even as they watched, a new constellation began to pulse with light, deriving its shape and form from echoes of their stars. Flashes of connections from their original asterisms ignited like a celestial strobe, like earth's first flash of chain lightning.

She hugged him close, and he kissed her forehead and said with a small laugh, "I'm not sure, but I think someone just said *amen.*"

Chapter Thirteen

Martin had returned to his assignment by the time Marley arrived at his doorstep to ask for his help. Instead, she found George alone, asleep at noon. As she stood in the doorway of his room, she considered that he might be ill and she sent the children to wait on the porch.

She gently shook him, and when he murmured Susan's name with a silly laugh, she realized he had a different fever.

"Get up, you lazybones!" she bellowed.

Alarmed, he jumped up, wrapping a blanket around himself. "Aunt Marley—what's the matter?"

"You tell me—I pass the schoolhouse and hear all sorts of business going on inside, but when I get here to ask Martin for help, he's gone and you're in here fast asleep!"

"Oh, he's not here."

"Well, I can see that. I'm not asking where Martin is. Why aren't you in school?"

He shifted from one foot to the other, and he glanced at the floor. "I was up late, helping Martin get ready to leave, but I guess I didn't hear him when he rode out."

"All right, then. You can take me to town. And I'll leave you with Aunt Ruth tonight, to make sure you get to school in the morning. Unless you'd rather stay with me and your Uncle Hawk?"

"He's with Mr. Thomas," he said, perplexed at her threat.

She fumed inwardly. Even young George understood how odd the idea of her and her husband sharing their home had become.

"Fine. I'll go on to town without you."

"Are you jok—pardon me, ma'am. I'll be happy to escort you. I wouldn't be able to sit down for a week if my father thought I let you drive a wagon to town with two children unescorted."

She bit back laughter. Once upon a time, Ray would've howled at such starchy behavior. But this, Ray himself had starched into the boy.

"Your father would not spank you. You're much too old for that. He'd find something much more painful. Anyway, I'll wait outside with the children."

George joined them in another five minutes, hastily groomed and dressed and stuffing a piece of cornbread into his mouth. In afterthought, he asked, "Are the children hungry?"

Marley spoke from the seat of the wagon as George climbed up beside her. Abby and Sam sat in a small enclosure she'd rigged in the front of the wagon, to keep them from wandering away. Not quite a cage ... more of a playpen. Abigail wouldn't try to climb out, but Sam was a handful.

"They've had breakfast, thank you."

Sam held out his hand. "Me, pease."

George smiled. "May I?"

She waved, and he put the last of his cornbread into the boy's mouth then took the reins. "Abby, are you still a little hungry? I have a little more left inside."

She knelt at the front of the wagon, smiling prettily at George, the ruffles of her cap framing her flirting. "No, thank you, Georgy. Can I sit on your lap?"

"Now you know your mama has to give permission for that, and I think I'm already in hot water."

Marley couldn't resist the charming grin on the young man's face at her daughter's winsome smile.

"Both of you, just sit still for a second." She stood up.

"I won't move," George said.

"Not you," she said, gritting her teeth.

"Oh, well then." He raised his arms in the air and gave a little shimmy for Abby's entertainment, and the child laughed.

Marley lifted Abigail over the back of the wagon seat, situating her beside George, and then she brought Sam up and into her lap.

With everyone settled, George drove the team over the rutted path to town. The spring rains had stopped a day or two before, and she gasped at the finery of the countryside.

Purple lavender, yellow black-eyed susans, wild bleeding heart, and rusty foxglove. As they passed alongside a small brook, she asked, "Now what's that, Abigail?"

Abby leaned forward, craning her neck. She wasn't sure the child would remember since the last time she'd seen it. "Skunk cabbage!" she said, wrinkling her nose.

"No, it all smells wonderful," she told her daughter.

She took a deep breath, inhaling till she felt the oxygen fill her and move through her giddy brain. How she loved spring. The season of promises kept, a reminder that God hadn't given up yet on this old world.

As they neared the town, they saw a wagon headed their way, heavily laden with supplies and a young family. Marley and George exchanged nods with them.

"Didn't they look tense to you?" George asked. "And they looked like they were in a hurry."

"Oh, I'd forgotten it was Publick Times," she whispered. "I usually keep the children at home then."

George gave her a skeptical look. "Oh, I see. Don't want them to be reminded that—"

"They're only children! They can't yet understand things like auctions."

"Well, when would it be that they can?"

"It won't be today. Go the back way. Do *not* go through the square. I will not have them see such things."

"You can't shelter them much longer. Children Abby's size are already picking worms off tobacco out on Westover. "

"Well they are at Rosalie, too! There's nothing wrong with good, honest work. Abby works as hard as I do."

"Not so some fat old white guy can get rich."

Marley gasped. "George! Where have you heard that crude talk?"

He went silent. Then he met her eyes in challenge: *It's true, isn't it?*

"It's wrong to hate anyone for something they have no control over, but avarice does make people ugly."

Abigail was afire with curiosity at their disagreement. "What's Publick Times? What's wrong with picking worms off tobacco, and things like oxens? What's avarice, Mama?"

Fortunately, Sam had fallen asleep with the rhythm of the wagon.

"Auctions, Abby, not oxen. I'll explain those another time. Publick Times are when people come from all around to do business and to attend court. And to buy and sell goods. Of course, with the war, everything's a bit chaotic. And avarice is greed, the worst kind."

"I forget greed. Is it like when Sam wanted more cornbread, even after he just had breakfast?"

George chuckled. "You got it, child."

As they turned down the small alley leading to the Trelawney home, George fell silent.

"Hush, Abby."

They could see the Palace Green between the houses, and there stood militia forces gathered around tents. They looked to be unpacking.

No—packing. And they were in a hurry.

"Help me get the children inside, George. I don't understand what's happening here."

He stopped the wagon quickly and helped Marley and Sam down, then Abby. Sam awakened, blinking in confusion. He pointed at the home before them. "Grandpapa. Nan."

They hurried to the door. Marley peered at the men she saw assembled on the Palace Green. One man, clearly an officer, called another. "Yes, General Nelson—right away, sir."

Thomas Nelson, Jr. This was the Virginia militia. Deep pride stirred within her for her native home. She looked at the men—most of them so young they were barely shaving, their simple homespun clothing likely the best they had. Young George was better armed and outfitted than some of them. She pressed her lips together and cleared her throat against the emotion.

They were preparing to march out, but at the moment she couldn't remember the threat facing them. The heroic stories of her childhood took on a depth and dimension as she continued to live within them.

Marley tapped on the door, then opened it. "Anyone home?"

In a glance she took in the state of the home—Thomas, too, was preparing to quit the city. Noise came from upstairs. "Yoo-hoo, dear! We're up here!"

This gay call came from Hannah, who seemed to be under the impression they were departing for a riverside picnic.

The sudden pounding of boots on the stairs caught her attention, and the sight of her husband struck her as it always did. He looked more like his old self than she'd seen in years. He crossed the room in four long strides and drew her to him, hugging her hard and kissing his son's head.

"Papa?" Sam asked, rearing his head back in suspicion.

Bronson gave a soft laugh as he reached out to give George a brisk pat on the shoulder, then took Abby from him.

The child hugged him tightly. "Papa! Don't be afraid! George took care of us."

"What's going on?" Marley asked.

"Arnold and Phillips are at Burwell's Ferry. Headed this way."

"The militia have to hurry, then."

"Exactly. And so do we. Phillips is under pillage-and-destroy orders from Cornwallis. He has over 2,000 troops. It took a fleet of 11 to get them all here from Portsmouth."

"Let's go, then. We'll take only what we need. You and George and I can all fit on the front of the wagon with the children. You can use the space in the wagon for whatever you need. What shall I take?"

"Father's wagon is loaded already. Take a look around and see if there's something meaningful to you that I've missed."

"Portraits. That's what you can't replace. We'll avoid Quarterpath Road on the return." She hesitated. "But wait. This house—"

She cut herself off, mid-sentence, declining to disclose what she knew. This house survived intact and little changed to the time of the Restoration, beginning in 1927.

But who knew what they'd taken out of the house. And this house in the original 1781 had no one named Hannah around to throw unplanned drama into the mix.

"Never mind," she said. "Let's play it safe."

Aileen, the old nursemaid who'd been with Thomas forever, was hastily packing items Marley assumed were sentimental to the family. She loved the old woman. Perhaps as old as Thomas, she still moved with purpose and vigor— though perhaps more slowly than she had 35 years ago.

Aileen had been Bronson's nursemaid, as well as that of his mother, Jennie. When Thomas had taken his young son to Bermuda decades before, Aileen had followed him, doting on the young boy as she had his mother.

Marley efficiently stripped the walls of art and the desk of letters and paperwork. She grabbed a basket and told Abby to fill it as quickly as she could with foodstuffs from the kitchen.

She opened a hall closet and found the painting of Jennie Trelawney covered with a blanket. She called Bronson. "Why is this in the closet? You surely don't think they'd spare it?"

He gave a tight-lipped smile. "It was in the wagon. *Someone* must have taken it back out."

Which was code for *your crazy-ass grandmother.*

As Hannah arrived, frostily noting their detection of her ruse, Marley spat, "How could you? That's all my husband has of his mother to remember her by."

She looked away, sniffing. "Aileen must have put it there."

Aileen gave Marley a smile and a shrug. "Aye, ye got me."

Over the past five years, the old woman had developed the patience and charity of Job. And she adored Marley, for the small feat of crushing the curse of the Dandridges. Marley's grandmother had a lifetime pass by association.

They soon filled the second wagon with belongings as well, and they set off. Bronson led the wagons into a path he knew through the woods to make their way back to Rosalie.

As they rode along, Marley fed the children bites of fresh cornbread and fried chicken Aileeen had packed for them. Sitting shoulder to shoulder beside her husband, she ached to touch him in some small way—but she'd grown skittish since he'd been home. He and George chit-chatted about matters at Rosalie—school, crops—and the many redcoats in the area.

She relaxed as the morning wore on, and she soon grew sleepy and leaned against Bronson's shoulder. She and their sleeping son leaned against him. She slipped her hand under his arm, clasping his bicep as she nodded off contentedly.

He shifted on the wagon seat, and she sat up. "Sorry," she said softly. "I wasn't thinking."

He transferred the reins to his other hand and put his arm around her, drawing her against his chest and kissing her hair. The warmth of his welcome overwhelmed her.

"All well over there, George?"

"Yes, sir. If we make it home all right, I'll never miss school again."

"How's that?"

"If I'd been in school this morning, I'd be writing an essay right now, instead of hoping we miss Benedict Arnold."

Bronson laughed. "Now you have something to write about. The morning you ran across General Nelson's militia preparing to elude the most infamous turncoat in history. Well, at least up to this point," he said, sending Marley a small smile.

"No, he's made himself a cliché along the lines of Little Jack Horner."

"Have you heard from your father lately, son?"

"He brought us home after Mr. Morgan's funeral—me, Martin, and aunt Marley."

Bronson went silent for a moment in confusion.

"He *did* look for you," Marley answered his unasked question.

"Ah. So he went back to the field afterward?"

"To tell you the truth, Uncle Hawk, I think he went right back to see Mrs. Morgan."

"You can call her Aunt Juliana, too, you know."

The boy shrugged. "I just don't feel like I know her well enough yet. Anyway, Brother Dan told me Father forgot something at Stonefield. Did you know he works for General Washington?"

"Indeed?" Bronson asked, noncommittally.

"He has papers that the Commander-in-chief signed. Martin said I couldn't tell anybody else about it. I knew you probably already knew, since you were both in the First Rhode Island."

"When you have a secret like that, you can't assume anything, George. But of course you're right trusting me and your aunt. Now these two little flibbertigibbets, that's another story. They're like little parrots. Tell them what you wish the village to—"

And at that same moment, they all went silent. They heard the sounds of horses and men conversing.

The spring woods were still in the process of budding out, and they were plainly visible from the Quarterpath, a few hundred yards away.

Bronson looked back at his father and gestured him to hurry, even as he pulled their wagon up behind a stand of pine trees in the midst of the barren woods. Thomas clicked the horses into motion, and the wagons pulled behind the pines as the redcoats came into view. A few officers rode into view.

"Why, they wouldn't bother us, would they? Civilians?"

"Father, what have they done over the past twenty years to give you cause to trust them? Especially Arnold?"

Thomas gave a grunt of agreement.

"It's just a few men," George whispered. "Officers, I think."

"They're an advance party. The others will be along shortly. Get under the wagons."

"Papa, I'm afraid," Abigail cried. Having lowered her voice to a whisper, it came out as a squeak.

"It's all right. There's nothing to be afraid of. Did your mother ever tell you about the time she single-handedly whipped the redcoats at the Battle of Great Bridge?"

Marley cast him an appalled look. "Of course I didn't!"

"My father said you did," George retorted.

"And they both told me as much," Thomas echoed.

"Well. Thank you *all* for your confidence, but I would rather my children not think of me as—"

"As a brave and capable example of womanhood?" Bronson asked, his gaze clear as he smiled at her.

And before she quite realized what she was doing, she leaned up to kiss him on the cheek. His hand rested at the nape of her neck as he held her close, lightly nuzzling her ear for a fleeting moment.

When she drew away from him, she felt her cheeks burning—and she saw him lightly bite his lip as he regarded her.

And, as love for her husband burst within her in the pine-scented, shaded wood, just for a moment she stopped to love her life.

Chapter Fourteen

Marley stooped beside her children. "Abby, I used to be afraid, too. With your father's help, I learned to have courage. And so can you."

And then they all heard it—the thundering of thousands of redcoats in the dirt of the quarterpath. If they were found out, Arnold or Phillips would undoubtedly destroy everything in the wagons and confiscate their horses. They would likely identify Bronson as an escaped prisoner of war and arrest him.

Sam's face puckered into a wail, and Abby took a deep breath. "Come, Sam! Let's look for worms under the wagon! If they come near, we'll throw them at them."

His eyes went wide in excitement. The children scurried under the wagon—and Hannah began wailing. Aileen stood to the side, her head bowed in prayer, her mouth moving silently.

Bronson cast his father a frantic glance. Thomas hugged his wife close, pulling his cape around her to drown out her soft sobs. The sight saddened Marley. Who was this stranger who had raised her?

"I'll watch the children," George murmured, slipping flat under the wagon with them.

Bronson drew Marley close to his side.

"There. You see that man—the haughty one with his rather large nose thrust high, his jowls carrying nuts for winter?"

She smothered her giggles against her hand as the rider led the troops along the quarterpath. "It can't be."

"Yes. That's Arnold. The man at his side must be General Phillips."

"He does have the ego about him, doesn't he? It's quite remarkable that one's ego could be so insurmountable that a man, otherwise sound of judgment, would commit the sort of treachery that would lay waste his name for all time."

He glanced down at her. "Exactly. That's precisely who he is. The sort whose opinion of himself is so inflated and in the same moment so flawed that he would destroy himself in his misguided pride."

She stood, relaxed, with her husband's arm around her and her opposite hand stroking the back of his forearm.

A single fife pealed out the lively notes of a familiar tune, and Marley felt his muscles stiffen.

"Does that tune have a name?" she asked. "I remember it, but don't know why."

"*The British Grenadiers*."

A few bars later, snare and bass drummers joined in. It chilled Marley's blood, to know their prey was her own loved ones. She had heard this song played in countless re-enactments on the Palace Green back in her old life. Never once had the reality of the jovial call to war truly sunk in.

"Isn't that what they play marching into battle? Seems an odd choice for a troop movement without engagement."

He didn't answer, and his arm around her dropped to his side. He stared blankly through the pine boughs at the troops, and the trembling began.

"Bronson," she whispered urgently, shaking his shoulder. Unaware and unresponsive, he merely stared. His breath grew labored and heavy, and in the pleasant April day, sweat beaded on his forehead. She hugged him and whispered in his ear. "You're safe. You're with people who love you. You're safe."

Presently he blinked and saw her. His eyes closed as he turned away awkwardly. For a long moment, he looked around as if for an escape route. His gaze rested on his father, a good twenty feet away, sitting on a fallen log beside Hannah, comforting her.

"Everyone's safe. Was it the music that reminded you?"

He glanced back at the troops—still passing in formation, the music fading into the distance. Her frightened shell of a husband had returned.

"Yes," he said finally. "The fife and drums."

"Please hold me," she said, searching his face for any tenderness. Perhaps calling on his sense of protection might summon his strength.

He looked at her and pulled her against him, still trembling. She hugged him hard.

"Perhaps we start a fife and drum corps at Rosalie."

He gave a shaky laugh. "Why, thank you, dear."

"You know what I mean. You confront it. You hear it over and over, under your own control, until it loses all power over you."

He held her, and she gently stroked his damp back until the music was far down the road and he was calmer. "Dear God, I miss you."

His broken confession moved her, and she drew him still closer. She raised her head and met his gaze. "I'm right here. I'll never leave you, my darling."

When they reached Rosalie, they arrived first at the old overseer's house, leaving Thomas, Hannah, and Aileen there. Hannah hugged her grandchildren and promptly disappeared into the house.

"Well," Thomas said, smiling. "Ever the doting grandmother."

In afterthought, Marley followed him. "Would you mind if Aileen stays with us for a bit? I'm—trying to help Bronson."

He patted her back. "Aye, child. Would you come in and see old Hastings? I know he'll be disappointed otherwise."

She glanced back at the others. "I'll be right back."

Hurrying into the only downstairs bedroom, she found Hastings sitting in a chair in the corner, his eyeglasses low on his nose.

"What are you reading?"

He looked up, smiling. She crossed the room, glad to see her great-grandfather. "My sweet Merrilea," he said, his gnarled hand pressing her to him as she bent to kiss his cheek.

"'History merely repeats itself. It has all been done before. Nothing under the sun is truly new.'"

"Socrates."

"Solomon. Ecclesiastes, to be precise," he said, setting the Bible aside.

She perched on a stool beside his chair. He gave her a steady smile, and she noticed that the throw across his lap was slipping. Straightening it, she pulled the stool nearer and rested her head on his lap.

He stroked her hair lightly. "When I look at you, my dear, I am comforted. It's as if my William sits at my feet as a child."

The reminder of the grandfather she'd never known—that whether she knew the details of it or not, she was a part of something bigger—comforted her, too.

"Papa, my husband is suffering, and I don't know how to help him."

"How so?"

"He was imprisoned on the *Jersey* for many months."

"Yes. I've heard. That he lasted so long is a testament to his mental fortitude."

"The stay did its damage, sir. At times the memories overcome him unexpectedly and in lifelike detail. He trembles when reminded. He has trouble breathing. I'm afraid he may do something dreadful if he doesn't heal. He hasn't slept in our bed since he got home."

He sighed deeply, pressing his palms together under his chin. He removed his glasses. "Merrilea, there's something I've never told anyone before about my past."

She waited.

"When I was but a boy, my father sent me to serve as a page to the Duke of Marlborough—John Churchill."

"Winston Churchill's ancestor."

"No, his son."

They looked at one another in confusion.

"Ah. Evidently there was another Winston Churchill."

"He almost singlehandedly saves the world in the twentieth century."

"Oh, my! Well, this nobleman did his humble part in the seventeenth and eighteenth. My father sent me to join him when I was but nine years of age. Lord Marlborough had lost his own son just two weeks before, and he was quite distraught about it when I arrived. In time, he came to dote on me. I traveled with him in all his battles, all over Europe."

"He saw service in the War of Spanish Secession, when England became the world's dominant power. Spain was ruled by an inbred idiot and France could not manage its money. I was there to see the British Empire come into its glory."

She listened to his tale of youthful glory, astonished. Never would she have supposed it of her genteel old great-grandfather. And then he grew pensive.

"The diamond in the crown of his military career was a treaty that expanded the territory in which England controlled the slave trade to include the Spanish colonies.

"At any rate, I saw it more than once, what you speak of. War is the worst experience any human being might suffer. Those who survive are driven to madness, drink ... even taking their own lives."

"But how can I help him recover?"

"If you can get him talking about it, let him know you're a safe confidante. Let him talk and talk. Draw him out. The more he talks about it, the stronger he will grow. And by the by," he added, in casual afterthought. "If you think of it, ask him if your father ever spoke of his service in the war."

"My *father*?"

"He was one of his professors, as I recall. And I understood he fought in the French and Indian war."

"My *father*?"

"I grow old and feeble. Perhaps I recall incorrectly. But I remember him speaking of fighting with *Major* Washington. Who we now know as our Commander-in-chief."

"I don't understand how that could have been. It doesn't fit with the story Hannah told us."

He patted her cheek. "Do not shrink your father to fit Hannah's mean *mise-en-scène*. Both your father and my Cassandra were adventurers of great expanse. You truly can't begin to scratch the surface of their escapades. If every one of them were written down, I suppose that even the whole world would not have room for the books that would be written."

Presently, a tap at the door caught her attention.

Bronson walked in, closing the door behind him. "Hello, Godfrey." He hugged him, then knelt on one knee beside his chair. "You look very well indeed this morning."

"My physician has visited with my favorite tonic: her winsome smile."

Her husband favored her with an intimate glance. "She has miraculous healing properties."

"Bronson, can you recall back to the time young Rob was your professor?"

"Of course. One of the most exciting times of my life—until I met his daughter."

"Yes, yes, all that. Can you recall him speaking of fighting in the war?"

"The French and Indian War?"

He nodded.

The question gave Bronson pause. "I do recall a professor talking about that very thing, now that you mention it. I hadn't connected that to Professor Miller until now. But he was the only one young enough to have fought."

He looked up at Marley with something like distress.

"What's wrong?"

"Nothing," he said, again lost in thought. "It just gives me a different perspective. He was very knowledgeable about military strategy and the intricacies of the global conflict in the Seven Years' War."

"Of course, he would have been."

"No. He seemed to have a greater perspective of the event as the conflict here in North America fit into the greater conflict on five different continents around the world. And, especially, its place in history. That was what made his teachings so unique. He seemed to have an almost divine understanding of our place in history. And he made it quite clear that if not for the Seven Years' War, France might not have been so stubbornly committed to what they're doing now."

"What?" Marley was confused. "What do you mean?"

"Oh, no, of course he didn't foretell the future, at least not explicitly. He simply left us with the ominous awareness that Britain's reign as a world power must end, or her tyranny would be unstoppable anywhere in the world."

Marley looked from one man to the other, then shook her head. "No. This simply doesn't make sense."

"How so?" Hastings asked.

"Nan explained to us that day that he was new on the scene in the mid-sixties. That he soon went about courting my mother."

"Perhaps he only arrived after he fought in the war."

"How many college professors do you know who were veterans? They're usually scholars, devoted to learning, not fighting."

Bronson frowned at her. "I would consider myself devoted to learning, yet I understood the need to take up arms against Great Britain's tyranny."

"I didn't say that well. I would tend to believe that most scholars lack the characteristics that make for a great warrior. They debate consequences to death and render themselves unable to act. Warriors never have that problem. They recognize a threat and act on it."

"I would say your father's case was unusual, but not impossible."

"I'm inclined to agree with Merrilea," Hastings said. "Not only on the argument, but that her father did not arrive at Rosalie a war-weary warrior. He arrived with nothing except a suit of clothing and a pistol, all of it fairly new. I say again, Merri, your mother and father were great adventurers who moved about in time. I've seen them more than once in my life, although they swore me to secrecy about the details. I submit that perhaps his experience of the 1760s was not chronological."

Bronson sighed and nodded. "Of course. That makes much more sense. I'm still living in a frame of mind where events are sequential."

"They are sequential," she said. "Just not necessarily chronological."

"You just want to argue," he said, his eyes sparkling.

She laughed.

Another tap on the door came. "Hello, Mr. Hastings," George said as he walked in. "Aileen's asking about whether we're staying for supper."

"Unfortunately, we do need to get home."

Marley rose. Reluctantly, she bade Papa goodbye.

Bronson touched her back lightly as they left the home. "I do wonder how well he understood the French and Indian war—and warfare itself—if he hadn't yet fought in it when he taught us."

"Well, if what Papa is saying is true, he might've fought just as sport—for the experience alone. He was a veteran in the twentieth century, he would have had military experience there. As well as the benefit of studying history from a 200-year perspective. All the traits you admired in him had to have come from the future."

"Except that the parents who raised him were people of the past."

"I don't like to disillusion you, but there are a lot of teachers and professors out there who don't know the first thing about anything—except what they've read in books."

At this, he nodded and had to agree.

Chapter Fifteen

Although Ruth was well into her fifties and Dan nearly seventy, their large home was often full. They were the first to take in any new child who joined the extended family, and they determined which family was better equipped to raise the child.

Ruth was preparing supper when Bronson and his family arrived, and Marley wouldn't have dared drop another hungry mouth on her—let alone six—without offering to help. She poured beer into mugs and passed them to the men, then apple cider for everyone else.

As Ruth ladled barley soup into bowls for the table, Marley sliced a hot skillet of cornbread and placed it in a basket, with fresh butter alongside.

"Ruth, I found a truant on my way to Williamsburg."

"Oh, my! A truant?"

George swallowed and nodded. "She means me. I overslept."

"You missed an exciting discussion on the French and Indian War."

"Did I."

"Now don't you get sassy on me, young man. It *was* exciting. Do you think all these French aristocrats would be falling all over themselves to help us beat the redcoats if they hadn't lost New France back in the 'sixties?"

"Guess not. Is it all right if I stay with you for a few days? At least till Martin gets back?"

"Begging your pardon, Ruth, he can stay with us after tomorrow. Just walk home after school, George."

For several minutes, they ate in contented silence. If there was one thing the war had given them, it was an appreciation for good food—something there was never enough of, among the soldiers.

After dinner, the children retired to the living room to play, and George was given permission to visit Susan.

"I hate to bring this up, Ruth, but what do you think should be done about that creepy old guy who came threatening everyone after the funeral?"

"What's this?" Bronson glanced at her.

Ruth pursed her lips. "Oh, that Loyalist trash, Gerald Grimewood. He came around claiming we needed to leave the state—said any freed slave does, six months after being freed."

"Well, it might not be a bad idea—for all of us. There's a huge world out there, and most of it isn't at war."

"That's exactly what your friend Ray said." Dan nodded at Bronson. "But isn't that what your father tried, when he left for Bermuda? Long as you live on God's green earth, you aren't beyond the reach of war. How'd that come out, again, for your father?"

"That man is the devil," Ruth said, spitting out the last word.

Marley raised an eyebrow. "I take it you mean Grimewood, and not gentle Thomas."

Aileen coughed gently, raising her eyebrows.

"Well, speak up, woman," Ruth said.

The old Irish servant glanced around the table. "You know the unspeakable thing he does, every night, at Black Oak?"

Ruth nodded. "I know. Half the county knows."

Bronson's jaw went hard. "No respectable landowner in Virginia does business with him."

"He doesn't need Virginia, as long as he's got all of England. And the more of those girls get children by him, the faster he sells them, the more land he buys, the more he builds out. He's an abomination on this land."

The woman's embittered rage troubled Marley. Ruth was one of the gentlest women she'd ever known, and this was unlike her. She was nervously nibbling her fingernails.

"How are you feeling, son?" Dan asked quietly.

Bronson hesitated. "Fine, sir," he said at last.

The older man gave him a long look, then clapped him once on the shoulder.

As they prepared to leave, Marley hugged Ruth. "Please stop worrying about Grimewood. We'll figure something out, between us all."

Ruth met her eyes, as if she were a foolish young girl indeed. "He will not drive me out of my home."

The children were exhausted from their long journey and eventful day, and they barely stayed awake long enough for Aileen to put them to bed. The older woman bedded down in the nurse's room adjacent to the nursery. Marley had never gotten around to getting a permanent nurse—but the thought sorely tempted her now. This arrangement would have the added benefit of getting Aileen out of Hannah's toxic path.

She put out a light blanket with pillows on the sofa for her husband. She'd given up pressuring him. If patience was all he wanted from her, then patience he would get.

Only as she washed up did she realize how tired she was. The days had grown longer, and the sun had barely set before she'd scrubbed and slipped into a light shift and into bed.

She was in a deep sleep when she heard the creak of the bed slats, and she lay unmoving. She opened her eyes and saw a lamp in the room. She turned her head and found Bronson resting one knee on the bed, shirtless. He was freshly bathed, his hair still damp. Somehow the sight of him, uncertain, brought back the night she'd first watched him bathe aboard the *Adventurer*.

She turned toward him, propping herself up on one elbow.

He hesitated, looking for more than words to explain. "I need you," he said at last. "I need to touch you, to hold you."

She nodded and waited.

"I should not be here with you. I may frighten the children, as close as their rooms are. I may repulse you, but I'm so tired, and I need to sleep—"

"Come."

She flipped back the covers on his side of the bed. The windows were open and she felt the coolness of the night on her bare arms and on her thighs.

He removed his trousers and lay them over a stand, then slid underneath the covers. For a moment, he lay on his side, watching her in the lamplight. Then he lay back, pulling the covers up over his nakedness.

She smiled at him. "That doesn't seem fair."

One side of his mouth went up in a sensual grin. She would have kissed him, but he spoke.

"I have a lesson for you."

"May I?" she asked, stroking the hollow under his shoulder.

"All I have is yours, Marley."

She lay her head there and, for the first time in three years, lightly brushed her fingers against his bare chest.

"Still need to plump you up a bit more," she teased. "Remember how well we ate on the *Adventurer*? I still remember that first morning, when Rashall brought me a fresh-baked ship's biscuit, and ham, and it was so delicious!"

"Er—you thought that was a ship's biscuit?"

"Wasn't it? It looked like one."

He laughed, and she rubbed her cheek against the feeling, savoring it. "It was a crumpet. Ray cooked for you himself."

"Ohhhh." She raised her chin. "No wonder there were no bugs."

His laughter spread until he could scarcely breathe. He hid his face in the pillow to keep from waking the children. When he looked up at her, his eyes sparkled. He brushed a strand of hair away from her face and turned her on her side, fitting himself to her lightly as he slowly sobered. "Marley, Marley."

"*Your* Marley."

He kissed her. "My Marley. Is the lamp all right with you?"

"Of course. What was your lesson?"

"It's a lesson I never stop learning—I learned again that my wife is the most fearless woman I've ever known."

He nuzzled into her hair lightly, his hand resting on her shoulder. She grasped it and brought his arm around her.

He spoke slowly, haltingly. "I sometimes—well sometimes I cry out in my sleep. Occasionally it's worse. Just go ahead and wake me up if I start making noise." After a moment, he added, "I am trying very hard, my darling. I'm doing the very best I can. I am ashamed it isn't better."

She fiercely brought his hand to her lips and kissed it. Then she turned halfway, to meet his eyes. "Then here's your bit of knowledge from the future. In history, the hellish ships of Wallabout Bay are the great unknown, unspoken shame of the British Navy. We teach about the heroes of Lexington and Concord, of Yorktown and all the other many battles. No one teaches this, however. No one talks about the many heroes who were lost as British prisoners of war.

"Forty-five hundred Americans will die in the battles of the War for Independence. Four thousand, five hundred, all together. And two and a half times that many—over eleven thousand—will die as prisoners of war, mostly in about a dozen prison ships in Wallabout Bay. That diabolical *Jersey* and the rest."

Bronson took this in. "George Washington sees prisoners of war as enemy combatants deserving of the same treatment we give our own soldiers, little as they have. Clinton, Howe, all of them, from the mad king down, see us as traitors and criminals and would not treat their foxhounds with such barbarity."

She wanted to ask him how he had done it. She had never heard the details of his escape, so frightened she had become of how different he was. Now, she had no interest in startling him. When he was ready, he would tell her.

As she comfortably turned in his arms, he followed her—just as if he'd never left for Rhode Island. And yet he nuzzled her hair lightly, teasingly—as if discovering her for the first time. It set her afire. She felt his shyness even as his hand smoothed down her arm, then lightly cupped her breast, his thumb brushing fleetingly over the nipple. She arched back against him, and his hand appreciatively roved over her rounded hips, then pressed her into stillness—but yet against him.

"One miracle at a time," he whispered, kissing the nape of her neck.

She smiled and murmured, "Not a day goes by that I don't thank God that you're here with me. I am your wife, and I will help you as much as you will allow. It's just that simple."

And Marley slept the soundest sleep she'd known since her husband had gone away to fight. If he made a peep that night, she didn't hear it.

She awakened to a tapping on the door. "Anybody home?"

Bronson was still in bed with her, but he recognized the voice as soon as she did.

When the door was thrown open, she celebrated the laughter and happiness on his face at the sight of the man who stood there.

"Ray!"

Chapter Sixteen

"I can see you're feeling better."

Rashall stood at the door, grinning at Hawk, who was shirtless and hanging onto his wife like a man overboard.

Hawk threw a dirty sock at his face. "Get out of here! And where've you been?"

"I'm sensing some mixed messages."

"Go away! Let us get dressed."

He closed the door, smiling at Juliana, who waited on the stairs, her arms crossed nervously. *I told you,* she mouthed silently.

"I've been up since before dawn. I started your fire and brought your water. Juliana helped me make an old-fashioned country breakfast for everyone. Let's go, let's go! We got hungry children waiting for my famous ship's biscuits."

He heard Marley muttering amid Hawk's laughter as he returned to Juliana on the stairs. He started down, then one step below, he turned, catching her by the waist.

She gasped and giggled, and he kissed her throat, his open mouth sliding to her ear. He had been in her constant, secluded company for several days now, and it wasn't easy to give that up.

"You know, I say this with no small degree of shame, but I've known a woman or two."

Hundred, he added silently.

She lifted her chin, giving him an unwittingly sensual glance, utterly undisturbed by this.

"And I have never needed one as much as I need you."

He lightly kissed her mouth.

"Would this ache then go away?"

When he felt her open mouth meet his lips in a brief, bold kiss, his breath caught.

"Not for long. I cannot imagine being apart from you in this world. It presents a conflict for my loyalties."

Presently he heard giggling at the foot of the stairs, and Juliana gave him a lazy smile, raising her eyebrows and looking past him.

There stood Abigail and Sam in their nightgowns. Abigail covered her mouth delicately as she tee-heed. Sam merely pointed and chuckled.

"Yep, he's his father's son."

He skipped the rest of the way down the stairs and grabbed Sam up in his arms. "Isn't it about time they breech you, little fellow? The gowns are nice, but I think you're big enough to be in some sort of trousers."

He laughed and waved his pudgy arms triumphantly, babbling happily in response.

They returned to the dining table, where Aileen served the children their porridge and began feeding Sam. As soon as they were finished eating, she swept them away.

"Seen and not heard, you know," she said with a merry twinkle as she followed the children back upstairs.

Soon they heard the thump of boots on the stairs, and a hastily groomed, brightly beaming Hawk appeared in the doorway. He crossed the room as Rashall rose, and as he hugged Hawk close, he couldn't help but notice how lean he'd grown. He was never fat, but the few years of his wife's cooking and the comfort of home life had filled him out— before they'd sailed north to Rhode Island.

Now, he was thin almost to the point of emaciation. "Cutting back on the pork pies, are we?"

Hawk laughed, and he schooled his own features into joviality. Was this the same man he'd left a year and a half ago when he went into Lafayette's service? His face was so angular, he seemed a stranger.

"Dining at the Hotel Clinton leaves something to be desired."

Rashall laughed. "All right. There's hope for you yet."

Juliana was pouring coffee when Marley arrived. "Where's that famous hardtack of yours, Ray?"

"Baby, I mixed up a batch just for you." He held out a plate to her, and she raised an eyebrow, ignoring his offering as she walked to kiss her sister and sat beside her.

"In my defense, I've never met anyone who would confuse a crumpet with a ship's biscuit."

"And I've never had a crumpet that lent itself so winningly to the confusion."

"Hey, hey!" Rashall interjected.

They soon fell silent as they dug into the scrambled eggs and ham and fried potatoes, and Hawk was the first to speak. "Have you been riding all night from Stonefield?"

"Most of the way. We napped a couple of times." He reached over and touched Juliana's hand. "Do you want to, or shall I?"

"Go ahead."

She sipped her coffee, her eyes sparkling the palest emerald green in the morning light. He still couldn't quite believe she was his. At last he noticed Hawk and Marley focused on them.

"We're going to be married."

Everyone at the table went into a joyful chattering, and he answered questions as best he could. "Soon as Dan can do it."

Hawk hesitated. "Sure you don't want to ... umm ...get married at Bruton Parish Church?"

"Have an Anglican wedding, you mean."

"Don't give me that. Why not?"

He calmly pressed his napkin against his lips. "I'm supposed to ask for the blessing of a church that didn't think I was good enough to be a priest because of my skin color."

"Just the way everyone's hassling everyone, that's all. I'd mind your p's and q's."

"*My* p's and q's?" he asked. "In this county, where the majority of its citizens are in bondage?"

Bronson stared back at him with an expression of amused skepticism. He extended his hand across the table. "I'm Bronson Trelawney. Perhaps you've heard of me from an old friend of mine who used to know me. You can call me Hawk."

He good-naturedly smacked his hand. "Who's everyone?"

"That contemptible beast who owns the countryside next to Stonefield."

"Oh, the fellow who—"

Juliana squeezed his hand gently, and he looked at her. *Not at the breakfast table, please.*

"Who married my parents, Hawk?"

"I suppose. But if you're concerned about acquiring the respect of the townspeople, it's something to think about."

"You've become so domesticated, my friend."

"And that isn't what you want? For the last five years we sailed together, all I ever heard you talk about was home."

He glanced at Juliana, then leaned over to kiss her. "Well, I found my home."

Hawk's dumbstruck gape went from him to Juliana. "Begging your pardon, sir, but I'm supposing that my beautiful wife's lovely sister isn't going to want to go traipsing about the countryside after Lafayette until this war is settled. Especially when you have your way with her a few thousand times and have her toting around a litter of little ones?"

Rashall gave him a steady smile. "And how are you, my dear friend? Are you up to explaining to all of us your adventures? When last I left you, the British had left Newport for the southern theatre, and the First Rhode Island found itself with little to do to while away the hours."

The normal animation of his friend dispersed like a bad humor deserting his constitution, leaving him ill at ease.

"Oh, no, you don't," Rashall put in. "Stop that right now. You were chattering like a squirrel."

"It isn't anything I have any control over," Hawk spat. "Do you think I like living this way?"

Rashall glanced at Marley. Once again, he saw that sensitive, walking-on-eggshells woman she'd been when they first found her.

"Look at your wife, man. Behold the frightened little girl you fished out of the ocean nearly six years ago. Look at the circles under her eyes, from managing her household as if she were a widow for the past three years. Do you remember her taking on the entire Royal Army dressed as a ragamuffin soldier herself? Are you proud of escorting her so far backward?"

Hawk's angry gaze clashing with his filled with confusion and shame as he glanced quickly at Marley, who tried to school her features back into placid contentment. Her awkwardness was pitiful. Watching her husband take in the truth was even more so.

She shrugged and shook her head. "It's just an old habit I used to have," she said, looking instead into her empty plate.

Hawk nodded, searching for words. After a long moment, he reached out to take her hand. "Aye, given you by a selfish bastard I hope to meet someday. God forgive me for becoming anything like that coward."

Rashall waited as his friend sorted through how to start. His eyes darted from Marley to her sister and back to his own hand covering his wife's.

"As you said, the British moved south, taking their destruction with them in the fall of 1779. By then the *Immortal* had been impressed into service for the patriots. I left the First Rhode Island, intending to come home and rejoin the militia. Jem and most of our men are fighting there.

"Instead, I was captured nearly as soon as I left. And I retired to Maison Clinton. Oh, the accommodations were nice enough at first. Portholes decorated with the finest iron latticework. No worry about ever gaining unwanted poundage, as the rotten foodstuffs they do give you are chock full of additional guests sharing the nutrition at no extra charge. And there are comrades aplenty crammed in to keep your summers warm, if not your winters. And if you die, you'll be buried with other patriots—in the very same mass grave. And worry not if your lot is to live another day. When your fellow inmates leave you one by one, you won't be lonely. For even if the one who's chained to you has cried and begged for death for days … and at last God grants that tender mercy, why, they don't bother removing him from the chain you share until—"

He stopped abruptly when his wife threw her arms around his neck, her body shaking with silent tears. He buried his face in her hair, and her hand smoothed over his head as if he were little Sam.

His jaw hard with suppressed anger and grief at the monstrosity of this noble war, Rashall glanced at Juliana and saw her large eyes pooled with tears. When he would have taken her in his arms, she took his hand and squeezed it instead, with a silent shake of her head.

At last, Hawk went on. "I … hm. I have nightmares about it sometimes. It's gotten better since—" he glanced at Marley, then went on, "well, recently. I was reminded I have the great fortune not to be alone in this battle. And the oddity of it is, the more I talk about it, the better I feel. It's as if the load is divided and shared by those who listen."

Juliana sniffed and rose. Picking up the coffee pot with a thick potholder, she refilled everyone's coffee cups. Until Juliana, Rashall had never noticed the many small tasks ordinary women did to create comfort in this world. His own mother was a different sort, perhaps even stronger than his father, and while she did the same sort of tasks, she expected her own menfolk to share in such tasks as other women did not. It didn't seem to be a matter of wrong or right—just different.

Juliana, so familiar with the ways of so many eras, was more comfortable with everything she did, it seemed. She knew who she was, and didn't have to prove anything to anyone. She who had a better perspective of all time than anyone he could imagine in this world, let others be who they were without trying to enlighten them. By her example, perhaps, she was at her most persuasive.

"Rashall?"

He looked up, startled at Hawk using his Christian name. For him, he was either Ray or even still Raven.

"I had an odd dream a few weeks ago. I dream often, always in a pattern. It begins in some unusual place, and then ends with me back in chains on the Jersey. This night, it began with the funeral of a man—a military man, I think it might have actually been our own Navy, if we had much of one. On the land before us were countless white crosses, spreading out for acres. It was a cemetery, but unlike any I've ever seen. And there was a bugle call playing, but the call wasn't familiar to me. Ray, the man looked like you."

"Was it me?"

"No. The uniform was unlike anything I've ever seen. Certainly not anything in our Navy or Army. It was white, with a stiff collar up against the man's neck. The top of the coffin was divided in two, with the top half open to reveal the man lying there. The bottom half was closed. His cap lay over a flag draped there. Much like the flag we fly today, but with many more stars—arranged in rows."

As Hawk stared into his coffee, recalling the details, Rashall saw Marley and Juliana exchange a glance.

"Now I had this dream the night of Enoch Morgan's funeral, so my father supposed I might be bothered that I left Marley to find her own way there with Ruth and the others. And that I've done so poorly in looking out for George since I got home."

He hesitated, then stopped, still not looking at him.

"Was he wearing a gold insignia?" This from Juliana. "With an eagle, clutching an anchor and trident?"

"Yes," Hawk said, startled. He shifted in his chair, leaning forward. "Those are the details I couldn't quite remember. How did you know?"

"And did he have facial hair? A mustache and small beard—just on his chin?"

"Yes—yes! That's the man. But how ... it was in a dream. I do not know him. How could you?"

She hesitated. "I have a photograph of him. I found it the same day you three first visited me, all those years ago."

"Photograph? What's that?"

Rashall saw the dread enter Marley's eyes. She understood. Juliana glanced at him, as if for permission, and he nodded.

"It's an image, like a portrait, but captured by a device. In the future, everything we do can be preserved to look at—or listen to—again later."

"Yes, I told you about that," Marley said. "But where did you find a photograph of a man that Bronson happened to dream about?"

Juliana gave that small sigh Rashall had come to recognize as impatience with slow people who didn't understand everything to be known about the past and future.

"We dream in symbols that are a part of our connection to all mankind—what they call the collective unconscious. Whether we even realize it or not, we're connected to others. This isn't theory; in the future, this is known to be true."

"That's interesting," Bronson said—not even remarking on the oddity of Juliana's explanations of the future. "But how does it relate to me dreaming of someone I don't know?"

"In the future, our families—meaning in this context the Millers and the Carlyles—are inextricably connected. Surely we learned that the day of Hannah's confession."

Marley merely stared, awaiting her next revelation.

Reluctantly, Juliana reached into the pocket of her apron and withdrew the treasure that she never let out of her possession. He had seen it during their trip here. She handed it to her sister.

"Do you know who these people are?" Juliana asked.

Marley held the photograph up to the daylight from the window. He watched the wonder steal over her face, and her hand covered her mouth. She nodded silently.

Hawk leaned close to her to inspect. "It's remarkable. All the details, so clear. You say a machine did this?"

"Yes. Called a camera."

"Who are they, my darling?"

She swallowed and wiped her eye, then held it out to him. "This is Mama. She had a birthmark at the corner of her eye, in the shape of a crescent moon. And this—" She choked up. "This is my daddy. He's bigger here than I remember him—

"'Our,' you mean," Rashall said.

"I'm sorry?"

"Our daddy. Juliana's, also, of course."

Her color heightened. "I'm sorry, I wasn't thinking. But look how muscular he was! Oh, Bronson, you do remind me of him in many ways. He loved the ocean, and he loved learning. He loved teaching, he couldn't help but do it. And this is our sister, Rachel. This was before we were born," she said, glancing at her sister.

Juliana nodded.

"Is this the man you dreamed of?"

Hawk glanced at the man, then at Rashall, then nodded. "Aye, that's him. Don't you think you look like him, Ray?"

"I can see it."

But Hawk frowned, now, as he looked at the photograph. "Marley—this is the man who taught me at William and Mary. There's no doubt of it. Except he looks quite a bit older here. Yet it was before you were born."

"I thought we agreed that he and Mama traveled a great deal through time."

"Yes, but think of how Hannah explained the events. He arrived at Rosalie somewhere in the early to mid-sixties, already established as a professor at William and Mary. He fell in love with your mother, and not long after that they traveled back in time to 1986."

Again, the worry entered Marley's gaze. "I see what you're saying. And Rachel was born just two years later, around the time this photograph was taken."

"He looks a good fifteen years older."

"Because he lived in another time and grew up there. When he returned to his own time, he looked younger—he was born in 1742, so he would have looked very young, Cassandra's own age. But when he was that age, his parents took him to the year 1953. He grew up—lived a life that I'm still not too well informed about, except through Marley. And *then* found a means to go back in time."

Rashall nodded. "So in this century, he still looked like a young man, but he had the life experiences of a man of 37 when he met your mother."

"Exactly."

"My, my," Rashall murmured. "Wonder if she was disappointed when they woke up here."

The four laughed, but Juliana raised a flirty eyebrow. "Some women like older men."

"Watch your language, young lady. Thirty-seven is just three years older than me."

He saw arousal move through her eyes as she stared back at him mysteriously, and he cleared his throat, straightening in his chair.

Marley was focused once more on the photograph. "And this must be our grandparents. I don't remember them, but your brother, Grey, talked about them. Daddy talked about them."

At this reminder of his brother, Hawk leaned back. Rashall knew that look.

"You're still back on this? That didn't happen that night?"

Hawk crossed his ankle over the other knee and gave Rashall a silencing look.

"All right. Just because your wife tolerates your moods and coddles you doesn't mean I have to. It *happened*, man. Three grown people don't have the same delusion. Guy walked out of nowhere into your cabin, looking like your father but not quite, identified your wife God knows how, knew things about all three of us that nobody else could have known ... and we *all three* just imagined it?"

"Time-travel," Bronson said flatly. "How can that be?"

Rashall saw the exact moment that his wife understood his implication that everything she'd told him about herself was a lie. "Er, uh … bright fellow?" He glanced between Hawk and Marley.

She laughed as she rose, in the busywork of clearing the table. "That's all right, Ray. He's made it clear to me he plays at believing my story. I just don't understand why the man I love would have married a liar."

He didn't attempt to deny his doubt, falling silent as she removed empty plates and dishes. Juliana joined her.

"You remember it the same way?" Hawk asked him, when the women began washing the dishes silently.

"You know, I'd laugh at you, as stupid as you've become, but this isn't even funny anymore."

"It defies logic. It *can't be* real."

Rashall glanced at Juliana. "Baby doll, we're all going to have to go back to Stonefield."

"No! No more time travel!"

The vehemence of her anger brought him up short.

"I don't understand."

She dried her hands on her apron even as she rushed to him. "Don't you see? We marvel at the lives others had, we envy what we don't have, we look on other lives, we burn endless hours that we can't get back in a place where we have no impact at all. Where by our own agreement we refuse to make anything better. Meanwhile, people in our own world hunger and suffer and die alone. Where we should have impact, we happily agree to have none, while we waste the little time we ourselves have been given entertaining ourselves with the endless possibilities."

"We were only there a minute or so. We came back in the next moment."

"We were in that time for several hours, Ray. It may not have felt like it to you, but they were hours that we'll never get back."

"No. It was just a minute or two. I looked at the clock before we left, and after we got back."

"No! Rashall, I've spent countless hours of my life traveling in time. That time—all of it—counts against my *actual* life, here with you. All right, think of it this way. Imagine if you and Bronson set out in a ship from the landing here at Rosalie. You travel the globe. Thousands of miles, for weeks and weeks, seeing wondrous sights. You arrive back at the same location on the landing. Does that wipe away the impact your voyage had upon you? That's the impact of space. This is the impact of time. Time is never *free*."

He began to understand.

"Uncle Malcolm told me that a long time ago, but I never fully appreciated it until I met you. And the moment I met you, I stopped the travel for that reason. Every hour we spend in another time is subtracted from our lives. It may not feel that way when we do it—when you're young, time feels endless. We quickly realize it isn't. Not even if we spend it in another era."

"Wait a minute," Marley said. "You travel through the portal here on Rosalie? And you were able to take Rashall with you? And then come right back?"

Juliana looked at her sister sadly. "There's a time-travel control center far beneath Stonefield. I've spent countless hours traveling almost any place or time you can imagine."

And then, he watched her explain the inexplicable to her sister and Hawk. The women finished the dishes, returning to finish their coffee at the table.

"So that's how Malcolm and Mary travel about, serving as guides to travelers?"

She nodded.

"But why Stonefield?"

"Why not?"

Her laissez-faire attitude, innocent as it was, annoyed Marley, and at last Rashall saw the significant difference between these two women. In any circumstance, Marley would always be the one to ask why and attempt to change, and Juliana would be the type to accept and move beyond.

"That's why you're that way," he said.

"What way?"

"Nonchalant. Detached."

The characterization clearly disturbed her. "You act as if I don't care about anything."

"You've never been allowed to care. It's been drilled into your head *not* to get involved—to leave no footprints, as they say."

She only gazed back at him without speaking.

Marley took up the photograph once more with a look of wistful longing, and Juliana leaned forward, looking over her shoulder. "Notice anything else?"

"What do you mean?"

"Look at the two babies," Juliana said. Rashall nearly laughed at her no-nonsense tone as she attempted to guide Marley, as if pointing out the sun rising over the eastern horizon.

"Oh, isn't that sweet. They form a little pink heart." Then she gasped. "That's your mother, Ray! No wonder she and Rachel were so close!"

"*There* you go," he said.

Then she shook her head. "But no, that's not right. Camisha never knew Rachel until she and her mother went to live with Shep, James Manning's older son. Max, I think he called himself then."

"Something happened to disrupt their friendship," Juliana said. "It had to have. This was ... before. You know."

The group fell silent.

"I wonder what happened to Camisha's father?"

Rashall glanced at Julia, and she nodded. Still, he wouldn't dare repeat the grisly details he'd read about in that article.

"He ... was killed in a manner similarly gruesome to that of your own parents. Jack Sheppard was even identified as a ... what did they call it. An interested person, maybe?"

"A person of interest."

"Precisely. They knew each other from the Navy. Apparently the Manning brothers—Sheppards, that is— traveled to 1976, as your grandmother said that day. Using your father's Phi Beta Kappa key to enable their travel. The older brother went to school; the younger joined the Navy."

"How could you possibly figure all this out?" Hawk asked, astonished.

"Oh. It's like your brother said. You can find out about people just like *that*. But the part about 1976, I deduced. The article just said Cameron and Jack knew each other from the Navy."

"Cameron?"

"My grandfather."

"Yes," Marley said. "I think I remember your mother saying she was named after him."

"Interesting that you remember that. She's always told me that, too. But the article said that his mother's name was Camisha."

"Your great-grandmother's name was Camisha?"

He nodded.

Hawk's gaze focused on something behind Rashall, and he looked over his shoulder. "What's wrong?"

"I'm not sure." He glanced at Marley. "Did you move our portrait from where it used to be on that wall? There's an ordinary bowl of fruit there, now."

She shook her head. "No."

"I wonder what happened to it?"

"Oh, probably one of the children pulled it down accidentally. I'm sure it's around."

The back door banged, and a breathless George rushed in, his face beaming. "It's time. Everything's ready."

Chapter Seventeen

Juliana sat on the edge of Ruth's bed, watching the older woman as she bent to slide open her bottom dresser drawer. She moved with deliberate, even regal, motions as she withdrew an item and turned to Juliana.

"I did your sister's hair for her wedding, and our dear friend Camisha's, thirty-five years ago now." She gave a small chuckle. "I reckon young Bronson, eager as he was, still brought the scarf back in better shape than old Ashanti. And all Ashanti had to do was untie it from around my girl's shoulders. Of course Bronson came from a long line of sailors, so he knew what he was doing, taking apart those knots.

"Lord have mercy, I was a different person when Camisha married her Ashanti. Didn't know how to spell my own name. I bless the day she came here. Just as if she was tied up in Mr. Grey's family from long before she was born, she worked the magic that it took to free us all. Him, most of all."

In her hands she held a small piece of folded fabric. She lay it across the bed beside Juliana and rolled it into a long, thin tube, with each end free and flowing. She gently turned Juliana and went on speaking as she began weaving the fabric into her hair.

"Juliana, you're a curious young woman, but I love you like you were my own. And I'm going to tell you, same as my mother told me, what this scarf means—to me, to you, to all people. This world is full of heartache. I expect you see that every day, same as I do, in all my little babies, snatched out of the hands of greed and captivity. I expect your mama and daddy, and his mama and daddy especially, saw it more than most."

"How do you know that, Ruth?" she whispered.

She smiled slyly. "You must know my girl tells me everything." Then she added, "But even if I never saw Camisha, I knew Cassandra Hastings' mama and daddy myself, and this beautiful hair didn't come from either one of those heads."

Juliana hesitated, unsure how to phrase her question. "Ruth, do you know anything about my father—ever being in danger as a child?"

"He lived a life of adventure, I saw that for myself."

"How so?"

She hummed. "I watched him and your mother and Hannah disappear into thin air one day—long while back." She went on working on her hair. "I never liked to go around those old ruins. Seemed like sacred ground, for the deaths of Mr. Grey and Miss Emily. Cassie stopped in at our house that day to tell me goodbye. She said she and her young husband were going away. I asked her to stay—Juliana, your parents were such fine people. You're aware they didn't even know what Hannah had done, aren't you?"

"You mean abandoning me grow up in the same time where my own parents would fall in love? No, I didn't know that. At least not until just a few years ago."

"Well, Cassie said they couldn't stay, that Rob had to get back to his teaching. When they left, they headed for the old ruins, and I ran after them, trying to stop them. By the time I got there, old Hannah was hugging Cassie. Then Cassie and Rob started to walk into the ruins, and Hannah grabbed onto Cassie. I yelled at them both and reached for Hannah, but she shoved me away. And honey, when I looked up again, they were all three gone.

"I don't mind telling you, I doubted my own eyes there for a while, until I talked with Camisha about it. I tried talking to Mr. Hastings, and he just looked back at me, clucking that proper tongue of his and saying, 'My heavens!' He told me to take off the next week and get extra rest. And darned if he didn't tell Dan something about it, for Dan made sure I didn't lift a finger to do anything."

"Ruth ... do you happen to recall ever seeing the Mannings on Rosalie, back in the '50s? Perhaps '53?"

Ruth grew grim. "I do remember that, because Camisha was here at the time. Let me look at something."

She crossed the room, opening her box of journals. She flipped through them, then withdrew one of the ledgers, paging through. She stopped, handing it to Juliana. "Here it is. I remember, because we were saying goodbye, and they wanted plenty of time to get to their ship without rushing, and we'd just finished a late breakfast. She had her children with her—well, except for Rashall, he was already off sailing with Bronson and that Michael fellow. Ashanti was with her, and they were on their way out. I remember they had to meet a ship at 6 pm."

"So you *saw* the Mannings? Which ones?"

"All of them. Then I looked up again, and it was only James Manning, that devil. His boys must have taken off somewhere."

"Do you remember what time it was?"

"It was in the morning—I'd say around ten o' clock. Why?"

Juliana shook her head. "Just trying to understand something."

She smiled as Ruth finished the weaving, then turned her face up to examine her handiwork with satisfaction.

"There. All done. All I ask is for you to return it when you're finished with it. That old scarf's been a witness to the beginning of more happiness than any piece of cloth has a right to. Now I know you're excited to get out there to that big, handsome man waiting for you, but I have one more gift for you."

From behind the wardrobe in the corner, she withdrew a quilt displayed on a stand. She carefully removed the quilt and walked to present it to her.

The quilt was a masterpiece of color and story, images sewn inside the wedding-ring pattern. Here, in a blue circle, she saw a baby's tiny brown hand; there, a cross and a date, likely representing a sacrament in his life; in still another, a broken heart—and her lips parted as she saw the date of her first wedding there. Facing her was a freshly sewn image of two hearts, with today's date. Still, quite a number of squares lay ready to admit more memories.

"Juliana, I started working on this the day I got the news that Rashall had been born in Boston. I made it for his family. First time I ever saw you two together, I knew you were meant to be together. It may have taken a little longer to come about than we would've liked, but you're together now. And let no man ever come between you again."

Juliana set the quilt aside and hugged Ruth close, unable to put into words how much this meant to her. It was like a journal written in a matronly art form.

Ruth took her by the shoulders. "Just one more thing. You may not know it, and he doesn't even seem to accept it yet. But your Rashall is set apart. He's called to lead his people, like my Dan, like Moses. He doesn't even accept right now that he *has* people to lead. Like Jonah, he's wrestling with God's will in his life—but in the end, he'll go to Nineveh. He may go in the belly of a whale, but he'll go. Just like we all do, sooner or later. And don't worry about what happened with your parents. We've all got exactly one life that's ours to live. That's what you want to focus on."

The riddles, Juliana tucked away in her heart for later. She knew that in time, she would understand.

As she reached to fold the rich, elegant quilt, Ruth shook her head. "I'll send it over to your place."

They were soon joined by Ruth's daughter, Sukey, who had loaned her the ivory gown she wore, with a green and gold stomacher that lifted her breasts almost shamefully for display.

Sukey inspected her, then placed a voluminous, sheer lacy ivory scarf over her head, arranging it to fall delicately over her shoulders and down her back.

Sukey held her hands and smiled. "I don't mind telling you, we'd just about given up on either of you ever marrying."

Juliana laughed and shook her head. "I wasted so much time in needless uncertainty."

"You didn't do anything wrong. A man like Ray is hard to focus, sometimes. On the surface, he seems like a jester, but there's a lot more to him than that. Well, we'd better get downstairs soon. I hear music from the meetinghouse."

The multitudes were gathering from throughout the countryside for the wedding of Marley's sister and Camisha's son, and the early May day had dawned clear and warm. The world seemed to celebrate the brief respite of peace and joy amid the destruction.

The door opened, and Marley stood there, smiling broadly. She closed the door and gave an appreciative whistle. "Well, I don't see you spending much time at your reception."

The women hugged, and Sukey patted both sisters. "I'll wait outside for you."

When the door closed, Marley hugged her. "I'm so happy for you, Juliana. Ray will be as fine a husband as Bronson. Why don't you just move in with us, until the war is over? Or at least until Ray's home?"

She smiled and squeezed her sister's hands. "I think I'm going to travel with him."

"But how can you do that? How will that fit his cover story? He's on the move all the time."

"I don't want to be apart from him. We've lost so much time already, time we can never get back."

"But don't you think ..." She stopped, struggling to find the way to say it.

"Marley, I love you for caring about me, but it would do us all a lot of good for you to accept two things about me. First, I know we'll have strife. And second, I don't care. Everyone in the world has problems. Ours will just be a different kind."

Marley gave her a long look. "Are you happy?"

"What kind of question is that? I'm happier today than I've been since the first day I met Ray. Yes, Marley. I'm happy."

They heard the elegant opening notes of Pachelbel's Canon in D on the bass, soon joined by a chorus of violins. She remembered Papa teaching her himself how to play the piece.

Marley hugged her once more.

"Never forget, Juliana, how much I love you. How proud I am of the young woman you've become all on your own, self-sufficient in the wilderness, and yet as poised as a queen. How blessed we are to have each other. Congratulations. In all of life, I wish you the very best of God's blessings."

Juliana, rarely overcome with emotion, was moved by her sister's praise and love.

At that moment, a tap came on the door, and Sukey opened it. "Papa is here for you. Are you ready?"

She sniffed and nodded, wiping at her eyes.

"Did you make her cry?" Sukey asked, casting an accusing eye at Marley. "That was your one job—to keep the bride from getting puffy eyes."

Juliana laughed. "I'm done now."

As they walked to the end of the hall, she saw Papa at the bottom of the stairs sitting in his chair, near the open door, his eyes focused on her. George waited with him. Ruth's family and their children and grandchildren filled the room and spilled out onto the lawn, all dressed in their Sunday best. Only Dan, waiting at the church, was absent. The room went silent as she descended the stairs, and Sukey's youngest granddaughter fingered Juliana's gown. She suspected the tot probably recognized it as belonging to her grandmother.

As she arrived at the foot of the stairs, Papa rose and gallantly kissed her hand. His eyes shone brightly as he held out his arm to her. "I am so proud of you, darling daughter. You are the crown jewel of my old age. It has been my pleasure to be your papa these twenty-eight years."

She lay her hand over his arm and he escorted her the short distance to the meetinghouse. George walked just behind him to look out for the frail old man, and Hasty's eldest son pushed the wheel chair behind them.

Sukey led the procession toward the altar, with Marley just behind. Sukey's granddaughter Betsy, just Abigail's age, and Abigail followed as flower girls, delicately strewing the aisle with the delicate, star-shaped nicotiana flowers, with hibiscus, and with sweet magnolia petals.

Papa led her up the aisle and stood before Dan, who waited—in a suit. The sight confused her; he normally wore vestments during services. Then she noticed that in place of the ornate Book of Common Prayer he usually read from during services, he instead held a simple Bible.

When she looked at Rashall, she knew the changes were on his behalf. He gazed at her with a solemnity that startled her. George silently took his place beside Bronson and his father.

Her breath caught at the realization of it all—Rashall was soon to be her husband. And she would make mistakes and ask his forgiveness and, she knew, be forgiven. She would tell him stories and change him and he would do the same for her. Perhaps they would be blessed with children. Perhaps they would be called to leave their impression on other children.

But leave their footprints behind, they certainly would—intermingled together.

The musicians—performing just off to the side, near an open window—finished and sat down, and Dan began with a prayer.

"Who presents this woman to be given in holy Matrimony?"

Papa bowed to Dan. "Her family, sir, in gracious gratitude."

He then turned to Rashall, stepping back a half step. As she perhaps knew he would, Rashall hugged Papa and helped him to his place in his chair. He then joined hands with Juliana, standing tall and strong beside her.

"Brothers and sisters, we are gathered together today for a joyous occasion. If any of you know cause or just impediment, why these two persons should not be joined together in holy Matrimony, you are to declare it now."

Out in the road, they heard a voice scream out. A woman's voice, Juliana noted. She and Rashall exchanged a startled look, even as Dan glanced toward the sound.

The sound of horses' hooves joined the woman's voice. "Wait! Rashall, wait!"

Dread entered Juliana, even as Rashall exhaled heavily. Nothing good could come from a development like this.

The women of the congregation, flipping fans furiously against the noonday heat, turned and craned their necks to see what was happening.

An usher stepped out onto the steps and held out his arm toward Dan. Then he laughed and looked back into the church.

"It's your mama, Ray."

"Don't I know it."

Laughter went around the congregation. Juliana exhaled in relief.

Old Hattie, sitting in the front row, harrumphed. "Lord have mercy. She's going to be mad as a hornet."

"Amen, sister," Rashall whispered, casting Juliana an anxious glance.

Presently the lady in question hurried up the steps, ignoring the usher's offered hand, her satin skirts swishing. She hurried down the aisle, and Ruth rose in the second row, waving at her. Everyone in the pew moved over to make room for Camisha and Ashanti, who trailed a few steps behind the cyclone that was his wife.

Camisha wagged a stiffened finger at Rashall. "You, I will deal with later." Then she bobbed her head in contrition at the pastor, even as she patted Hattie on the shoulder and kissed her. "Forgive us for being late, Brother Dan."

As casually as if her tardy arrival were from the next house over rather than 600 miles up the coast, she folded her hands in her lap and focused on Dan. He opened his Bible and began to speak.

"Our inspiration this morning comes from the Book of Matthew, chapter 24, beginning with verse 37.

*"But as the days of Noah were, so shall also the
coming of the Son of man be. For as in the days that
were before the flood they were eating and drinking,
marrying and giving in marriage, until the day that
Noah entered into the ark, and knew not until the
flood came, and took them all away; so shall also the
coming of the Son of man be. ...*

"We live in a wicked, war-torn land. Now we're having a joyous moment this morning in our meetinghouse, where we come together to celebrate the wedding of this couple. But in the next town over, up the coast, down the river, men are fighting and dying. Our young men are with them. They're being taken as prisoners of war. Some come home. And those who do, they come home with scars. Some scars you can see, some scars you can't. Some come home missing an arm, or a leg, or both. Some ... well, some don't come home at all.

"They're doing that to improve this old world. They're doing it for freedom. They're doing it for equality. Now freedom and equality are worth fighting for—of course, they're worth a lot more when all men have it, rather than just some."

Amens went around.

"But when this war ends, another one will be just over the horizon. For that's the way of this world. That's not to say we're supposed to just lie down and die, or hide in a closet and hope for the next world. We *have* the hope for this world. We're here today to bless others, to remind them that the kingdom of heaven is nigh.

"Here in our little town, we have blessings more than most of the people in the entire world. We're free. In the next town over, down the coast, up the river, men and women and children are still held in chains.

"And yet, our Christian brothers and sisters in chains are richer and freer than those who hold them in bondage. Because you see, they're fighting a war, too, just like us. While we're here, all of us traveling on this short byway, we serve a mighty general, one whose troops wear the armor of God. Our loins are girded with truth, and our breastplate is righteousness. On our feet we wear the gospel of peace. We take with us the shield of faith to protect us from the darts of the wicked. We wear the helmet of salvation, and the sword of the Spirit," he said, holding up his Bible for emphasis.

"And now, I ask for a second time if there is anyone here today who knows a reason or impediment that these two should not be joined in holy Matrimony."

Only the stirring of fans broke the silence, and when Dan held out his hand to the couple, Rashall took Juliana's right hand between both of his and turned to face her.

"I, Rashall Ashanti Adams take thee, Juliana Juste Miller, to my wedded wife, to have and to hold from this day forward, for better, for worse, for richer, for poorer, in sickness, and in health, to love and to cherish, till death us depart; according to God's holy ordinance, and thereto I plight thee my troth."

Anticipation tingled along her spine as he spoke his vows. She repeated them, a smile lighting her face, her thumbs lightly caressing his palms and wrists as she spoke. She saw the expectant excitement in his eyes, and she wanted so much to hug him. *Rashall's wife.* The reality of this moment thrilled her.

Bronson produced the rings, which they exchanged— identical posies carved inside said, *Always and forever I am thine.*

Dan solemnly pronounced them husband and wife, and Rashall turned to her as if contemplating a gift he wished to unwrap slowly.

He lifted the lace scarf, revealing her to his hungry gaze, and he lowered his mouth to hers. She could feel the chaste restraint in him as he resisted his own impulses. He pressed his cheek to hers, whispering against her ear, "I love you more than my own life. You are everything to me."

"Brothers and sisters," Dan said, turning them toward the congregation, "Please welcome Mr. and Mrs. Rashall Adams."

The congregation erupted with joyous exclamations of happiness and applause. Juliana slowly absorbed it all—she was sure no time-travel version of this moment would ever do it justice.

Chapter Eighteen

The newlyweds turned to briefly greet Camisha and Ashanti, then walked to the steps of the church, where they formed a receiving line. Many of the women ducked out the side door to the dining hall to put the finishing touches on the dinner buffet.

Little Dan and Hasty had been responsible for the meats, and the heady scent of smoked and grilled beef and pork, chicken and duck, wafting over from the dining hall, helped the reception line move fast.

Finally they moved toward the dining hall, and Juliana grew even more aware of Rashall's nearness. His hands never left her for long; she found it mystifying that he could infuse such outwardly respectable caresses—a lingering brush of his palm over her waist here, his fingers curling near her breast, or down the line of her lower back *there*—with utterly carnal pleasure.

For the most fleeting moment, Enoch Morgan crossed her mind, like a bad dream from which she'd only begun to awaken. She still didn't quite understand why he'd ever married her to begin with, but she celebrated that it was far in the past.

At the edge of the dining hall, Ray suddenly captured her hand and pulled her around the corner of the building. There, he pressed her against the building, his upper arms framing her face there as he lowered his mouth to hers.

"I ache for you," he whispered, his open lips brushing her ear, then biting her earlobe lightly.

She sighed at the sensation, and his hips arched against her. Her laughter fell away at the frankness of his hunger. She gasped in anticipation at his boldness, his hard strength.

"Perhaps we should take a short break before joining the others," she suggested. "Where are we tonight?"

"In one of the newer houses, far down close to the river. But there's no such thing as a short break with you tonight, my darling. Possibly ever."

"Let's make a quick showing and then say goodnight. Surely people will understand."

Reluctantly, she grasped his hand and pulled him away back toward the crowd, where she saw Marley, Bronson, and Thomas standing near his mother. She was tapping her toe as she watched him arrive with a silly grin on his face.

"I wondered where you'd run off to," she said, dryly.

Ashanti stood beside his wife, and only then did Juliana notice how thin he was. She'd met him only once, a couple of years ago, but she remembered him as a much more muscular man—was it a failing of her memory?

Then Rashall turned his gaze on his father as they all greeted one another. "Father, have you lost weight?"

"Just a tough year."

Only then did she recall that they'd lost their oldest daughter only a year ago. When she looked again at Camisha, she saw that her face, too, was thinner. For a woman who never seemed to age, she had done her share in the past five years.

"Is Parks here?" Rashall asked. "I didn't see her come in."

"Yes—off there with Sukey. She has little Ashanti and John with her."

"Shonny is here?" Marley asked, as if he were a celebrity. "And little John? Abby'll be thrilled. Is Taleeb still fighting?"

She nodded.

They rejoined the rest in the dining hall, where plates had already been served for them. She noticed Rashall watching her as she nibbled at a crab cake, and she leaned close to him, her breasts nestled against his arm.

"You know, I'm exhausted. Do you think we could perhaps freshen up and rejoin the others after a nap?"

His lips brushed her forehead, then lowered to her ear. "The quicker you finish that dinner, the quicker I can put my mouth on you, baby."

"Where?" she asked, imagining that mouth on her.

"Right here, if you don't stop tempting me."

She laughed and leaned back, seeing his roguish half-smile as his eyes slipped down over her.

Bronson and Marley arrived at the table with Camisha and Ashanti, and the younger man sat beside Ashanti. "How are you, sir?"

Juliana watched the exchange, wondering if he'd get the truth out of him.

"Better than most, son." He clapped Bronson on the back.

He leaned back and met his eyes squarely. "Are you, sir?"

"I'm alive and with the people I love, I just watched my oldest son marry a smart, beautiful woman, and I'm about to have a feast. That's more than most of our men out there fighting have been able to say for six years."

Marley hugged him. "That's one thing I've always loved about you, Ashanti—your joy."

"Ask my wife, she'll tell you. I didn't come by it naturally."

"Where are the children?" Camisha asked. "Little Abigail and Sam?"

"Father's here—he's on his way over—but the children went home with Aileen," Bronson explained.

Marley shook her head. "God forgive me, but I really wanted a night on the town."

Rashall laughed. "You always did know how to live it up. Ask Hawk. Whenever we hit any port as youngsters, the first place we headed was the local meetinghouse dining hall."

"Well, this is a fine night on the town for me. Even if it is only 2:30 in the afternoon. I even get to have blackberry wine. When did you all get in, anyway?"

"Just now. We came mostly by coach."

"Had to be here for my boy's birthday," Camisha added.

Juliana looked at her husband in surprise.

Bronson's shoulders sank. "I knew it was around here somewhere, but the master of intrigue over here never mentions it."

"Not even to me," Juliana put in.

Ray shrugged. "'Tis nothing, the passage of time."

Bronson laughed at his suddenly philosophical friend. "Haven't looked in the mirror lately, have we?"

She was certain her husband would have parried a far funnier, perhaps viler, quip—but he only smiled at Bronson, who shook his head as if for a lost cause.

Marley slapped gently at Ray. "You could have at least let me know so I could do a cake for you."

"Oh, I have everything I need, right here." He covered Juliana's hand with his own. "Plus Hattie said the wedding cake's chocolate."

She laughed.

"I noticed Dan isn't wearing his cassock," Ashanti said.

"His is not an Anglican church."

"But he's always followed an Anglican order of worship."

"Not always. Only since I gave him the book, after I was ordained. Or after I *thought* I was."

"Why didn't you want to marry in your own church, at home?"

Ray ignored the challenge in his father's question, instead turning to put his arm around Juliana's shoulders. "I am home."

As if he hadn't spoken, Ashanti went on, "The church where you were baptized?—confirmed?"

Ray's gaze dropped to the table even as he sat up straighter in the chair. Clearly he didn't want to confront his father—especially in his frailer state. "Begging your pardon, sir, I have a higher loyalty to the God Dan serves than an organization that obeys man's *sinful* laws over God's."

A charged moment passed between the Adams men.

Camisha lay her hand over her husband's, soothing him. Ray had told Juliana of the conflict that still plagued the couple over their son's expulsion from the priesthood. Ashanti had let it go; Camisha had not. As a result, the two attended different churches in Boston.

Juliana was stirred at the look of complex love that passed between the couple before she slipped her arms around his neck and hugged him close. What triumph, to pass through what they had known over their lives together and find themselves more deeply in love than ever.

She saw Camisha quickly wipe her eyes as she kissed her husband's jawline. What was wrong? Perhaps this was grief over Helen; she'd lost her daughter only the year before.

"At any rate," Ashanti said at last, "I congratulate you on your marriage today. But I mostly admire that you'll have no trouble remembering your anniversary."

Everyone laughed—except Camisha, who studied her right hand. She straightened and removed the ring there, holding it out to her son. "Helen's wedding band. She would have wanted you to have it. Let Juliana wear it."

"No, Mother. You keep it for Parks. I bought these posy rings years ago, and Juliana loves them."

Juliana noticed a figure silhouetted in the door. "There's Martin."

Rashall waved him over. "When did you get in?"

"Just now—look at you! Congratulations, brother."

"Will you join us?"

"Unfortunately, I can't. I have to ride right back out." He extended a letter to Ray. "The major-general's asking for you."

Juliana's heart sank. "Not so soon."

"The other express riders aren't as entertaining?" he asked, breaking the seal.

"Which major-general?" Camisha asked.

He threw his mother a glance, his eyebrows raised.

"Tell me it's Lafayette. Tell me."

He scanned the note there, a ghost of a smile crossing his face, and held it out to her.

Her jaw dropped inelegantly as she scanned the letter. With a frown of confusion, she read aloud.

My Dear Vicar Adams,

Kindly Favor Us With Your Presence At Your Earliest Oppty, Sir.

Our Punctuation Suffers Dismally.

Chased by Those Who Do Not Give a Filip, We Still Seek Your Benediction.

Yours Sincerely, ~~L~~ lafayette

She smiled. "A riddle, wrapped in a mystery, inside an enigma. Are you a courier, or an English tutor?"

"That's his idea of wit. And … he failed to capture Benedict Arnold and fears being tracked by William Phillips. Not exactly written in cipher. Tell him," he went on, glancing at Martin again, "that the vicar has taken a bride. He's French, he'll understand that."

"Aye," Martin said.

Camisha handed the letter over to Marley. "He's pretty witty. The history books don't capture that so well."

Rashall smiled. "Very clever. Good Lord, the fellow's a decade younger than I, and though he's only spoken English for even less time than that, he works the language as if it were his native tongue. As well as being an able and honorable soldier. I understand why Washington loves him so."

"So you've forgiven the general?" Marley asked.

Rashall hesitated. "I've come to believe that in this whole enterprise, Washington's the only man who's indispensable. And even the best of us are imperfect."

Bronson nodded. "Aptly put. He's fighting a war against a collection of men steeped in seven-hundred year old tradition and vanity and all its attendant ego. Whose leaders, by the way, bicker worse than the lowliest stable hands. Clinton and

Cornwallis were supposed to be good friends, and now they can't even communicate with one another. Arbuthnot, Clinton's admiral, is even worse. It's a testament to the Royal Navy and Army that they've accomplished as much destruction as they have. Well—that, and Arnold's personal vendetta against Washington and the rest."

Juliana put in, "And there, Arnold fit right in with the British military leaders—the victim of his own vanity."

Bronson nodded. "Exactly. And then there's Banastre Tarleton out there, an utter cad, slaughtering men who have surrendered as a rule rather than a heinous exception. They call him Bloody Ban for a reason."

"Bronson, honey, how have you been? You look like you might have put on a few pounds, and I'm pleased to see that."

As Camisha abruptly changed the subject, his gaze flickered over Marley, and color rose to her cheeks. "I'm doing much better since I visited my personal physician."

Camisha laughed, glancing at Marley. "Now we don't need to hear *all* the details."

He laughed. "No, you don't understand. Just being able to sleep through the night is a great medicine."

She stared back at him with gentle wisdom.

Juliana sought a way to ask about Ashanti's health, but others had failed twice already.

"What about you, baby?" Camisha asked Martin.

"I'm working with Ray. But as soon as this war's over, I'm heading for Ohio Country."

"Ohio? What in the world for?"

"Because this is a slave state, ma'am. Ohio isn't."

"Ohio isn't a state at all, it's the frontier. Do you want to have to carve a living out of the wilderness, or use the education you've gotten to make a life for yourself? Come to Boston."

"It's legal there, too."

"Well, it's being edged out by case law. And you're a free man. Maybe you could study law and help us all move the process along a little faster."

He gave her a cynical smirk.

"You straighten out that face right now," she said, without the least trace of amusement, and her thirty-year-old godson quickly obeyed.

"But Mother Camisha, Boston has no cause to feel superior. They allow blacks their freedom, but ... equality? That's another kettle o' cod."

This had given her something to think about.

"And I hear talk about Spanish land grants in Texas."

"To Spanish citizens," she added, with a comical frown, as if he were stupid indeed.

"No. They're allowing Americans to settle there."

"Martin, that isn't true. At least—if they are allowing it, you have to become a citizen of Spain. And it's still a raw and rugged land."

"They've had missions there for fifty years already."

"Do you even speak Spanish?"

"No," Ray put in. "But he does speak Lakota."

George and Martin dissolved in laughter at the ribbing, but Camisha scowled at him. "Don't you mock that boy's heritage. He has the blood of warriors flowing in his veins."

Her godson beamed at the praise.

"He's also got rocks tumbling around in his head over this Ohio business, but that's for him to figure out on his own." Rashall rose from the table, taking Juliana's hand. "And with that, dear friends and family, I adjourn with my bride to *rest*."

Bronson raised an eyebrow. "I doubt you'll get much rest."

"No less than you got on Thanksgiving weekend, six years ago."

Marley smiled and blushed at the gibe.

"Ah, well then," her husband said. "You'll need rest to recover from all your resting."

"George? Come with us."

They found a quiet table and sat there. "Son, we've talked about this over the years. Your mother passed away from the smallpox, is that right?"

George nodded.

211

"Do you remember her?"

"Yes, sir, I do."

"Tell Juliana about her."

"Well, she worked a lot. She worked in the kitchen. She had a hard life. I don't remember ever seeing her laugh."

"Do you feel like you knew her very well?" Rashall asked.

"Her mama took care of me, when I was little. I love her because you're supposed to love your parents, but I didn't know her very well, if truth be told. It wasn't her fault."

"Do you know how important you are to me?"

"I think I do, sir."

"I love you, and you're my son. I pray for you and hope for a productive, meaningful life for you doing the work God has for you to do. I know you don't know Juliana well yet, but she wants everything for you that I do, or I wouldn't be marrying her. Have you thought about what you'd like to call her?"

"Yes, sir. I call you Father. I'd like to call her Mother."

Tears filled Juliana's eyes. "Can I hug you, George?"

He laughed. "Well, sure."

As she hugged him, she said, "Now we're not going anywhere—we're right here, if you need us. All right? And in a couple of days, we'll start working on making a home for us all as a family. You can help your father with ideas for that."

"I'm glad to hear that, ma'am. I'm happy my father finally married you."

Laughter boomed from Rashall at that. "I wanted it even more than you did, believe me. You're with Brother Dan and Ruth tonight, correct?"

"Yes, sir."

"Good. We'll spend some time together tomorrow. Work on your studies."

And with that, they quit the dinner reception.

Chapter Nineteen

As they walked out into the road paved with gravel and crushed oyster shells, Juliana marveled at how the town continued to grow. A bank of clouds foretold of a storm coming in off the bay, and she felt a delicious breeze steal through the muggy afternoon.

Ray held her close as they strolled, and he led her to a small, pretty cottage not far from the river, in the shelter of a stand of pines. The windows had been opened and when they entered, Juliana was surprised at how much cooler it was than the crowded dining hall.

Nervously, she walked through the home, taking it all in. The flooring was polished oak throughout. A large main living area held a brick hearth, and a small kitchen and water closet completed its cozy comfort. The spacious bedroom also was dominated by a brick hearth.

Rashall went about the place, lighting lamps and candles.

"I never thought I would love anywhere more than Stonefield, but I love this little home. Whose is it?"

"Dan says it's new. They're using it for guests at the moment."

He leaned back against the bedroom door, his hands behind him, his long legs before him. Juliana found herself inspecting him with breathless anticipation. Startled at her own boldness, she looked away, finding the quilt Ruth had given her earlier draped over the end of the bed.

"Isn't it lovely, Rashall? Here's the square of your baptism ... here's the *Adventurer*. It's like a biography."

She looked back at him, finding a small smile at his lips. He walked to take the quilt from her and hang it on a stand nearby. "Look. Someone thought to leave champagne, in what might have been ice at some point. Fortunately they left a selection, along with foodstuffs. What do you think about a glass of your old favorite?"

"But I don't want you to drink it if you don't care for it."

He took a deep breath as he poured a glass of blackberry wine for her and of rum for himself. "Let's sit here in front of the hearth," he said, carrying their drinks to the small table beside the oversized leather armchair.

He sat in the chair, and she joined him on the stool near his feet. "You're joking."

He took her hand and brought her to her feet. Slowly, as if he were beginning the most chaste dance, he settled her onto his lap.

His breath caught in his chest and he smiled in pleasure as she curled up against him, sighing contentedly.

"I never knew such a simple embrace could be so ..."

"So?"

"So ... *mmm*," she murmured. Her fingertips fumbled at the silk stock, her breath teasing his throat as she worked.

A moment later, he loosened and removed the stock in a single motion. She lowered her lips there, tasting him.

His free hand roved over her back as he regarded her.

"What?"

"Wondering how you might take to camp life."

"Do you mean it?"

"I can't see any alternative. I have to go back. I can't leave you behind. I hope having you as a wife doesn't reveal another streak of selfishness within me. I'm bad enough as it is."

Thunder rumbled in the distance. "How do you think you'd deal with sleeping in the open in a rainstorm?"

"With you?"

"Always."

"Like a baby."

"Is it starting to feel a little chilly to you?"

"So much for sleeping in the rainstorm, eh?"

Again he set aside his drink and ran his open palm up over her thigh to her hips, then to her waist. His glance fell to her breasts, swollen invitingly over the edge of the stomacher.

"What do you think about a fire in the hearth?"

"I'm in favor of it."

"Then again, we may have to shut the windows to keep from entertaining the countryside."

She blushed. Then, with a smile, added, "Promise?"

As he walked toward the hearth, he gave a great laugh.

She unfastened her dress and wriggled out of the stomacher and dropped it all at her feet. She stood there in her shift and stockings and shoes, her arms crossed under her breasts.

"Thank God for whoever prepared this place," he said, lighting the laid fire in a few seconds with a candle.

He straightened and turned, and the easy grin left his face. She daintily stepped out of her gown, her eyes meeting his, then picked it up and lay it with the quilt. She held out a hand to him in innocent invitation.

He was there in a moment, sweeping her up against him. He drew her body full length along his, and she grew enflamed at the contact.

The emotions that flooded her left Juliana speechless—and yet hungry to share with him.

"Stop," she whispered.

He laughed, lightly nuzzling her throat with a line of kisses. "Funny girl."

"I just want you to understand how much this means to me."

He met her eyes in the burgeoning flames of the fire and the flash of oncoming lightning against the windows facing the river. "Believe me, my darling, I understand. This moment is all I've imagined a wedding night should be."

In the end, she could not put into words all the yearning she'd known, and she certainly couldn't tell him how many times she'd revisited their few, precious memories together. She was left to rely on gestures. Her slender fingers trailing along the smooth edge of his freshly shorn jawline, and unbuttoning his jacket, then his shirt, and drawing them both aside. Her frankly approving gaze as she took in his broad shoulders, his muscular chest, a light sprinkling of hair that she couldn't resist smoothing with her fingertips. And her open mouth learning the taut, male planes of his body. With each gesture, she whispered, not quite aware of it, her love for him.

And she felt his restraint as he allowed her discovery. When she reached the buttons of his trousers, she curiously ran her fingertips down. A shame, that a married woman, let alone a woman as widely traveled as she, should have no knowledge at all of this place on a man—but she was so grateful she was learning of it from Rashall.

"Juliana," he whispered, his hand covering her wrist.

She glanced up at him. "I know it's not very ladylike of me, for this time, but I'm just so curious about you. About your body."

The expression on his face could've meant anything—a bit of wonder, a bit of confusion—but he only gave her a tender smile. Gently, he set her hand aside and smoothly unbuttoned the trousers, pushed off his shoes, and let the trousers drop, tossing them aside and turning halfway to remove his socks.

She didn't realize she was holding her breath until he turned back to her, and a great sigh of wonder left her at the sight before her.

Her curiosity still unquenched, she lightly touched him. Such a marvelous combination of textures. Hard, fierce; soft, tender. Instinctively she understood that such a beautiful array held countless levels of sensitivity, and she licked her lips, anxious to discover them all.

As her mouth moved over him, tasting, learning where his pleasure lay, she inhaled his arousing aroma and tasted the exquisitely thin, sensitive layer of flesh here and there.

He responded with unusual reserve, absolutely silent as his hands smoothed over her hair, caressing her as she enjoyed him. When her hands lightly stroked and cupped him, he stopped her, catching her hands in his.

"Did I do something wrong?" she asked, looking up at him.

He brought her to her feet without answering, his expression quizzical—as if she were from another planet.

Then, in a flash, he skimmed her shift over her head and allowed his gaze to drift over her. She smiled, unable to forget the terrible marriage she'd endured with Enoch Morgan, and grateful for the unanswered prayers that enabled her to appreciate the man before her.

"You are unspeakably beautiful."

He kissed her, his large hands spanning her waist, his mouth gentle as he explored. His hands cupped her breasts, and she tasted his sigh as his thumbs encircled her large, pale nipples, stirring them into hard wakefulness. The pleasure he gave her, with knowing lightness—almost teasing—made her breathless, and she gave a soft moan.

"I love that so much," she said with a breathless laugh.

He nibbled her earlobe, his thumbs still teasing her with strokes as light and insistent as a feather. His palms molded her breasts as he stroked. "You like that, baby?"

She arched against him, her body hungering for a firmer touch. "More," she whispered. "Or let me kiss you again."

"We've got all night, Juliana. And I'm in no rush."

"But I've wanted you for so long—I've thought of this so many times."

His hands slipped from her breasts down her back, cupping her hips and drawing her full against him, so that she felt him seeking entrance between her thighs.

"Have you?" he asked lightly.

"Oh, yes."

"How many?"

"I don't know. Almost every night since we met."

He stopped and leaned back from her, his eyes once more lit with wonder. "You're a mystery, Juliana M—" he stopped.

"Juliana Adams," he said with relish. "My wife. Such an erotic pleasure, to discover each nuance of you."

Once more, he led her to the large chair. Arranging a light cotton throw over it, he sat there, his legs spread in invitation, sipping his rum. "Let's finish our drinks."

She sat across his thighs carefully, looping one arm around his shoulders and resting her other hand over his hard length.

"Now baby, how are you going to drink your wine if you're pleasuring me?"

"Sip of rum, please," she said, giving him a sensuous grin.

He tilted the glass against her lips and she let a large drink run down her throat, setting her afire. She licked the last drop off her lips.

"How I love your mouth. More so than anything I ever imagined."

"So you did, too? Imagined ... it?"

He laughed and cupped her breast, his other hand stroking her back. His fingertips brushed her nipple, then slipped down her slim waist to spread his hand over her generous hip.

"I absolutely adore your womanly body. It's taking everything in me right now not to just turn you around and slip right in. I can have your breasts and pleasure you while I'm inside you as well."

She gasped at the image his words conjured.

"I'm guessing that colonel of yours never even imagined having you that way."

"He never ..."

"I'm so sorry, my darling. Forgive me."

Again he kissed her, and the sensation conspired with the rum to set her afire. She turned in the chair, straddling him, then presented her breasts to him.

And his mouth was there in a moment, his hands kneading her hips, then one hand slipping to cup her other breast and tease her nipple again.

Her hand slid down between their bodies, taking him in her hand, excited and nervous about the size of him. He seemed unaware how large he was.

He hummed against her breast, tightening her pleasure, and she cried out. Then she whispered, "I must have you. Now."

His hand slid along her thigh and then between them, at last touching her. "Ah, baby, you're so ready for me. Well, I hope you're ready for a long night."

His middle finger slipped along the flesh between her thighs, quickly finding that center of pleasure, and he teased her a bit before exploring the opening.

He stopped.

"Juliana—how can this be?"

"How can what be?"

"You're a virgin."

Her head dropped in embarrassment at the revelation. She'd thought he might not notice—or even be able to tell.

"The rumors were true."

"About?"

"Never mind. Let's go to the bed."

"What rumors?" she asked, even as she stood up.

"Not about you, it's Morgan. He ... wasn't interested in women. Lafayette said that likely he married you as a ruse."

He stood up and scooped her up in his arms, then walked the few steps to the bed and carefully lay her down. He drew back the covers and she quickly scrambled into the cool, clean sheets.

He hastily shut the windows facing the other houses and returned to her.

"My wife," he said, his eyes trailing all over her body. "I shall enjoy making you mine—and becoming yours."

His mouth knew every inch of her, and she grew joyful that he enjoyed it as much as she had enjoyed kissing him. He seemed to find special pleasure in suckling at her nipples, in using his tongue there, teasing their hardness.

His mouth lowered between her thighs, entirely covering the most sensitive part of her until they both felt the pressure building within her. And only as she felt that pleasure did he replace his mouth with his hand and slipped between her thighs, knowingly breaching the fine barrier there in one thrust.

She sighed his name. "I'm not sure I can take all of you."

"We've got all night, sweetheart." He knowingly massaged her even as he thrust lightly, rhythmically, making his way deep within her as another wave of pleasure built.

"I think I'm going to—" she gasped, biting her lip.

"My God," he gritted out, biting her throat as he sank within her. "Tell me you love me, my love."

She whispered her love to him as his strokes grew shorter, harder, as he molded her breast, as her pleasure washed over her once again.

He stopped, gazing at her in adoration in the fading daylight.

Only then did he begin to find his own release, as the storm arrived outside the windows, its sheets driving against the river, the tiny home buffeted with the winds and rain.

And only then did Juliana understand that at last, she, too, had found her home. She would not fear the winds or the rain, for God was in them. She would not fear the storms of war, for God was with her. She would not fear the hatred of ignorance, for God had blessed her union with this man, the man she had loved since before time.

As they dozed in one another's arms, with the lightning storm rolling into a more peaceful cadence, Juliana heard a loud crack. Rashall raised his head, listening. When nothing else followed, they drifted back to sleep.

Chapter Twenty

Rachel looked homeward toward the southland. She could see only as far as the Jersey horizon beyond Staten Island. Above Staten Island lay Wall Street, then Chelsea, then Midtown. Above that, ending immediately below her, lay Central Park North—part of a park unchanged over the past two hundred years. She huddled more closely into the woolen scarf around her throat and head as snow flurries flew harder in the darkness just before dawn.

The city was beginning to awaken. It gave her pause, how little this part of the city had changed even in her lifetime, in the past four decades. Oh, of course the trivial changed. Restaurants came and went with the trends. Businesses opened and closed with the technology. But amid upheaval and violence, celebrations and laughter, terrorism and trading, New York City lay as indifferent to time as a Dickens truth, this place where the rich grew ever richer and the poor, ever poorer.

On the street below her, poor women on their way to the subway pushed their babies in strollers as they had a hundred years before—and a hundred years before that. Rich men hurried past on their way to earn yet another fortune.

Only four stories high, this building had once been divided into private apartments. When Emily and Tate bought it, they restored to it its previous understated beauty as a nineteenth-century mansion. Irritating Tate to no end, his manager had ignorantly sold something to a developer called airspace rights, assured that it wouldn't impact their privacy. Developers had then built a cantilevered building beside him that, ten levels up, extended over their rooftop patio.

Rachel smiled at the memory of Tate's response. He'd promptly fired his manager, bought out the developer and put the kibosh on the whole thing, leaving it a testament of folly to those who still saw human beings as commodities, even well into the twenty-first century.

She glanced up, seeing the colorful mural that Tate had commissioned to reassure his daughters of his constant care. Painted into the concrete overhang of the unfinished development, it was a 40-feet wide Tate at his most carefree, making a face at Cammie as she'd snapped the photo it had been painted from.

Now, each time his family looked up, they remembered the larger than life man who'd adored each one of them. Her heart ached at Emily's loss. She couldn't imagine; when she herself had traveled from 1746 to 2016, thinking Grey and Emily lost to her for all time, she had felt as if she'd fallen into a circle of hell. Emily, still a vibrant young woman, with a trio of daughters to raise—she couldn't begin to imagine what she was going through.

And to contemplate what they were going to ask her to consider—something she herself wasn't sure of—would perhaps be too much. Yet they had to ask.

She heard the click of a heel against the rooftop flagstone and turned. Her husband stood there, a lower corner of his charcoal grey coat folded back in the sudden, sharp breeze. He lowered his head and walked toward her. The wind tousled his salt-and-pepper hair. At sixty-five, he was as handsome as ever, and she silently thanked God for the miracles that had kept them together.

"Are you ready?" he asked.

"Are you sure this is the right thing?"

He thought. "As sure as anyone could ever be about such an explosive prospect."

She gave a soft sigh. "These children have been through so much already."

"All the more reason to remove them from this place, for all time."

She remained uncertain, and the last thing she wanted was to present a discordant note to Emily and the children. "How do you know it'll work out right?"

"You read the same journals I did. One of those was written by your own sister. Now I don't know how it came into her possession in the twenty-first century with her writing in it—or perhaps it's only complete now that she's been back there herself, to have written of that period. You saw how many different women contributed to its history."

She glanced up once more at Tate's mural. Truth to tell, when they realized the import of their reading her own sister's writing—where Marley had also mentioned Juliana—they skipped those journals. She was not equipped in any way to know her sisters' fates.

"Rachel, you were the one who pointed out to me that your parents weren't even supposed to be in this time."

"And now we're taking back into history children that aren't supposed to be there. And what about the Trelawneys— all the people you freed? How will that work? How do we know that—"

"I don't!" He turned his face into the snow that fell faster and faster. "I don't know that any of it will work. I only know in my heart that we have to try."

"And what, then, about the threat Jack Manning made on his deathbed?"

He squared his jaw. "I will not live my life looking over my shoulder."

"Well. Emily has three daughters to raise. You would have her do that amid a war-torn country?"

"Every time has its own unique dangers. And war is timeless. War lives in all ages. We don't know that a tyrant from our own age won't bomb this building in the next ten minutes."

"All right," she said with a weary sigh. "Whither thou goest, and all that."

He sent her a wry half-smile. "That's the spirit."

They descended from the rooftop on the wide, maroon carpeted stairway, stopping in the kitchen.

"Where do you suppose the servants are?"

"Sleeping, if they have any sense," Rachel said, yawning.

They'd arrived only a few minutes ago and let themselves in with their spare key. Grey brewed coffee as Rachel walked quietly down the hall to Emily's room. She tapped softly on the door. "Emily? Are you awake? It's Rachel."

With no response, she gently opened the door.

The master bedroom looked out on the courtyard behind the home, and Rachel noticed in the thin gray dawn a bright red cardinal looking in on Emily, snow whirling about him.

Emily lay on her back, toward her side, one arm under her head, her other hand clutching a tattered tissue.

Rachel crossed the room, sitting on the bed beside her. The younger woman's eyes opened; disoriented, she looked around in sudden anticipation. As if, Rachel suspected, hoping it was all still a bad dream.

Blinking, she finally focused on Rachel, and even as disappointment crossed her face, she reached for her, hugging her hard. "Oh, Rachel, I'm so glad you've come. Where's Papa? He came, didn't he?"

"I left him making coffee. He might be waking up the girls. How are you?"

She sat up in bed, reaching for a silk dressing gown. Even in this era, Emily still had the same ineffable quality of grace and archaic elegance as her father. No matter whether he was dressed in his interpreter's costume or a pair of jeans and flannel shirt, he was the epitome of refinement. The eighteenth century didn't wash out.

"I slept almost through the night. I woke up at 3:15, as usual."

"But you went back to sleep all right? And you've stopped taking the medication?"

She nodded, lowering her head. "I've stopped it. I suppose it's huge sign of progress, that I was able to sleep through the night."

They rose from the bed as they heard the children's voices in the hall. Cammie rushed into the room and threw herself into Rachel's arms. "You came—and you made Papa come! I'm so happy!"

She laughed. "Honey, I didn't have to make him, he wanted to come. We missed you."

Soon after came her younger sisters, stair-steps to Cammie. Together, they were a giggling mass of excitement surrounding Rachel, and Emily shooed them out. "Breakfast first, girls. Perhaps we can talk Papa into making pancakes."

By the time they reached the kitchen, Grey had already poured coffee for the women the way they liked it. Inviting his granddaughters to help make special pancakes for everyone, he sent Rachel and Emily down to the sunroom on the next level to relax.

Rachel kicked off her shoes. She loved this room, for in the winter, when it should've by logic been cold and drafty, the heated floor made it one of the most welcoming rooms in the house.

"How are the girls?"

"As well as could be expected. They're all sleeping in Cammie's room these days."

"Well, hey, that's an improvement. At least they've made it out of your bed," Rachel said with a smile.

She gave a rueful laugh, then took a steadying breath. "I just wish there was a manual to tell me what to expect. When it stops hurting. When I'll stop reaching for him when I wake up. When I'll stop calling his phone, just to hear his outgoing message."

Rachel looked out to watch the snow falling steadily. "Sweetie, I've never had to go through what you're going through. I was blessed to completely forget my entire family until I was old enough to bear it—and later I had your father to help. And you, of course."

She sipped her coffee, then selected her words carefully, meeting Emily's eyes with steady kindness. "But once I lost someone. She was my dearest friend. You actually knew her. Do you remember Camisha?"

She frowned in confusion. "You mean that preschool teacher of mine?"

Rachel reached for her phone, finding the old photos she'd transferred there. "This is Camisha. These are photos from before you were born. These are scanned in from when we were little. Gosh, those photographs are fifty years old, now. But here's one of us at Raleigh Tavern—just before we came to Rosalie."

Emily pointed toward the entryway. "I have that photo by my front door—and the old portrait, with ... but Thomas Jefferson is in that portrait, isn't he? Rachel, I thought she was my preschool teacher."

"Honey, you never went to preschool. Your father home-schooled you. You could read and write and were fluent in French by the time I met you. And you were only six years old."

"Papa? But how could he do that and work in Williamsburg?"

"Do you not remember seeing Camisha when we visited Rosalie a few years back? Cammie was playing with a little boy."

Alarm entered her eyes. "That was real? I thought I must have dreamed it. They were there, out of *nowhere*. And we never talked about it."

"Emily, do you remember Sukey?"

Her face lit up. "Yes! Camisha said she was my girlfriend. And her little brother, Dan. They had to pick worms off the tobacco plants in the field." She gasped, her face filling with fear. "Rachel, that couldn't have happened. We lived in Williamsburg when I was growing up. How do I remember a tobacco farm?"

"You're remembering Rosalie."

"Rosalie? That's the old plantation out near the James River—the ruins. They haven't grown tobacco there for years."

"They did when I met your father. When you were growing up there."

"You've never told me about that, Rachel. I've asked you so many times."

"Because I thought you were old enough to remember on your own, eventually. So you do remember Ruth's children."

"Ruth! I remember her as well. She was so nice, and so pretty."

Rachel walked to the doorway of the sunroom, where Grey had left the suitcase containing the journals. She opened it and withdrew the old books.

"This is a set of old journals your father found. They were at the home where I first grew up—Stonefield. You might have heard us talk about it."

She placed it on the table where they sat and gestured to the woman's portrait centered on the cover. "Look at this woman, Emily. Do you recognize her?"

"She looks like Ruth."

"That *is* Ruth. Open it and read the first page."

Rachel prayed, as she opened the book, that it would prove to be a healthy diversion from her depression, and not an insurmountable mental barrier. Grey might never forgive her if this backfired.

"'For our children's children,'" she read.

"Go on."

"'This is the diary of Ruth Freeman Trelawney of the events beginning July 4, 1746. July 7, 1746 ... Mr. Godfrey Hastings has been teaching me to read & write. He gave me this diary as a school lesson. He says it will get better over time ... July 8, 1746 ... I was sad already that my friend Camisha was gone, sailed up to Boston to be with her husband's family. Then two nights ago the awfulest thing a person could imagine happened. There was a fire up at the house, and by the time we saw it, we couldn't do nothing but watch it burn. ... First we knew something was wrong, Mr. Thomas was screaming and crying and running like a crazy man behind the house, and his little Bronson screaming and crying and Dan and the other men had to keep him from going in the house. I had to take the baby from him, I was so afraid of what he might do. Then we found out. Mr. Grey, and Miss Rachel, and poor, sweet little Emily—they was in that fire. Those good people, they died in that fire. I don't know how to tell little Dan and Sukey, they loved that child like she was they sister. Come to find out, Old Nate saw the whole thing! He saw that James Manning, that devil of an overseer Mr. Grey ran off. Well, Old Nate saw him sneak into the house with a torch and a kettle of whale oil. Then, little Miss Emily went and ran inside, like she forgot something. Mr. Grey ran in after her. Miss Rachel, she ran in after him. I expect if he hadn't had the baby, poor Mr. Thomas would have gone in after all of them. I feel for that man, I do. He's rich as sin, and he's lost every last person he loved, except for that little baby boy. And in sparing that little baby boy from man's sinful destruction, God is merciful. ..."

"Grandfather," Emily whispered. She looked up, tears streaming down her face. "How can this *be*?"

Rachel knelt beside her. "Do you remember, then?"

She nodded, her hand across the lower half of her face, weeping silently as she closed the book. "Are you telling me we traveled in time here?"

She decided against trying to soften the blow of the news; the feasibility of time travel had progressed no closer to reality today than it had thirty-five years before. "Yes. The U.S. government has been working on this for years, to keep the technique out of the hands of the wrong people. It's the nuclear power of the next century. Your father found a place far underground at Stonefield, where time travel is possible. He showed me, just before we came here."

"My head hurts."

"You probably need to eat some breakfast. Ready for pancakes?"

"This is surreal."

Rachel nodded. "When I first traveled back to your time, it took me a while before I believed it. When we came here, you eventually forgot all about it, and we let you forget as well."

"Why are you telling me now?"

"Because, I'm starting to believe that most of our problems stem from all three of us being from another time. It's more complex than that, and I'll explain it all, later. Why don't we go have some breakfast?"

"Wait. Camisha is still in the eighteenth century?"

"She wanted to stay—to try to make things better for the future."

"How could a preschool teacher do that?"

"Well, I wouldn't knock a preschool teacher. They're raising the next generation. But Camisha was a lawyer—one you remember because she loved children, and she dearly loved you. In fact, she helped save your father when he was tried for a crime he didn't commit. But when I realized she stayed in the past even after we returned to this time, my heart was broken. It was as if she had died—she *had*, in my life."

"How did you get over that?" she asked bleakly, leading them back, finally, to her original question.

"Well. First, I tried to be patient with myself—and I'd suggest you do the same. Second, I forced myself to accept it. Those things you're afraid of—waking up without Tate, missing him when you least expect it … try your hardest to make peace with that being a part of your life."

"Rachel, do you suppose I could travel back in time and change things … so Tate wouldn't die?"

"I wish it were that easy. With things that happen in this world, we don't know everything. In time, we'll understand. In time, you'll find that even the blackest moments can lead us into a life that's still rich and rewarding—and happy."

"Why do you believe that? Look at all the suffering in the world."

She smiled a bit. "Camisha knew just how to answer that. 'Don't blame Dad for the mess in the playroom,' she said. A lot of life's suffering, we bring on ourselves. A lot of it is just life. But I believe it because I know it firsthand. He's always faithful. Don't lose heart, baby. Ask him for help."

In the other room, she thought she heard a noise. "Grey?"

He didn't answer, and she could hear him upstairs, laughing with the girls.

"And there's that. I keep hearing noises in this creaky old place. It's probably one of the servants, to tell you the truth. But the girls are letting their imaginations get the better of them. Some kid at school said their dad's a ghost now, haunting them. Bullies, even at times like this."

Then came a sudden loud noise she couldn't quite place, and the slam of a door. She and Emily rushed to the foot of the stairs.

"Grey! Get down here, now. And have Cammie keep the girls up there."

The intruder could be anyone from a fan to a home invader, but how they'd gotten past security was a mystery. The home was gated and guarded.

She heard Grey's footfall on the stairs and put her arm around Emily as they edged toward the entryway, where they'd heard the sound. Grey put his arm across them, holding them back. He walked into the entryway, still holding his arm out as a warning.

He walked into the long hallway to the entryway. "Dear God," he murmured. "What in hell is this?"

They followed him. Rachel heard Emily's quickly stifled cry, but she fell silent instinctively at the sight on the wall.

An antique oil portrait, still in its ornate frame, was impaled on the wall with a dagger, buried to the hilt. What kind of person was strong enough to drive a dagger through canvas and into several inches of oak in a single thrust?

They studied the portrait. A couple and their toddler in a garden, the man in a navy wool dress coat, bronze buttons to the waist, tails at his knees, black trousers, and white stockings over simple buckle shoes. One hand lay on the woman's shoulder.

The woman, sitting in a chair, was pregnant and wore a lilac dress with white lace at the cuffs and neckline. A contrasting flowered burgundy drawstring skirt underneath showed at the front. A straw bonnet was tied at her chin. One hand lay on the shoulder of her child—possibly a girl, though she knew the dressing customs of toddlers back then, all of whom wore gowns, offered no guarantees. Her other hand lightly rested at her shoulder on her husband's fingertips.

The handle of the dagger, where the blade had been thrust, rested on the woman's belly.

Rachel went dizzy. She had seen this woman before, through the time portal at the ruins of Rosalie. She was her sister, Merrilea. And the young man with her was her husband, Bronson Trelawney. She recognized him from the duplicate portrait Emily had hanging at her entryway—of Bronson, Rashall, and Camisha with Thomas Jefferson. The original belonged to Helen Carlyle.

Grey turned to face them, his face grim. "Jack Manning's arrived at last."

Chapter Twenty-One

From the peaceful seclusion of Ruth's front porch, Camisha watched the rain. The day's events had been exhilarating and exhausting, and most of the town were in their houses, fast asleep. Camisha couldn't sleep.

Now Rashall was married. Only Eston, still off with the Rhode Island Regiment, and Parks, her baby, were left—although Parks was engaged to a young soldier.

The front door creaked, and she turned to see Ashanti walk outside in his dressing gown and slippers. She'd sewn him the silk gown several years ago, and he had filled it handsomely back then. Now, it hung loose on him—something in his wilder dreams he expected her to ignore.

When he saw her, he shook his head. "What do you think you're doing out here, all by yourself?"

She smiled. "Still think someone's going to snatch me as a runaway? I couldn't sleep."

He rubbed his hand along her shoulders as he joined her on the bench. "And you know I can't sleep without you."

Several moments of silence passed—nothing but the whisper of the rain. Finally, she could no longer ignore the opportunity afforded her by their solitude. "Why don't you see the doctor while we're here?"

"We have the best doctors on this continent at home."

"I thought maybe you just didn't want people knowing your business."

"You've already told me they're all frauds. That eighteenth-century medicine is a combination of amputation and demon possession, with some purging and leeching thrown in to make it look reputable."

She pursed her lips and looked at him, not even attempting to hide her fear.

He softened. "Baby, I'm fine."

"You've lost weight. "

"Am I supposed to have an appetite when you can't stop crying?"

"Granted, I miss my little girl. Haven't been great company."

After a long moment, he said, with gruff tenderness, "She was my little girl—you know that. Parks is yours."

She looked down at her folded hands.

"And no man could wish for a better companion."

"Look, I'm afraid. You need to be honest with those of us who love you. The only way you can do that is if you see a doctor. And any doctor is better than no doctor at all."

"All right, I'll see Doctor Boylston, soon as we get home. I promise. But I don't think that's what's really bothering you."

She looked into her husband's light hazel eyes—nearly green. It was what she'd first loved in him. The honesty in those eyes. Taking his hand, she kissed the back of it, then the palm, thinking of all the work this man had done to make a life for her, for all these years.

"I don't deserve you," she said. "So much I have to be grateful for, and I'm only depressed at the sadness in this world. All those little children I thought I was doing some big noble thing for, stealing them away from places like Black Oak. For what? Death instead by smallpox, dysentery?"

"You can't mean to compare life as a slave to life as a free man?"

"It all seems empty, this place where we live. Filled with grief. Happiness seems so undeserved."

Presently, he asked, "Baby, do you remember what you said when you accepted my marriage proposal?"

She welcomed the distraction. "I think I compared our promise to the vows Ruth and Daniel took. Back when they were still enslaved. I said the auction block couldn't sever their vows, and time would be powerless to destroy my promise to you ... to honor my vows until I draw my last breath. And you said—"

"And when the last breath leaves my body, it will be your name."

"This whole life is gone before you know it. Camisha, you taught me that just one thing matters and lives on after us. Only one thing we do can live on. And that's the children."

And even as he spoke, the sentry shouted, "Riders!"

They rose at the sound of horses—and not too far away.

Ashanti rushed to the door and called for Dan and Bronson. He stepped inside the main room of their home, grabbed a rifle from the rack and hastily loaded it. He handed it to Camisha and loaded another as Bronson and Marley hurried out with their own firearms, followed soon after by Dan and Ruth.

Men began pouring out of their homes, most armed with muskets, a few with rifles. At close range, the musket was a better choice. Rifles were designed for distance.

Camisha moved to stand beside Ruth, who was the better shot of the two. It was not unusual for the women of Rosalie or elsewhere to protect themselves thus. Those who were married had children, and many men were either away fighting, or had only recently returned.

Still, Camisha was wary. Were the riders killers without scruples, like Banastre Tarleton? Or would they turn out to be friendly patriots, come to warn them of another threat?

By the time the riders arrived, one firing his gun in the air, they had a welcome party waiting and they screeched to a surprised halt. Several men stood with their barrels trained on the newcomers; the rest easily held their muskets across their chests, ready to fire if need be.

Camisha did not know the half-dozen men who arrived, but two were dressed in the finery of wealthy men. Both were older, one carrying a torch. The rest looked to be militia men.

"No need for gunfire," the leader of the group said. "This won't take long."

"Who are you, and what's your business here?" Dan called out, without anger or threat.

The man slipped down from his horse, reached into his pack and walked to a tree. He opened a sheet of paper and nailed it to the tree with two sharp raps of a hammer.

"We are here on behalf of the sheriff of Williamsburg, to formally give notice. You have six months to sell your land and leave the commonwealth of Virginia, or be taken into custody as lawbreakers, your property confiscated."

"*What are your names.*" Ruth repeated evenly, as if the question were a death threat. She knew well that before the war, the main purpose of the militia around these parts was to round up runaways.

"I have informed you of our purpose here. You will desert these premises by December 31, 1781, or be taken into custody and tried for violating the laws of Virginia. Good night."

As quickly as they'd arrived, the men reined their horses around and rode back toward Williamsburg.

Camisha frowned. "Why do you suppose they waited until after dark?"

"I can tell you one thing. They did *not* expect to be looking down two dozen muzzles. I'd venture to say it might have gone a little differently otherwise."

Bronson dropped off the porch, walked to the tree and removed the paper. He glanced up to notice Rashall and Juliana approaching. They studied the post and returned to the porch.

Men from all over the town walked to them, asking for details about the post.

Dan walked to the center of the gravel road and called out, "People, go back to bed. We'll gather at the meetinghouse in the morning at daybreak for more discussion."

Rashall reached his mother and kissed her forehead, and she looked at Juliana. "Honey, do you not shoot?"

"I can, but Ray can take care of me."

"Is that so? Him galloping around the country with Lafayette?"

"Mother, please. Are you all going to bed?"

"I won't be able to sleep for hours," Camisha said.

When they returned to the house, no one pretended interest in sleep. Ruth walked into the kitchen and poured cider for all.

"Now what?" Ashanti asked.

Camisha jumped right in—she knew only one sensible solution, and she wanted to get it out before the conversation went elsewhere. "I know this isn't my call, but we could move all of you home by winter. Things'll be quieter near the end of October, but if we go overland in groups, you could be settled in your new homes long before then."

"I *am* home," Ruth said flatly, then sipped her cider. "I am fifty-four years old, and I've lived here most of my life. That devil Grimewood came here from Carolina not ten years ago. And you can bet he was behind that stunt tonight."

"How do you know?"

"I just know."

Rashall spoke up. "That wasn't a stunt. And he has Virginia law on his side."

Bronson lay the page out in the middle of the table. "This isn't even a legal document. It says, effectively, 'Get out like we told you to."

Camisha leaned forward, reading. "'By order of this writ, all original slaves named and receiving manumission in Grey Trelawney's will, as well as all their descendants and spouses, are hereby ordered to leave Virginia by the end of this year, 1781.' Huh. What do you know about that. You'd think with something like this, the sheriff might have affixed his signature to it. Or maybe even had a real live judge sign it."

Bronson nodded.

Rashall rolled his eyes. "You don't mean to tell me that you think if we ignore them, they'll go away."

"Of course not. I'm just saying no one has to start crying and packing their bags tomorrow."

"That's easy for you to say. When was the last time you were asked for your papers?"

"Must we have this argument again?" Bronson sighed.

"Of course not. I'm merely weary of this issue continuing to be an issue for the foreseeable future—well, at least as far as Mother can foresee. I truly am considering taking Juliana to France."

"A honeymoon?"

"A life."

Everyone stared back blankly—everyone, that is, except Bronson. He seemed to know what Rashall was thinking.

"There's no slavery there. Lafayette assures me I could make a good home there. The biggest challenge, unfortunately, is the monarchy. For all its major flaws in slavery, the United States is grounded in the unalienable rights of the individual. I don't see that in France."

"No." Camisha bit it out without even considering consequences. "You must not. At least, not if you're expecting a tranquil life."

"But Lafayette—"

"Trust me. No. We have our revolutions to fight—the French, theirs."

His lips went tight as he considered her, then all at once he relaxed and smiled at her. Unfortunately, she recognized that; he was dismissing her opinion entirely.

The table fell silent.

"There's one sure-fire cure for this," Camisha said. "And it's the only one I can think of."

All eyes turned to her.

She shrugged. "It's a long shot, but if you're dead set against coming to Boston, somebody could ask the governor to grant special permission for you to stay."

"Jefferson?" Thomas asked. "Good luck finding him—the Virginia legislature is living like highwaymen these days, on the run, the wanted men they are."

"I could find him," Camisha said.

Rashall and Ashanti exchanged a smile, and she intercepted it. "You *doubt* me?"

Ashanti quickly shook his head. "Camisha, you can do anything you set out to do. You always have."

She shook her head, her face taut with tears. "I'm not going to sit here and be mocked. You two *men* sit there and ponder what miracle you're going to pull out of your pocket to rescue five hundred free black men in the heart of Virginia's tobacco plantations, plus their wives and babies. Maybe you can waltz every one of them through that portal out there and into a time where people of all skin color can look at each other with love instead of suspicion. Does anyone here know when that time might come to pass? Well? Do you?"

"Mother—"

"I'm going to bed. And what are you doing here, anyway? You two are supposed to be over in that honeymoon cottage, making me another grandbaby. And once I get my hands on that baby, you just try taking him or her to Paris. Just you try."

She tried her hardest to toss off her threat with the teasing sass they expected from her, but the tears still threatened. She swallowed and left the table and went to bed.

જી

Marley had made breakfast for the household by the time Camisha made it downstairs, and the young mother mixed her a cup of coffee, just the way she liked it.

Odd, how the random memory of stopping to pick up a cup of specialty coffee on her way into court, in her old life, came back to her. For a moment, the fresh sensation of the memory alarmed her—as if she'd somehow daydreamed the past thirty-five years while she was waiting for the barista to deliver her double espresso.

"You coming to the meeting?"

"What do you think is the best answer to this?"

She sipped her coffee, then finally spoke. "I think it's for Ashanti and me to go to Monticello. And we both know it still

238

won't be enough. Nothing can be enough in this world. France isn't a bad idea, but France is blowing through their entire national fortune, to wipe out Britain as a threat in the future."

"That's the hardest thing to get through to them. While I know Lafayette admires our ideals in principle, we're almost beside the point. The point is shutting down the British."

"And France is going to be no place for anyone, let alone a young mixed couple, for the next two decades."

With that, they left Aileen to manage the kitchen while they made their way over to the meetinghouse.

Dan brought the meeting to order with a prayer for wisdom in discernment for the assembly. "Now most of you who are here this morning saw the riders last night. Did anyone recognize any of them?"

Negative murmuring.

"I'd like to begin the meeting with some words from Hasty, speaking for our brother Martin, who's away serving the Continental Army at the moment."

Hasty stepped up to the podium. "I understand more than many how much we all love our home here, and take pride in it. It's as nice a village as any in the Tidewater. We educate our citizens, we worship freely, and we're healthier than many, since we started purifying our water and collecting rainwater in the cistern. I don't mind telling you, the thing I miss most when I'm away from home is having a good, cold drink of water whenever I want it.

"But I can understand what my brother Martin says, that we should all head west—out where slavery isn't even an issue. That's what his plan is, whenever this war is won—and he's looking for others to join him, on his journey into the frontier. So no matter what else happens, know that's one option. Thank you."

He returned to his seat, and Dan rose again, holding out his hand to Rashall, who quickly joined him.

"My idea is for us to consider moving to France. If we sell this land and its homes, the proceeds will give all of you passage to the new land and a very generous start there.

One of the women stood up. "I've heard that Paris is a very dirty place. We all know that even in this country, large cities with dirty water and messes in the street are breeding grounds for fevers."

"Of course, that's a risk everywhere. We can always teach people what we know, though. And Paris isn't the only place to live in France. The one very strong benefit of living in France is to be free from the threat of slavery. We don't know what will become of the lands on the frontier; perhaps they, too, will accept slavery."

This generated a great deal of positive discussion, along with questions Ray responded to as if he were preaching about the promised land. Hearing her son speak warmed Camisha for his intelligence—but her poor old heart couldn't bear the thought of losing him, too, to a land thousands of miles away. Or, worse, to the brutal revolution looming on its own horizon.

"No place is perfect, of course," he conceded, at last. "And France is but one of many options."

With that, he returned to his seat.

Dan then introduced Camisha, and she walked to the podium, her mouth set in a line to attempt to control her sadness. She determined to speak simply. It had been years since she'd even attempted persuasive speaking, the sort that had once saved Grey Trelawney's life. She no longer found interest in such theatrics.

And then she heard her voice, just as if her old friend were speaking from over her shoulder. *That mouth is as much a part of you as your nose. You couldn't turn it off if you tried.*

Thirty-five years had passed since she'd last seen her friend. She thought Ashanti had filled the gaping hole in her heart, or perhaps Ruth. But no one was Rachel. Only Rachel would be able to understand what she was going through—with Ashanti, with Helen. With this.

She cleared her throat and spoke softly. "My suggestion is for my husband and me to ride to Monticello and secure approval from the governor for a permanent, binding exclusion for the Rosalie Trelawneys. He is an opponent of slavery."

"He is also an owner of slaves," someone called out.

"As are others fighting for freedom in this country. Let's focus on what we have in common. Let's focus on what we're trying to accomplish here. Let's focus on the preservation of a community of free black people in a commonwealth that has over time adopted a slave economy. Aside from just protecting your own home, Rosalie would continue to serve as the example it is, that a tobacco farm can be much more profitable, its workers much better educated and valuable to the community, when workers are properly valued, properly compensated, and allowed to make their own choices in life. And is it too much for a young family to expect a basic, safe home rather than the shacks that these people—"

She stopped, shaking her head, finding her veneer of detachment slipping. She noticed Ashanti in the front row as he watched her cautiously.

"My little girl. She was telling the truth. Slaves live like beasts of burden. No human being has a worse life than a slave in this world. What is the point, for those of us who live free in this world? How much better do those little children we've ransomed from the slave plantations have it? How can anyone be happy, when … we still suffer. Our children still d…"

She broke down in tears, there in the pulpit. Ashanti rose from his seat and walked to her, taking her in his arms. He didn't try to move her as all the grief of the past thirty-five years came out—losing her little Martin, Booker, Helen … and then that Rashall, talking about going to France, of all places. She didn't even attempt to move from Ashanti's arms. He held her without awkwardness before the assembly, even slowly rocking her, as he would've comforted their daughters.

And then something happened.

Ashanti's gruff bass voice sang out four notes. "Oh, happy day …"

The room remained silent. Again he sang out the words, a little more strongly, as he fought his own emotions.

This time, their son answered, rising to lead the responsive singing. "When Jesus washed ..."

"Oh happy day ..." Juliana joined him, with Marley and Bronson falling in a note or two later.

Ashanti went on. Ruth had made her way to the upright piano at the front of the room by the first chord change and joined in. Parks stood, leading in her clear, sweet contralto. Sukey joined her.

Then, the most powerful voices of their choir quickly added to their song with fierce joy. "He taught me how ... to watch, fight, and pray ...

"To watch ... fight and pray ..."

"And live rejoicing... every day..."

Presently, the strength and fight rose up within her, and she raised her head, joining in the responsive singing as her family continued to carry her. The singing went on for some time, as the assembly were reminded who they were. And at last, everyone was seated, leaving Camisha and Ashanti in the pulpit.

She gave her husband a look that he hadn't seen in her in a long time—joy. He nodded and began to speak.

"If it pleases my wife, I'd like to leave after this meeting for Charlottesville, with as many as would like to accompany us. We can't afford to tarry. His term as governor ends this week."

Thomas rose. "I'll go. I can still ride well. We'll take my finest mounts. I can furnish anyone who'd like to come."

Hasty and several others volunteered, and the meeting concluded with a prayer.

"I have one other item to add," Dan said. "As a community we've debated in the past on incorporating as a town—whether we even can right now is beside the point. But I'd like to propose for consideration that we name our town to honor the woman who's done so much to make us who we are today. And I know she'd never stand for us taking her name, but perhaps that of the woman who raised her—and who she raised. Those in favor of naming our community Helentown, Virginia, signify by saying 'aye.'"

The building shook with the sound of unanimous approval, and emotion filled Camisha and her husband alike.

As they mounted up and departed for Charlottesville, Camisha thought of Rachel—in their goodbye at the old slave cabins, when she'd hurried to warn her about James Manning's escape, all those years ago. *"Have you forgotten who you are?"*

"No, Rae," she whispered now, in joy and peace. "I've remembered, same as you."

Once again, she had remembered. Thanks to her husband, she had remembered.

Chapter Twenty-Two

In the end, it was only dumb luck that found them in the right place and the right time.

Bronson and Marley were crossing the short stretch of land between the village and their own home with Rashall and Juliana, Aileen, and the children in the wagon. Will sat on the seat between him and Marley, his head in Bronson's lap.

They passed in front of the old Rosalie ruins. Aileen crossed herself just as she did each time she visited their home, more from superstition than reverence. This was the place, after all, that had taken her little Emily, and her father, and the young miss who'd restored them to Thomas.

He glanced over and saw Marley gazing backward toward the arched entryway that still stood where, as she remembered it, she'd seen her own sister on that Thanksgiving before their wedding, six years ago.

And even as he followed her gaze, a woman appeared there and crossed over near them, just a dozen feet away. She looked backward at a man who followed behind her. They stopped only when they stood on this side of the ruins.

As if out of God's first breath of thin air, they had appeared. And then they looked up, noticing the wagon full of passengers.

Holy mother of God.

Rashall gave a funny little high-pitched gasp.

Aileen, fortunately, was by now occupied once more with the children, and he hurried the wagon on another hundred feet before stopping and jumping out. "Aileen, can you drive the team on to the house with the children? The rest of us need to check on something."

"Yes, sir, of course. But stay away from those ruins. That land is cursed, I tell you."

Bronson gazed up at the old woman who'd raised him as she took the reins from him, averting her gaze from the ruins. She was the closest thing he'd had to a mother, and he looked at her now as if for the first time. Her vibrant red hair had long since faded to white, and her arthritic hands were still active, though slower. How he'd taken his old nursemaid for granted through his life. She had simply always been there—as she had, no doubt, for his mother.

"Yes, ma'am. I only wanted to check on a lost sheep I noticed along the ridge. Juliana, Rashall, would you come with me and Marley?"

She kissed her children and jumped down from the wagon, watching until Aileen put the wagon into motion and was well on her way.

They turned back toward the ruins—and saw nothing.

"What? Didn't you see what I saw?"

"Aye."

"They're in the trees there," Ray said.

Then they saw the couple again, glancing at them from behind one of the ancient live oaks where they'd ducked.

The men walked forward with their wives, their attention rapt on the other couple—who emerged from the trees and began to walk toward them.

Bronson grabbed at his wife as she broke away from him with a sob, racing to the other woman, who met her halfway.

Juliana ran after Marley.

Instinctively, all three men stopped, allowing the women to meet in the middle.

"Dear God, can it be?" Rashall said.

Bronson swallowed against the hammering in his chest. It could not. It simply could not be. The trembling began in his fingertips.

At attention at his side, Will whined, then barked at him. When he still didn't respond, the dog nipped lightly at his ankle, demanding his attention.

Bronson focused on the dog, dropping to one knee to stroke his fur as Juliana had shown him. His trembling subsided, and his heartbeat began to slow. What a smart dog he was, to have been trained when to sense he was about to have an episode.

"Everything all right?" Ray asked.

He nodded. "Who do you suppose that is?"

"You know who it is, Hawk," he said, then took a deep, bracing breath. "We met him five years ago next month. It's your brother and our sister-in-law. Let's go say hello."

"Is it really you?" Marley was asking as they approached. "You were dressed in modern clothing, before."

The woman nodded, tears in her eyes. "Little Merri. And could I be lucky enough to hope this might be Juliana?"

Juliana nodded silently, and she was the one who crashed through their polite distance—as if aware of each second of the clock ticking past as they dallied. She grabbed Marley's hand and pulled her to their other sister and hugged them both around the neck.

The women went silent, then, and Bronson walked toward his brother. "Are you—"

"We've met before. I'm your brother, of course."

Bronson laughed to dislodge the emotion in him, but the sound came out a strangled sob, and his brother caught him with an arm around his shoulders.

"I take it you're both fighting for freedom, one way or another," he said, holding out his free arm to hug Rashall.

"You don't know the half of it," Ray said, casting Bronson a look.

Grey attempted to interpret what wounds his brother might have suffered as he glanced over him. Instead, Bronson looked toward his wife, who was by now holding out her hand for him.

"Bronson, this is my big sister, Rachel. Rachel, this is my husband. We have two children, but we sent them on to the house with Aileen."

"Aileen is here?" Rachel said. "Your mother's nursemaid? Oh, what a pleasure to see her again!"

Bronson saw the physical resemblance between her and Hannah—both stunning beauties. But there the resemblance ended. This woman seemed to have a level head on her shoulders, as if unaware of what a beauty she was.

Belatedly, he responded, "Yes—and mine as well. I was afraid what the shock might do to her if she saw you and Grey. She's hale and hearty, but not as robust as she once was."

Rachel smiled. "Oh, Bronson, she loved you and your mother as if you were her own children." She abruptly closed her mouth, as if afraid she'd brought up an unpleasant topic.

"Thank you," he said. "That's a comfort to hear."

"Rachel," Marley went on, "this is my husband's best friend, Rashall Adams."

Her voice caught as she reached for him. "You're Camisha's son. You're the pirate she talked about in her last letter to me."

He laughed heartily, hugging her. "That's my mother. Raid a few Spanish and English merchant ships, and you're branded for life." At length, he withdrew. "You will never know how much that woman loves you. I've heard about you my whole life. I'm even named after you—and believe me, being named after a woman is something I don't often admit to."

"Oh, I'm so excited to see her again—even for just a few more minutes. Where is she?"

Ray looked from Juliana back to Bronson. "I'm so sorry—she just left this morning for Charlottesville. With my father and Thomas as well."

A moment of sharp disappointment passed, then the blow was softened. "Well. At least I get to see my sisters *and* their husbands. It's an abundance of blessing that I never expected."

"Wait—did you say Thomas?" Grey asked. "Not our father?"

Bronson nodded. "Yes. He's alive and well. Aged, of course, but neither his mental or physical faculties are overly diminished."

A smile lit Grey's face. "I never would have imagined that."

"Well, let's retire for refreshments," Bronson said. "We can take you back up to where the Trelawneys live, or risk Aileen's life by bringing you home. What shall it be?"

"The Trelawneys," Grey repeated. "You mean the people who were freed after the fire."

"They've built a village you'll be proud to see," Marley said. "They named it after Camisha's mother. And they adopted your last name as their family name. Oh, Grey, there was this wonderful set of journals the women had kept over the centuries that told of their struggles. Unfortunately, it was lost when I traveled to this time."

"Then I have some news that may please you," he said. "It's a long story, but I found those journals and they're now in the legal possession of the Foundation. I made the gift in your name. For all time, a gift of Merrilea Miller Trelawney."

The joy that swept her expanded through Bronson—and he marveled at the feeling, a smile crossing his face as well.

He was falling in love with her all over again.

That was what he'd been going through, for the past few weeks—as he struggled with the temptation to make love to her, against the chasm of distance that had grown between them over the past three years. New love was growing, an even deeper love than the love they'd known so far.

Marley pressed her fingertips against her mouth, quieting the storm of emotion within her, and she shook her head. "You have no idea how happy that makes me. I thought it was lost to posterity in some police junkyard."

Bronson clapped his brother on the back and turned toward their home. "Come. Come to the house. Aileen often naps with the children. I doubt she'll object if we offer the suggestion. We'll introduce her later."

The sisters walked ahead of the men on the way to the house, and everyone waited outside while Marley hurried inside to check.

She opened the back door, inviting them in. "They're at the head of those stairs, so if we go toward the front of the house, we won't disturb them."

Marley prepared refreshments while Bronson gave the others the grand tour. She caught up with them in the drawing room.

"This is Lottie Chesterfield's home," Rachel said, a smile of wonder settling on her face. "It's where Camisha and I stayed, our last night in the twenty-first century. But there was a portrait then of Thomas—not a very flattering one."

Marley mused over this. "Perhaps your knowing him changed him."

Grey gave a great laugh. "You have that right. And me as well. If not for Rachel ... Well. Let's just say she restored that relationship to something perhaps better than brand new."

"There was a terrible rain storm that night," she went on. "I heard someone calling my name—pretty unnerving, like a little girl. And I looked out into the storm and saw Emily under my window. To this day, I'm still not sure who she was. I don't know that I believe in ghosts. But I followed her into the Rosalie ruins, and the next thing I remember, I was back in time."

"Who was Lottie?" Marley asked.

"She said she was the last surviving Trelawney." She smiled. "Maybe she's one of your descendants."

Marley's face went white. "How could that be, if you met her before I went back in time?"

Rachel laughed and shrugged. "I was just kidding—but she had to be someone's descendant. She was the most curious little lady, wearing this wig nearly sideways—good grief! She probably wasn't much older than I am now."

"That I don't understand," Rashall said, parsing his words thoughtfully, as if aware he could easily insult someone. "I thought you girls were only a few years apart in age."

"Well, we were, in our natural lives. If much of anything in our lives has been natural."

"Rachel traveled to 1746 one night in 2016," Marley said. "I remember seeing her and Camisha on the street in Williamsburg, that day. Nan and I traveled the very next day to 1775. Meanwhile, she, Grey, and Emily all traveled back to 2016—seemingly in the next moment."

"But it isn't," Juliana said. "All of that time travel is real time in our lives, even though we may come back to the very next second, when the travel ends."

"How do you know so much about it?" Rachel asked.

Grey glanced over. "She lives at Stonefield. She would have to know about that system there."

"You know about it?" Juliana asked.

"I bought the property after Marley and your grandmother never returned."

Marley asked, "Grey, why haven't you visited for the past few years? After your last visit, you sounded pretty agitated."

He stirred his coffee absently, glancing at Rachel. Abruptly, she went serious, and he sighed. "I *was* agitated. Who here recognizes the name Jack Manning?"

Marley spoke. "We all know who he is—he's the man who … who killed Mama and Daddy. Also the son of James Manning, who used to work for you, and who had an affair with our grandmother."

"*What?*" This from Rachel.

Marley rubbed her forehead, then took a deep breath. "How to sum this up. I don't know how much you two have figured out on your own, somehow, in your time. So here goes."

And she proceeded to explain the rich, crazy tapestry of their family history. "Now I don't know everything—or, well, anything—that happened with Mama and Daddy. I know they traveled in time, and I think Daddy knew about the labyrinth. But Nan met James Manning after her husband died—even while Thomas was courting her—and he used her to try to get revenge on Camisha, for destroying his life. Apparently, after he set fire to Rosalie, he disappeared with his sons and reinvented himself. Along the way, our parents traveled in time. I know nothing at all about that, beyond his teaching at William and Mary when Thomas Jefferson attended. And that at some point after our parents met, Jack Manning met our mother."

"Your parents would have met as very small children," Grey said. "Gideon and Sarita—your father's parents—worked at Stonefield for William and Hannah—your mother's parents."

Rachel frowned over this. "You know, I remember that night—I remember Jack Sheppard. Manning. He was evil personified. He was planning to come back and kill us as well. Whether he was doing it for his father or whether he was just embittered because our mother had rejected him, I don't know. And the meth no doubt helped. He killed them out of pure bloodlust.

"But Max, his brother, was different. I think that every single thing he did that related to our parents was to protect his brother. I grew up with the guy—all he cared about was making money. I'm not saying he was innocent. He made Camisha's life as a little girl a living hell. But he wasn't a killer. He was a manipulator."

"So both Mannings are dead?"

"Yes. And we come to the purpose of our visit," Grey said.

"Visit?" Marley echoed, heartbroken. "I thought you'd come back to stay."

"Oh," Rachel said gently. "No. Emily and our grandchildren are still back there. At least at this point. We have some things to tie up—and I'm not sure Malcolm will allow it, anyway. Grey has his fingers in a lot of different nonprofits—the sort of work Camisha used to do."

"Well, you'll never know how happy I am that you came."

Grey withdrew a package from the worn leather satchel he carried. He looked from Marley to Bronson. "Before I show you this, I should warn you that you're going to find it very upsetting."

Bronson cleared his throat, then took his wife's hand in both of his. "All right."

"I suppose I should give you some background. Do you remember when I visited you three on the *Immortal?* Well, I had received a phone call from a hospital administrator back in our hometown, who told me that an old man in their care was asking for me. He was very ill and was expected to die shortly. Naturally, I hastened to visit the man.

"Turned out to be Jack Sheppard. Almost ninety years old. I didn't recognize him. He seemed quite addled—not looking me in the eye, not even aware I was there. Then he looked at me and spat in my face. Well. You can imagine my chagrin. I mean, what *is* the etiquette in such moments?"

"Did the person who called you tell you his name?" Bronson asked.

"They said he was a John Doe, supposedly no memory. I told him I was leaving and turned to go. He said he wanted to offer his confession. I suggested he ask for a priest and, again, turned to go.

"And then he said, quite clearly, 'All right, then. I'll see you again in another few years.'

"For thirty years, I'd watched just one small part of the hell he'd put this family through, and I had no patience for his games. I told him if he had anything to say, he'd best say it, as there'd be no more ill-conceived vengeance at his age.

"And then, he smiled. And he said something that chilled me to the bone. He said, ''Tis already done.' Since he could not best me, could not hurt Rachel any more, in the past, he had chosen to do so in the future. He spoke in riddles about Camisha, and now I've come to believe that he felt he carried out his vengeance against her by killing her father. I'm not certain of this, just a theory. At one time I was even convinced the entire thing could just be another game. He lived in a mental prison of imagined slights he felt the need to avenge. And, during the period when Cameron and the Millers were killed, he was also taking a wide range of drugs, but *not* taking prescribed medications. He punished the girls' mother and father for her rejection of him. He punished Camisha by killing her father. Now, there's this."

He unfolded a piece of fabric he'd wrapped around the object, and now he revealed what lay there.

Bronson frowned. "It's that portrait we were missing, Marley—remember the other day, I mentioned it?"

She nodded. "I see nothing terribly horrifying about this. How did you find it?"

Grey turned it around to her, unrolling a small cylinder in another scrap of cloth. "It was mounted on the oak wall in the entryway at Emily's townhome in Manhattan. With this," he added, revealing the dagger, leaving it lying on the cloth. He pointed out the inch-wide cut in the cloth over Marley's pregnant belly in the portrait. "Right here."

"Did you show it to the police?"

Rachel gave a gentle sigh. "Marley, think. They would start asking us questions, and when they got to the 'Do you have any idea who could have done this?' we would reply, "Yes, as a matter of fact. There's this guy from the eighteenth century who killed my parents, and then he might have killed my best friend's dad, but you won't be able to do anything about it, because he's crazy. Oh, and he died five years ago. And his brother was Max Sheppard, one of the most brilliant computer minds of the twenty-first century. So what do you think we should do, officer?'"

Marley shook her head with a smile. "You always were the smartass. Even when I was just three."

"I'm sorry. And it's not funny at all, I know. Evil people do evil things. It's just … cops hear crazy stuff all day. We didn't see any point in dragging Emily through it all, with everything else she's going through."

"What happened to Emily?"

And she told them.

Bronson said, "So this vile person, at some point in his misbegotten existence, in the recent past, in fact, found his way into our home and stole our family portrait. And the dagger— is it something meaningful to you? I don't recognize it."

"It's from a display Emily has in her apartment entryway. It's meant to replicate the display in the Governor's Palace."

Bronson nodded. "But it's not a—what do you call them, Juliana?"

"Final artifact."

Soon, they heard noise on the stairs, and Aileen peeped in, waving at Marley. "Afternoon, mum. Thought I'd start supper. Ah, I see we have guests. I'll make up the spare bedroom."

"Yes, these are distant relatives on my father's side from the north," Bronson explained. "Mr. and Mrs. Grey."

He saw the imperceptible shake of his wife's head, even as she murmured under her breath, "Good to know what a poor liar I married."

"I have other worthy qualities," he said with a grin as Aileen crossed the room and curtsied.

"Hello, sir. Mum. Happy to make your acquaintance." She narrowed her eyes and gazed at the two for a second glance as her memory saw past his lie, then she dismissed it. "Please let me know if I can help make your stay more pleasant."

As she turned and headed for the kitchen, the others exchanged smiles. "It's not as if she would be expecting Grey to sit down to supper."

The evening passed in joyful camaraderie, dampened only by their having just missed Camisha and Ashanti. The shortness of their visit—they would leave in the morning, to ensure they were back well within 24 hours—somehow only made the moments they shared tonight much more precious.

When they'd washed and brushed their teeth for bed, Marley opened the window to let in the cooler night air. "Should we let the children sleep with us?"

"No. Will's in there with them. He's a brave and capable guardian. We can only make so many concessions to fear, and I will not have my children's bravery and courage compromised just in case a lunatic happens to make his move."

"Are you sure you're all right without Will?"

He threw back the quilt, folding it at the bottom of the bed, then pulled back the sheet.

"I have my wife." He gestured for her to slip in before him. "Wait. Remove the gown."

He saw her flush with pleasure as she debated how to answer him. Then, deliberately, she straightened before him and drew the gown up over her head, discarding it across a chair.

He leisurely inspected her in the lamplight. Then, again, he held out his hand in invitation, and she slipped into the bed, turning to watch him. His gaze never leaving her face, he removed his own clothing, watching her perusal.

When he stood naked beside the bed, she eagerly reached for him, and he took her hand and kissed it, turning her on her side, away from him. Leaning over her, he ran a long, lingering stroke over her beloved head, her shoulder, her arm, her breast, her waist, her rounded hip, her strong thigh.

He slipped in behind her, allowing himself the pleasure of full contact. He kissed her throat, murmuring in her ear, "Ray is in the next room, and I do not intend to entertain him tonight."

She abruptly turned in the bed, throwing her thigh across him and rising over him to offer her breasts to his ministrations—a gesture he could no longer deny himself.

Silently, he pleasured her with his mouth, placing his hand lightly over hers. When she moaned, he let his hand slip down to her shapely rear and lightly spanked her there—once, twice.

He cupped the back of her head, pulling her down to him and whispering in her ear, "Can you be silent? Otherwise, we shall enjoy one another the first moment they leave."

"Yes, please. Please. Please."

She grasped his wrists, again directing his hands to her breasts, and she grasped him, lowering herself astride him to tease him.

He gave a sound of pleasure against her nipple, his hands kneading her hips as he lifted her, more purposefully teasing every inch of her sensitive flesh.

"Shh," she whispered in his ear, rotating her hips over him. "Don't want to entertain Ray."

"Let me taste you. Come sit up here—on my mouth."

Instead, she whispered a blunt command in his ear, and he slid into her narrow passageway. He gave a long, deep sigh as she began to move over him. But within moments, her movements grew more eager, and her breasts swayed with seductive rhythm in the light that played over her body.

Abruptly, he pulled her close, his mouth covering her breast, then he rolled her over, and slipped her thighs over his shoulders. He moved with quick urgency as she nervously bit her lips, soft sighs of pleasure escaping, and he reached out, placing his hand over her mouth.

Her eyes flashed with a fire of arousal at his teasing domination, and as she moaned softly, he released her mouth and placed his own there, kissing her deeply.

He whispered almost silently in her ear as his fingers slipped between their bodies, touching her. "I love you so, my darling. I love you …"

He saw her eyes glisten as he felt his pleasure building, and in the end it was his own joy that he wanted to shout from the rooftop. He felt her pulsing around him in release, and a moment later he slipped to her side, tucking her close against his chest and curving around her in protection. "Dear God in heaven, I am so thankful for you in my life.

He whispered to her his love as they drifted to sleep.

They awakened to a piercing scream in the nursery.

A child's cry, then another, followed the scream. Bronson leapt out of bed as fear seized him. He grabbed his dressing gown and threw it on halfway out the door. Marley was only a few steps behind, followed by all of the others.

They arrived in the open doorway.

Above Sam's crib was a modern photograph—of Grey, Rachel, a young woman they assumed to be Emily, and three young girls—their granddaughters. It was impaled on the wall with a bloody knife, the blood dried and flaking.

Rachel and Marley were both trembling and on the verge of tears. "What is this?" Marley cried. "How could anyone have gotten in here—without even awakening the dog?

Bronson pulled the portrait down off the wall, and Marley grabbed Sam to comfort him, then drew Abby close. "Mama, what's the matter? What happened?"

Fortunately, the child hadn't seen the portrait before he pulled it down. Aileen's blood-curdling scream had likely awakened both children and set off their fearful tears.

"That's not one of our kitchen knives," Marley said. "Is it familiar to you, Bronson?"

He nodded, glancing at Ray, who also recognized it. "Aye. It was my knife. It's the knife I ... dispatched Percy Snaveling with."

Juliana grimly looked at the knife. "He died?"

"Aye."

She exhaled slowly. "It's an artifact."

"An artifact of what?" Rachel asked.

"A final artifact. It marks the time of a person's death—and events that occurred around that. We are connected to the time by the items that surround us."

"You remember the items we were given in the labyrinth?" Grey asked Rachel.

"Ah. Of course."

"What's the most important event that happened near the death of that Snaveling fellow?" Juliana asked.

"We rescued Ray."

"No," Ray said, stricken. "I mean, yes, that happened, but something more lasting was that we met George that day."

"Then this might be an artifact to use if you wanted to travel back to that time. There would likely be many others."

The couples looked at one another. Bronson reached for his frightened daughter and brought her into his arms, letting her rest her head on his shoulder.

Juliana said softly, "Someone's been in the labyrinth."

Chapter Twenty-Three

The end of the day neared, and the sight caught Camisha unawares. They had been traveling the old highway through the hills of the Piedmont to Charlottesville, and had passed through Richmond early the day before. Her husband traveled just ahead of her; ahead of him, old Thomas, leading the way. On either side of her, as if a royal entourage, rode Hasty and Silas, Ruth's son and Hattie's grandson. Bringing up the rear was George, Rashall's young son, who'd begged to come along as lookout. Her old joints ached, and she yearned for the high-tech sleep mattress she had taken for granted, forty years before. The thought made her smile as she nodded sleepily.

They passed under a low-hanging line of trees, and she looked up.

Clouds across the sky exploded with purple and orange, the sun hovering above the horizon for a moment before its swift descent. Just ahead lay the end of the Piedmont, the Blue Ridge Mountains. Beyond that, stretching out in surreal mists, stood the backbone of the Shenandoah Valley, the Massanutten Mountain ridge.

The men stopped at the sight.

"Sweet Jesus," Ashanti whispered.

"Amen." She had driven through these mountains more than once, in another life. She had viewed them from an airplane descending into Richmond. She had read news stories where insane, greedy developers were dynamiting the mountains to get at their coveted fuels. She remembered noting the grandeur of this vista, but not with the visceral reverence and wonder filling her now in the cool of the approaching evening. She had forgotten how much she loved the mountains. Before her, silhouetted in the sunset, her husband might have been leading her into the Promised Land.

In minutes the sun was gone and the sunset faded into darkness, and they hurried along the old road into Louisa. There, perhaps, they would find decent lodging for a few hours.

"How far do we have to go?" George called—just like any teenager. *Are we there yet?*

Thomas answered, being the leader and the only man in the group having traveled this far west. "We're about 40 miles from Charlottesville."

A lantern burned at the wooden shingle hanging near the side of the road, a crude painting of a cuckoo clock beneath the arch of words: *Cuckoo Tavern.* The place looked crowded.

They waited with the horses while Thomas and George entered. He soon exited. Casting Camisha an apologetic glance, he reported, "They're full. They said we're welcome to camp anywhere on the lawn. There's a nice location just over there."

"I'm so tired, I could sleep in this saddle," Silas said. "Not sure I didn't, along the way."

Camisha tried to think as she stared at the tavern sign. Something about the entire scene felt vaguely familiar to her, but she was so addled with fatigue, she couldn't clear her thoughts, let alone her memory.

It was still early in the evening, but they were all exhausted. After they ate a filling and welcome bowl of rabbit stew from the tavern, they found spots near one another under a circle of growing oaks. Ashanti lay on his back, and she curled up against his side, gazing up at the starry night.

"I see our stars out there," she said, teasing him, reminding him of their courtship, so many years ago.

"I'm that sleeping one right over there," he said, pointing.

"Sweet dreams, baby."

"Always of you."

She smiled against his chest. How many thousands of times had she heard that tender goodnight of his? Had she ever truly appreciated it as much as she should've?

"I love you, Mr. Adams."

He kissed the top of her head, hugging her hard.

She'd scarcely fallen asleep when she heard the pounding of many horses, and she awakened to find Ashanti and the others already awake, watching the approach of nattily-dressed British soldiers in white trousers.

"Green coats," a man on the lawn whispered in awe.

Ashanti gave a look of perplexed caution, uncertain what that meant.

Camisha could just make out the green of the officers' coats as they led their horses past a cresset full of burning fatwood to the watering trough and dismounted. She grabbed Ashanti's sleeve. "That's Banastre Tarleton," she whispered close to his ear, raising a finger toward the most dandified among them. "He's a merciless killer. God, protect our boys against him."

"I remember Bronson talking about him."

As the man near them had recognized him, Camisha remembered why this was all familiar. Even as she began rousing the rest, the other man was hastily rolling up his bedroll.

"Stop it, woman!" Ashanti murmured. "Be still! You know they'd soon kill us as look at us."

"No," she said. "That man there is Jack Jouett. We have to follow him, and quickly. He'll be riding fast to warn Jefferson. *That's* who they're after."

Tarleton had awakened the entire lawn, and his soldiers ignored the other travelers as they walked into the tavern seeking sustenance.

In the time it took for Camisha to hurry to her feet, Jouett was saddling his horse. "We have to go *now*," she said, shaking Thomas's shoulder. "And we have to keep up with that man."

"But—"

"Trust me. You'll see soon enough."

Jouett mounted up and ambled off unnoticed by the British, then quickly sped into a gallop. Thomas understood as well as Jouett. Tarleton's Raiders, all on the best mounts they'd been able to steal from Virginia's plantations, were well within a day's ride of Monticello.

As he rose and quickly rolled up his blanket, the others followed suit, and soon they were off.

They rode their hardest to catch up to him—just close enough to keep him in their sights. And it was a tough ride. He headed due west over an old, forgotten road, grown over and obsolete but a shortcut that Tarleton might not even know, unless he had slave guides with him.

As they rode, Camisha reflexively prayed for strength for old Thomas, for her husband, for the men and for George—but mostly for the horses that had barely had time to refresh themselves before the hardest ride of their lives. And she gave thanks that Thomas had planned as well as he had—using the first opportunity when they arrived at the tavern to refresh their water and stores.

The month of May would have already made many of the sources of drinking water they might come across a fertile breeding ground for bacteria. As it turned out, they had little time to stop and refresh themselves. Jouett set a punishing pace, but she knew he had to, if they were to make it in time.

She tried to remember the details of Jouett's ride. She knew that the storied Shawnee fighter and captive Daniel Boone, newly elected to the Virginia legislature, would also be captured by Tarleton, but released unharmed soon after. Beyond that—and a niggling sensation that the Virginians weren't too anxious about the cutthroat headed their way—she remembered little.

Knowing Jefferson and his genteel brethren, they wouldn't have been in too much of a hurry either way. Old Godfrey came to mind, and she smiled despite herself as she imagined what his reaction might be to the news that Banastre Tarleton was on his ass.

Oh, my word! We must make haste, mustn't we? That would be about as excitable as he'd get.

She wasn't completely certain, but she suspected that Jack Jouett thought they might be a party of Tarleton's men after him. They faithfully matched him, move for move. This only inspired him to ride harder, faster.

And the faster he rode, the faster they rode. Fear clawed at her, and she had the forethought to pray, quite seriously, for surefootedness for all their mounts. The Old Mountain Road was narrow and overgrown with brambles and thick vines, and it took skillful horsemanship to keep the horses steady on the cluttered path.

Camisha had enjoyed spirited riding in her youth when she and her mother had accompanied Rachel to Max Sheppard's Austin ranch, but riding lit only by the light of the full moon in rugged territory was new. Exhilaration began to edge out her weariness as she caught her second wind, stopping to relish the moment she was living, the sort of thing she'd dreamed of more than once, growing up. For a moment she remembered that—she'd even told Rachel about it when it happened.

"How could you stand to live back then? They had no toilet paper. Or toilets, for that matter!"

She smiled at the memory. She sure missed that girl.

She was thankful she'd worn a set of Ashanti's clothes for the trip—the wilderness was no place for a woman to be discovered riding unchaperoned with a band of men.

Hours passed before Jouett disappeared before them. They rode right past him where he'd turned off at a creek, as he dismounted his horse and hurried into the woods.

Thomas raised his hand to slow them, and they turned back, reining around to where Jouett was hidden behind a tree—relieving himself.

"Captain Jouett!" Camisha called, before she quite realized what he was doing.

"Camisha," Ashanti said in a low scold, explaining, just that simply, what was going on. She covered her mouth with a giggle.

They waited until Jouett hurried for his horse as she drank at the water's edge. Their horses, too, drank.

"Kind sir," Thomas called. "We are friends, patriots like yourself. We seek Governor Jefferson as you do. May we follow you?"

"You've proven you may," he responded. "But I cannot slow down for you. I hope your mounts are up to the task."

Hasty put in awkwardly, "D'you mind if we … er, quickly, that is …?"

"Yes, yes, hurry."

The group dismounted and quickly took care of their business, then hurried to catch up again as Jouette rode off.

Thomas, now by happenstance riding beside Camisha, called out to her, "Not to ask the odd question, but who is this fellow we're following across the countryside?"

"Young captain in the militia—Jack Jouett. He knows a shortcut to Monticello."

"Ah. Well. Aren't we clever."

And on they rode.

Thomas was beginning to grow pale by the time they reached the Rivanna river, in the deepest darkness before dawn. The horses crossed the shallows and they rode out, up a thickly wooded hill. And then, in the moonlit night, they saw the iconic mansion as they reached the top of the hill—Monticello.

Jouett rode up to the door and jumped off, leaving not a moment to chance. By the time they reached the mansion and dismounted—with Ashanti and George helping Thomas down—the captain was banging the door with both hands, shouting loudly. "Raiders on the way! Tarleton's dragoons! Open up, sir!"

Presently a servant opened the door cautiously, peering out. Jouett pushed his way in, shouting up the stairs, "Governor! Governor—come quick, sir! Your life and those of the legislature are in danger! Banastre Tarleton is on his way!"

Camisha and the others reached the entryway behind Jouett, looking and smelling like a band of bedraggled gypsies.

They peered in at the governor of Virginia, the third president, and the author of the Declaration of Independence. Not to mention a whole host of other accomplishments, including founding the University of Virginia.

And fathering her own family.

He descended in a dressing gown, carrying a lamp, and he might have already been awake.

"Come in, come in," he said, and the servant lit candles then closed the door behind them. "I take it you've come a long way. See that their horses are cared for," he said, aside, to the servant, who nodded and hurried to the back of the house.

"Would you like refreshment?" he asked, as he led the group through the house to the dining room. A man and a woman were already at work, preparing for breakfast.

"There's no time for that, governor. I was at the Cuckoo Tavern last evening when who should appear than Banastre Tarleton and a great number of cavalry—hundreds. They were still approaching when I rode out. I was followed by these people, whom I'm sorry to say I don't know."

Jefferson peered at Thomas. "But you, I do know. You were a burgess, some years ago, as I recall. I sat in on many a conversation when you visited while I was growing up. And I believe I went to school at William and Mary with your son."

Thomas bowed as he introduced himself. "Our business is not quite as urgent as this gentleman's, sir. It is most imperative that you secure your family and the legislature."

"Well, my family has yet to breakfast, so we shall do that, and then make these arrangements. And your name again, young man?"

"Captain John Jouett Jr., sir, with the militia here in Charlottesville. My father has a tavern across the street from the courthouse, so I knew your assemblymen must be there."

"Ah, yes, of course. The Swan Tavern. Well, make yourself at home while I dress. If you've come from Louisa since late last night, you've ridden hard."

"I cannot, sir. I must get into Charlottesville, to warn any I can. Tarleton is on his way here, sir, with all haste."

After a quick exchange of horses, he was gone again.

A servant showed the visitors a room where they could wash up, and when they returned, it was to hot, fresh coffee. Soon, they began to smell the aroma of biscuits and bacon cooking. When Jefferson joined them again, elegantly dressed for his morning escape from the gallows, they were served a hearty Southern breakfast of shirred eggs, bacon, ham, *and* sausage.

"Madame, I believe I know you as well. Forgive my poor manners. I met you in Williamsburg, just a few years ago, with Thomas's son, Bronson, and his new wife, as I recall. And perhaps your son was there as well?"

Camisha blinked. "Sir, I'm running a little slow on sleep, but ... are you not concerned about your personal welfare? We do not need to be entertained."

"May I never be so fearful that I am a poor host for my guests," he said. "My wife and children are dressing, and another guest will accompany them to a friend's house, until I can assure their safety. In the meantime—is my memory failing, or am I correct?"

"Well, yes. And I thought my mama was the epitome of Southern hospitality—but she never entertained guests while a cutthroat was breathing down her neck. Sir, this is my husband, Ashanti, and my grandson, George. Our friends, Hastings and Silas. And, of course, you know Thomas."

He nodded. Again he coaxed them to join him at the table, and they did. Color had begun to return to Thomas's cheeks, and he ate a hearty breakfast with the others.

Camisha withdrew the letter she'd penned for Jefferson to sign, along with another sheet of blank paper. "Sir, we are here today for an urgent cause that only you can accomplish."

"I will do all I can."

"There is a community of free blacks, living near Williamsburg. They were freed and deeded the estate of Thomas's eldest son, Grey, when he died. It's quite a substantial amount of acreage, and they've worked hard to improve it."

"That's good to hear. I should like to free my own slaves as soon as is possible."

She nodded, not trusting herself to speak. *Then do it, damn it! Forget the damned shirred eggs and multiple estates that go on for miles, and set them free!*

Of course, it wasn't that easy, and she knew it. But for this particular forefather and his love for wine and gracious living, it would literally be impossible. Not even at his death would he be financially able to free them—let alone during his life.

"Ma'am, would you like some fresh biscuits?"

Startled, Camisha turned. A child appeared at her elbow, smiling at her with upturned hazel eyes. A beautiful little girl, with a sparkling smile—perhaps eight years old. She was transfixed by the little girl's winsome smile, and she didn't know why.

"Thank you, yes," she said, accepting the basket and placing one of the biscuits on her plate as she passed the basket on.

"Thank you, Sally," said the governor, patting the child on her shoulder with a fatherly gesture.

"Sally?" she repeated as the child smiled adoringly at Jefferson. "Are you Sally Hemings?"

The little girl curtsied. "Yes, ma'am."

"Why, yes. You know the Hemings?"

"I believe we may be distant relatives." A safe enough excuse. She cleared her throat to steady her emotions.

What the hell was she doing, thinking he would be a likely person to sign such a document? He was the most deceptive of racists, those who loudly railed for rights for blacks while dismissing them as incapable of fending for themselves.

She desperately tried to clear her thoughts. Briefly, her mind went back nearly forty years, to when she was a young lawyer doing pro bono public defense. Her first client was a gang member who she was certain had likely committed heartless crimes against people far weaker than himself—and there was nothing, nothing in this world, that she hated more than a bully. Her mentor, an old judge who sang in her church choir, told her simply that it wasn't her job to sit in judgment of her client; just to argue the facts that supported his innocence in the particular case before the court.

Now, she grimaced at the delicately formed shirred egg in the morning light coming through the nearby window, trying to focus on what, exactly, her argument was. She didn't have to convince him to free the Trelawneys. They were already free. In a sane world, they wouldn't have to be riding across the country to get permission to live in the little village they'd built from the ground up.

Thomas seemed to be reading her mind. He reached past Ashanti to cover her hand and squeeze it. "Do I need to remind you again that you argued successfully against Peyton Randolph, the very King's attorney in the colony at the time?"

She looked at the old man—what a friend he had come to be, not only to her and her family, but to all those at Rosalie who had relied on his support for legitimacy through the years.

She focused herself. She only needed to convince Jefferson to let them stay in the community they'd built over the decades. She knew well his belief that blacks should be resettled to their home countries; that this was a belief that even some blacks believed in fervently. She would have to convince him, instead, of their service to this country, this commonwealth. In short, she had to convince him of the revolutionary idea that *this*, the only land they'd lived in their entire life, was their home country. It was her only hope.

"Sir, more than half of the Trelawneys at Rosalie—like both Hasty and Silas, here—were born on that very land. They've worked the land diligently. They now cultivate some of the finest tobacco in the Tidewater area. Not only that. They've worked even harder to educate themselves, at first grabbing every used newspaper they could find to help their children learn to read. Now they have their own school. Their own library. They attend church every Sunday, they pay taxes promptly, they give to the poor in their own need, they serve in the militia and in the Continental Army.

"You're not old enough to remember Grey Trelawney, of course. He died when you were just a tot yourself. But he was once a slave-trader. He saw nothing wrong with it, until he stopped to look at the people whose lives he destroyed. The families he destroyed. Oh, he was a *benevolent* slaveholder, if you think there is such a thing. But no one who can claim ownership of another human being should ever consider himself benevolent."

She paused, allowing the thought a moment to sink in. The man before her would be remembered as the most famous benevolent slaveholder known to history.

"And Grey immediately set it aside and sought to free his bondsmen. He died not long after that, and in doing so, his goal was accomplished. After he died, they decided to take his name as their own in gratitude for the chance that he'd given them all. You see, Governor, he had understood, having watched his bondsmen grow into a community, that *this is their home*. Most of them have no memory of Africa. They don't know the customs. They don't know the languages. These people are Christian, sir. They fight for independence in this land, sir, just like every other patriot in this land.

"I'm asking you, sir, to sign this letter I've written up for you, or to pen an irrevocable order in your own words, that the Trelawneys of Rosalie, in James City County, Virginia, and their descendants, be afforded for all time the full rights of free citizens to remain in Virginia, for meritorious works done during their decades in this country—thirty-five of those years lived as free men and women in Virginia.

"And sir, on top of that, I'm asking this as a personal favor because of the work my son, Rashall, is doing as a ... er, *courier*, shall we say, gathering intelligence for Major-General Lafayette as well as our Commander-in-chief, General Washington."

Jefferson gave her a long, shrewd look. "Your son works for Lafayette?"

She nodded. "Yes, sir."

Thoughtful blue eyes looked out toward the rising sun, and they all heard the noise of his family coming down the stairs.

She glanced at Ashanti, who squeezed her hand in encouragement—as if to say, *Good closing argument.*

Then she saw Thomas wink at her reassuringly.

Jefferson looked up. "You realize that today is June fourth ... and that my term ended yesterday."

She gave an audible sigh of disappointment. All this distance, putting Thomas through such a stressful night ... "Oh, sir, I'm so sorry, I didn't know. Please, be on your way. The men will arrive soon. Thank you for listening to me."

He glanced at her even as he reached for a bottle of ink and quill that she suspected was never far away, and he read what she'd written, wrote a few lines beneath it, and signed it. He presently passed the finished document back to her. Despite all she'd seen in her life, the scrawled *Th. Jefferson* thrilled her.

He had added his own note. "And irrevocably, the Trelawneys of Williamsburg are industrious free Americans welcome in Virginia or any other state of their choosing—forever. Dated June 3, 1781."

Jefferson's wife, Martha, entered then, with three little girls behind her—her daughters Martha and Polly, and Sally between them—Camisha's own ancestor. She was only mildly surprised to have realized that this child, a slave, looked as white as the half sisters with whom she was about to sit down to breakfast. What a confused, ridiculous world she lived in.

She ached with everything in her to hold that child to her heart, and to thank her for everything she'd endured that she and her own children might know freedom.

What a world it might have been, she thought, if any of our leaders in this or the next century had had any sense about human relations. They would have given people incentive to marry other races. Maybe they'd give folks another ten acres for every beautiful mixed baby they had.

Imagine how much less strife, she marveled, when we saw all kinds of interesting people emerge in the human tapestry. Race would have been nothing. Instead, our leaders clung to the lie of race to serve their own greed. And in that greed, they kept us in the darkness of hatred—as they would attempt to do for nearly three more centuries. Until the people said, *Enough.*

Chapter Twenty-Four

The three sisters stood there on the old, overgrown lawn of Rosalie—now, little more than a field—attempting to put off the inevitable.

The youngest watched as Marley, lips pressed tightly together, took a deep breath and spoke. "I almost wish you hadn't come at all. Forgive me. I had no idea it would hurt so much. You were still just that little girl in my memory and now, I know you. And it's as if you're ..." She shook her head, dissolving in silent tears.

Rachel nodded, abruptly hugging both sisters close. "I know, but I'm not. I'm alive and well, just ... elsewhere. Something I've learned from all this is that everything really is happening at once. Time is ..." She tried to find words to describe it.

"Time is a construct of God to put order in the universe, and seasons in our lives," Juliana said.

"Yes. We *will* meet again. Ask old Ruth about 'someday in Glory.' She's the one who taught me. I love you, my sweet little sisters—so much. Take care of one another, and love each other."

As the younger women returned to their husbands, Juliana and Rashall watched Bronson attempting to negotiate with his brother.

"I will not let you leave until you assure me you'll be back when you say. Jack Manning means to settle this—and until we do, we live in fear. I now have four men from Rosalie flocking about Aileen and the children, and I'm still uneasy."

He spoke as if Grey and Rachel were stepping through the entryway of the old plantation house for dinner—rather than walking through a dimension in time to go forward nearly three centuries.

Grey nodded. "Your Friday night at midnight. At the labyrinth. By then you should know more about the dagger."

"'Tis mine, I'm certain. The blood must be Snaveling's."

"Did you leave the knife in him?"

"What difference does that make?" Bronson asked, as he tried to remember.

"You remember having lost track of the knife soon after his death. If you kept it, you certainly would have cleaned it of Snaveling's blood. I think the blood may be someone else's— perhaps even someone Manning himself killed."

"Honey, we have to go now. We only have a few minutes to spare." Rachel checked the pendant watch that had been her passport to this time. She flashed a wry smile at the women. "I can't take him anywhere. He just goes on and on."

The reality of Grey's travel sank in, and Bronson hugged his older brother hard. The sight brought tears to Juliana's eyes. How different they might have been, had they known each other through the years.

"'Tis but a sojourn," Grey said.

And she wasn't sure whether he spoke of this separation— or life itself.

The older couple moved to the entryway of Rosalie, stopped for a moment to look back at their loved ones, then faced the old ruins. Grey placed his arm around Rachel's shoulders. They gazed into the portal for a long moment, and then walked through—dissolving into nothingness.

Bronson clapped Rashall on the back. "Let's go."

Having access to Thomas's horses made the ride to Stonefield much swifter than their long, meandering hikes. The

June day was already hot and muggy in the Tidewater. As they rode through the village, as busy as a hive, several waved as they passed. She heard the choir practicing in the meetinghouse.

By the time they forded a shallow, stony spot in the Chickahominy River late that day, she was as weary as the others, and had begun to be unnerved by their supernatural comings and goings. Truth to tell, she wasn't quite sure Uncle Malcolm would approve of it, although Grey had reassured her that he had. It made her wonder what Malcolm was up to.

They made camp once, to rest the horses and nap. Late the next day, they rode through a rainstorm on their last mile, and arrived at Stonefield soaked and chilled.

"I miss Will," she said, handing out towels.

"Thank you for leaving him to protect the children," Marley said.

"Oh, he's much better off there for now. Is anyone hungry?"

"I'm too tired to be hungry," Rashall said. "I think we should get a good night's sleep."

Bronson nodded. "But just for my own sanity, why don't we secure the place up here, and run down and check to make sure we're alone."

"There's another exit through the root cellar," Rashall told him.

When Juliana opened the window seat, revealing the circular stairwell, Marley shook her head in disbelief. "The years I grew up here. I never knew that was down there. How obedient and dull *was* I?"

"It might not have been open for you. Mainly because of either our grandmother, or Jimmy, her abusive partner."

"What do you mean?"

Juliana hesitated. "Well, usually the system tells you if there's an anomaly in time—that is, you may already exist in the time you're trying to travel to. It usually has to do with conflicts in your own existence. Perhaps, because of the ethical issues with Hannah or Jimmy, the window seat was closed. Or if the system is a creation of the government, they might have physically closed it off at some point."

"Our father was in the Navy—do you suppose he was a part of its development?"

Juliana shrugged. "Anything's possible. Come with me."

Marley and the others followed her down. "There are 674 steps. So don't worry. It takes a few minutes the first time."

Partway down, Ray stopped them. She had to lean backward to hear him speak down to the others. His deep voice was hushed.

"What if someone's down there?"

"What do you think?" Marley asked. "You're both armed, aren't you?"

"That's not exactly the point."

Bronson and Rashall exchanged a look, and Ray shook his head slowly.

"Yes, that's true," Bronson said, as if he'd read Ray's mind. "No one down there can be up to any good. The best we can do is defend ourselves and send him away. Live to fight another day, that sort of thing."

"And that goes double if it's Manning."

Marley frowned at Rashall. "But he needs to be stopped— and the only way I think you're going to stop him is to kill him."

"No," Juliana said. "When we kill him, his deeds are frozen in time. Whatever he may have done in the future."

"But this is before that future." Marley said.

"Not on his lifeline. He's skipped around, who knows where, doing who knows what. *This* is what's meant by an anomaly. People are meant to live a linear life, not pop in and out of millennia as if they're shops on the square, leaving imprints behind, everywhere they go. Our grandmother unleashed a lunatic in time. We should have learned from her mistakes."

"Dear God, I'm so tired, I can't think. I understand now."

They continued down and at last caught on to the rhythm, and soon they arrived at the stone floor. Silently, they peered around. She saw the wonder in Marley and Bronson, and the alertness in her husband. He scanned the area nearest them, then joined her as she led them through the passageway.

Marley emerged under the labyrinth sky, her eyes widening. Juliana saw the place through her eyes—over the past two decades, she'd almost come to take the vista for granted.

The cavern seemed to stretch out forever, its sky overhead showered with the constellations that represented the people of all time. The endless, serpentine passageways on the ground disappeared into the distance. Cool mist rose in tendrils from the ground as it always seemed to. In this time before electricity, this system somehow existed. She had attempted to understand that before, but for her, it was as impossible a concept to comprehend as forever.

As the others absorbed the sights around them, she murmured softly, "It's a wonderful place to sleep, in the summer. I used to come down here every night in August with Will, especially when I was afraid, or lonely."

Marley looked at her. "Were you here all alone?"

"Oh, no. I had Will."

Compassion filled her sister's face at Juliana's cheerful response, and she hugged her. Juliana wasn't quite sure what she'd said to upset her, but she was pretty sure she was being pitied, and she never liked that.

Take care of one another, and love each other.

Juliana remembered Rachel's words and hugged her sister.

Rashall had been uncharacteristically silent, and she saw him gazing up, worry etched around his mouth. She followed his gaze, finding the small constellation that had been born when he proposed to her, the last time they visited this place.

It was still shining brightly—but one of the other asterisms connected to him had begun to flicker. "What does that mean?" he asked. "The last time we were here, that grouping had a slow, steady rhythm and a bright silver color to it. Now it's in distress."

"I'm not sure. It's probably just a temporary condition. Sometimes they do fluctuate."

"Do you think my parents could be in danger, wherever they are? Is this sky ... er, is its information current?

"Yes. That's why we saw the new formation just as we were engaged. They call that 'real time,' she said with a chuckle. "Real time indeed. Oh, I almost forgot!"

She reached into her pocket for the small bundle wrapped in oilcloth. She unwrapped the dagger that Grey and Rachel had brought with them from the twenty-first century.

She approached the reader and it glowed purple in the shape of the dagger, startling Bronson. Once again, the system didn't speak to her familiarly, as it did when she was alone. She placed her hand on the reader.

"Good evening, Juliana. Present your artifact."

"I do not wish to travel tonight, but I would like to identify this item and whether it's a final artifact. If so, I wish to return it to its rightful place."

"Present the artifact."

Careful not to handle it without the oilcloth, she pressed the artifact against the reader and stepped back.

A few moments later, the voice spoke. "No index entry, no travel available with this item. Organic matter contains the DNA of Robert Miller and Cassandra Hastings Miller. Fingerprints on the item include those of John Manning, Sheppard Manning, Grey Trelawney, and Bronson Trelawney."

"What do you mean, no index entry?"

Several seconds passed in silence.

"What does that mean?"

"The item was formerly an artifact but was used in the murder of Robert and Cassandra Miller. Multiple anomalies occurred during its use, resulting in a permanent stack failure. System self-restored after catastrophic crash."

"Stop speaking in technical jargon!" Juliana interrupted.

No response.

"Please explain to us what happened in English."

"The system allowed travel that should not have been authorized, by a traveler who was not adequately authenticated, resulting in a fatal system error."

"Please!"

"The traveler, John Manning, also known as Jack Sheppard, bypassed system protocol in an unexpected system event. Artificial intelligence has recovered and restored all system information. The item was neutralized as an artifact and no longer enables travel."

The group looked at one another, attempting to take it all in.

The system added, "The murder of the Millers was a violation of terms of service. We regret any inconvenience this may have caused."

Juliana looked as if she'd been slapped. Marley shook her head. Bronson frowned, attempting to understand. "Any ... *inconvenience*? Why ... *what* ...?"

Marley shrugged. "It's a supercomputer—a very advanced supercomputer. I can't imagine this coming from anywhere except the Department of Defense. It may be able to recognize you, but it's having a difficult time saying in plain English, 'We screwed up. He shouldn't have known about time travel, let alone been enabled to do so by one of your dumb relatives.' The verbiage is legalese. Not sure who they're expecting us to sue at this point for, oh, the deaths of our parents."

Rashall was rubbing his temples. "I say we go to bed, get up early and go from there."

The others chimed in their agreement. As Juliana attempted to retrieve the dagger, the reader flashed, and she jerked her hand away. A cylinder descended from the cavern ceiling around the reader—something she'd never seen before. A moment later, the cylinder vanished again. The dagger was gone.

"Where's our knife?" she asked.

"The item has been isolated in suspended containment and can no longer be accessed. We regret any inconvenience this may have caused."

"All right," Bronson said, leading them back to the stairs. "That's about all the fantastic tales my beleaguered brain can take in tonight."

They arrived back upstairs, and Juliana brushed her teeth, grateful for the rainstorm that had washed away the grime of the ride, if not their exhaustion. As she slipped into bed beside her weary husband, they soon found themselves falling asleep. But just before she slept, the thought came to her, and she asked the question aloud.

"Ray?"

After a long moment, he murmured, "Hm?"

"What about Sheppard Manning? What were his fingerprints doing on the knife?"

He turned over on his back, drawing her to his side. "He was the more sane of the two—correct?"

"That's what Rachel said. He was the one who raised her."

She tried, but she had to let the thought go. Sleep had claimed her at last.

Chapter Twenty-Five

"Our Commander-in-chief is without a strategy," Lafayette said. "And as glad as I was to learn of your wedding, Martin also brought news of Phillips' death."

"It isn't as if you required my comfort, sir," Rashall said.

"No, but I had tucked away a bottle of brandy to celebrate, and it went undrunk."

He winced. "Oh, sir. My apologies indeed."

"You alone can appreciate the sacrifice."

Rashall nodded.

"However," Lafayette added, leaning near, "I do thank you for the ... er, charming company, you have brought. Tonight we shall drink the brandy to celebrate. Other wives travel with us, but none so comely nor delightful."

He nodded, his eyes drifting to where his wife stood, helping the company cook dish out rabbit stew. They'd considered having her disguised as a male aide of Rashall's, but the complications had been endless. Even now, he smiled inwardly at how the men would react to see him casting such adoring glances at another soldier. Heavens, the stir that would make.

"But do you notice the few none-too-adoring looks, sir?"

"How so?"

"Consider Wainwright, there."

"Not this again. Well. Pity the boy, he does not come from the brightest lineage."

Wainwright sat alone before a fire, cooking a squirrel he'd caught and skinned. Little more than a rat. Quite literally, he would rather starve than eat the cooking of what he saw as the white wife of a black man. Never mind that the black man happened to be the good friend of the major general.

A long moment passed before Lafayette took a deep breath and leaned back against his pack where they sat on the ground in a circle of oaks.

"My friend, consider this moment. We sit in leisure at our noonday meal. We have a meal Louis and George would do battle over, served to us by a woman you happen to adore. Last night's rain storm washed us clean—a state, you assure me, that's in fact quite healthy. And it washed the countryside free of humidity so that this hour we enjoy a cool breeze. Our bones are intact, and William Phillips abides with the angels— or the opposite. The other men find your wife as much a delight as I do, and the only feeling they have toward you is envy. And should we instead focus on the knowledge that Cornwallis, Tarleton, and Simcoe all roam the countryside in search of us?"

Rashall leveled a look at his friend and commander. "In truth, Louis and George would battle over which is better— cote de boeuf or Sunday roast."

The Frenchman gave a guttural groan. "Oh, you cannot compare the two! Cote de boeuf is a tender gastronomical wonder. What the English do to beef should be punishable by time in the Bastille."

He stopped, noticing Rashall's amusement, and smiled himself. "I have missed you, my friend." And then: "I say it again—you should come to France. There are very few Wainwrights there. People would look at you and see only a young couple in love."

"You tempt me mightily, sir. I as much as announced this intention at my wedding, and I might have mentioned my own suicide, from my mother's reaction."

"Why? She does not like the French?"

Rashall took a deep breath, knowing the danger involved in warning people of their fate, even with the best of motives. "I believe that she observes your work for the equal rights of mankind in this country and she sees in your immediate future a revolution of your own, perhaps as violent as this one."

"Your mother is a wise woman. It is inevitable. So you saw her at your wedding. Is she in Virginia now?"

He laughed. "Believe it or not, she's in Charlottesville, lobbying Thomas Jefferson to declare the freed slaves of Rosalie permanent residents of Virginia."

"This is remarkable why?"

"The slave codes say that any freed slave must leave the commonwealth within six months of emancipation."

"And they were freed…thirty years ago, I think you said?"

"Thirty-five."

"Pah. Slave codes. An entire insane set of principles based on greed and ignorance. The sooner it dies, the better."

"All of its principles are deeply embedded in this country. The very idea of race itself as being more than a social construct, for example. You don't think the fair Bostonians believe that blacks are truly equal, do you?"

Lafayette frowned, as if fearing his English skills had failed him. "Pardon?"

"There is just as much distrust of blacks in the northern states—perhaps more, for its deviousness. At least the contemptible slave owners of South Carolina admit that the economy depends on free labor. The most free-thinking among the north believe that blacks should be freed and returned to Africa. What connection do American blacks have with Africa other than its role in selling its own brothers into bondage?"

Lafayette nodded. "What you say is true, when I consider it. And you are right that its insidiousness disguises it. People oppose slavery—but look at the segregation in New England."

"There you go. Sir, I do wonder how useful I am to you with Arnold now back in New York."

"I understand your reordered priorities and release you from service if that is your desire."

"You're joking. You've hanged men for deserting."

"Men, yes. Not you."

"Why, thank you."

"You are my friend and you have a very delicious morsel of a bride."

"Sir!"

Lights twinkled in Lafayette's eyes. "You know I adore my own Adrienne. Do not be simple-minded. I mean delicious morsel in the most respectful of terms."

"But of course."

The Frenchman went on, his passion rising into a rant. "Soon this thing will come to a head. But it will not without the attention of the Comte de Grasse and Rochambeau. Fortunately our Commander-in-chief is a humble man and, while he requires loyalty and devotion, he recognizes the need for what he does not have. He has no navy to speak of. What few ships Virginia had, Arnold destroyed at Osborne's Landing. Only now, after years of training with von Steuben, does he have any kind of an army—certainly not equal to England's. And I continue to be shocked at how little his very own homeland, this Virginia, supports him in his noble fight. They seemingly would rather have their fine horses seized by their very enemy than to give them to those who fight for them. And so we plod along as sitting ducks while Tarleton's men heartlessly plunder the plantations, wreaking his terror astride the finest Virginia stallions."

"The only saving grace we have in that area is that the Loyalists have no interest in fighting, either. That surprised Cornwallis. The King had believed that, especially in the South, they would willingly take up arms against their patriot brethren."

"Yes. And now, our commander must recognize that the fight is here, on Virginia soil. He is obsessed with New York— and I fear it will continue until we are surrounded and slaughtered.

"This devil Cornwallis is much wiser than the other generals with whom I've dealt. He inspires me with sincere fear, and he troubles my sleep. I learn from him—and only hope that these people do not pay for my lessons."

Nearby, one of the younger soldiers was humming a popular tune. Presently, he began to sing, and several others joined in.

> *In a chariot of light from the regions of day,*
> *The Goddess of Liberty came;*
> *Ten thousand celestials directed the way,*
> *And hither conducted the dame.*
> *A fair budding branch from the gardens above,*
> *Where millions with millions agree,*
> *She brought in her hand as a pledge of her love,*
> *And the plant she named Liberty Tree...*

The sound of a horse's hooves bearing down broke off their song, and a rider rode into camp—Martin. He brought his horse to a halt a few feet away and swung off, bowing and saluting to the major-general and handing him a letter.

"There was a skirmish at Charlottesville."

Rashall stood, alarmed. "What do you mean? Was there a battle?"

"Tarleton was there. He learned that the legislature had retired there from Richmond and swarmed in. A captain of the militia named Jouett noticed them near Louisa and rode through the night to warn the assembly.

"Tarleton must have rested his men, for Jouett outpaced him by a couple of hours at least. It's rumored Jefferson ran like a coward to Carter's Mountain, rather than staying with his assembly."

Rashall grabbed his arm. "But—Mother's up there, with Father and Thomas and two of your brothers. Did you happen to hear news of them?"

"I did not. Tarleton captured some of the assemblymen, most of whom he paroled on the spot. Jefferson was his prize, but he escaped."

Lafayette looked up from the letter. "Clinton is telling Cornwallis to take up a position in Portsmouth or Yorktown. How many weeks ago did he say he did *not* support such a move? And I'm supposing that he's frustrated at Cornwallis's sense of authority and autonomy. He hints without saying so outright. These men exhaust me. They alternately despise and defer to one another."

Martin nodded. "Cornwallis is in Williamsburg. He has seven thousand men with him."

"And us with perhaps four thousand, including Anthony Wayne's troops," Lafayette mused, folding the letter and tapping it against his other palm.

"Then my task now is to flip a coin over Mad Anthony, who no doubt has taken it in his head to engage the general with his paltry command, all of whom would rather be enjoying a lovely New England summertime than sweltering in this southern Purgatory. I am a divided man with Wayne, who is indeed mad ... and yet sure enough in his audacity to inspire the sanest among us."

He put the letter away and stood, shaking his head. He looked at Rashall with a fond smile. "Go home. Take your bride and ride for home. Hope that by the time you are bored and have a little one underfoot, this war will be won and we might toast one another. As for me, the brandy shall have to wait."

Chapter Twenty-Six

Grey parked at the curb in front of the old frame home. The woman inside had lived there since her daughter had vanished, thirty-five years before. She herself had grown up in the home.

As he helped the children out of the back, he instructed Cammie, "Now you're in charge of your sisters, all right? You know how old Mama Helen is."

In fact, she was 83—but sometimes it was hard to tell. She had the energy of a much younger woman, especially when they visited. He prayed that what he had to ask her today would not be more than she might be able to bear.

"Of course, Papa," Cammie said. "I'll look after them."

"Did you bring your books and crayons? We're on a tech-free vacation, you know."

"I know, Papa. I saw you get lost on the freeway."

"Good show."

The truth of it was, they were attempting to wean the children off of their gadgets. Just in case.

As Emily took charge of the children, he walked ahead with Rachel up the sidewalk. He fit his key in the lock and turned, tapping at the door even as he glanced inside.

But he heard her singing before he saw her.

"Mama Helen?"

"I'm in here, honey."

He stepped aside to let the family pass. The last time they'd visited Helen had been at Christmas. She had become an adopted grandmother to the children—as well as a mother to Tate, who'd never known his mother. No small coincidence to Grey that a singer whose meteoric rise hung on a single song about a lost family, had in fact grown up in foster homes, never knowing his own family. By the time he met Emily— while making an appearance at a foundation Grey had begun for fatherless boys—he'd written, recorded, and sold several platinum collections. His music was highly sought after, because each collection told a story—unlike the individual releases virtually all musicians recorded today. The cover story about him on a major news magazine last year was titled: RETURN OF THE ALBUM: TATE SOTHERN REVIVES THE ART OF MUSICAL STORYTELLING. Other artists had recently begun to release music in collections again.

Grey cleared his mind of those thoughts. *I'm thankful we had him as long as we did. And I'm thankful to believe that he loved the family we gave him as much as we loved him.*

They walked through the living room and into the kitchen at the back of her home. He remembered the last time they'd visited Helen with Tate along; he'd been thrilled with the old woman's home, and Grey understood why. It just felt like *home*.

For the love of God, why was Tate inhabiting his mind again?

The room probably looked much the same as it had a hundred years before, except that Grey and Rachel had made certain the appliances were state of the art. Yet still designed in the mid-twentieth century lines Helen loved. So Helen had what, hopefully, felt to her like her old Frigidaire icebox and her old Cookmaster stove.

She rose from the table, smiling. It always startled Grey a little, when he noticed she'd gotten a little older. He'd seen her just weeks before. He'd known this woman longer than her own daughter had, and while he couldn't have loved her as Camisha had, he loved her as he would have loved his own mother.

The children reached her first, of course, and she bent down to hug them as they hugged her legs. Cammie, growing up fast and always tall, still only reached her shoulder.

"Are you children hungry?"

"Did you make sugar doodles, Mama Helen?" Lucy, the youngest, asked.

Cammie rolled her eyes. "Snickerdoodles, Lucy."

Helen gave Lucy a wide-eyed smile as she reached for the cookie jar and placed it on the table. "I sure did. Miss Camisha, You know how to serve up cookies and milk for you and your sisters. You can relax and play your games right there, or go on in to your playroom, if you like." Then, as the girls ran to the playroom: "Can I get you older children some coffee?"

They hugged and chitchatted and soon settled in the cozy living room. The words for describing the style were quaint and ironic—mid-century, they still called it, when they were firmly in the middle of another century. And *modern*. Now, at least, they called it *retro modern*, whatever that could possibly mean. The couch was a bright yellow, the chairs blue and green, their wooden legs straight and plain. Many of the knick-knacks, such as the large wall mirror behind Helen, were older, from Helen's mother's own childhood. Although her cherished, embroidered armrest doilies of a duck and her ducklings were perhaps even pre-World War II, they seemed to complete her homey décor.

Emily reached into her bag and withdrew the small package she'd brought for Helen, setting it aside for now.

Small talk had never held much allure for Grey. Despite his genteel upbringing, he had quickly acquired a fondness for the directness that came so naturally to his wife. It had taken him a little longer to develop the trait on his own. But the woman before them reminded him of her daughter, and he understand why Rachel was so fond of her. She, too, was plain-spoken and direct. And, thanks to Rachel, Emily had never lost her tendency to be too blunt.

So with all four as direct as they were, it made sense that for a long moment, they were entirely silent, merely looking at one another in expectation. They weren't here just to catch up. They had a purpose.

Finally Helen laughed. "It seems you have something to say. Am I mistaken?"

Rachel looked to Grey, and he shook his head. "No, Helen, you're correct. I'm just not sure how to ask."

"Baby doll, any question you have, just ask me. But none of us are getting any younger, so maybe you'd better get it out."

"Papa, why not begin with our gift?"

"Yes. That's best. Go ahead."

Emily held out the gift to Helen. "I hadn't ever seen this before Rachel showed it to me, so I don't know whether you've seen it."

She made a great show of delight over the gaily wrapped gift and opened it with care. "It just looks so beautiful."

At last she revealed the photograph and gasped. "Oh! It's my Cameron! And Cassie and Rob, and his parents. And of course, you girls," she said, smiling at Rachel.

"So you ... knew my family?"

"We were the best of friends."

Rachel looked at him, confused—clearly unsure what to say. *Why the hell didn't you tell us?* seemed a little harsh.

Helen gave a soft chuckle. "Oh, I'm sorry, baby doll. I didn't want to stir up anything painful for you."

Rachel shook her head. "I'd have given anything to hear the smallest story about them."

"Well, this night, we went to a banquet at Annapolis. Rob and his father both wore their dress whites. Cameron had been an officer, too, but by then he was prouder of being a police captain. We were living in Boston, by then. Moved up there to be closer to his mother. We took my mother along, too, but after ... well, I never liked the cold weather, and neither did Mama, and so after Cam was gone ... we moved back to this house of Mama's. He'd left me comfortable enough so that I didn't have to worry anymore."

"Wait."

Helen looked at Rachel.

"Max always acted as if he was saving you and Camisha from a hellish existence. You were fine?"

"We were well enough off, I could send her to law school."

"I thought Max did that."

"Did he *say* he did?"

"He hinted that he gave you the money. I don't know whether Camisha knew the truth or not. I thought you were there because it was a better life."

"Hannah had signed over her rights. I'm not judging, maybe he bullied her, too. He was good at that, you know. Honey, we were there because I loved your mama and your daddy and you didn't have anyone in this world to protect you from that man."

"So you *know*?"

"Anybody with eyes to see knew he was a bad man. Bully a little girl till she couldn't say her own name. I just wish we'd never left Virginia."

He smiled. "All right. Do you remember the first time we visited you? Or at least the first time I met you?"

"Of course I do. You brought me the letter from my little girl. And the portrait of her." Subtly, her gaze moved toward the wall just beside her, where the painting hung.

Rachel had been glancing at the portrait since they'd sat down—of Bronson, Rashall, Thomas Jefferson—and Camisha, hovering behind them with a smile.

He saw Rachel look down, gathering her strength. And likely remembering her friend.

"We never talked much about that," he said. "I was sure that when you wanted to talk about it, you would. But you never did."

"Honey, what do you want to know?"

Thirty years of proper English upbringing surfaced, numbing his tongue. He looked to Rachel in desperation.

"Helen, what did Camisha say in her letter?" she asked. "We were vague about what had happened because we didn't want to upset you—but you read her letter and never spoke of it again. We honestly don't know what she told you."

"Well, I recognized the man in that portrait as our third president, didn't I?"

Helen reached into the drawer of the end table and withdrew the letter, handing it to Rachel. *Mom* was written across the front. She gently opened the letter.

"Read it out loud, Rae, will you?" the old woman asked softly.

She looked up quickly, and he knew she was remembering that only one other person had ever called her that.

Christmas 1746

Dear Mom,

I write this today with the hope that someday you may get it. I will look for ways to make that happen as soon after the date I disappeared as possible. I know you'll be worried when we haven't spoken even one day.

It was the hardest decision I've ever had to make, and yet it was never mine to make. You always taught me to stand up for myself and my loved ones. Mom, I'm married now to a free man who was born in 1714, in Boston. He's a good man, a strong Christian, and he owns a couple of shops here in Boston where he makes a good living. His brother is a gunsmith, and the entire family works for the abolition of slavery. Mom, I think you would be thrilled to know that we befriended none other than Crispus Attucks and helped him escape his enslavement to a new life as a sailor. He promises to come back and see us when he returns to port, and I believe he will, although it would be terribly dangerous, as we still see public notices demanding his return. We are building a home in Beacon Hill, and we are very happy.

I am pregnant with our first child, and I miss you so much. Every day I miss you. Every day I have questions, and I don't know who to ask. I'm meeting people here, but I'm afraid. I don't want you to worry about me, though. You taught me to be strong and have pride in who I am. I keep wanting to tell you how much I miss you, but please just know that I think of you and pray for you every day.

I see much needless suffering here. People drink dirty water and get sick and die. They don't bathe because they think it's unhealthy to do the very things that would save their lives. And people in my old life think they have it hard if they are inconvenienced and miss an appointment.

I know how difficult all of this must be to believe, but I am hoping, by the time you get this, to have found a tangible way to prove that it's true. I am not sure as I write this what that will be, but I'll think of something. My only regret in all this is that I did not know in advance what would happen. I would have hugged you a little longer, the last time I saw you. I would have told you, again, how much I love you. I would have thanked you for all the sacrifices you made in your life so that I could have a good life. We both know what a terrible person Max Sheppard was, but I also know you stayed so that I could have a good education, and I thank you for that, and so many countless other things you gave, that I can never even remember, let alone repay.

Please know that when my first daughter is born, I will name her after you. You were always the most beautiful woman in the world. And I look forward to that day, so I can hear your name spoken again, in happiness, in my home.

I pray for you every morning and every night, Mom. I will always cherish the memory of the sound of your voice. And I hope for that day when we're all back together in Glory.

I love you, Mom
Camisha

Rachel accepted the handkerchief Emily passed her, and she dabbed at her eyes. She swallowed, folded the letter, and handed it back to Helen.

"Did you have any trouble believing it?" she asked.

Helen shook her head thoughtfully. "No. It just hurt to know that somehow, my little girl had already been gone on to heaven for a long time. It's just not natural, losing your children before you were born."

What she said wasn't amusing, but he could see so much of Camisha's reflective humor in her that he almost laughed. She had a gift for absurdity.

"Well, what if there were a way for you to see her again?"

Helen looked at her fearfully. "I don't believe in any such thing as séances or black magic, Rachel. You know I'm a Christian woman."

"I know that. I wouldn't suggest it."

"What if we told you we visited the eighteenth century a few days ago?"

At Grey's question, she seemed to fear he was mocking her. "What do you *mean*?"

"Just that. If we could take you to visit her, would you want to go?"

She looked at each of them for a long moment. "I don't understand what you're asking me. She's dead, son. She's gone to live with Jesus. Is that what you're asking me? Because you know that's up to the Lord to take me, not me to decide. Lord, if it was up to me, I'd have been gone thirty-five years now. Day I heard my baby was gone."

"I know." Rachel reached out her hands. "But think about the fact that Camisha *did* go back to a different time in history. What if we could take you to where she is, the same way?"

Her eyes narrowed in a shrewd stare. "Me go back."

"Yes."

"How?"

"Well, don't worry about that for now. But would you want to?"

"Go see my baby?"

Rachel nodded. "She's my age now, Helen. Same as she would've been if—"

"Hand me my purse. How soon can we leave?" She stood up from the chair.

This time, Grey laughed.

"Now you have to think about it. There are some rules to time travel. You can't stay longer than a day, or else you'll spend the rest of your life there."

"You were there longer than a day, weren't you?"

"This is different. When you plan a trip, you have to follow some rules. You have to be prepared."

"Oh, I see what you mean. I was just thinking I needed to refill my blood pressure medication." She stopped short. "Now what about that?"

Rachel took a deep breath. "I won't lie to you. You know how backward medicine was back then. They didn't even have vaccines. Some people, like Camisha, are brave enough to inoculate their families against some diseases, like smallpox. But things like artificial hearts and overnight organ replacement, like we have today …"

But Helen was already shaking her head. "That's all right. I'm an old woman. If I can just be with her for five minutes—just to hug her, one more time—I can die a happy woman."

Rachel looked at Grey, tears standing in her eyes. He nodded. Where had he heard that before?

The rest of his plans had to be left unspoken, for now. It was too large for discussion. The wheels in his mind went into motion, calculating all they had left to do.

Transfer the foundations they'd established into trustworthy hands.

He thought of the man who'd adopted Rachel, as he so often did. For all the evil he had done, his money had done a great deal of good since it had come into her possession, years ago, when he died.

His mind went back to planning. They would need to sell their homes. Determine whether any trinkets were worthy of attempting to take with them. Visit the pediatrician to make sure necessary shots were current. He was distracted at the prospect of the doctor—should he and the other adults visit the internist once more, for the road? Both he and Rachel had had preventive replacements the year before.

He shook his head free of the distractions as the children ran into the kitchen, ready for cookies. "Papa," Cammie called, "don't forget our gadgets need recharging, when our break is over."

Without a doubt, the hardest preparation would be to de-tech the children. Technology could a blessing—heavens, how he would miss hot showers and cold A/C—but increasing AI had insinuated itself into each nook and cranny of their lives, partly under its own power. Now, it was up to him and Rachel and Emily to teach them that joy was far superior to entertainment.

Chapter Twenty-Seven

Marley stared at her husband pacing the oak floor near the window seat. "Why don't you sit here and rest? You're probably going to need your energy tonight."

He sat on the sofa beside her, tapping his fingers on his knees.

She couldn't blame him. They were both people of action, and they'd been reduced to endless waiting. Waiting for Camisha to return from Charlottesville with word of her success. Waiting for Grey to return, to put an end to the persistent threat of the Mannings. Even the war seemed to be in a macabre minuet, with Cornwallis chasing Lafayette, who was waiting for the arrival of Mad Anthony Wayne, the general from Pennsylvania. And everyone awaited the grand entrance of the French fleet—Cornwallis with healthy dismay, Lafayette like a child at Christmas.

"Let's leave him a note and go on down," Bronson said, rising again.

"The descent only takes a few minutes, and there's nowhere to relax down there. What if he's been delayed?"

"Then I shall go on, myself."

"Oh no, you won't."

"I can at least conduct a scouting mission."

"Bronson, you know I can be helpful."

"No, in this case you cannot. The Mannings are playing a mortal game of whist, and they seem to hold all the cards."

"I don't think his brother is involved. I believe it's more a game of chess, with a lunatic making up rules with each move."

"I do not care a whit the metaphor used."

"I'm just reminding you that both of their fingerprints were on that dagger, not just Jack's."

"And I'm reminding you the lunatic held a dagger above our sleeping son and daughter, and I do not wish to wait for him any longer."

With that, he crossed the room in two strides and climbed into the window seat stairwell, quickly descending out of earshot.

Marley scrawled a note to Grey with a sigh, weary. The nib of the quill broke, and she swore, rummaging in the drawer for a knife to trim it. "Writing with damned birds' feathers," she muttered. "No wonder we have to rely on the French to fight our battles for us."

Her life seemed to have become a disquieting combination of long stretches of desert with periodic monsoons. For a mad moment, she yearned for the old comforting sensation of working in a dig. Oh, it was tedious, sometimes backbreaking, work, but in those moments, elbow-deep in historic Virginia soil with her mind at peace, she knew she was where she was supposed to be on this earth.

With that, her spirits sank as she recalled her last visit to town. Unconsciously, she had begun to avoid Williamsburg. Each visit was a new reminder of the work she had left behind, and the long, sleepy era stretching out ahead for the village, for the rest of her natural days. Like others whose shops had vanished with each visit, she no longer had a reason to visit the old capital. They still had market days, but they were nothing like they'd been before, when people had come from miles around to attend court, to settle business—to spend money. That revenue stream had trickled up the James into Richmond.

And in her own time, had it been any better? Sometimes there seemed to be so little interest in history—in learning the lessons of the past. Her job had been a labor of love—like all her fellow workers at the Foundation. But too many others her own age preferred to deny the past, to pretend it had never happened. How many in her time piously railed against slavery of the past—ignoring the tens of millions enslaved around the globe in their own, enlightened time, imprisoned and toiling in menial jobs and in the sex industry, even in this very country.

Doctor Goodwin came to mind—the rector of old Bruton Parish Church who'd started the whole thing back in the 1920s. She gave a wry smile. What a complex vision he had had. Living in a sleepy old town that time forgot, he'd seen instead the vibrant eighteenth century village underneath it, and understood what had to be done to make that vision a reality. It had consumed the rest of his life. She wondered if he had ever wished he'd just never set eyes on Williamsburg. The possibility chilled her.

She left the note under a bowl in plain sight of the lamp on the table, checked that the front and back doors were barred, and followed her husband down into the cool darkness below.

She emerged on the stone floor below, hurrying through the passageway. The sight of Bronson stopped her. He wore faded jeans and a button-down shirt, neatly tucked in and buttoned to his chin and wrists. She bit back her amusement, her heart warmed.

"Swing and a miss," she said as she approached him. She unbuttoned the top two buttons of the shirt and then the cuffs, folding them back a couple of times. She pulled out the tails of his shirt, smoothing the rumpled fabric.

She stepped back and gave him a critical look. A moment later, she was flooded with heat at the sight of him, watching her uncertainly with an utterly sexual, if unintentionally so, expression. A few wispy, light brown hairs emerged at his collarbone, and the jeans reminded her of her husband's powerful virility. Thank God they hadn't given him a tux.

"My sweet, dorky husband," she said, re-buttoning one of the buttons in afterthought. "You're so steeped in ideas and principles, I don't think you know how hot you are."

"Miserably so, but at least 'tis cool down here. I shall miss you so."

She tiptoed to kiss his cheek and whispered in his ear an erotic clarification of her meaning. His arm came around her shoulder, pulling her close as his other hand moved down her back to draw her against him.

"As soon as I get back," he said. "Be ready."

"Please be safe. Are you sure you'll be all right?"

"Didn't you say I'll be back in the next moment?"

"So I'm told. As you may recall, I liked it better here, so I never *went* back."

The clinical voice interrupted them. "Present your artifact."

He held an item against the reader. A moment later, looking back at her, he vanished. She blinked—he couldn't have known he would disappear without finishing their goodbye.

Only then did she realize she hadn't even asked him his destination. She peered at the reader, but it had already concealed the artifact he'd used.

She glanced into the sky absently, waiting for his return. Her thoughts returned to Williamsburg. There was perhaps a bit of irony in her delight in settling here in colonial Virginia during its most exciting time. She had forgotten that she would also have to watch the decline of Williamsburg. Perhaps it wasn't so much forgetting as it was not appreciating the pain experienced by those who had cherished this old town. She was not alone in her depression over the extended sleep of the grand old town.

And again Goodwin came to mind, and she wondered if ever he became discouraged—especially before he began to see the fruit of his labor. His passion for the project had made him a perfect head of fundraising for the restoration, but it had to have been a grind after a while for a man of God also running a poor parish church.

An inspiration struck her. Bronson would be back any moment, and she was seized by the rare opportunity to act before anyone could dissuade her. Juliana had traveled extensively; why shouldn't she take just a short trip, herself?

She stepped up to the reader and placed her palm there, barking out her desired destination. And in less than a minute, she was dressed appropriately. She was traveling to a time long before the famous "DAVIDS FATHER" telegram when John D. Rockefeller Jr. had officially set the Restoration in motion.

"Return passage guaranteed via today's *Virginia Gazette*, in the portal below the columns of the court."

She pressed her artifact onto the reader.

The next thing she knew, she lay crumpled on the steps leading to a porch. Snow flurries whistled through, and the sky promised more. She gathered up the purse she'd been given, noticing the folded *Virginia Gazette* just inside, and snapped the purse closed.

Her clothing and wool coat were in place; time travel, she saw, was much more civilized when a bit of planning went into it and one arrived clothed at one's destination. The sudden, crushing headache, however, appeared to be unavoidable.

Relief filled her as she recognized the courthouse behind her, with four columns supporting the pediment. The detail distracted her. These columns were yet another eccentricity of Williamsburg's Big Sleep period that folklore had insisted were to have been a part of the courthouse originally. They'd added them after the courthouse partially burned down in 1911.

She looked closer—you couldn't tell that they were rigged from bricks, covered with concrete. Only an archaeologist from her time would have known the truth, from the stories of the Restoration. It saddened her, to think of the once great center of academia, philosophy, and prosperity jury-rigging outward architectural elements—wrongly—for the sake of fitting into a world where, much more notably, a corrupt belief system had been exposed and rejected.

She came to her feet quickly, lest her odd arrival be noticed.

She realized she could not have been noticed. The street was empty. Her heart sank as she looked out on the Duke of Gloucester Street of February, 1924.

A hideous line of telephone poles marched down the wide green median on Duke of Gloucester. A few Model-T's cluttered the curbs. Concrete roadways and sidewalks lay like nameless gravestones marking the demise of the oyster shell-studded paths Jefferson, Washington, and Lafayette had trod.

On either side of the street lay recent nineteenth-century homes as well as rotting, swaybacked buildings well over a hundred years old. Well-kept colonial homes had been tricked out with Victorian gingerbread trim by residents anxious to keep up with the times. More Southern porches than Mayberry. It was like arriving at a reunion of brilliant old classmates, only to find them sporting party hats and noisemakers, doing the hokey pokey.

She began to panic—beyond the impact of the ghastly architectural nightmare. She couldn't get her bearings. She turned—and turned again—attempting to remember where she was. The Raleigh Tavern should be—no, of course. It had burned to the ground late in the nineteenth century. What was she looking at?

Calm down, dear. You have 24 hours to get to ...

And then she did panic.

Where was her return time portal again? The voice had said it, and she'd been so amused with its clever ring that—was it county colonnade? She should have asked for them to repeat it. A system like that, and they didn't print out a boarding pass of some sort?

She stopped and took a slow, deep breath. It would come to her. It would have to. Or else she'd have to steal a horse and head to Rosalie, hoping beyond hope not to run into her own descendants on her way to the portal.

She was going to have to sit quietly and let her mind relax—that would bring it back to her.

Dear God! What a terrible joke this would be, to travel in time on a whim to possibly the most depressing time in Williamsburg history—and then get stuck here.

Unless, again, one were an archaeologist. In which case it would be far and away the most exciting.

With running water and electricity. She sighed in pleasure at the idea.

Then she remembered she had a purpose here, and she focused. At least she knew east from west. She turned and headed west.

As she started down the street, the snow fell harder. She'd made it two-thirds of the way when she heard the flat sound of an orchestra on an old gramophone coming out of one of the houses. She smiled as she walked down the old street—it almost felt like she'd fallen into an old Frank Capra movie.

She followed the sound and turned her head—someone in the Geddy House was playing a waltz, and she heard the words:

Sleep, sleep, sleep
How we love to sleep

She raised her eyebrow at the lyrics. Apt indeed.

She spotted Bruton Parish Church just a little farther on, and entered the church silently. Cool and unlit, it exuded a peaceful aura, and she felt herself yawning. The entire town seemed under a spell.

Then she noticed an older, white-haired man sitting in the front row, leaning forward, his elbows on his knees, and his head cradled in his fingertips—in prayer.

She stepped forward, sitting in the pew across from him to offer her own prayer for wisdom.

She recognized the man as none other than Doctor Goodwin, and she glanced toward him out of the corner of her eye. He nodded and jerked back slightly, catching himself, and she was amused to realize he wasn't praying—he was dozing.

All at once he sat up straight, his eyes widening—surprised himself. Then he saw her, and he coughed. She fought the urge to laugh.

"Ah! Please, accept my apologies. That waltz just relaxes me so—all those Fred Waring songs. Not particularly ecclesiastical, but easy to dance to," he said with a laugh.

"Are you Reverend Goodwin? The rector?" she asked, well aware he disliked being referred to as a doctor.

"I am."

"Marley Trelawney."

"Happy to make your acquaintance. Fine old Williamsburg name."

"Do you sleep all right?" she asked, concerned that he might be sleepless over the task facing him.

"Well enough, I suppose. At least, I ought to. It seems a sleeping spell has been cast over our little Lotusburg."

"Lotusburg?"

"Ah—after the mythological story of the islanders who ate the lotus plant and slipped into a happy, sleepy apathy. A dozen years ago, the town slept through an entire election. The Richmond newspaper enjoyed twitting us over that, dubbing us Lotusburg."

"Oh, of course. I did hear about that."

"It was deserved. Who sleeps through an election? And perhaps that isn't even the worst of it. People who know better now slumber our way through the atrocious changes being made in the name of progress. I'm as modern as the next fellow, and I'm sick to death of the call for gasoline pumps on every other corner."

"You lived in New York for a while, didn't you?"

"Fourteen years. It might have been a hundred, for the damage they did while I was gone."

"Who?"

"Everyone, here and there. Just thinking they were beautifying their homes with the facile trends of fashion, they continued the destruction of an irreplaceable part of history. I take it your husband has an interest in the old days?"

Marley was well-adjusted, but the assumptions of men of the past still occasionally irked her. Raising the next generation was an important task, but women enjoyed work, also.

"Well, yes, but I myself am an archaeologist. The restoration and enduring legacy of a historically accurate, eighteenth-century Williamsburg is my life's work. Now and, more than ever, in another hundred years, we must ensure that the tiny village survives to tell the tale."

"Indeed! In fact, the women of Williamsburg first raised prominent interest in this, by restoring the magazine in 1889 and founding the Association for the Preservation of Virginia Antiquities. Perhaps you'll be willing to join in our effort."

The suggestion startled and tempted her, but she quickly recovered from her bout of insanity.

"I'd love to, to be quite honest. But my husband would likely protest." Ironic, for her to have imagined sexism in his assumption—when it was her own love for her husband and family that would keep her where she was. "I am concerned, though, at the task before you."

"I do feel overwhelmed at times. Working for Doctor Chandler raising money for William and Mary is interesting and engaging. I met many in New York with connections to—er, well-heeled circles. But restoring the entire town to its old glory is something so far greater in scope than restoring my parish church—or even the grand old Wren building. And imagine the challenge of convincing my employer at the college to delay that restoration until I can convince enough benefactors to support this greater—almost impossible— vision that, at the moment, is mine alone."

She nodded, feeling the weight of his worry.

"Sir, your employer—Doctor Chandler, that is—has been invited to speak at a Phi Beta Kappa banquet in New York. It's important that you speak at this banquet. Dr. Chandler may suggest this on his own, but if not, you must do so."

"What do you mean? Why?"

"For many reasons—but the most important being that there will be in attendance another Phi Bete whose acquaintance you must make. A gentleman named John D. Rockefeller Jr. Sir, he's the only one who's ready and willing to help you. He may require a bit more convincing, but it's important for you to attend, so you can meet him."

He studied her cautiously. "Is that why you came here today?"

"Not the only reason, but perhaps the most important."

"How do you know this?"

She hesitated. "I'm a Phi Bete myself, as was my father, and Mr. Rockefeller, as well. When I heard of the meeting, I felt sure you'd want Mr. Rockefeller to know of this opportunity. He's a philanthropist, and he cares about the future. This important effort must be carried out—in order that the future may learn from the past."

He looked up suddenly. "Ah! I do like the sound of that. 'That the future may learn from the past.'"

Marley gulped. She thought she understood the paths of time travel. That slogan had existed before she traveled in time—in fact, long before she was born. For a moment, her mind was lost in a chicken-or-egg tangle before she let it go.

"Yes. That the future may learn from the past," he repeated. "Thank you. In the future, God willing, we won't make such foolish mistakes as to create counterfeit concrete columns of the court."

And as he spoke, relief flooded her. *Columns of the court.* That was her portal.

He went on, "If I can somehow find a diagram to map how the old town was laid out, of course."

"There's a map at the college than can aid you. A man found it over ten years ago in a library from Norfolk that he purchased. It's drawn to scale—mostly—by a French military officer in 1782."

"Is that true? Are you certain?"

"Yes. Without a doubt. Reverend Goodwin, please allow me to thank you for your passion for this project. Someday I know that what you see will come to pass. And there will be nothing—*nothing*—like it anywhere else in the world. And it will be a reminder of a time when men and women worked and sacrificed to create a land where—someday, that is—all men will have the same opportunities."

She turned to leave, then once more stopped. "But the disagreement you may have with Mr. Rockefeller over electricity and indoor plumbing—heed his advice. Visitors will gladly pay someday for the opportunity to visit the restored colonial village—but not if they have to use an outhouse."

He laughed and bade her goodbye, and she walked into the street, back toward the courthouse. She stopped before the

Geddy house, where a young lawyer named Vernon Geddy had been relaxing to the sound of Fred Waring's orchestra in the winter night. He may have played an early record on a phonograph or he may have listened to it on the radio. He might have felt quite sophisticated for owning the technology. Throughout the ages, mankind prided themselves in their technology. Gadgets that in another ten or twenty years—or one—would be laughably out of date. Technology began its swift death as soon as it was born.

Perhaps Geddy had taken his wife for a waltz around the living room—she would've attempted to brush him off, laughing, and their children would have clapped and giggled gleefully to watch their parents acting so silly, in love. Love grew and changed and thickened in some areas and thinned in others—but it never died.

Love for her husband and gratitude for him and for their children rose up within Marley so full to overflowing that tears came to her eyes as she stopped, for just a moment, to realize life, here in this other time. She wished her husband was with her, to share it with him. She would never be able to describe the cold, the smell of dinner cooking, of fires warming the homes, the subtle sounds of the evening—the wind, the trees, people moving about in their lives. Or the anachronistic jumble of a visual feast that 1924 Williamburg, Virginia was.

And she understood why Juliana had stopped her travels when she met Rashall. Now, she hated Bronson missing any part of her life.

She returned to the courthouse steps. The snow had stopped falling, and she stopped to look around her little town in the waning winter light.

She turned away to the columns, found the portal, and stepped through, back into the labyrinth.

She stopped short, startled. Malcolm and Mary stood there, neither looking at her. She grew alarmed. "What's wrong? Where's Bronson?"

"I'm right here, darling," he said, coming into view from behind her. Thank God—he was dressed in his own clothes.

And then she saw a wound on his jaw—perhaps three inches long. He noticed her alarm and smiled. "'Tis but a scratch."

Relief flooded her at his joke. Thank God for long winter afternoons when re-enacting Monty Python clips served as entertainment.

"It's you we're concerned about, Merrilea," Mary said.

"Why?"

"Why did you travel today?"

She considered that. "I thought the Reverend Goodwin might be discouraged. I miss the Williamsburg I knew. I don't mean in my own time—I mean … *Williamsburg.*"

Mary nodded. "I see. All three of you sisters are intelligent—but you concern us the most. Rachel has a healthy fear of time-travel, almost to the level of superstition. Juliana is a sophisticated traveler, having enjoyed the activity since she was a child. To the point of boredom, in fact. And never at her most curious did she fully appreciate its innocent power."

Malcolm straightened. "Your grandmother, on the other hand, was at the opposite end. She lacked the awareness to understand its power. And she unwittingly placed that power in evil hands. Her actions resulted in anomaly after anomaly— that, fortunately, all of your husbands are now working to undo. Do you understand what an anomaly is?"

"I thought I did. In this context, it's a deviation that threatens the natural existence of a person or persons."

Malcolm sighed. "Yes. That's precisely correct, of course. That's where the problem lies with you."

Terror filled her, knowing her grandmother's fate as a result of her cavalier attitude about the time travel.

"Please don't take away my memory of my family—or of my sisters. I don't know what I've done, but I swear to you I'll never do anything wrong like that again if you'll just tell me what it was. I was worried about Doctor Goodwin, and I just wanted to make sure he was all right."

"Calm down," Malcolm said. "You've done nothing wrong. But both of us want you to understand who we are—and why we are the way we are."

"What do you mean?"

"Doesn't it strike you as odd, that we appear the same today as we did five years ago?"

"I thought perhaps you lived outside of time."

Mary's eyebrows went up. "Yes. Precisely. I wasn't always this age, Merrilea. I'm not a saintly angel."

Marley grew cautious. If they weren't angels, and they didn't age, what *were* they?

"Who are you?"

Malcolm exchanged a smile with Mary. "You frightened her. No need for that." Turning back to her, he said, "We once were as you are, living our own lives."

"What happened?"

He leaned against the stone wall, gazing up into the stars. "I'll spare you the needless details. I was an old man wishing to make a difference in the world, in a big way." He laughed, shaking his head, as if at his own foolishness. "Mary was—er, a woman looking back on her choices in life, trying to undo the single choice she thought mattered the most."

Marley saw the transformation go over Mary's face—as if she were a young woman again, confronted with the endless options offered in life. "Decades after I ended a relationship with a young beau, I could see into his life through the technology of the era. I saw that the man I had once thought was rootless and not appropriate for marriage had in fact become a model husband, father—even grandfather."

She stopped, remembering, then went on.

"I chose to go back to that moment in my life when I let him go. And I changed my choice ... with disastrous results. I thought he was the love of my life. What I did not know was that I was not the love of *his* life. I was meant to make that choice as I originally had. In making this choice with what I thought was hindsight, I changed the path of his life, destroying his entire family. We soon parted again, and he met his love much later in their lives, a bittersweet blessing. They remained without the children that they both had wanted, but still in love. I meanwhile, was forced to live with this knowledge as I relived the same life I'd lived before. When I came to the age I had been before, my life was frozen in time."

"What about you, Malcolm?" Bronson asked.

The old man cleared his throat. "No. I will not make this about me."

"But ... you were doomed, I suppose, to the existence you have now? And yet you seem content—can you at least tell us what it is you *do*?"

"We watch the night sky," he said, his chin rising as he looked up into the firmament, "for signs of disquiet. Occasionally, as with Merrilea's sister Rachel, it improves a person to visit another time. We manage all the logistics of those visits.

"But know this," he added. "Those who look back on the past with contempt or nostalgia do a disservice to their own time, their own lives. How often have we looked back and thought we could save the world, if only we could go back for an hour? 'Would they not listen, if we could warn them of their misdeeds?'

"Do we think those who lived in that time were not striving to make those changes already? And is the world we live in such a nirvana of perfection that there aren't changes we shouldn't be making to our own lives—to do what we wish we could do, were we able to change the past?"

Bronson grew grim as he listened. "You're telling me to dissuade Grey from his mission."

Malcolm took a deep breath as he shook his head. "*No*. I'm telling you to live your life, aware of the gift you've been given. If you're convinced that it's part of your life to correct an anomaly, determine what is anomaly and what is *not*. Judge carefully *where* the anomaly occurred. Strike at the root."

"You mean the earliest location."

Malcolm's eyes narrowed. "You're a clever boy, you can figure it out."

With that, Malcolm and Mary disappeared into the maze of the labyrinth, to continue their endless penance through time.

Chapter Twenty-Eight

The steamy night clung to them as they trotted the last mile of backroad, cooling the horses. As they arrived at Rosalie, they swung off their horses and hurried to the rain barrels for fresh water. Juliana grabbed two pails to water the horses, and Rashall took the pails from her, kissing her forehead.

"Why don't you just keep me company while I brush and water the horses and put them down?"

Juliana stretched in the doorway of the stables. "It's good to be home."

"You know, as silly as it sounds to have to say this, we probably ought to start thinking about making a proper home for ourselves."

"Don't you like Stonefield?"

"I love it. It's just so remote, so far removed from everyone. Wouldn't you like to live nearer your sister?"

"Of course. I do love Stonefield, though."

"We can build a home just like it. What about the little honeymoon cottage?"

She smiled slowly as he brushed the horse. "Not much room for children."

"Well, if we lived here, we'd have more little ones than we'd know what to do with. No interruptions at all."

Soon, they'd put the horses in their stalls for the night.

"Feel like a swim?" she asked, walking toward the river.

"How deep is it out there?"

"You know the answer to that. You sailed a large ship up to the shore the day we met."

"Exactly."

"You were a sailor. Don't tell me you can't swim."

"I can swim fine. I just don't want to be foolhardy as dark as it is out here." After a moment, he said, "Don't tell me you swim out here when you're alone."

"It's one of the things I love about the place, Ray. I know it as well as the back of my hand. I feel as safe at night as I do during the day. Would you mind if I took a quick dip? It's so hot, and I just don't want to get into my nice clean sheets filthy."

In the end, he gave in, slipping out of his clothes as he watched her undress in the moonlight, innocently unveiling herself to him. *God, how I love her.*

They seemed to have so little time together. They'd had no honeymoon at all to speak of—and for all he would love whatever time they had together tonight ... well. For even that, in fact, he was thankful.

She dove into the water head first, and he waited until she surfaced before stepping into the cove in the James where it flowed alongside Stonefield.

He remembered that afternoon, years ago, when they'd visited just after Bronson's wedding. He remembered his first glance at her when he walked into Stonefield that day. As he swam to the surface and joined her, he brought her close, kissing her lightly as he treaded water.

"Do you remember when we met?"

Her eyes sparkled in the moonlight. "You were adorable."

"I was a dolt. A lovesick twelve-year-old would have been wittier."

"I saw the wit in your eyes."

"Well, you'd have had to. It sure wasn't on my tongue."

She laughed and swam for the steps leading up the path. He watched her emerge, savoring every moment with her. He scrambled out of the water, padding after her, and sighed at the luxurious sensation of cooler evening air against his body as the water evaporated.

"Never let me contradict you again. This is the perfect end to a long, rough day."

At the door, he rinsed his feet with rainwater and stepped inside on the mat, quickly finding a towel in a cabinet. He gently rubbed it down over Juliana's head, her throat and shoulders, her back, and the other lines of her body before he quickly toweled himself off and drew her close.

He didn't have to ask her about her interest in supper. He had no other pressing engagements, no one clamoring for his time. It was only him and her, a husband and wife, learning how to care for one another, how to pleasure each other.

He carried her into their bedroom and lay her face-down on the bed and lit a couple of candles. He glanced up and saw her lazily watching him. He gave her a long, slow backrub, ironing out the kinks in her upper shoulders and back. Just as he almost finished, she turned, lifting a thigh around him in swift grace and blunt invitation.

He accepted it all.

Covering her mouth with his, her body with his, he entered her, pouring out his love to her in softly whispered words. She responded with innocent ardor, her fingers lingering lightly over his muscled arms and chest, then exploring everywhere.

Within minutes, consummated in every way imaginable, they dozed, and then slumbered, and then slept.

Rashall heard the light tap on the door before Juliana. He quickly slipped into trousers, grabbing a shirt and the lamp as he headed for the front door. "Who's there?"

Bronson and Marley impatiently called out as they banged on the door again. "Let us in, we're tired."

The grandfather clock chimed nine—they'd barely had time to fall asleep.

He shoved the bar back and opened the door. "My life has officially become surreal. Let's stay quiet, I think Juliana's still asleep."

Hawk and Marley entered, and he slid the bar back again. Dark circles shadowed his eyes.

"You look like hell."

"I just need a couple of hours sleep," Hawk said, yawning. "Grey's meeting us here at midnight. I wasn't sure if you'd be here or not."

"What happened to your face?"

"Ray, I haven't slept in three nights. I've got to lay down." He sank onto the chesterfield, grabbing a pillow from a chair.

"They got into a knife fight," Marley said as she spread a light blanket over him. Hawk was already asleep. "Some other guy was with Manning."

"They actually found him?"

"Grey's done a tremendous amount of work to put this together. The goal is to engage him as late as they can in his lifetime, but before he kills Cameron Carlyle. Go on back to bed. I'll wait here."

"And engaging Jack Manning means killing him."

"Not according to them—but that's how they expect it to go."

"Honey, don't you want to sleep? Go on in and lay down in Mary's bed. She isn't here tonight."

"I may do that in a minute."

"So what did they learn from that trip?"

She shook her head. "Only that they didn't go back far enough. Grey theorized that Jack Manning had probably been in the future for a while before he had the idea to travel farther into the future."

Rashall nodded. "I get it. There's no relationship to when he went far into the future—except that it happened after he had access to Stonefield. And *whenever* he went, he just said nothing about it for decades, until he died. But he had to go far enough ahead to know about the labyrinth—and especially, that Grey knew about it. That Grey would have a way to compare notes with us here."

She absorbed this. "Yes. The only way to control the time-travel is with a final artifact connected to the destination."

"And you can't get your hands on artifacts from the future outside of the labyrinth. When did Grey buy Stonefield?"

"I think he said a year after he and Rachel first left 1746."

"So we think that Jack Manning discovered the labyrinth … while you and your grandmother were still living there?"

"I don't think so. I think he was in a mental institution at that point." She rose, leaned over and kissed her husband, then walked to Ray and kissed his cheek. "I'm going to take you up on that nap. I'll see you in a couple of hours."

☙

"Rashall."

A soft tap came on their open bedroom door. Grey stood just outside the door. He nodded and walked away.

He was awake and up in the next moment.

He leaned over to kiss Juliana lightly, who slept on. She unconsciously lifted her cheek to his kiss and sighed in her sleep.

Hawk sat drinking coffee before the cold hearth, perusing a page. "Malcolm's outside. Makes me feel like the girls are a little safer that way."

Grey tilted his head. "He's not exactly who you'd pick as a second, is he?"

"I sense he's much tougher than he seems," Rashall said, pouring a cup of coffee and joining Hawk, who handed him the page he'd been examining.

"Or at least Jack would believe that. I can't imagine Malcolm not accosting him at some point. He yelled at Juliana when she was a little girl for visiting Baby Jesus in the manger." Hawk raised an eyebrow, sipping his coffee.

Grey laughed. "Did she? How fearless that girl must be!"

His heart stirred with pride. He loved that Hawk enjoyed that story—and that it impressed Grey. He didn't need to tell them that she'd seen it all, and the immense potential in mankind—as well as their aptitude for evil—terrified her. Fortunately she'd seen the miraculous in small kindnesses as well as landmarks in the spiritual history of mankind.

Malcolm entered, checked the doors and shutters by habit, then bade them goodnight and disappeared into his room.

In minutes, they were in the labyrinth, dressing in different clothing.

"What is this fabric?" Hawk asked, buttoning his shirt. "It feels like silk, except ... odd."

"They sure like their colors, don't they? Switch shirts with me, Hawk. You have two. I can't wear a shirt covered with flowers."

"We need to stick with what we were given," Grey said. "Besides, I don't think that's two shirts. I think it's a shirt and a jacket. See, it's made of the same stuff."

"But it looks like a shirt. See, it has cuffs, and a yoke. And ... pockets on the breast? Curious."

"Stop complaining."

"Why did they wear two shirts?"

"It's something called a leisure suit," Grey snapped. "Can we please focus and stop worrying about the clothing they wore?"

Silence.

"I just don't understand the pockets."

Grey sighed. "Are we ready? Take hold."

They grasped each other's wrists, and he pressed the artifact into the reader.

They arrived on their backsides in a grassy lawn.

"All right. Right there—the monument of the woman, holding the chain? That's our portal. You both have artifacts as well. If we get separated, that's how you get back home. Do not wait. Just assume that the others have made it out. Meet back here in twenty-three hours, to be safe."

But both Rashall and Hawk were transfixed at the sight of the monument—at the very top of the list on the stone column was the name CRISPUS ATTUCKS. A woman fashioned in bronze, raising a broken chain in her right hand, and in her left, an American flag. Near her right foot lay a crushed crown.

And at its base, a bronze relief of the massacre itself, an artist's depiction of how Michael might have looked.

"It was inspired by a painting of the French Revolution. Liberty Leading the People, lighting the world, and all that."

"The French *what?*" Rashall asked, riveted on the phrase.

"I spoke out of turn. It doesn't take much to figure it out, considering the great Lafayette and his brethren, but I shouldn't have brought it up." Then he noticed his brother, still gazing at the relief. "I'd forgotten. You two actually *knew* him, didn't you?"

"He was brother, father, friend," Hawk said. Rashall had nothing to add.

They walked down Tremont Street the length of the Boston Common. Rashall suddenly shook his head. "I don't think I should have come here. I grew up right around the corner. It's much more crowded and ugly, but I don't want to accidentally see something I'd rather not know."

"Don't worry." He opened the door to a nondescript brick building, and they followed him. "First, a quick chore."

They soon entered an office, where Grey spoke quietly to the woman at the desk. She glanced at the men, then nodded. "Yes, we have an opening. What do you need?"

"Every shot available. We're going … abroad for a period."

Rashall grew impatient as they sat waiting. This place wasn't as unpleasant as the place Juliana had escorted him to, but he was already anxious about getting home.

"What are we doing here, anyway?" he asked.

Grey shrugged. "I thought we ought to take advantage of modern medicine while I have you here. We're getting you both inoculated."

"My mother already inoculated me."

"That's just smallpox."

In another few minutes, they were freshly inoculated and out the door. Grey stepped off the edge of the walkway, looking into the busy street and raising his hand. Rashall's mouth fell open at his indifference to the machine rolling at him.

The machine, a conveyance of some sort, stopped beside them, and Grey opened the door. "It's a taxi. A ride for hire."

They climbed in, and Grey read an address from a slip of paper. Rashall was sandwiched between them, and Hawk slammed the door.

"You sure about this? It ain't the best part of town."

"I'm certain."

With that, the driver shot away from the Common like a cannon ball. Hawk held onto the door. He braced his hand against the back of the seat in front. Several minutes passed as they moved—very fast—through the city.

He noticed music coming out of the front of this taxi thing. The driver reached to adjust a dial, and the music got louder.

Once I was a boogie singer playin' in a rock and roll band

The driver, wearing a slouchy gray knit cap and smoking a tube of tobacco, bobbed his head along with the tune as the song grew louder and odder.

Rashall looked from Grey to Hawk and back again. "Did he say 'white boy'?"

The driver nodded, momentarily lowering the volume. "Yeah, man. Cool song." He turned it up louder.

"Cool?"

"When something's cool, it's good," Grey said.

"And when something's hot, that's also good." Hawk nodded along with the driver, keeping time. "Quite melodious, isn't it? Appealing rhythm."

Grey raised his eyebrows, fighting a smile.

Rashall collapsed in laughter as he slid down in the back seat. "Something's cool, it's good, something's hot, it's good."

"Would you three can it? I'm tryna hear the song."

Rashall went silent, glancing at the others. "Can it?" Hawk whispered.

"He means, be quiet."

"Tryna?"

"Aw, man, it's over. Never mind. Here's your stop."

"Wait." Rashall grabbed Hawk as he opened the door. "What are we *doing*?"

Grey signaled to the driver. "Keep the meter running."

"Not in this part of town, son. I'm getting out of here. You go, or give me another address."

"Can't you just drive around with the meter still running? Pretend I sent you to a better part of town. Go around the block."

The driver looked over his left shoulder and pulled away, muttering. "Laugh over my funky music, send me the hell into Dot, crazy mothers. Melodious, my ass."

Grey leaned toward them, waiting until they were focused completely on him. He kept his voice under the sound of the music, which made it tough to hear clearly.

"Two men share an apartment in that building. The elder is named Max Sheppard and the younger is Jack. I know nothing about them beyond that. This is the first location I've been able to find of their existence."

Rashall explained, "Hannah—Cassandra's mother—told us that they traveled using Rob Miller's Phi Beta Kappa key, at the Rosalie portal, at some point in the 1760s. Do you remember if she said a year, Hawk?"

"It happened while I was at William and Mary. So at some point between '59 and '61."

"And she said Cassie was there. When was that?"

"I remember what she described—Cassie visiting the classroom, and Jack Manning becoming angry. I don't remember that actually happening, though."

"Perhaps she lied?"

Grey slowly shook his head. "I don't think so."

Rashall went on, "You don't understand. This woman would lie to Jesus Christ, and him knowing her up and down. I don't think she has a real firm grasp on reality."

"Well, not anymore, that's certain," Hawk agreed.

"What do you mean?"

"Malcolm and Mary took away her memories of anything related to time-travel. She remembers nothing of raising her granddaughter, of traveling to the twentieth century, nor of traveling back to the eighteenth."

Grey paled. "Why?"

"She ... well, I think in the modern colloquialism, we would say she broke the terms of service."

After a moment of thought, he shook his head. "No. I discussed this at length with Malcolm and told him my intention. He approved. We're fine."

"I would have remembered her, though. Hannah said Robert invited the whole family. They would have stood out, as women in the classroom were rare, except as servants."

"Then he visited later. Cassandra herself would have only been fifteen when you left school."

Hawk was given pause. "I probably know Hannah the best of us, and I'm going to say she told the truth—as much as she ever does—but that her memory in this case was faulty. She remembered being embarrassed that Robert was taking care of Cassandra in the classroom, and that it upset Jack. And those were things she wouldn't have admitted lightly. That's just her personality."

Grey swore. "I'm going to have to research more."

"Can't we dispatch them here and be done with it?"

Rashall's eyes went wide as he looked at Hawk. "Kill them in cold blood?"

"They're known killers."

"Jack is," Grey said. "Max is just a controller. Remember, Rachel grew up with the guy."

"In other words, someone who wouldn't dirty his own hands with blood, but hire someone else to do his killing for him. Like, oh, his lunatic brother."

Rashall raised a hand. "I say let's go meet them, if they're there. Perhaps we can give them a chance to repent."

The Trelawney brothers turned to gaze at him as if he'd spoken in Martian.

Grey sighed. "You're your mother's son, all right. All right, driver. We're ready. I don't suppose you'd be of a mind to keep the meter running after I pay you, and circle the block?"

The driver gave a short laugh as he delivered them to the spot, and they climbed out as Grey paid the fare. Night was falling, and Rashall's suspicions were confirmed when he noticed disreputable characters eyeing them.

The taxi pulled away. "You do have your blades, don't you?"

Rashall laughed. "Think we'd be here if not?"

"Just remember I'm not as spry as I used to be, and I haven't been in a fist fight in thirty-five years. Damn. Just recalled the last time was with James Manning."

The men entered the apartment building, walking past two men smoking in the vestibule. Rashall recognized the smell—hemp was grown in his own home state as well as Virginia, but the varieties some smoked for pleasure were rarer. And this smell was distinctly the same.

The men looked at him, and he gave them a short nod. "Hey, man," they said.

They passed through a glass door and walked down a hall. "Hey, man," Rashall echoed, practicing the greeting. Grey shushed him.

They walked up four flights of stairs, then passed apartments occasionally noisy with music, laughter, and arguing. At the end of the corridor, they stopped before the apartment where the letter E dangled crookedly.

"I don't like this positioning," Hawk whispered.

"They're cornered. We aren't," Grey said.

"If they have a gun, that's an awful long hallway to get down without them hitting one of us."

Rashall knocked on the door.

Presently, a shuffle inside sounded. "Who is it?"

"Acquaintances of your father," Grey said.

"My father's dead. Go away."

Grey knocked, loudly. "Open the door."

"I'm with the church, Jack," Rashall added, to reassure him. "We aren't here to hurt you.

The door opened a crack as the man took a quick glance at them. When he attempted to close it again, they blocked it, then shoved it open.

"My brother isn't here."

The man who stood there was young, slim, and neatly dressed. Rashall looked past him at the few boxes stacked behind him. He glanced at Hawk—none of them expected the tidy apartment, or the polite, suspicious young man who stood there.

"Sheppard," Grey said. Clearly he recognized him, despite the years separating him from the man Grey must have known.

His hair was as black as his father's had been, but had already begun to show premature greying. He was perhaps in his mid-twenties.

"Should I know you? You couldn't know my father, so I know you're lying."

"Don't ask me how, but I did know James Manning."

This startled him. "You *couldn't* know him. What do you want?"

"Where's your brother?"

"Visiting some friends. Then we're headed out of this hellhole." He crossed his arms and spoke frostily. "If you knew my father, what was he like?"

Grey considered this. "He could be a bit of a brute."

Sheppard snorted. "He was a monster. Asshole, I think, is the term. If I thought I was to become someone like him, beating my family, I'd put a bullet in my brain tonight."

They fell silent—even Grey seemed surprised by this.

"But if it's true, how did you know him? If you know him, or knew him, you know what I'm asking you."

They glanced at Grey, who answered. "I can't explain it, but I knew him. All we came here to do, today, is to persuade you to live your life honorably. Trust in God for any vengeance you feel in your heart. Forgive those who hurt you."

At this, the man went silent, his gaze focusing on each of their faces in turn, as if memorizing them.

"Look, I don't know what you want from me, but I don't have time for it. If by some fluke what you say is true, tell that man we're both dead. We stayed here for a reason. Now, we have a new life, and I'm doing my best to help my brother get over the abuse he piled on us both."

His voice was flat, his face stony.

Grey exchanged a look with them. "He abused you?"

"Everybody who knew him knew that. That you don't says it all. Who the hell are you, anyway?"

"Don't you recognize me from the trial in Williamsburg? I'm sure you would have been there. The entire county jammed the place."

"What trial?"

"My trial for murdering my wife, Letitia Trelawney. Whom your father drowned."

"Grey Trelawney." Sheppard's cool exterior vanished, leaving him pale and fearful. "You couldn't be."

"Not to worry, he did me a favor. I do want to make something clear to you, however. If your brother harms a hair on the head of anyone dear to me, I will track you both down and kill you on the spot. Know that now."

"He's harmless, I assure you."

"He's a killer. Commit him to a cell now. He cannot be trusted among civilized society."

Sheppard Manning waited a long moment. "Goodbye."

"I mean what I've said."

They turned and walked away, and the door closed behind them.

They headed downstairs wordlessly. Out of nowhere came a man rushing headlong up the stairs. He stopped abruptly as he nearly smacked into Rashall.

"Out of my way—" he said, completing it with that loathsome racial epithet.

The man who stood there couldn't be more than twenty. His thick, black hair hung to his shoulders, and he was fully bearded. He was the spitting image of the older man Rashall had shot on Duke of Gloucester Street.

Rashall's jaw dropped in mock surprise. "Hey, man, are you talking to me?"

"Out of my way," he said, repeating it all again.

Rashall turned to Hawk. "Did he call me what I think he did?"

Hawk shrugged. "Doesn't seem too smart, granted."

Grey shook his head. "No. Leave him alone. This is Jack Manning."

"Hey, man," Rashall said, liking the term and how it rolled off his tongue. "How long have you been in Boston? I used to live down around the Common."

Hawk sent him a subtle smirk at his *hey, man*.

A knife appeared in Manning's hand, and before either man had time to move, Rashall had knocked it away and grabbed Manning by the throat, shoving him against the wall. The knife went clattering down the stairs. Only when it came to rest on the landing a couple of feet below did Rashall realize it was covered with dried blood. *What the hell?*

"You do look like your father," Rashall said, forcing his attention back to the man before him. "An accursed fiend."

Jack stared at him impassively, pretending courage. His breath was coming in gasps as Rashall tightened his grip around his throat. "Oh, yeah?"

The words came out in a fearful squeak.

Grey nodded. "Yes. Not quite his height, but otherwise very much so."

"We'll tell you, as we told your brother: Fear God. Leave vengeance to him. Now get out of here."

Manning hurried up the stairs, as they paused on the landing. Ever the dandified colonial gentleman, Grey pulled out a handkerchief and picked up the blade, hastily wrapping it and slipped it into his boot.

"He's already hard at work, racking up those frequent evil miles," Grey said as they hurried outside, into the street.

"What's a frequent evil mile?"

"Never mind. Very bad attempt at a joke in this parallel universe where evil is damned hard to kill. Heavens, look at that. Our little fellow stayed around."

The taxi pulled up, and they piled in and drove off.

"What made you stay?" Grey asked.

"I didn't. I just got back from another fare. Some weird guy, looked like Charles Manson, except scarier. Black hair."

"That's who we were there to see," Grey said. "Where did you pick him up from?"

"That creep's your pal? Get out."

"He's not a friend. We were there to—never mind. It's a long story."

"Where to?"

"Nearest police station. I found a bloodstained knife I want to turn in."

"No," Rashall said. "Let's get closer to the monument first."

"Good thinking. Do you know a police station near the Common?"

He nodded and pulled away. "Where did you say you picked him up from?" Hawk asked.

"I didn't. I don't rat out my fares."

Hawk sighed as he looked at Grey, who explained, "His customers are often morally suspect people who have committed crimes, and he doesn't cooperate with law enforcement."

"Hey, man," Hawk called. "Who said I was law enforcement?"

"Let me give you a piece of advice. If that isn't your knife, drop it on a vacant desk and get the hell out of there."

"Why?"

"Because the person who reports a crime becomes their first suspect."

"Ah. Yes, quite right. Perhaps you should wait for us, then."

Soon they arrived at the police station. "And don't have the brother do it," the driver said, as he pulled the taxi over.

"What?"

"You," he said, jabbing a finger at him, "Stay here. Let one of them take it in."

Rashall sighed in frustration. "Am I to understand that two hundred years later, we are *still* not looked on as equal?"

The driver raised his hands. "I ain't saying that. I'm just saying, better safe than sorry."

Grey climbed out on his side. "I'll be right back."

Hawk and Rashall exchanged a nervous glance.

"I'm just saying," the driver went on, "time to test the system ain't when you have a bloody knife with somebody's fingerprints all over it, and they might just be yours."

"Excuse me?" Rashall began, but Hawk shut him up, pointing at Grey, skipping down the stairs to the sidewalk. Hawk opened the door, and they made room for him.

He climbed back in.

"You get it back in there?" the driver asked, pulling away.

"Yes. Take us back to the Common, driver."

Chapter Twenty-Nine

Bronson said a silent prayer for strength as Grey pressed the artifact into the reader.

The crushing pain piled onto the headache already there, and he opened his eyes, relieved and terrified at the sight before him. They were still in the labyrinth.

"All well?" he asked Ray, who nodded.

Grey led them out through the root cellar—avoiding the subterranean maze. "We'll wait over here for them to arrive."

As they left the root cellar, they heard a bloodcurdling scream from the woods. Grey pushed them both back, flat, against the side of the stone house. A young girl—perhaps no older than fifteen or so—raced toward the two-lane highway on the other side of the woods.

"Damn!" Grey exploded. "We're too late. I always arrive here."

"You've been here before?"

"I just visited to see what I could learn. I quickly left. There are sights that can't be unseen—and certainly no little girl should have had to see. God knows what the young lady who just ran away saw."

"Who was she?"

"A babysitter—a nanny. I've tried to discover her name, to no avail. I don't understand why Hannah wasn't babysitting."

"I can answer that. She'd remarried, and her husband had some health problems and died right after Juliana was born. I'm just not sure exactly where she lived. Somewhere near Williamsburg, I assume. Professor Miller was on sabbatical, and they'd only recently purchased and refurbished Stonefield."

"Ah. That makes sense. Rachel oddly has no memory at all of who the babysitter was, and I've always been curious about that."

They watched the full moon rise into the eastern sky as they waited.

At that moment, they heard children inside, screaming—even the baby. Instinctively, he lunged forward, until his brother and Ray caught him. "You cannot. You'll kill him if you see what he's doing."

Bronson paled.

"The scars they bear on their cheekbones—Jack Manning put them there, with a penknife."

"I do not have the strength to bear this," Bronson gritted out. "These are our wives, those little girls crying, begging for help against this animal."

"Yes. And if you would be reunited with them in a better time, you—will—do—nothing."

He retched behind the stable nearby, then returned.

Ray turned away, shaking his head, covering his ears—and silently weeping.

"Just wait. Be strong."

The minutes seemed interminable—but soon enough, an engine started, then faded.

"They're gone."

"Now what?"

"We wait more. The children will leave."

"Leave? Go where?"

"You know, don't you? They spent a month in a vacant farmhouse—right over there. Rachel had convinced herself—and Marley—that their parents were just sick, and would come for them as soon as they got well. And those little girls somehow managed to keep themselves and that little baby girl alive during that time as well."

He stopped, placing a hand on each of their shoulders. He gave them both sober stares. "You cannot talk to them, or stop them. They went through this long ago. We cannot disrupt this part of it, at this point."

"How can you be so detached about this?"

"At the moment, arguing with you does help."

Bronson fell silent.

Then they heard it—an unusual sound, like something rolling along. Grey held his index finger to his lips, and they pressed themselves into the shadows against the house.

Grey inched along the edge of the house until he reached the dirt path that Stonefield backed up to. He watched the little girl who would someday grow up to be his wife, pulling the wagon that contained her newborn sister, with her younger sister, little more than a toddler, trailing along behind, running in the hot August night to keep up and glancing at her baby sister occasionally to check on her.

Bronson pressed his hands to his face and turned away. "Dear God!" He choked out. "When I remember their grandmother casting them across time from each other, so soon after they'd been through *that* ... and now this."

Rashall just stared, disbelieving. "Dear heavenly Father, please help them. Be with these brave little girls, and keep them safe and healthy and lead them back to us."

Bronson clapped his hand on Rashall's shoulder in agreement with his prayer. He saw something fall from Marley's hands, and again he started forward instinctively.

"No," Rashall whispered. "Remember? That's the miniatures that belonged in the double locket. Hannah will find them and that helps the police find the girls."

The little girls walked on in the moonlit night.

The three men who stood there had known the scourge of the whip; had known the illness and torture of warfare; had known imprisonment, and hunger, and the loss of those they loved.

But tonight, as they watched three little girls flee in fear for their lives, they knew pain, and they wept.

Grey wiped his face with a handkerchief as he turned back toward the house. "I remember a detail in the room that may help us come back to an earlier time."

"I'm not going in that house, and neither are you," Ray said. "And Hawk sure as hell isn't. That's his history professor lying dead in there. And *he's* that same little boy who was born on your slave ship, Grey."

"There's a takeout food order that may have a receipt—that would serve as an artifact to get us back before the murders."

"Don't you understand?" Rashall asked, angry. "We need to go back to the source. Hell, if we could go back to the day James Manning was born and drown him, that might work, but I'm not fond of infanticide—not even for monsters."

"What's your solution, then?"

"The key Rob Miller had with him, that they used to open the time portal."

Bronson nodded. "Yes. His Phi Beta Kappa key. He shouldn't have even brought that with him into the 18th century. That began the Mannings' time travel, and that's the only way to end it."

"How did they get it?" Grey asked.

Rashall answered. "James Manning stole it from Rob's room. He planned to find my mother and you and Rachel and kill you all."

"Just as they all three were going through the portal, he saw Camisha there at Rosalie, in the distance, and he stepped back. His sons went on—and I expect tonight we learned why they never came back. He was as brutal to them as he was with the rest of the world."

"That key is the source. Grey, you could spend the rest of your natural life in the future stamping out wildfires he started in time ... or we can reverse it all."

He hesitated. "Then Sheppard never had any interaction with Rachel. How does she meet your mother? Who, then, leads her back in time to meet me?"

"You're making a joke, right? That *those* two women could be kept apart?" He shook his head and placed his hand on Grey's shoulder with grim comfort. "Juliana has a portrait—a photograph, I think she called it—of my mother, and her parents holding her. Right beside my mother is Rachel, with her parents holding her. Beside them are Rob's parents, with his mother holding onto him like only a mama does. Look at what Manning threw at them—and they still became best friends." He smiled at both men. "Some friendships are just meant to be."

Bronson nodded. "Let's go home."

As they turned back toward the house, they stopped short, again faced with the daunting knowledge of the terrible scene that lay inside. And without speaking, they went instead into the root cellar.

They found their way back through to the labyrinth. "Plenty of time left on the meter," Grey said, glancing at his watch. "Do we want to go ahead and knock this out?"

"I need to see my family," Bronson said. "I don't know if I'll ever see her again without thinking of that little girl, toddling along after her sister in the gravel, in those thin little shoes, three tiny little girls, all alone in the world. Nobody looking after them except God."

Ray nodded, looking at him. "You know, that's wise advice for us all. If each time we grew tired, or impatient, with our mates, were we to think of them as small children, needing help ... perhaps we'd find more patience."

"I have something to tell you both."

Bronson smiled. "And you couldn't have gotten it out in the taxi?"

"Hey, man," Ray said, shaking his head.

Bronson cast him a glance.

After a long pause, he said, "I'm bringing my family back."

He couldn't have understood him correctly. "Back here? For good? To live? Or just to visit?"

"To stay. As soon as I iron out my cover story."

"Cover story?"

"It was my death that enabled the people at Rosalie to be freed. My sudden reappearance might complicate things."

"You're right there. There's a plantation owner who loathes everything about the Trelawneys of Rosalie. He's trying to force them all out of the state."

"Which one?"

"Fellow lives up by, well, here. Named Grimewood. Owns Black Oak Manor. My parents and Thomas went to Charlottesville to try to get an exemption."

Grey nodded. "Well, he's not alone. None of these fellows know how to make a profit without free labor."

"And yet all the people of Rosalie prove to them daily that with hard work and education—and rewards for your labor—it can be done—if you don't take baths in French champagne."

"Speaking of Rosalie ... would you mind if we lived with you, until Rachel and I can work out living arrangements?" Grey asked. "I know it would be quite tight—three more adults, three more children."

"We have five bedrooms. We can work it out. Do you want me to start planning a new place for you—perhaps out by our house? I keep trying to get Ray out here, but Juliana loves this old manse."

"Yes! Or you can wait till I'm here to help. Nothing too large, but a few good-sized bedrooms for the girls, anyway. And if there's room, perhaps we'll make a nice library. Not that I suppose I'll have any books at all. I will miss my work. I feel I've been useful in filling an uncomfortable niche, teaching people about my earlier life. But we can talk about all that later. For that matter, the house can wait until we get here. For now, I know you miss your lovely wives as much as I do mine. I'll be back as soon as I can."

Chapter Thirty

On this most festive of days, Juliana lifted her face in joy at the first hint of autumn: a cooling breeze whispering through the leaves of the old sycamore. She stood in the cool, aromatic darkness of a tobacco barn, watching her husband and Bronson with Dan, Thomas, Little Dan, and George, all of them just outside the door, sampling the Trelawneys' latest creation.

Little Dan gestured toward the various stations in this, the fermenting barn. "We sweat the tobacco leaves for a minimum of eight cycles, to remove all traces of bitterness. Then we age those leaves."

"Do you use spring water to ferment?" Thomas asked.

Little Dan winked. "Now you know I'm not going to give away family secrets, sir."

"But I'm part of the family!"

The men laughed.

Thomas nodded. "I vow, it's the finest I've ever tasted, bar none. West Indies be damned."

"Thank you, sir. We've been developing this particular blend for a few years now."

Bronson examined the cigar, handling it with sensuous ease as he brought it to his lips again. A twinkle lit his eyes as he glanced toward his wife, who stood with Juliana and Sukey.

The women were touring the tobacco programs as part of the town dedication ceremonies.

Juliana blushed at that look, but her sister simply shook her head.

"Oh ..." Marley said, aggrieved at him for reasons not quite clear to her. She suspected an inside joke between the couple. "You better bring some of those home, so we can try them, after the children are in bed. With some rum."

He held the cigar out in invitation, the lit end facing him. "Try it now."

Marley looked toward her sister and Sukey, then noticed Ruth and Hattie watching them from a rocking chair under a tree, mending. "He knows how unbecoming it would be for me to smoke around a bunch of men."

"Be the first to break the mold. Show the rest of us how it's done."

Marley smiled broadly at her sister and walked to her husband with a little strut. Juliana glanced over at Ruth's sewing circle. You could hear a jaw drop.

Then, as Marley took the cigar between her fingertips with confident grace, Ruth chuckled out loud and elbowed Hattie, both of them beaming in approval at her pluck.

The local ladies garden club, this wasn't.

"Oh, my goodness!" Marley exclaimed, nodding at Little Dan with enthusiastic approval as she tasted. "This is better than Rashall's."

"I *knew* you two were pilfering my cigars on that voyage," he said, shaking his head.

"Ruth, these would taste wonderful with your blackberry wine."

Ruth wagged a knitting needle at her. "You naughty, naughty girl. You're going to get us all started on another bad habit. The wine's bad enough on its own."

Marley turned to Juliana and held out the cigar to her in invitation, but she just laughed and shook her head. She took one more puff, then walked to her husband's side, leaning against him, and whispered in his ear. As he replaced the cigar in his mouth, his eyes narrowed with a rakish grin, and he hugged her close.

Sukey laughed softly. "So *that's* how it's done," she murmured.

The two women laughed together, and when Marley rejoined them, she said, "I heard you laughing at me. What were you saying?"

Sukey hugged her. "Oh, no, honey. Nothing so harmless as idle gossip. We were out and out *envying* you."

Marley smiled. "Anybody can smoke a cigar."

"That's not what we were envying," Juliana said with a silly giggle.

Marley's eyes went wide in disbelief. "You're joking, right?"

"What do you mean?"

"If you think your husband is as starchy as all that, you have a *lot* to discover about him. He's funny, and risqué, and warm, and down to earth, and ... oh, Juliana, he's just a very special man. And *so* sexy."

Juliana wasn't sure what to think about Marley's effusive praise, until she recalled that they'd first become friends in the close quarters of a ship. And it intrigued her—was her own husband the type to teach his wife how to smoke a cigar?

The aroma of meats cooking in the open pit wafted their way just as the pitmaster called out for dinnertime. Her father-in-law arrived and bent over to offer her his arm. "Would milady care to join me for dinner?"

"Well, considering I can't smoke cigars, I'd be delighted."

"Is it that you *can't* smoke cigars, or that you *won't* smoke cigars?" Marley called out after her.

They wound their way through the serving line to fill their plates with the bounty of summer harvest and savory meats. Country ribs, smoked brisket, yam chutney, roasted Brussels sprouts and corn on the cob, cole slaw, freshly sliced melon and fat, ripe plums, spiced peach pie ... far more than she'd ever be able to have even a taste of.

As she found a seat between her husband and her father-in-law, Juliana thought of the troops throughout the countryside.

She remembered the delight they'd had when she had briefly joined their company with Rashall, helping with the cooking and laundry duties. She'd never worked so hard, nor had such a grateful audience for anything she'd done in this life.

When she'd asked Rashall what the men usually ate in camp, he'd been encouraging but vague, reassuring her they weren't starving. She could tell by a simple glance at most any of them that this wasn't true.

Hasty, sitting across from her and Rashall, dug in happily. "I'm heading to meet up with the militia, first thing in the morning," he said. "So I'm fattening up, tonight."

"What do you usually eat when you're in camp, Hasty?"

The question, asked just as he sat down and eyed a healthy portion of beef ribs on his plate, animated him. "Well, we're supposed to get meat, bread, vegetables, milk, and whiskey. What that translated to, if we were lucky, was whatever salt pork we could get our hands on, some cornmeal, and a gill of whiskey. And when we weren't lucky, what we would actually eat was squirrels, or—"

"Hasty, who's leading the militia you're a part of?"

"Why, Ray, it's General Nelson. You know that."

"I know. I just wanted to hear you say words that didn't spoil appetites."

Hasty stopped, his mouth gaping. He shook his head at her. "I'm so sorry, Juliana. I wasn't thinking."

"I asked the question, Hasty. I genuinely wanted to know."

She closed her mouth. She wasn't sure she had what it took to be the wife that Rashall needed.

She shook away the unhappy thoughts as Dan announced grace. Rashall took her hand and stood with her at his side, and she bowed her head as he led the prayer.

As they ate, Dan spoke quietly to Rashall. "Son, can you tell if you've been given any more guidance about the subject I raised with you recently?"

His question was not for the table at large. She and Rashall had discussed it more than once, and she'd offered her support as well as her concerns.

"I have, sir. I'm privileged to accept God's call."

Exclamations of joy went around the table. His mother, sandwiched between his father and Ruth, simply bowed her head briefly.

"Now you know you can't live way up the river if you're going to lead these people, son."

"Yes, sir. Bronson's helping me plan out our house. Then Silas and Hasty will do the construction."

"Sounds like you've been given the guidance of Solomon, son."

"Just lucky to have good friends."

"Are you through with your commitment to the Marquis?"

He hesitated, glancing from Juliana to his parents. "No, sir. In fact, I'll need to go back soon. Cornwallis may be attempting a maneuver in Yorktown that, if he does, will fail, spectacularly so. He and his commanding officer, General Clinton, have communicated poorly for the past year, and I believe this may be their doom. Clinton tells him to turn right, and by the time he receives his message, he's been marching left for months. Now, he's expecting the Royal Navy to rescue him from an increasingly perilous position—foolishly, I believe. It's no strategy to take when the person ordering the Royal Navy about remains incommunicado."

"And the French Navy?"

"Comte de Grasse is juggling commitments he has to the Spanish, in Florida; and orders from his King; amid favors to General Rochambeau. It is the Major-General's hope and expectation that the French fleet will descend soon."

He stopped, lowered his voice, and went on. "Sir, between us, there is no hope at all for an American victory without this intervention."

When the two men had finished their dinner, Rashall said, "Would you join me for a cigar and a short walk?"

"Now that sounds mighty fine, Ray. Let's take that pretty wife of yours, too."

Ray offered the older man a cigar. He declined, so he put his own back in his pocket as they strolled away.

"I didn't want to bring this up in front of others, but I'm not without concerns over the people here in the village."

"How so?"

"You don't see?"

"I mean, which concerns. There are so many."

"The free black men and women, thriving in a slave economy. That's my first concern."

"And?"

"The second being how they fit into a brand new country being founded, already at odds over the rights of blacks."

"Any other concerns?"

"My marriage. I know God has blessed our union. But—"

"There's no but."

"Sir?"

"God has blessed your union. I'm not trying to be overly simplistic, but everyone has problems of one sort or another. One important item you neglected to mention is that all of you, every last one of us, here on this land today—well, except perhaps old Thomas's wife, Hannah—we're all well-educated. Now we may not have gotten it from the palace tutor, but we use the same books they do, and we love those books a whole lot more than some. Ray, that's an advantage you'll have over almost all people you meet of any color. Most of this country can't even write their names.

"And you're blessed by your mother. Smartest woman I've ever met. 'Boil the drinking water.' 'Wash your hands.' 'Inoculate your children.' Three simple rules and our children are already outliving children of the wealthy in this area.

"Sir, I worry about these people, in this country."

Juliana saw the frank concern etched in her husband's face.

"Are we just building castles in the air for them?"

He might have thrown water in the older man's face. "You know, Solomon tells us that life is empty. But his point is that God gave us this earth to enjoy, and we don't have much time here. So let's enjoy the time we have. That's not to say live in debauchery, but I don't believe for a second that the good Lord put us here to suffer."

He chuckled, touching Rashall's shoulder. "And I don't know how to break it to you at this late date, but my parishioners are used to living their lives in praise, not fear. Most of these people work hard all week, and they'll be looking to you to uplift them on Sunday mornings. If you plan on scaring them, well maybe you and I need to talk out this transition a little more."

Rashall nodded. "I agree completely, believe me. My mother taught me about joy every day when I was growing up. She reminds me every minute I'm with her. But she'll be the first to remind you that even in Boston, which is supposed to be the most enlightened place in this country, blacks sit in the balcony during church services. Whites and blacks can't marry. For that matter, they haven't gotten around to outlawing slavery up there, either."

"Ray, I do see your point. My point is that, well, it's like the old hymn says. I'm just a stranger here. Short is my pilgrimage, heaven is my home. Time's wintry blast will soon be past. I shall reach home at last. Heaven is my home."

"Yes, sir. But ..."

And he stopped protesting.

Juliana saw the wonder move over her husband's face as he understood he was in the presence of a true man of faith. He had seen God work in his life, time after time after time. He lived it. He believed it. When he glanced at her, she could only nod in understanding.

"Thank you, sir. I'll do my best to live up to your example."

"Son, let me tell you this—the less we focus on ourselves, the more we trust in God, the more we grow. 'He must become greater, I must become less.'"

As the sun began to sink into the horizon, the drummers gathered around near the dance area they'd cleared. They began performing, soon joined in by a flute. Then two of the older children joined in with pennywhistles, and old Isaiah perched near the drummers, plucking his banjo. George, always with an aptitude for music, added subtle body to the song with the Jew's harp.

The fingers of the children flew joyfully over the pennywhistles, and the song became a lively, raucous folk song—a bit Irish jig, a bit Scottish country dance. The music took the town by the hand and brought it to its feet in the clearing. And because they were within walking distance of the James River, the dance quickly became the Virginia reel.

Joy filled Juliana as she clapped along in time, tapping her toes, until her husband grabbed her hand and pulled her along into the midst of the throng. She laughed in pleasure as they lined up with the rest, turning and do-si-doing and galloping as darkness fell about them and the mounted torches were lit.

The gathering danced with abandon, whooping and shouting as they went.

An uneasiness filled Juliana as she heard a rumble. Rashall saw her face. "It's just thunder," he said as he reached her again. "Not to worry. Storm's on the way. We'll finish this dance, first."

The dance continued, the music growing louder, until suddenly she heard a distinct scream. "Riders!"

That was the rumble she'd heard—half a dozen or more men on horseback, bearing torches.

People continued to dance even as Juliana and Rashall fell away, hastily steering people toward the meetinghouse. Rashall directed her, "Go inside."

"No. Look at all these children."

She quickly hurried the children and other women into the meetinghouse as the men stood to face the riders.

Men arrived on horseback from the direction of the Quarterpath, hollering almost as if part of the dance. They rode in fast, through the town, dismounting only long enough to break windows and ignite curtains.

A rider rode straight toward the crowds, and the men and women—and children—rushed to get out of the way. The rider reached the school house, broke a window, set the drapes afire, then tossed a torch inside. Then a second and a third.

A moment later, Ruth emerged from the meetinghouse with a rifle and a pistol. The pistol, she fired into the air. Then she hoisted the rifle. "Next one touches a single building in my town gets a ball between his eyes."

The riders swung their horses around to leave. "Let this be a warning to you. Get out of Virginia, or you'll get worse," one yelled.

Instead of leaving the way they'd come in, they rode toward the crops, one still brandishing a torch. He drug it along through the grass as they cut through it on their way out, lighting the field that would spread the quickest. Just as he rode out, he tossed the torch into the tobacco field. They'd had no rain for weeks, and the hot, parched tobacco, ready for harvest, lit as easily as a pipe.

The men and women there understood the men had just set a field full of riches afire, and before the men were gone, they were already rushing to beat out the fires. Their first concern was the crops. They could rebuild a house, but it took a lot longer to grow a field full of tobacco.

They could not put it all out. Men rushed in every direction—some to the school house, to stamp out the fire that was already spreading inside, some to the half-dozen homes in flames, some to the fields.

Juliana grabbed her shawl, dipped it in a barrel of river water, and hurried with Sukey to the fields. They beat at the fire, coughing against the smoke that rose, choking them. "Be careful!" she cried. "The smoke can kill you. Watch your skirts. And stay on this side of the fire."

Where was that storm Rashall had promised now? They could use some rain. She heard its rumble—she even saw a flash of lightning, which they didn't need—but there was no rain.

Hasty arrived at the edge of the field, coughing, covered in sweat and ash. "Has anyone seen my father?"

"No," Juliana said. "Perhaps the school? Rashall's right over there in the tobacco, he might know."

Hasty sprinted to him, grabbing him by the arm. He signaled to Daniel, Little Dan's eldest though still in his teens, and the young man ran with them. Big Jim, their middle brother, emerged from one of the fire-damaged homes and followed.

She and Sukey dashed after the men to the schoolhouse, but before they reached it, they heard Little Dan screaming for Hasty.

Smoke poured out of the schoolhouse. She covered her nose and mouth with the wet, ashen shawl. "Over here!" Little Dan choked out, wracked with coughing.

Then they saw—Dan, stretched out on the floor, overcome by the smoke.

"Get out of here!" Rashall ordered Little Dan. "We've got him. Daniel! Hasty! Let's go!"

Sukey cried out as she saw her father, unconscious, and Juliana quickly grabbed her and pulled her back outside.

Little Dan ran to the door, gasping for breath. The other men bent to carry Dan outside, onto the grass.

"Hawk! Where are you? Need some help here."

Rashall fought for breath himself even as he dropped to the man's side. He opened Dan's mouth and inspected for obstructions, then pinched his nose and placed his mouth over Dan's. He breathed into the old man's lungs as his mother had taught him long ago. He paused long enough to rip open Dan's shirt and placed his ear over his heart.

Little Dan faced Rashall. "What can I do to help?"

Hasty knelt at his father's feet, resting his hands at the top of his father's worn old shoes. The sight troubled Juliana. All Dan had given to lead these people in this terrible era, and he didn't even own a decent pair of shoes.

"Hawk! Somebody find Hawk!"

Fear gripped Juliana, and as she looked around, she saw Bronson racing from the far end of the homes they'd torched.

Sukey trembled beside her, and she took her into her arms, stroking her back silently as the woman whispered, "God, help my daddy, please help my daddy."

A moment later, Ray placed the heel of one hand over the center of Dan's chest, straightening his arms and joining his hands, thrusting down in even, sure strokes.

Bronson arrived at last, dropping to his other side and speaking softly to him. Rashall nodded. Bronson took over the breathing for Dan, while Rashall continued compressions.

Marley joined them on Sukey's other side, hugging them both.

She wasn't sure when Camisha and Ruth arrived. They were just suddenly there, their dirt-streaked faces blank as they stared. Camisha tried to hug Ruth, but she shrugged away, kneeling at her husband's head, stroking his forehead lightly. Ashanti stood at his wife's side, his head bowed against hers, their hands folded together in prayer.

Rashall and Bronson went on with stubborn faith, breathing for the old man, compressing his heart, while the women prayed. While the people of the town gathered silently around the scene, staring in disbelief at what they saw. Praying as Dan had taught them over the past thirty-five years.

In the torchlight, Juliana saw the sweat soaking Rashall's back as he took turns with Bronson pressing against Dan's chest.

And then Ruth reached out and touched his arm, stilling him. She shook her head.

He spoke softly to her and continued the compressions, and she grabbed his arm, a sob catching in her throat.

"Please, honey. He's gone. I ... well, I felt him hug me just now, and he's gone on."

Juliana and Marley supported Sukey as she wept. Soon two of her youngest daughters approached from the meetinghouse, and she wiped her eyes, opening her arms to them.

"What's wrong with Grandfather?"

Sukey took the children aside, gathering strength because she had no other choice. Her husband was gone, her father was gone. Juliana watched in amazement as she mustered her inner resources to comfort her children.

Another young man who'd been hovering behind them since they pulled Dan from the smoke-filled building walked up to Ruth. "Sister Ruth, I believe this is yours. This was under Brother Dan."

She looked at the book he held out to her, and she took it, gazing blankly at it.

The Book of Life.

She remembered Rashall telling her about the old man showing him the book that named every child they'd ransomed from captivity, and his pride at his wife's accomplishment.

Then she noticed Camisha, gazing at Ruth. Silent tears streamed down her cheeks as she gazed at her friend, as if waiting for the signal that she could help her. No signal came. The tears seemed captured within Ruth's chest—as if she'd been strong for so long, she didn't know how to do otherwise now. As if she knew she had to be strong enough for both of them now, for her family.

Ruth rose, looking around at the others, her face almost lighting in a smile, out of habit. The wife of a pastor, doing a thousand unnamed and unnoticed, thankless tasks every day, content to toil in the shadows and be the helpmate of a man of God.

Sudden confusion filled her eyes. Utterly at a loss as the people waited for her to speak, she whimpered, her face collapsing into tears as she turned away.

Camisha murmured to Rashall, "You boys get Dan into the parlor at the parsonage. And keep the door closed until he's presentable." She glanced at Juliana, gesturing at the throngs gathered there. And she rushed to Ruth's side.

Dan's sons, along with Rashall and Bronson, carefully lifted Dan and bore him to his parlor.

Juliana took a deep breath, asking quietly for wisdom as she turned to the crowd.

"Please, go to your homes. If your home was damaged tonight, please stay with your closest kin. Is there anyone here who doesn't have a place to sleep tonight?"

No one responded, and she continued, "Please keep Dan's family in your prayers. I expect we'll meet in the morning for services."

Hattie appeared at Juliana's elbow, her face wracked with worry. "Miss Juliana—that is, Mrs. Adams—I help with those who pass on. Should I go on up with the other ladies and prepare Brother Dan?"

"Yes, Hattie. How many boys do you need to help—carry water, and such?"

"Two's plenty."

Juliana quickly appointed two of the stronger, more helpful boys to help them.

As the crowd dispersed to their homes, she looked around the village. As burning and pillaging went, the destruction wasn't much to speak of. They'd not known of the fermenting tobacco—the field was where the riches lay, or so they'd thought. So the tobaccos they were fermenting for special cigars remained untouched. It was hard to tell in the dark the extent of the damage to the homes, but at least the damage was distributed enough that people weren't homeless. All told, they could replace the houses in a few weeks' time with boards and glass and a bit of paint. A few rows of tobacco wasn't the end of the world—and the burned grass would be tilled and make the ground richer.

But as she watched old Hattie hobble up the steps of the parsonage with her helpers in attendance, she knew that the loss of the Trelawneys tonight was immeasurable.

Chapter Thirty-One

Emily herded her children into the car, ignoring the paparazzi across the street. Her driver hovered nervously. "Are you sure you'd not like me to accompany you, ma'am? The skies look nasty."

"We'll be fine, Bobby. Please don't worry."

"And—going without your security detail? That can't be a good idea. You'll be so isolated, your phone may not even work out there."

She smiled at him as she climbed into the driver's seat. She never missed her father while Bobby was around.

"Hence the term 'roughing it in the wild.' Don't worry. We'll be back Sunday. If we aren't, send out the cavalry."

She steered away from the curb and did a U-turn to head out toward the old bridge leading into New Jersey. Bobby stepped into the street, standing between the car and the paparazzi.

"Mom, who's Oginga Mboya?" Cammie asked.

"He was a leader in West African history. I'll find out more for you."

She could never think of the place as anything except the George Washington Bridge, but they'd renamed it a few years ago to placate a group of social engineers. The memory of George Washington's extended campaign in New York to win independence from Great Britain, the lessons she'd learned about his starving troops' Christmas in Trenton, the old portrait of him crossing the Delaware—it was all gone in the modern collective unconscious.

Not long after the renaming, it had been discovered that their chosen figure had three wives. On went the search for a perfect man, one who'd accomplished anything without a sin or two in his lifetime.

And still, nearly three hundred years after this country's founding, poor people—black and white alike—lived pathetic lives, cut short by violence, and too many found their identity in faraway lands. Emily never put into words her thoughts on the reason for this. With the best intentions and the most innocent of company, her comments could be overheard or misquoted and set the social media world afire and put at risk the foundation Tate had begun not long after she met him.

"That's okay, I'll look it up."

She reached out and touched Cammie's hand as she reached for her device. "No technology this weekend."

"Oh, right. I forgot." She looked into the back seat.

"No, don't mention it to them," Emily said. "They're not thinking about it right now, and if we're lucky, they'll both fall asleep."

"Didn't we just have another tech-free weekend?"

"And wasn't it nice? We got to talk to one another much more, and we got to bake our own bread, and learn how to do canning."

"Yeah, that bread was the best I've ever tasted."

"Things are always more satisfying when you've worked hard for them."

She had her best mom voice on. She had one job these days, and that was to wean her children off of the luxuries of the twenty-first century.

As it turned out, all three children drifted off another half hour into the trip while Emily found her way into the Catskills. She'd never driven this trip, although she was confident she could get them there. She wasn't as confident that they'd continue to do well without their fingertip connection to the entire world.

This was a generation who were practically androids, as hooked up as they were to the most sophisticated gadgets of the day. Her children were probably worse than most—although she worked hard to keep them from becoming spoiled, keeping them away from the Internet had been a tough job, thanks to Tate.

Tate had started them off on that. His technophilia had been his only trait that she wasn't fond of. He was completely linked up with whatever the technology magazines wrote about. In this, he was much closer to his own generation—even Rachel's, for that matter—than to Emily. Now, thanks to Rachel's directness, she knew why. She'd spent her formative years without electricity or running water.

Nervousness filled her as she thought of the incredible truth—and in the next moment, she smiled at what Tate would have had to say. He wouldn't have been satisfied until Grey took him to the place where he could travel into the future. But even that, he would have found interest in only as an offshoot of technology.

As for herself, she had always missed the time she came from, although she hadn't known why. When she had learned those lessons about George Washington, she had wept over the stories of his soldiers. Their bravery astounded her.

And it helped her understand her father much more. His work was real. While her peers mocked people like Papa and his co-workers as dressing up like actors every day and confused about who they were, he *knew* who he was. That identity informed and empowered his work. He brought Williamsburg visitors to tears because he told the simple truth; his own mortification and regret over his past couldn't have been conveyed by an actor.

The thought of Papa was crowded out by sudden worry at the road before her. Sleet had just begun falling, and she hated trying to drive on slippery roads.

Camping was the closest to traveling in time that her children had ever experienced, except in an occasional historic children's book. No one loved camping more than Cammie and her—and her father—but would children who had been raised to take running water for granted survive in that world?

Their immune systems were another concern. Not so much that they wouldn't survive, but that perhaps they might carry a germ back to the past that would wipe out the town. She'd tried to avoid giving them antibiotics whenever she could, but had they perhaps developed resistance to mutant bugs of this century that hadn't been around three hundred years ago?

She considered pulling over as she surveyed the narrow path ahead. Had she taken a wrong turn?

She drove over a bump in the path, and Cammie stirred. She sat up, looking around.

"Are we there yet?" Lucy called, from the back seat.

"Yes!" Cammie cried. She pointed happily at a bright red marker tied to a post at the side of the road. The rag was almost obscured by the elements and snow that had just begun falling. "There's your bikini top!"

The sight brought a welcome smile to Emily's face at the memory.

"I remember, you said something to Daddy about how you'd never be able to find the cabin if our lives depended on it. So he said, well, we'll fix that. And he reached into your beach bag and pulled that out and made a naughty joke and you scolded him."

Emily exchanged a look with her daughter.

"Mom, do you think he knew?" she asked, her face filling with pain at the memory.

Emily wondered, too. But to reassure her daughter, she gave her a tranquil smile. "Of course not. He couldn't have known. But maybe God knew we'd need a happy memory to guide us."

Once more the thought of her father returned to her. It saddened her to know that their return to the eighteenth century would end a truly inspiring career educating visitors about his life. How lost so many were in anger and hatred, rejecting the truth that could guide them.

"Yes, Lucy. We're almost there."

&

Rachel sat with Grey at the desk in his library, videoconferencing with Tate's lawyer, Montgomery. He was tapping into his laptop as Grey spoke. Beside the desk sat a court reporter, recording the conversation on her steno machine. It always surprised Rachel that they still used the same shorthand machine that had been invented so long ago. Montgomery was recording the meeting in video as well, for everyone's protection.

It just made sense to keep good records when people met to give away billions of dollars. Soon, Montgomery would no doubt be glad he'd made the video for other reasons.

When Tate had drawn up his will, not long after his marriage to Emily, she had surprised him by refusing to allow herself to serve as his prime beneficiary. Instead, his foundation was, with Grey serving as executor. Now, with power of attorney from Emily, he was consolidating those funds into a trust controlled by a board.

"And the properties in Jamaica?"

"Montgomery, what part of 'everything' don't you understand?" Grey asked with a smile.

Montgomery raised his eyebrows as he stopped typing, looking at Grey. "You know I have to itemize it. Five years from now, when you come back to me saying, 'but I meant to keep that pretty little cabin off in the Catskills,' I don't want to have to commit hari-kari."

Grey smiled blandly. "It's hara-kiri."

Typing again, he returned, "Say it however you want. I pronounce it suicide, and it's something I'm not in favor of, especially when it comes to me."

There was no surprise that while Grey and Rachel had accumulated some wealth due to her consulting business and his shrewd investments over the years, the bulk of wealth they had to dispatch had come about from Tate's estate. Now, it fell on Grey's shoulders to ensure that all of this wealth went into irrevocably protected funds. His main strategy was bypassing the technology of the day and imposing strict constraints on financial transactions to slow them down. Equal in importance was his insistence on tying a board of trustees to financial decisions. It would be difficult, if not impossible, for anyone to defraud the new foundation with such safeguards in place.

Even Montgomery, Tate's personal lawyer, would be able to do nothing without signoff from the board, after they left.

This particular detail they imposed to protect not the money or the beneficiaries, but Montgomery himself.

"Where are you planning to go, Grey?"

"We're going off the grid."

"Even Tate's kids? How are you going to educate them?"

"We will."

"You didn't join a cult, did you?"

He and Rachel laughed, but Montgomery just stared at him. "It's just the oddest thing I've ever seen. And I know I'm paid to do your bidding, but … it just seems awfully final. I don't want cops sniffing around, asking me why I didn't see the signs."

"We don't either," Rachel said. "Hence the language."

Imagine the attention that would be focused on this man after the entire family disappeared from a remote old house in Virginia without explanation.

"All right. Now you want everyone from Jay down to Bobby—except me, of course—to have a fully funded retirement fund, based on their current salary. Retirement at 65?"

"No. Retirement as of now."

He stopped typing again and stared at the ceiling. "Okay. So that means Bobby, who's 39, gets an annuity that adds up to his salary beginning at 65, plus his current salary times 26."

"I don't think it would work out precisely that way – the interest should begin funding some part of the salary at some point before 65."

"Right, right. Understood. But you want them to be paid a salary for no work."

Grey sighed. "They won't *be* working."

"That's what I'm saying." He went on typing. "You know Jay is already a very wealthy man."

"As a result of his own hard work. He made Tate a very wealthy man, too, and, now, our daughter a wealthy woman." Grey squeezed Rachel's hand.

Montgomery gave a mild smirk. "Not for long, she ain't."

"If she cared about that sort of thing, she wouldn't have refused to let Tate give her his entire fortune."

"Montgomery," Rachel said, "All we're trying to do here is help life go on without us here."

"All right. Now, about his bequests to other nonprofits."

"Leave those intact, of course."

"Even 30Mill? The foundation to fight human trafficking?"

She saw Grey inhale and exhale grimly. Tate had founded that with thirty million dollars—as he said at the time he did, a dollar for every slave alive in the world today.

"Especially that."

"Got it. Now, let's go on to yours. First, this CCA Trust."

This was the foundation Grey had set up and slowly funded over the years to provide better legal advice for youthful black offenders. As far as lasting impact went, it was the closest he could get in this century to replacing Camisha Carlyle Adams.

Joy filled Rachel. She couldn't wait to see her again.

"That goes into Tate's Emmitt Till Fund."

"And the 'great' scholarship—the Grey and Rachel Trelawney fund?"

"That stays independent," Grey said. "College scholarships for underprivileged children in Appalachia."

She had never lost sight that, but for Max Sheppard's wealth, she might never even have been able to go to college. She'd been luckier than most orphans—her father had been a decorated Navy vet, which had given her access to scholarships. But just up the road a bit from where she'd been born, children were still born without hope in old coal-mining country, now infested by drug addiction. More than a few of them were vets themselves.

They had never been able to have other children, so she socked away everything out of her consulting business into investments and funded a trust for educating other children.

And then, Max Sheppard had died. He had unintentionally left her as his beneficiary, and with no one else to contest the will, she and Grey had inherited everything he owned, including his company. With a portion of the proceeds from its sale, her paltry little foundation took on a life of its own.

"I have some properties I'd like to add to that fund," Grey said. "And Emily has instructed me to include all of her New York properties as well."

Rachel stared at him, speechless. A moment later, she turned away from the video screen, moved to tears at the gesture by her husband and daughter. The Central Park North townhouse alone was worth hundreds of millions of dollars.

When she could speak, she asked, "Are you sure you shouldn't reserve that home as a museum? They restored it to its original state."

Grey looked down at her and slowly smiled. "Eh, it's just an old house."

His joke made her smile. In recent days, he'd begun growing a beard and mustache to make his return to Rosalie less problematic. Most, she was certain, wouldn't remember him. Those who were old enough to remember him would never have expected him to walk down the street. But he didn't want to take the chance of ruining anything among the people of Rosalie who'd been freed thirty-five years before.

Her feelings were mixed. The facial hair was certainly sexy enough, but Grey's face was beautiful and expressive, and she disliked that being hidden.

"Folks, I think that may be it. I'll get these printed up and overnighted to you. Think about it some more. Take your time, and when you're good and ready, and I mean *really* good and ready, get them signed and notarized and send them back."

Grey said, "Actually, I have one other item I might want to add. The disposition of our home in Williamsburg. Give me till tomorrow morning. I need some more details, first."

Montgomery turned aside to speak to the court reporter, and she stopped typing and left the room, closing the door.

He sipped his coffee. "I just wanted to try, one more time, to ask for more details."

"And we'd love to help you out there, but you know we can't."

"Can you just tell me why you can't ... tell me?"

Grey took a deep breath. "I would love to—if I could do that without being locked up."

"Rachel? Blink once if he's got a gun on you."

She laughed. "When I think back on it, it was my idea."

Grey nodded. "That's true—it was."

"I would feel a little better about this if I could see you were holding out even a few hundred thousand. I'm only hoping this means you've got plenty of cash sewn into a mattress somewhere. Grey, have you seen a doctor recently?"

"For what?"

"Just a general health checkup, you know." The discomfort on his face left Grey confused.

"I don't know what you mean."

"All right. Let's just say I'm just trying to make sure that you're of sound mind and body."

"Not that it's any of your business," Rachel interjected, irritated at his line of questioning, "But we both just had a full checkup last week, as well as full organ replacements within the past year. Our doctor's name is Fullerton, he's here in town, and we've instructed him to release records to anyone who asks. Knock yourself out."

Grey raised his hand. "Okay, if you really want the truth. I'm from the eighteenth century, like Rachel's parents were. And it turns out this has caused some ripples in the space-time continuum, so we're moving back to the eighteenth century to live out our lives. Plus we prefer the clothing they wore back then. It makes nooners so much easier."

Rachel exploded in laughter. "Grey!"

"Fine." Montgomery straightened his tie and squared his shoulders. "Just trying to show you I care about you, man. Next time just tell me to mind my own business."

๙

Grey left the house after sufficiently apologizing to Montgomery for teasing him. He had no patience with the litigiousness of this time, and he knew that personal decency aside, other lawyers would have made a point of putting the question on the record, as he had. But he had also been one of Tate's closest friends for most of his life, and he had spoken out of real concern, so he hadn't deserved to be the target of Grey's dry humor.

He grabbed his great coat and walked outside and into the cold. He loved their small house in Williamsburg so much, he couldn't imagine leaving. But he'd found in the past four decades that he could tolerate almost anything as long as Rachel was with him. Without her, he could tolerate little for long.

An old song had been playing in the background at Montgomery's office, and it stayed with him as he walked.

The streets were quiet, but not quite deserted, as he walked toward the grand old house Thomas Trelawney had once lived in. His relationship with that man had been afflicted, to say the least. His first thirty years in life, he had felt nothing but disinterest and rejection from the man. When he'd barely come to know him, he'd fallen out of his life without warning. And that, he would always regret.

He opened the gate in the white picket fence around the Trelawney home, walking up the flagstone path. A small group of die-hard tourists had braved the cold for this last tour of the day, and the lady of the house was speaking in soft, genteel tones, dressed in colonial finery. The family who lived here were not employees, but merely residents.

And Trelawneys.

He looked up at the home. He'd lived in this town, walked these streets, passed this house, for thirty-five years now. But he could never forget the years he'd lived at Rosalie, when he visited town only to be reminded of the man who had rejected him. Of how he'd foolishly hung onto his righteous anger for so many years, ignoring Thomas's attempts to reconcile. Until Rachel, he had rejected Thomas with the same—worse—finality as that man, and had never seen the hypocrisy of it.

He stood in the shadows as the woman finished her talk. Usually she dealt with the mundane story of her life as a modern woman living in the old capital, but today she waxed romantic.

"My ancestors played a part in governing Williamsburg, in preserving it, and in working on its restoration. I am deeply proud that today, you will find many Trelawneys of vastly rich pasts living throughout this great land, from New York City to Napa Valley, from Seattle to Sarasota, from Williamsburg, some say, all the way to Paris."

Something grabbed his heart and squeezed hard, and he struggled to maintain his composure. How he would miss this place—this mission! Truly he had come to believe that this work of his had given meaning to a wrongheaded and disordered youth. That he might give warning to a modern world where slavery still went on—where dishonorable men still made fortunes from the suffering of children, women, and even men.

His eyes widened as he realized her talk had finished, and the visitors were drifting away. While he stood at the foot of the steps and they waited for the others to leave, he turned, looking out onto the town, seeing it as his father might once have.

He had resisted the urge to learn the fate of Thomas. Born the same year Williamsburg had become capital of Virginia, he had lived at least as long as the old town itself. In that day and age, it was an accomplishment in itself.

At last, he turned. "Good evening, Grace."

"Grey, how have you been?"

He accepted her daughterly pat on his sleeve, and he nodded. "It does get better."

"I don't know if you've ever spoken with my husband, Ethan. He's out at the moment, but he's a fan of your work."

"Oh," he said, never quite sure how to respond when he heard such things. For him, it was akin to being a fan of a person's eye color. "Well, I appreciate that," he said, and it felt stiff and awkward coming out.

"Do come in. Benjamin is expecting you."

She closed the door behind him. "Clara was my mother-in-law. She mentioned you while she was still alive. Always very cryptically, I must admit. Are you actually one of our relatives?"

"Distantly so." He gave an enigmatic smile, a tip of the hat to his interpreter persona.

That story made such meetings more comfortable. Although he and her husband were both Trelawneys, Ethan could not have been a descendant of his. Ethan had to be a descendant of Bronson and Marley.

She turned to call up the stairs, "Benjamin, Mr. Trelawney is here. He's headed back for his final few weeks in a couple of days, but he's here now. I suppose you're aware he has a job offer in New York."

"Yes, I'd heard that. I'm hoping to change his mind."

She directed him to the sofa, and he couldn't help but remember the last time he'd been inside this home, in 1746. It had been the days following his brother's birth. So much strife and turmoil—and joy—in those days. He'd come to love the small babe in the short time he'd cared for him, and he'd looked forward to helping his father with all the responsibilities and duties that went into raising a motherless boy.

But that wasn't to be.

He glanced toward the stairs, somehow still expecting his father to descend any time.

Grace left to fetch refreshments, and a studious young man descended the stairs and walked to him, introducing himself.

He was nearly as tall as Grey, with pale blue eyes and dark blond hair, and it was impossible to miss his resemblance to Bronson. His face wasn't yet nearly as angular as his brother's or his—both he and Bronson had their father's good bones—but he'd likely grow into them as he aged.

He had to be his descendant. Unless Thomas had fathered an unknown child, he couldn't have come from anyone else. He and Rachel had only Emily, and her children were all Sotherns, younger than this young man.

They sat in chairs before the fire, and Grace returned with cider.

He sipped his, then jumped right in. "I understand you're graduating this summer."

"Yes, sir. I'm considering going on to law school. I also have an offer at a bank in New York."

"What law school?"

"Harvard. I just received my acceptance letter."

"Why Harvard?"

"Well ... aside from it being ivy league, it's also a family school. My mother's father went to school there."

"And your father?"

He chuckled. "No, he went to good old William and Mary."

"Ah. As did several signers of the Declaration of Independence."

"Yes, sir."

Oh, the sound of that: a polite young man who knew as well of the many Harvard graduates who were signers.

"And another of those signers also happened to be the first law professor in the United States—and it wasn't at Harvard," Benjamin conceded. "It was at William and Mary where George Wythe taught Thomas Jefferson, John Marshall, and Henry Clay."

"William and Mary must also be a family school."

"Yes. My father is pushing for me to go there."

Although he was as driven by money as many men were at that age—Grey included—he was intelligent and knowledgeable of American history, and he was a Trelawney.

And it gave Grey pride to know that his family name lived on in this young man.

"Well, I can see you also have an interest in American history. I've read with interest your op-ed pieces—those published here in the *Gazette* as well as those published in the *New York Times* and elsewhere."

"Oh, yes, sir. I do indeed. You don't grow up in Williamsburg without an appreciation of American history. As many signers were aristocrats, there were many, many more farmers' sons who fought and died for independence."

"Have you taken any history classes as an undergrad?"

"No disrespect to my school, sir, but I wouldn't. I've been fortunate to grow up living in a history lesson, surrounded by scholars who have devoted their lives to education. My parents made sure I understood how everything that happened in this little town fit into world history. I know American history."

"And yet you want to be a banker."

He faltered, fumbling for a satisfactory explanation.

"Believe me, I'm not judging," Grey added. "You literally wouldn't believe what I did to get ahead when I was your age."

"Took up slave-trading?" he quipped.

Grey tilted his head. "Enough about me. The salary you'll make in New York puts what you could earn here to shame. But what if I were to offer you, say, five years of what they've offered you in salary to agree to accept a position here?"

"They'd match my salary?"

"That's not at all what I said. Are you planning to get married soon?"

"Haven't met the right girl."

"Well, take your time on that. So you don't have anyone else to take care of except yourself. Correct?"

He nodded.

"Your debt situation?"

"None. Why?"

"My offer is to personally give you five years of your New York salary to accept a position I've created for you. It's a management position as well as a character interpreter."

"I'm not a good actor."

"I'm not concerned about that so much right now. But I do need for you to agree to accept the position for a minimum of five years—preferably ten. You could easily make your career here in that time, and the cost of living is much lower than Manhattan. And you'd be able to invest that money to stabilize your future income more quickly. After five years, if you're still interested in going into banking, you'll still be able to find something there."

"What about Harvard?"

"Well, that's the decision you have to make. But I can tell you that you'll get a fine law degree right here, just a stroll down Duke of Gloucester Street to the other end of town. You'd be busy, to be sure—classes, a full-time job, and part-time interpreting."

He rubbed his jaw, thinking. Grey felt joy leap within him—he was interested.

"Now I know how tempting the glamour and glitz of New York is for a youngster, so you'd be able to take extra time off in the winter, when they're slow, to visit the city if you like. I think you'll find New York much more pleasant as a visitor; residents pay a great deal in taxes. Oh, I almost forgot. My wife and I own a small home here in Williamsburg that would be yours to use, as long as you work here."

"Permanently, if I stayed?"

"Yes. Now they do have requirements for residents. Of course, you're already familiar with those, growing up here. I'll work out an agreement that gives you permission to live there, free of charge. If you stayed here permanently, you would eventually own the home. It's just a small cottage, not large enough for a big family, but it's comfortable for a couple and three children. Any more than that and you'll be very crowded."

"When do you need an answer?"

"Now. If you aren't interested, I'll need to find someone else, and I'm on a tight schedule."

The young man sipped his coffee, then looked at him.

"This isn't a lifestyle to choose for getting rich," Grey said. "You make very little money and perform a unique service for people you'll probably never see again—and who usually don't realize at the time how much they're getting out of you. The entire place *is* an educational foundation. As you know, we're an authority for people around the world looking to learn more about this era. You'll be an expert yourself within five years, and yet you never stop learning new details. You'll watch people stunned to learn how people had to live back when our country was founded. Astonished at the bravery of young men and women working for freedom in the new country. And heartbroken to learn what those who were enslaved went through, in this most bitter of ironies, while fighting for freedom for others."

After a long, sober moment, Benjamin asked, "You're retiring, aren't you? You want me to take over your position."

"In a manner of speaking. For reasons no one can understand—but that have nothing to do with any special talent of mine—I am uniquely equipped for this. It has been my privilege to serve in this capacity for this many years. And I would train you myself, so you needn't worry."

"Your character's very popular. I don't think I could adequately fill your shoes."

"You needn't. I have another character you can play. My grandson, working as an abolitionist with all the challenges of the same era. Slave codes, hatred, the false theology supporting slavery … it goes on. After having read your op-ed pieces on subjects related to its periphery—and, especially, to human trafficking in our world today—I believe you're as uniquely equipped as I was thirty-five years ago."

Benjamin set his coffee cup on the saucer and held out his hand, dead serious. "Mr. Trelawney, you have a deal. When can we start lessons?"

"Let's begin now."

Chapter Thirty-Two

Rashall sat across from the marquis in his tent, smoking Trelawney cigars. "Cornwallis is suffering. His men are sick and he's burning through provisions. Especially with the unplanned responsibility of feeding those who were freed or who escaped from the plantations."

The marquis nodded. "I had thought that he might try to cross down and escape to the Carolinas, but he seems content in York."

"Considering he's slaughtering his horses, I'd say he's hardly content there."

"Well. Meanwhile, General Washington merely hints at joining us. He needs to come and put an end to this. When their own kinsman arrives on Virginia soil, imagine the excitement that will give the troops—especially his own militia."

He spoke with his usual intelligent alertness, now combined with frustration.

By this, the third week of August, he and his men had made it down to the juncture of the Pamunkey and Mattaponi at the York River.

"When a general is to guess at every possible whim of an army that flies with the wind and is not within the reach of spies or reconnoiters, he must then walk in the dark. Should a

French Fleet now come in Hampton Road, the British army would, I think, be ours."

"I understand he's been in Santo Domingo since April. Do you still expect him?"

"Indeed, I do. I expect that on some fine morning not too far in the future, General Cornwallis will arise and look out his window and spy the entire French fleet lined up in the Chesapeake Bay. It has become clear that Lord Cornwallis is entrenching at York and Gloucester. The sooner we disturb him, the better."

"Rider," called a soldier outside the tent. They exited, and Rashall was grateful for the breeze that moved over him in the sticky, oppressive heat.

A courier he knew from northern Virginia rode into the camp at full speed, pulling his horse to a quick halt.

Lafayette looked at the letter, then, as he broke the seal and opened it: "Oh, most glorious—Agh—I nearly swallowed my cigar!"

He eagerly scanned the letter, exclaiming in delight as he read aloud, "'Comte de Grasse was to leave Saint-Domingue the third of this month with a fleet of between 25 and 29 sail of the line, and a considerable body of land forces. His destination is immediately for the Chesapeake.'" He seemed to burst with happiness, and he exhaled as if in ecstasy.

Rashall's chest shook with laughter, and he said softly, "I can't imagine a Frenchman becoming so aroused over the notion of ships arriving with troops instead of, say, women."

Lafayette laughed, his eyes flashing. "Nor will you ever see it again, I'm sure." He signaled to the rider. "Come back. I will have mail for you in five minutes."

"What sort of troops do you think he'll have?"

"Three thousand. Three thousand French troops soon will be ashore and marching to Williamsburg." He shook his head with a smile as he prepared his ink and sharpened his quill with a penknife. "Think what you may of France, there is gravest dislike of Britain's tyranny throughout the world. We are not their only enemy. When it comes right down to it, this revolution of yours is quite incidental to the bad blood between France and England."

"And how does all this affect the French fleet?"

"Do you know of Galvez?"

"The Spanish governor of Louisiana?"

"None other." He jabbed his quill toward the letter from Washington. "He is now in league with de Grasse who, it seems, has been doing more these past weeks than enjoying island breezes. Galvez sent one of his officials, Francisco Saavedra, to meet de Grasse at the capital city of Santo Domingo to contrive a plan for defeating Britain. The Spanish agreed to fund this entire war effort by the French fleet and planned to use pesos arriving from mines in Mexico to do so. However, the ships had not arrived and other funds were not available.

"Instead, Saavedra appealed to Cuban citizens to raise the funds, and raised half a million pesos within hours! He says that the glamorous women of Havana gladly donated their diamonds to the cause of American independence."

The men laughed together in excitement. Rashall sighed— he was happy at last to have a home near his loved ones rather than roaming an endless blue horizon. But at times like this, he craved the smell of salt air.

Lafayette reached for pen and ink and quickly wrote a note. He sprinkled pounce on it to finish the ink, then tossed it away and sealed the letter, addressing it to Anthony Wayne.

"That stops Wayne from joining Nathanael Greene, and instead to connect with us. Now, to call up the militia without alerting our prey."

His next letter, he addressed to the new governor, Thomas Nelson Jr.—who also happened to command the Virginia militia and whose home was on the Yorktown peninsula. "Six hundred militia seems like a goodish number to me. What do you think?"

Rashall nodded. "Any more would give the plan away."

"Their first task will be to destroy all the boats on the Roanoke River, to prevent that crossing into the Carolinas. Ah.

And of course I must write Admiral de Grasse to apprise him of the state of the American and British armies."

He wrote a final letter to the Commander-in-chief he adored, thanking him largely just for letting him be a part of this moment. Lafayette was now certain that both he and Rochambeau were on their way south with the troops.

He handed the mail to the rider, who tucked the letters in his pack, mounted a fresh horse, and rode off.

Lafayette soon gave orders to break camp. They, too, would be marching to meet up with Wayne.

As Rashall prepared to ride out, Lafayette turned from the officer he was directing and waved at him. He dismounted and walked to the marquis.

"My friend, I expect time may get away from us in the coming weeks. The players are making their entrances. The leisure hours you and I have spent laughing over undrinkable coffee has cheered my heart during dark times and will again in dark times to come. While I hope we will yet share that brandy, for now, still, it must wait."

"Then I'll look forward to that."

"You will bring your bride to Auvergne soon? You are welcome at my estate anytime. Or lovely Paris? You have many countrymen here who came as visitors and never left, but you know I am too French, and I am certain I will soon be ordered back to France by my king. And I am not as strong as our Commander-in-chief, who can be away from his beloved Mount Vernon for six years. I miss my home, and my family."

He extended his hand and when Rashall reached out to accept it, the Frenchman clapped his other hand on Rashall's shoulder and they hugged.

"I understand. Only home is home. I would love so much to come and meet your family and perhaps we may. But I've learned that my work is here. This is my home. This is my land, and it appears I'm going to have to fight for it."

"That does not come naturally to a lover of life, but when someone threatens your very existence, we have no choice, do we?"

"No. We don't."

"Well. It has been a pleasure sharing with you the demise of William Phillips, my father's killer. Now, with all the letters you have watched me craft with hideous punctuation, I'll spare you that indignity for the next letter I write. I shall ask our Commander-in-chief to return the favor you and your kinsman have done for your countrymen—the ability to live your life in liberty and peace."

Rashall smiled at his flowery goodbye. "Man, I'm going to miss you."

The marquis gave a bright smile. "Then I shall look forward to our brandy. In this life—or the next."

With that, he snapped off a salute. Rashall returned the gesture and rode away into the darkness toward Yorktown.

He took a circuitous route to the town, to appear he was arriving from the north—rather than just upriver 35 miles. When he rode into the British camp, the sentry recognized him and waved him through, and he made his way to Cornwallis's tent. The general was asleep, so he grabbed the opportunity for a nap. He opened his bedroll under a tree not far from the tent and fell asleep within moments.

"You there." Rashall heard the quiet call at the same moment he felt a thump on his backside.

He scrambled away, coming into a crouch in a moment.

A redcoat stood there, his musket planted in the ground between them.

"Your folk are over there." He hooked a thumb in another direction.

"My folk." His gaze followed to the place, not quite within eyeshot. He could guess his meaning. At the moment, fresh from time spent with the most broad-minded thinker he knew, he lacked the interest in arguing with ignorance.

For some part of his life, Rashall had labored under the misconception that the British weren't the awful people he knew some Americans could be. Then his mother had explained to him that hatred and ignorance were the same, the world over.

He rose, straightening with a broad smile. "You know, that accent always fools me. But that could be because it makes you sound so intelligent and sophisticated."

The soldier gave a nod as he gestured again toward the distance. Apparently Rashall's accent made his insults come out sounding like compliments.

A bleary-eyed Cornwallis emerged, nodding at Rashall in recognition and repairing to a nearby tree. Packing up his bedroll, he made as if to trail off to the distance as he'd been told.

"Jim! Where are you going?"

"Oh, this here fella told me I ought not bother you, hanging around, catching forty winks outside your quarters."

"Nonsense," the big man said, frowning at the redcoat. "Come in, come in. I hope you bring good tidings. Is my commander headed south with reinforcements?"

"No, sir, I'm afraid he ain't. But I do have good news."

"Indeed." The man stared back evenly.

"Admiral de Grasse is headed to New York instead of here, and he only has a handful of ships. Between eight and twelve, is what I'm told."

"How can that be?"

"He's stretched too thin, and his fleet will be split between here, Florida, and elsewhere. The Spanish are making demands on his time."

"Florida." Cornwallis digested the implications of that.

Rashall had to work to keep the smile off his face at that thought. What he would give to see this man's face in that moment Lafayette had described—when he awoke with the French fleet outside his window.

Your folk, my ass.

Chapter Thirty-Three

He moved swiftly and silently on bare feet through the dark, paneled halls of Black Oak. A harvest moon high overhead illuminated the hallway through the windows of a parlor.

The house was still.

He headed straight for the master's suite at the end of the hall. His tread was so light and smooth, any chambermaid watching might have thought him a wraith. No one was in the house except for the master—his prey—and a young girl who was his own kinswoman.

He opened the door soundlessly and slipped inside, leaving the door ajar. On a pallet on the floor beside the window, a young girl lay facing the wall, sniffling. If he were a lesser warrior, the anger flooding him would have overpowered him.

He rushed to kneel at her side, slipping a hand over her mouth. He was not a man to soothe a woman at his best moment, and this was not that moment. His powerful body was taut with anger, and the little softness in him had left him.

Her large, liquid dark eyes gaped at him in terror, and he shook his head. "Go. Now. Say nothing."

She rose and glanced at the bed in fear, inching toward the door. And she hurried away.

He rose over the prone, fleshy figure in the bed. He paused to consider the options before him. It was not in him to kill a man without provocation. But the old buzzard who owned this palace had not been content to abuse those people he owned. Last night, he had violated a maiden he'd found bathing in a spring. She was promised to his brother. The vulture had brought her back with him to this place. He looked around the room in detachment. So much—and yet nothing but dishonor.

He was no longer a violent man, but he had learned many ways to kill a man—many of them silent. Many more, painful. He pondered for another minute, remembering the shame of the young maiden, trembling against the wall. It would bring him neither pleasure nor displeasure to end this man's life; it was simply a chore. But her suffering and humiliation cried out for justice, and his brother had told him to make him suffer.

In the end, expedience won out when the old man stirred in his sleep. A bronze statuette stood on the night stand, of a young brave reaching for an eagle taking flight. He lightly grabbed it and brought the base down with the swift force of a boulder falling.

Calmly, he washed his hands in the water that stood in the basin and dried them on a towel. He crossed the room and slipped out of the window, down the huge old elm tree there, and away, back to his canoe in the river.

Chapter Thirty-Four

The news raced down the river quickly. Ruth sat under the tree with Hattie, tatting lace doilies, when it reached Rosalie.

Camisha sat with them, reading a recent *Virginia Gazette* aloud. She'd spent more time in Virginia this year than she had since her childhood. She stopped, looking around for Ashanti. Last she'd seen him, he was helping the men refurbishing the fire-damaged homes.

"Either of you see where Ashanti got off to?"

The women shook their heads and continued with their work. Uneasiness filled her.

A shrill scream came from the river road. Susan, Ruth's granddaughter, came barreling at them with her slim arms waving.

"He's dead! He's dead!"

The women set aside their sewing, and others nearby in the village began to gather around.

Camisha closed the newspaper and stood, alarmed. "Who's dead?"

"Mr. Grimewood."

Hattie gasped.

"Is he now."

Camisha swung around at Ruth's toneless remark. She resumed her tatting, unmoved.

"Yes, ma'am." Susan came to a quick halt, breathless.

"Where did you hear this?" Camisha asked.

"Martin told me."

"How'd *he* know?"

"I think he said he heard it from a chief along the river."

"What happened?"

"Oh, look—there he is now. Martin!"

But he was already headed their way, flush with excitement. "Did you hear the news?" he asked, when he arrived. Then he noticed Camisha, and stopped short.

By now, a good-sized crowd was beginning to assemble in the shade of the old tree.

"Susan tells us Gerald Grimewood is dead. I take it he died of pure evil poisoning?" Hattie asked.

Martin looked around at the crowd, especially the youngsters who'd gathered, then back at his mother. He cleared his throat. "I heard from old William Natocawh that Grimewood ... er, kidnaped, one of the maidens. It's suspected that she herself may have killed him."

Ruth went on tatting, tapping her toe to a melody she hummed.

Camisha frowned. "A little girl. Killed that hulking brute, as evil as sin and twice as mean?"

"He was sleeping at the time."

"What'd she do it with?" her voice rose in doubt.

Again he cleared his throat. "A little statue."

"A little statue," she repeated. "How big is little?"

"Yea high," he said, holding out his hands perhaps a little more than a foot apart.

She dropped her cross-examination as the others plagued him with questions. Ashanti appeared from the crowd and came to her, even as she moved away from Ruth and Hattie.

"What're you thinking?" he asked.

"Hate it when you read my mind. Makes me wonder if I'm always so transparent."

"It's just me. Nobody else noticed anything."

"Martin, could you come and help us with something?"

He gave her a long look, missing the question someone had asked him. "Yes, ma'am. I'll be there in just a moment."

"Now."

He swallowed as he walked to her. "Yes, ma'am."

She steered him out onto the path toward the fields, with Ashanti on his other side.

"What were you doing at Black Oak?"

"I wasn't at Black Oak. I heard the news from William Natocawh."

"Then where were you when you heard the news, and why were you *there*?"

"I can't answer either of those questions."

Ashanti's hazel-green eyes blazed. "Son, you'd best answer both."

"Sir, that is classified information that frankly neither one of you even need."

They went silent, watching him dubiously. One corner of Camisha's mouth twisted.

"You know the Lakota are a peaceful people."

"Not when they're attacked, they're not. And neither are any of those natives around here."

"Grimewood has a harem of hundreds."

"Don't ask me why he did it. But I believe it."

"Oh, you do."

"Old William told me, and I trust him."

"How was he killed?"

"Struck in the back of the head with the statuette I mentioned. Old William said it's made of bronze."

Camisha heard the details dispassionately. All other things being equal, Grimewood deserved to die. But she had no intention for her Martin to become a vigilante in this world; there was simply far too much evil for him to ever be able to keep up with.

"Do you expect me to believe some little girl did that?"

"No—I didn't say I believed that. That's just what Old William told me. I think his son may have done it. They don't want any sheriff sniffing around."

"Son, did you kill that man?" Ashanti asked.

Martin looked at his godparents, both of whom had stopped walking to gauge his reaction.

"No, sir. I did not."

They nodded and turned back toward the group.

"That's not to say I didn't want to."

"Goes without saying," Camisha said with a nod. "Vengeance is mine, says who?"

"The Lord, ma'am."

"You better remember that. Now get on over there and celebrate your hero's welcome. Half the people there are going to think that if a brave did the deed, they might as well believe it's one of ours."

Martin gave a subdued smile as he nodded and took off back for the crowd.

"Let the boy crow a little bit, I say," Ashanti said. "Do you think he did it?"

After a long moment, she said, "I don't know. I mainly hope that he wasn't anywhere near Black Oak for the past week. That crowd with the torches'll come around here with a rope."

They walked past the tobacco fields, toward the old ruins. Her heart ached at the sight. How she missed Rachel. She dreaded going back to see Ruth at the moment, certain she had something to do with Grimewood's demise. The simplest public defender who'd seen what she'd seen from Ruth would've drawn the same conclusion. How she could've done it was what was a bit beyond her grasp.

"Baby, how are you feeling?"

"I'm a little tired. Mrs. Adams, I think I might be sick after all."

His casual broaching of the subject terrified her. It meant that he, too, was afraid. So she followed his lead.

"Do you have any pains? Say, along your arm or shoulder?"

He laughed. "Madame, I am sixty-seven years old. I'm a lot healthier than Dan was, but you know I love your meat pies and your *everything* puddings. But that's all right. I'm half convinced that when I go, you're going to run my carcass over to one of the plantations in the middle of the night and find an ornery old smart-mouth to take my place."

"That's not even funny!"

Fear moved subtly within her, and he turned his head down to kiss her mouth. In this time, there was absolutely nothing they could do for him.

"Oh, honey. Don't look like that. Not one of us knows our time here. Let's enjoy what we have. Maybe God'll heal me."

"How can you joke about that? He's done it before. He's done it for us before—more than once."

"Camisha, you know that when I'm joking the lightest, I'm praying the hardest."

In the field where she'd first met this man when she first arrived in this time she had loved all her life, she turned and threw her arms around his waist. She hugged him hard as she turned her face into his chest. His arms drifted down over her back, and he held her silently.

As they prayed the hardest.

"You suppose—we might sit here a bit?"

Alarmed, she helped him down. "What's wrong, Ashanti?"

He didn't answer. He collapsed at the edge of the entrance to Rosalie—not far from where she'd first seen him.

She screamed his name. Then she screamed for Rashall.

She fell to his side. His eyes were closed, and she cried out his name again. He turned to look at her, smiling as if he didn't quite see her. On a soft breath, he said, "Camisha."

Chapter Thirty-Five

Rashall stood at the altar of the meetinghouse. The cathedral in St. George's, in Bermuda, had been a magnificent work of art, filled with stained glass, statues, and icons, the exposed wooden beams of its ceiling resembling a ship's keel, as if he were still right at home on the *Adventurer*. The common church architecture reminded all who entered of the Christian journey.

The meetinghouse—the church hadn't even named a proper saint to pattern its mission after—was as straightforward as these people. A simple, large wooden cross on the altar differentiated the building as a house of worship.

He knelt at the communion rail and prayed for wisdom, prayed for courage, prayed for success. Malcolm had sternly warned Grey of all the issues facing him, and that although he would allow their travel, he would not take part in it.

When he rose at last and turned, his wife and Hawk stood there, waiting for him.

He came to her and reached for her hand, drawing her in gracious ease. "We'll be back before you know it."

For a long moment, she said nothing. At last, she kissed his cheek. "I know that. Just remember to avoid everyone except the Mannings. If you can get the Phi Beta Kappa key from them—and make sure it's neutralized, so you don't wind up stuck in the bicentennial—bring it back."

"Isn't that a must?" He exchanged a glance with Hawk.

He nodded. "Or they'll merely travel at a later time."

"Exactly."

"Do you feel pretty sure of what you're doing?"

"Juliana, we went over this dozens of times last night. Yes. I'm sure."

"All right. Remember: you have to get back to the labyrinth—or through the portal—in twenty-four hours. And be sure you're using the right artifact. And if you hear a very loud heartbeat in the labyrinth, go fast. It means your time is almost up. And while you're back in 1753, avoid everyone who knows you. Ruth said—"

Behind Juliana, he noticed Hawk covering the lower half of his face, stifling laughter at her nagging.

"Sweetheart, please."

She gave him another worried hug, then he kissed her and watched her head for the schoolhouse to join Marley. They were finishing the last details of preparing the place to resume classes.

Hawk handed him a haversack as they approached their horses. They mounted and trotted off past the ruins.

"Explain to me again why we can't just go through the portal right there and come right out? That's how Grey traveled, when he came to us on the *Immortal*."

"No, it isn't. He was using the labyrinth. They own Stonefield in the twenty-first century, and the labyrinth's still there."

"I know all that. But why must we use the labyrinth? It's so remote."

"Did you not sleep last night?"

Hawk gave him a dour glance.

"We can't use the portal because we don't have artifacts. We need to be there at a specific time. And in the labyrinth, we can get there when we want to."

They rode in silence for several minutes, until they reached the river road. "Just eager to get to where we can live our lives," Hawk said.

"How is your condition?"

"My...?"

"Your nerves."

"Oh, that. Much better. I still have occasional spells, but talking with Marley is like a tonic. And she helps me identify what can bring on an episode and we work on defusing that. Will is also tremendously helpful with that. She makes sure we all eat well, and I take Abigail riding and work to exhaust myself to help calm my dreams."

At that moment, they heard a rider approaching, calling their names. They stopped and turned. Martin, coming in out of nowhere, hell-for-leather. The terror on his face alarmed Rashall.

"Your father collapsed," he said. He hesitated, then said, "He's in bad shape, Ray. It happened about three, three and half hours ago. He's in Ruth's house."

Ray and Bronson exchanged a long look. "You go on back. Tell them we're on our way."

They spurred their horses the rest of the distance to Stonefield, and when they arrived, they found Grey drinking coffee at the hearth. "Do you two have any idea how hard it is for me to be here instead of in the Chesapeake Bay? All told, there are nearly thirty French ships of the line in the bay to do battle with Graves and his fleet."

"Grey, my father is gravely ill," Rashall said. "Do you think there's any possibility for ...?"

The news spurred him into action. "Come on. I was already planning a short excursion for them both tomorrow, to the doctor. Dear God, I hope we're not too late. It's such routine surgery, in the future. Why didn't I do this yesterday?"

They flew down the stairwell to the labyrinth. Rashall and Bronson were able to gain passage only as observers, so they followed along.

Rashall grew impatient with his terrified mother as he impotently watched her bicker with Grey about his plan for her husband. Oddly or not, she didn't seem the least surprised to find Grey Trelawney there, but she insisted on going along.

"Camisha, you're not thinking clearly, and I know you trust me. Please, let me do this. There are too many details to worry about if you try to go. I don't have clothes for you, and please! Just trust me! I can't promise you they can save him, but you and I both know he *will* die if you keep him here."

In the end, she agreed, standing there weeping outside the ruins. "I'll stay with her," Rashall said.

"She can't see you."

"I think she'll know."

And he watched as Grey lifted his thin father in his arms and disappeared into the twenty-first century with him.

Ruth arrived, trying to comfort her about Ashanti being with Dan now, and they'd look out for one another, and other such encouragement that did no more than terrify her.

Rashall couldn't bear watching his mother cry so fearfully—it was something he'd never seen this strong woman do. She looked so much like Helen or Parks here, it broke his heart. He put his arms around her, stroking her back, shushing her softly, murmuring reassurances.

Slowly, she calmed. "You know, Ruth, it doesn't make sense, but I think he's going to be okay. I just feel calmer."

Rashall stood beside her, lightly stroking her shoulder blades to keep her calm.

"Where *is* he?" Ruth asked.

"Bronson took him to the doctor," she said after a long pause—not bad, as white lies went.

"Well, that's good news. Why don't we go on inside, or even go into the meetinghouse and pray?"

She hesitated. "I'll be right there, Ruth. I need just a moment alone."

Then Rashall understood her worry—how Ruth was going to react when Grey appeared out of thin air from the portal with Ashanti.

"I'll be right there," she said. "You go on, now."

And sure enough, even as Ruth walked into the meetinghouse, Ashanti walked out of the ruins, alone, robust and whole.

Grey stood on the other side—able to see her, although she could no longer see him. Bronson stood beside him.

Camisha exploded with ecstatic joy as she threw her arms around her husband's neck. "What on earth did they do to you?"

"I'm not real sure. I thought I was dreaming—Grey Trelawney was there. I was in a doctor's office. They laid me out on a table, and this big contraption came down and next thing I knew, I was walking out of there with about four scars on me, but no pain at all. Baby, I feel like I'm 20 again."

She laughed, gently petting him, kissing his cheek fondly. It was a side of his mother that Rashall had never seen.

"Oh, by the way—he said to tell you he'd come for you tonight, so you could get it done, too. Camisha, is this a dream? Are we gone onto heaven, maybe?"

They walked away, arms around one another, as they mused over the philosophies of heaven.

Chapter Thirty-Six

Astoundingly, as if nothing had happened, Grey went on, "Today begins the single most important sea battle of this country—if not the world. And here we are, traveling back to the none-too-remarkable 1753."

Rashall exploded with an emotional laugh. "You just saved my father's life. And you act as if it were nothing more than a sneeze."

"I did nothing. It took a couple of hours to arrange it... the most difficult part was getting him there in time. I admit I was afraid we might not make it."

He brought out the artifact that had brought them there, and they returned to the labyrinth in the next moment.

"I think I just used up a year's worth of adrenaline."

"You have no idea how lucky you were to grow up with your mother. You know so much more than any normal kid growing up in the eighteenth century did. Now, where were we?"

Rashall exhaled. "The drudgery of 1753."

"Oh, yes. That again."

Bronson said, "Look at it as a battle in time. The most important of your life."

Grey nodded noncommittally. He may have been a sailor as a young man, but for thirty-five years he'd been a historian.

Rashall understood well how his own mother's love for history had changed her life.

They headed down to the labyrinth. Grey ordered their travel, and they presented their palms for verification.

"Destination is inaccessible. An anomaly exists."

The men went silent, surprised at this wrinkle. Rashall sighed. "It's me. My mother's there."

"Do you remember when this happened? Two men vanishing?"

"I wasn't there. I was with Hawk and Michael, chasing pieces of eight."

Grey turned to the machine. "Where's the anomaly?"

The machine was silent.

"I know it's my mother. She's the conflict." Rashall stepped forward, placing his hand in the reader. "I'll observe only."

"What does that mean?"

"No one can see me. At least no one in the time. Not sure if you two can. Can other travelers see me if I observe only?"

"Group travelers are visible to each other."

"But—we'll *need* you."

"Two of them and two of you. You can do it."

"Then why are you even going as an observer?"

"I can at least try to help—warn you if I see something you don't, or whatever. I just know I can't stay behind."

"All right, then. You go in an hour early and scout out the environment. See if you can find the Mannings."

Rashall arranged his travel, then changed into the simple homespun of a farmer from an earlier era. Checking one last time for the return artifact in his pocket, he raised his destination artifact, a simple handkerchief, to the reader.

The rich, pungent aroma of the tobacco fields awakened him. Steeling himself against the inevitable headache, he bolted to his feet in a field. Not so bad this time.

He looked around for a moment, orienting himself. Workers were in the fields picking weeds—one, only a few feet away. He waved at the worker, who looked in his direction without reacting.

It was true. No one could see him as he hurried down the path toward the river road. Even in this time, just twenty years after its inception, the town had expanded and improved in countless ways.

He had no time to marvel over the improvements the people had made. He loped off toward the river. And there he saw three men disembarking from a small commercial ship. The two younger men, he recognized right away from their trip to Boston in 1976. The older man, he would never forget: James Manning, whom he would kill a decade later outside the Raleigh Tavern.

He walked right up to them, to hear what was being said. Their tones were subdued; their words too inflammatory and ignorant to bear consideration. In the end, their plan and their goals were exactly as Grey had surmised.

They meant to kill him. As well as the woman who'd saved Grey's life—Rashall's own mother.

Knowing that, Rashall found a new respect for Grey; he was risking his life here.

"Father," said the older son, "will this finally set your mind at ease?"

"My mind is fine. They made me sound like a common criminal. They ruined my life—took everything I ever loved."

Caught up in his self-righteous rage, he paid no notice to the two young men standing before him. Was he so obsessed with his revenge that he completely lost sight of those two boys?

No. Rashall remembered Hannah explaining how angry he'd been when his boys vanished forever.

Sheppard scrutinized his father, who stood, scanning the deserted path of the town. He saw, in the distance, the ruins of the mansion he'd destroyed with fire two decades before.

"But sir, you're a wealthy man now, and it's been so long since ... the incidents in question. Can't you just put the thoughts of it away?"

Without warning, Manning slugged his eldest son in the jaw. Sheppard reeled back, catching himself from falling in the dust. He didn't fight back. Sheppard seemed to be a highly intelligent man, as well as slender and cool-headed. He was the type to be deadly while smiling.

Jack, on the other hand, had inherited his father's brawn and hot temper. If he didn't know any better, and he didn't, he'd say Sheppard and his father weren't physically related. Maybe the boy's mother had had a lover. Maybe that explained Manning's violence with him. Or maybe the man was just hateful to everyone.

"We're going to find that black wench, do away with her, and then deal with Trelawney. I don't care if I have to try it a dozen times to do it. I'll get it done, all right."

Suddenly the folly of their mission flooded Rashall. These men knew the secret of time travel. Retrieving the artifact would slow them down—but it wouldn't stop them.

Rashall spotted Grey and Hawk arriving just across the road, leaning against one of the houses. While he was invisible to the rest, they were quite visible. Hawk had cut his hair and both men had grown beards to reduce the chances of being recognized. The only person they had to worry about was Camisha. The others here thought Hawk at sea, a teenager, and Grey, dead. Even Camisha wouldn't be expecting to see Grey here—at this point in her life, she didn't know about the time portal on Rosalie.

Rashall crossed to the other men. "They can't see you at all?" Grey asked.

"No." He gave them a long look. "It occurred to me standing there that it's not enough to get Rob's key back."

"How so?"

Rashall rubbed his temples. "They know the secret of traveling in time. Apparently the portal only became activated—or active again—when Rosalie burned down. If they can't get to you without an artifact from the future, they can certainly get to my mother."

"Not if they don't know she's still here."

"They'll learn that today. She's got to be around here somewhere."

"Your recommendation, then?"

"Engage them."

"I cannot kill them in cold blood."

"Think back to those little girls pulling that red wagon." Grey's eyes were expressionless.

"Not one of us can kill a man in cold blood, no matter what a favor to humanity it would be. James and Jack lack basic civility. Sheppard is obedient enough, but he's no killer. Either of the other two will fight you over nothing at all."

Even as Rashall spoke, the three men passed them on their way to the ruins. They sprang into motion, taking a shortcut only Grey would have known, through the cool pines and oaks and maples that led down to the water.

Grey strode toward the rear entryway with calm assurance, Hawk and Rashall right behind him. Grey planted himself in the entryway with the others at his side—one warrior unseen. Manning approached him, his jaw hardening in resolve and intimidation. They met like small, determined armies squaring off at battle lines.

"Might I be of service?" Grey asked.

"Out of my way."

Rashall recognized it, then. The sound of his mother's voice and—high, lilting with girlish giggles, his sister Helen's voice. This, he had not expected. Everything within him wanted to turn to look at her. With steely resolve, he focused on the men before him, and her voice fell away. The moment was at hand.

"I do hate to be a bother," Grey went on. "But I'm watching the property for a relative. And as it turns out, the ruins of the mansion are quite dangerous. If you attempt to enter, you might be gravely injured."

"I said, begone."

Grey met him face to face. "I never liked you, Manning."

Standing so close, Manning could see the fierce glitter in his eyes—but would he recognize the man he thought he'd killed, thirty-five years before?

"You would have killed my little girl. Is there no end to your evil?"

His face lost all color. "It can't be. You died."

"You heard the rumors, didn't you? That I didn't die?"

Manning's throat worked to swallow. In a flash he reached for his knife. He stepped back, balancing himself on the balls of his feet as he moved around Grey. He took a false swipe at Grey, then another.

A third time, his hand sliced through the air as well as Grey's sleeve, drawing blood. Grey took a step back, putting space between them, and again leapt forward. Manning deflected the blow and returned with another thrust. Grey knocked away the knife and drew his own, driving it deeply into his heart.

Manning tried to speak. His eyes went glassy, and he dropped to his knees, then to his side. Grey withdrew the knife, wiped it on Manning's shirt, and replaced it in its scabbard.

"I do hope that's the last time we have to kill him," Rashall said.

Grey nodded. "Devilish hard to kill, wasn't he?"

He had moved so swiftly, shocking Manning so completely, that the other men barely had time to do more than stare. But now Jack, his eyes round at his father's lifeless form on the ground, gave a guttural scream.

He drew his knife and circled Hawk, attempting to disarm him mentally. Lightly, as if playing, Hawk shifted on his feet, carving a bloody, superficial X in the center of Jack's chest.

"You think that's funny?"

"No," Hawk said, easily keeping pace with him as he continued to move around him. At this point, he was waiting to make his move. "I'm pondering the best way to dispatch you. I can't stand the sight of you. You may be young, but you're already evil, and you only get worse as time passes. The X is for killing one of the finest, most brilliant men I've ever known."

He reached out and cut a purposeful line down Jack's arm. "That's for killing his wife, the mother of three of the finest women I've ever known. And for filling my wife with fear."

"I'll kill you both for what you did to my father."

"He wasn't worth it, trust me."

Sheppard spoke. "Jack, give me the knife. He's right. It's not worth the fight. You and I can go on and be free of the old man now. We don't even need to go to another time to do so. Or we can still go, if you like. The future must be a better place."

"No, I'm afraid that's not quite right," Grey said, speaking as if he were slow-witted. "Or weren't you paying attention to me when I told your father? No one is allowed in these ruins. I'm just partial to the arrangement of bricks as they are."

"I'm not going to fight you," Sheppard said. "If that's what you want, you can keep waiting."

Hawk focused on controlling Jack—and yet provoking him.

"Jack. Give me the knife. We'll go somewhere more fun."

As Rashall watched Sheppard with his brother, he suspected the dynamic between the two was more dangerous than he'd thought. He'd thought—along with Grey and Hawk as well—that Jack was the most terrifying kind of killer, with Sheppard merely trying to clean up for him afterward. Watching them now, he suspected Sheppard might well have more control over him than anyone thought. Grey had said he was a controller, not a killer. Now, Rashall wasn't so sure they weren't one and the same.

In a moment, Jack raised his arm and brought the knife down toward Hawk's chest. His own heart rose into his throat even as Hawk blocked the stroke with his blade, in the same motion slicing Jack's arm and flicking away the blade. It clattered to the ground, and Sheppard quickly knelt and retrieved it, tossing it back to Jack. Unfazed by the wound, he continued attempting to get through Hawk's defenses.

Grey cast Sheppard an even look. "So you're not quite so eager to walk away from this as you pretend to be."

Sheppard said nothing.

Grey approached him with his own knife loosely in his hand. "I grow short of patience."

"You're an old man. I won't fight you."

"Let's not bicker about age." His knife was up and out.

"I don't have a knife."

"Try looking in your lower right pocket, there." He cut a long, diagonal line across Sheppard's shirt, left shoulder to right waist.

Sheppard smoothly withdrew his knife and jabbed it toward Grey's midsection. Grey pushed him back.

"I take it you've killed your share of men, then."

Sheppard said this, even as he was distracted by his brother's fight. Jack's knife skills were adequate, and Sheppard watched closely as they fought.

Then a sudden sickening noise came from Jack, as Hawk slit his jugular. The man fell to the ground, and Sheppard fell at his side. Already, Jack Manning was dead.

Sheppard came to his feet, facing Grey. He took a fighting stance even as he spoke. "How do you know we've not left a warning in history to ourselves to avoid this moment?"

Rashall was alarmed at his familiarity with the possibilities open with time-travel.

"You can never kill evil, Trelawney. Do you truly believe my idiot brother was the danger to all of you?"

Grey jabbed his blade at him. "If I have to rid the earth of you ten thousand times, I shall do it. Blatant hatred is less destructive than the evil that you are. Your evil speaks honeyed words and smiles treacherously at your enemy while plunging a dagger into his back. Your benevolent prejudice is a tool of Satan. How many have you already killed that we know nothing of—as you would have killed my entire family?"

In the next moment, Grey's blade was at Sheppard's throat. He met Grey's eyes evenly, then took a step backward and howled with a blood-curdling, demonic rage as he drew the blade across his own throat.

Shocked, Grey recoiled, staggering away from him.

Sheppard collapsed in the field over his brother's body.

The three men quickly dug a grave near the ivy within the ruins of Rosalie, put the Mannings there, covering it with broken brick. Rashall hoped the ivy spread quickly.

They stared at the grave, and Rashall spoke. "The threat may never be fully gone."

As they prepared to go through the portal, Rashall stopped them. "Just two minutes," he said.

He walked down the street, unnoticed, until he saw his mother—fifteen years younger. She and her eldest daughter were laughing over something, and Rashall's heart filled to overflowing at the sight of Helen again, young and beautiful. Before she married Taleeb or gave birth to their children.

He walked to his sister and inhaled deeply of her aroma. He lightly touched her, rubbing her shoulders, leaning over to kiss her forehead. "I love you," he whispered.

How he missed her—had missed her, for the past year. He kissed her temple and felt her turn her head up, as if listening.

"Mother, where do you suppose Ray and Hawk are?"

His mother laughed softly. "Oh, baby doll, they could be anywhere. Why?"

"I caught a scent of something that smells just like Ray. I don't even know what it was—but I sure do miss him."

"I do, too. Don't forget to pray for him."

"I'll remember—always."

And even as she said it, he remembered his wife's words, not so long ago: *If you go merely as an observer, you won't remember. You remember going, but nothing about what you saw.*

The realization pierced him with double-edged pain; now, knowing he would never remember this moment. And for times to come, how much comfort the memory would have brought him.

Rashall understood the treachery of this glamorous pastime of time-travel and why his wife had abandoned it. And he understood what Dan had tried to tell him.

Life's moments were not meant to be looked back upon, with nostalgia or grief. Without realizing its moments, seizing them as they came, life was empty, meaningless. Like a rose or a song or manna in the desert that rotted by day's end, they were meant to be consumed with a glad heart—with gusto and delight.

Chapter Thirty-Seven

Grey leaned against the corner of the stables, watching a younger, terrified version of himself. Now, he sought wisdom for what was to come.

As he prayed, his focus changed. He watched the men in the laborious process of weighing anchor. How hard they worked, these men who hoped for so little. Benjamin Crowell, as fine a sailor as he'd ever known, had lost his entire family to smallpox just the year before. Yet there he was, scrambling into the shrouds to adjust a flapping sail to his captain's liking.

God truly had blessed him throughout his life—even during those times he neither recognized nor deserved it. Even now, the man he once had been, lost and empty and seeking what he knew not, stood shouting orders at his men. He saw the storm off over the southern horizon, somewhere out in the bay, and knew that the man he once had been was working along with his sailors to beat that storm.

All would fail. Tonight, he would be dodging lightning on his way to Rosalie. And there he would disembark and find his beloved Rachel. The memory still brought a smile to his face.

The *Swallow* soon caught the breeze and continued back down the river toward a storm he had yet to face.

Now, he watched the group outside the home, preparing to enter. William, the slender, pale son of Godfrey Hastings, knelt to welcome young Rob to his new home, and Grey saw the exact moment when resentment entered the eyes of the blonde mistress of Stonefield. It wasn't that she disliked children; she was swollen with child herself. He suspected it galled her that anyone besides herself should capture a moment of her husband's attention.

"William, the boy be a servant. You needn't treat him otherwise."

Grey sighed. How he disliked Hannah Hastings. Old Hastings had deserved so much better in a daughter-in-law. He couldn't fathom how such a young woman could have become so tart so early in life; as he watched, she wasn't yet twenty. She brought to mind none other than Letitia Trelawney. The memory of that fiend he'd once been married to crawled down his spine in a shudder of terror.

"You," she said, crossing her arms over her waist as she faced Sarita. "Water in the rain barrel yonder, flour in the kitchen. Tea be late."

Gideon watched her without reaction, but he knew how the man felt about his wife being addressed thus.

The comely, shapely older woman smiled gently and even curtsied—even though Hannah had already disappeared into the house. He knew from her own testimony that she was still happy in love, happy to be free, and looking forward to raising a large, happy family. He knew from his own research into his wife's ancestry that although she had wanted more children, she would never have another besides Rob.

Sarita looked around, and William gestured toward the side of the house. He patted Rob on the head as he showed Sarita the place, filling the bucket himself and carrying it back inside.

Grey contented himself to wait until the family went to bed, and he filled the time carving a name into the gigantic stump that stood near the wood yard. He left uncarved the last letter.

And as if he'd been waiting for that, Gideon walked out onto the back porch to enjoy a cigar and gaze at the stars. The sight comforted Grey—how often had he done exactly that with his own men?

"Gideon," he said, walking out of the shadows.

The man came to his feet, watching him warily. "Who are you?"

"Gideon, I'm going to tell you the truth. Be patient. I am your own old captain, coming from another time to warn you of a matter of some importance."

They stood in the dim light of a half-moon, and Grey wished he'd shaved his beard—although Gideon had seen him unshaven over their years together. The man didn't believe him, of course.

"There are four other men inside, and we are well armed."

Grey raised a hand. "No, there aren't. You're alone with your young family in this new place where I left you not four hours ago. You're afraid, because you've realized your new mistress is cruel and self-centered."

"Anyone could know as much."

"All right. You were born in this same county and went to work for me five years ago. You met your wife in Saint-Domingue and fell in love with her, along with half your fellow seamen on the *Swallow*. You spent several years of salary for her freedom, which I foolishly accepted rather than paying you instead, when it was you who demonstrated to me Christian love."

Gideon began to grow less fearful, but the suspicion remained. "How can this be? As you said, I just watched you sail away. Here you appear, decades older, yet yes, looking like yourself. Tell me something about you that only we would know."

"I prayed for my wife's death."

"Sir, that's no secret. We all did."

They laughed together. As quickly, Gideon sobered, shaking his head sharply. Grey half expected him to slap himself in the face to try to wake up.

"I'm here to warn you of something important—as important as your love for Sarita." Gideon raised his chin, and Grey went on. "In another four years, something truly miraculous will happen to you, and you will be transported to an entirely different place. Eventually, you will meet a young man named Cameron Carlyle. When you do, you'll remember this conversation. Honor your instincts to care for him. Throughout the rest of your life, protect him and preserve his friendship with young Rob."

"He'll be a friend of Rob's?"

"Sir, he'll be a friend to all you love, more than I can tell you, more than you can even guess."

"Why would you come from another time to tell me this?"

"Your life depends upon it. My life—all that I hold dear—depends upon it. Beyond that, I can tell you nothing. I cannot tell you the real threats you will face in the coming years, but I can promise you that your faith will see you through, and your boy's friendship with him will mean everything."

Gideon offered a cigar to Grey, but he shook his head. He then looked toward the river as he puffed his own cigar. "I already miss my mates. I'd trade nothing for my beloved Sarita, but the friendship on a ship is nothing short of brotherhood."

'Twas true enough. And yet, for Grey, he had never felt that kinship. He was always apart, emptiness a constant companion. Until he turned away from his despicable life. How thankful he was for his own Rachel, for showing him the truth. And Camisha. And this man, with his love for a woman Grey would have sold for little more value than a milk cow.

"Come with me." Grey led him to an old stump nearby and carved the *e* at the end of the name he'd begun earlier.

"When you awaken tomorrow, you'll come out here to chop wood. And you'll find this name carved here as a reminder. Pray for this young man as you pray for your own son. Every morning, every night. When the time comes, make him promise to always keep his family near yours—and require the same of your own son. It won't be hard, at first. But during those times when friends grow apart, he and Rob must remember the importance of their friendship. For them and their families, it will, literally, mean their very existence."

He left Gideon in the dark, disappearing down the root cellar. He had just one task left.

ꙮ

Ashanti lay in the dark coolness of their bed, flat on his back, musing at God's great gifts.

He rose quietly, watching his wife. She slept tonight, and he didn't want to upset that. When he left the small home they had on Rosalie, he walked outside, gazing up at the stars.

Dear Father, what happened that day? Did I truly see Grey Trelawney? I cannot remember, but I feel like a young man again. Please calm my fears. Please help me know what to do.

Then, as if in some kind of none-too-funny response from heaven, he saw Grey Trelawney emerge from the old Rosalie ruins.

He sighed. Maybe he'd died in bed, and Grey was some cosmic angel, come to take him home. That would just be his luck.

Grey spotted him. "Come with me," he called in a stage whisper.

Ashanti frowned. Funny was one thing, but this wasn't funny. Curiosity got the better of him, and he walked to meet Grey. "What are you doing here?"

"Hasn't Camisha told you anything in the past thirty-five years? Don't you remember the other day?"

"She's told me plenty. Nothing that made me think you'd come knocking. And all I know is that I feel better than I've ever felt in my life"

"Good. Rashall told me you were sick, so I took you to the doctor."

He squared his shoulders. "You what. Wait. How have you talked to Rashall?"

Grey was silent for a long moment. "I owe my life to your wife. I owe my happiness to your wife. And I owe your wife's happiness to you. So I've got a lifetime of favors I'll never be able to repay either one of you. And in the end, I'm a selfish bastard who lost a man who was like a son to me, to a bad heart, in a world where replacing an organ is *nothing*. And I've got exactly one night to help Camisha the way we helped you."

"What are you babbling about?"

"We're coming back, tomorrow. I've promised never to use the labyrinth again, and nothing is more sacred to me than my word. I have tonight only, to help Camisha, if she'll come with me. Just bring her out here while she's still half asleep. She won't even remember it."

Ashanti glanced back at the small home where he now lived with his wife. Something had soured her on Boston—perhaps the loss of their daughter, perhaps something else. But here they were, in the revolutionary war zone, on the eve of a battle brewing in Yorktown.

"Tell me something that makes me know it's actually you."

"Oh, for crying out loud, not this again. All right, one time I kicked you off Rosalie."

Ashanti laughed. "Yeah, you thought I was trying to stage a rising."

Grey gave him an even look. "Go get your wife. Now."

He returned to the house, where Camisha still slumbered peacefully. "Baby, wake up—wake up!"

"Mmm. You're in a frisky mood." She nuzzled against him.

"That's what I was trying to tell you. We have to hurry. I had an organ replacement surgery."

She reared back, eyeing him suspiciously, still groggy. "Huh?"

"Don't you remember? Grey brought me back. He told me …" He stopped, instead taking her hand and bringing it to his chest, where she'd already felt the small incision, already healing with surgical glue keeping it in place. "And here," he said, yanking her hand down to his right rib, then around. "New liver, new kidneys, new lungs."

She laughed, low in her throat. "Oh, this is the funniest dream I've had in a while."

"Baby, *get up*. He's ready to take you, too. I don't know how he did it, I don't know how he's here. But it's real. I thought I was dreaming, too, but I can tell you right now, I feel like a new man. There's no soreness, I'm not tired, I feel like—well, if I had the time, you know exactly how I'd show you how good I feel. I'll show you when you get back."

Her laughter was small, as if trapped in fear and hope. She closed her eyes tightly, then opened them again, staring at him. More than once in her life, this woman had seen miraculous healing. She'd even seen the simple hygiene she forced on everyone who would listen—and some who wouldn't—*seem* like miraculous healing.

"Is it true?" she whispered, her voice tight with tears as she hugged him. "Maybe we died and this is heaven."

"I am feeling way too carnal for this to be heaven." He pulled her out of the bed and toward the door. "Let's *go*. He has to take you."

"Will I see Rachel again?"

"My heavens, woman. You've been given a million pounds and you're asking if you can have two pence. Trust me!"

She stopped, in a moment deflated.

He stared back at her. "What now?"

In a moment, she was in tears, inconsolable. He waited. He could almost hear the seconds ticking away. "If he could do this ... why not Helen? Why didn't He save my little girl?"

The old grief awakened. It had come to be an unwelcome resident within him. He didn't care for it, he didn't want it there, still, but at least now he could tolerate its presence. And he knew her complaint was not against Grey Trelawney.

"You know the answer to that, Camisha. We *don't* know. We're only human beings. My darling—can't you just accept that He knows our hearts, and that in time, we'll understand? In time, we'll be with her again."

"Well of course he knows my heart," she said, as if he'd accused her of heresy. "And I do thank Him for you being here with me. You have no idea how grateful I am for that."

A sudden rapid knock on the door startled them. Then it opened, and she gasped at the sight of Grey, standing there before her. "Is it true?"

"Will you stop asking that and *go* with him?" Ashanti ushered her out the door, and they ran to the portal. He released her hand, and she stopped, digging in her heels when Grey would have pulled her after him.

"I won't go without you."

Ashanti knew he couldn't accompany them—something about a promise Grey had made to Malcolm—and they didn't have time to explain it to her. And Ashanti gave Grey a look, and together they shoved her through the opening into the twenty-first century.

Chapter Thirty-Eight

In the pleasant late September afternoon, Marley walked up Duke of Gloucester Street holding Abigail's hand, with Bronson on her other side, carrying Sam.

"Mama, who *are* all these people? They're falling out the sides of the town."

"This is the French Army and the Continental Army. Generals Washington and Rochambeau have arrived from New York to help Generals Greene and Lafayette defeat Cornwallis." She touched her husband's arm. "All well?"

He hugged her with his free arm. "Truly could not be better. I've never seen such rejoicing in this town."

Nor will you again, she thought. No need to say such things; they both knew the truth. They'd seen the people deserting the old burg, week after week, for Richmond. For those who loved the town, who remained, this was the greatest of farewells by the Commander-in-chief.

"Did you know that General Washington just now visited his home at Mount Vernon for the first time in six years?"

Confusion filled Abby's face. "Where did he sleep?"

"He's been at war."

"Were you at war together, Papa?"

"Well, we were both in New York," he said. "But I was a prisoner of war, so I was held captive by the enemy."

Abby gasped. "How did you get home?"

"I escaped."

"Did the general escape, too?"

"He didn't have to. He was smart enough not to be taken captive."

"Papa, you're smart." She didn't buy his joke.

"Look, Abby, there he is! Look, Sam! Bronson!"

Marley was so jubilant, she didn't even realize she was interrupting her husband's conversation with their daughter.

He chuckled. "Yes, I see."

They had reached the Palace Green, which was filled with tents. She pointed toward the simple brick house halfway down the green on the left, where George Wythe lived. Washington sat astride his chestnut with the white blaze on his face.

"Children, that's his horse, Nelson. He's his favorite horse, because he's so calm during battle. Oh, isn't he a handsome figure on horseback? He's going to be the first president of our country."

"How do you know?" Abby asked.

As she looked toward the child, she caught Bronson's smile on her. *Well?* He seemed to ask.

"Everyone loves General Washington. They'll very likely suggest him, when the time comes."

The men were lining up to ride out to Yorktown, and Marley was rapt. She almost wished she'd left the children at home with Aileen. Any other time, she would've been delighted to explain this experience to them as she'd done for so many visiting children during her work for the Foundation.

"Do you remember why we came to town, my Marley?"

"Hm? What?" She stopped, realizing what he'd asked. "Ah. Yes, of course."

There on the right, she saw the old house, just as she'd seen it so many times when she'd worked in this village. For a moment, she remembered those lonely days of her life. If she had had any inkling of what lay in her future—well! She wouldn't have believed it.

Her husband led them to the door and tapped.

The door opened—and there stood Grey, with Rachel close behind. He glanced around the street outside as if by habit, then welcomed them inside.

Quickly, the thought of war was displaced by the reality of her family. Thomas and Hannah were still out with Papa, which certainly kept him on his toes.

"Can't quite get used to the simple idea of living life without a lunatic snapping at my heels. Marley, how is this guy keeping you from joining in with the drilling on the Palace Green and Market Square?"

She shoved her index finger toward the Wythe house. "*George Washington* is on Nelson, less than a block from us."

Grey raised an eyebrow. "I take it you mean the horse, not the governor."

"What? Oh, don't be silly. Can you believe that? George Washington, right outside our door!"

"Uncle Grey, Mama and Papa said you have a little girl."

"Well, our little girl is all grown up. But she has three little girls, right upstairs."

Marley shooed her along, and then she noticed the young blonde woman descending from the stairs. "This young lady must be Emily."

Emily smiled as she crossed the room, hugging Marley. "I turned forty-one last year, so you're the young lady here. But thank you."

"And this is my husband, Bronson."

Emily's mouth dropped, and she quickly covered her lips with her fingertips. "The last time I saw you, you were only a couple of days old. I barely remember it—but I do remember adoring you."

"We called him Ambrose," Grey said.

"How do you like your husband's disguise?" Marley asked.

Rachel took a deep breath, sending her husband a judicious glance. "I understand the need for it. And I look forward to finding it in the bathroom sink one morning. Oh," she said with a sigh. "No more bathroom sinks."

"Maybe we can invent them," Marley said. "Move progress along a little more quickly. Bronson briefly had one as well. Cover up *those* cheekbones?"

Rachel's eyes went wide. "Exactly!"

Bronson sighed. "I don't have beard on my cheekbones."

"You know what I mean," Marley said. "You're handsome men. It covers up your smile."

Emily looked from one man to the other. "I can't believe you two are complaining because your wives think you're too handsome to wear beards. What kind of world are you living in?"

Rachel interjected, "They like to pretend they're above such things as vanity. Believe me, they're both eating this up."

They all laughed. "Want to go outside and watch them preparing to march out?"

They stepped outside, surprised to find the troops already filing out—the fife and drum corps making the sober parade a bit more festive. About a hundred men, or a few less, would die during this siege.

And American independence would be won.

The British would continue to press the war for another two years. But Cornwallis's surrender at Yorktown sealed the fate of the states formerly known as British colonies.

They sat on the lawn, watching the troops until the town was empty.

"We have a surprise for Camisha," Grey said. "She hasn't gone back to Boston, has she?"

"No. I haven't seen her for the past few days, but she's still here. She and Ashanti and Parks have been living in the town that the Trelawneys built. They call the place Helentown. Why don't you come home with us?"

"First thing in the morning. It's just a huge undertaking, with the children."

"It's going to load up your house, when we get moved in."

"All right. We'd better get started, to be home before dark."

&

Camisha accepted the quilts from Parks and placed them across the box of new linens. The wagon was full of winter goods Marley had ordered from Ruth, and she and Ashanti and Parks were expected there in another half hour.

On a normal day, she might have had an attitude about Marley's insistence on them all coming today, but she'd felt terrific for the past few days—and she wasn't sure why. She'd awakened a few days ago feeling like a new woman. Not even her cranky old hips had been bothering her. She didn't understand it, but she was happy to give credit to God and leave it at that. She felt new energy in the morning, and she slept better at night.

And God above be praised, Ashanti couldn't get enough of her, waking her up in unspeakably delicious ways and putting her to sleep as if he were seventeen instead of pushing seventy. No *wonder* she was in a good mood.

That first morning she'd woken up feeling better, she'd found half a dozen odd welts scattered around her torso, as if from bug bites, but they healed in a couple of days, so she hadn't given it another thought.

Today, she and her husband and daughter set out for Marley and Bronson's home with all the goods Ruth had sold her. When she arrived, she saw Rashall and Juliana sitting on a bench outside, sipping tea.

"Well, look at the lord and lady of the manor," she murmured with a grin as Ashanti stopped the horses and she jumped out of the wagon seat.

And when, she wondered, had she last been able to *jump* out of a wagon seat?

She reached into the bed of the wagon and withdrew a stack of towels. "While normal folk are out earning an honest living, you two seem to be living off of fairy dust. Or maybe pirate treasure? Now that couldn't be, could it?"

Her son winked at her. Juliana merely smiled that beatific smile so characteristic of her. At least—since she'd married Rashall. Had she been so goony when she'd first married Ashanti?

Her jaw fell at her son's flippancy. "You better not have any ill-gotten gains."

"Oh, they're well-gotten," he said. "Just ask General Washington."

"You know, in all seriousness, Daniel filled a lot of roles in this community. You're going to have to work a lot harder than you seem to …"

And then her attention caught on the door as it opened. She went silent, unmoving, at what she saw there. At *who* she saw there. It couldn't be.

The woman, overcome with emotion, tried to smile and instead made a funny little grimace, wrinkling her nose. Her hair—still in that damned French twist—didn't have a single lock out of place. Silver threads were sprinkled throughout, but she was the same. Lord, she was the same.

Camisha dropped the towels, unaware of anything but her girl. She cried silently as she ran up the two steps to the door. The women nearly knocked each other down in their haste to get to each other.

No words were necessary. They stood there without moving, just weeping in happiness into each other's hair. All the moments of happiness and heartbreak and life that they'd missed over the past thirty-five years apart, wishing for just this moment. Just one more hug.

When, finally, they drew apart, Camisha pulled up her apron and wiped at her wet face, swollen with tears. "Please tell me you're going to stay for supper."

Rachel burst out laughing. "Supper and breakfast, too. But I brought a small gift for you with me, and if I don't get out of the way, she might knock us both down."

Camisha blinked in surprise as Rachel stepped aside. And she cried out at the sight of the slender old woman who took Rachel's place, reaching out to pull her close with gentle grace before her arrival had quite sunk in.

"Mom?" she whispered, hugging her mother, dissolving in tears once more as her mother held her—exactly the way she had held her when she was a child. "Oh, Mom."

Her mother wouldn't let her go. She just stroked her daughter's hair, crooning soft endearments, murmuring praise and thankfulness for a glimpse of Glory.

"Mom, let's go sit down. I don't want you to be overtaxed. We don't have any EMT guys here."

"Now that doesn't matter one little bit. Grey had me fixed right up, just like you."

"And just like me," Ashanti said, joining them with a smile.

Her mother cast a critical eye over him—exactly as she would have inspected a date when Camisha was growing up. He had a good sense of humor about it, bowing deeply before her as he introduced himself.

He didn't mention that he and Camisha had been married far longer than Camisha had lived with her mother. She knew herself that mothers didn't think that way. The expiration date never ran out on the my-baby warranty.

"Well, you do seem to make her happy," her mother said, hugging Ashanti. "And where are my grandchildren?"

"Right there's one," she said, introducing her to Parks. "And I somehow feel you might have already met Rashall."

"That is one handsome young man," she said. "And young Parks here is a beauty, just like her mother."

They made their way inside, and she saw Marley. "Yeah, I've got your rush *towels* outside."

"You don't think we'll need towels, with this crowd?"

"I think you're mainly going to need Ruth's blackberry wine. The rest'll take care of itself." She looked around. "Who do I have to thank for this bounty of miraculous surprises?"

Rachel pointed to her husband, who innocently and obliviously was pouring a cup of coffee. He turned and found everyone staring at him.

"Grey Trelawney, you handsome thing. Come here right now."

He came to hug her hard. "No big deal at all."

She burst out in laughter. "Honey, you say that when someone picks up the check at lunch. Not when they make miracles happen. But I don't understand what my mother meant by saying you had her fixed up—just like me. Pray explain, sir."

He pulled her aside to do so. She gasped. "You mean to tell me I have a new heart?"

"No. You have new knees, hips, heart, lungs, kidneys, liver, and the minor organs as well. It's done easily in our time with simple robotics."

"Why are we speaking so softly—as if it were a criminal act, rather than a miracle?"

He hesitated. "Because I can't bring anymore miracles in, and my wife has two sisters and two brothers-in-law who lack the luxury."

She sobered. "Not even Bronson?"

"I did ask him. He declined. He recognizes the line is drawn somewhere. So he drew it. At least I had them immunized."

"Camisha? I have a young lady you might like to meet—who happens to share a name with you."

Camisha looked toward Rachel, who had her arms around a young girl of perhaps eleven.

"Hello?" a voice called from the door. "Anyone home?"

Camisha waved at Rachel, then smiled at Grey as she recognized the voice and started toward Rachel. "Now it's your turn, friend. Try not to give him a stroke."

Pleasure lit his face as he walked toward the front door. She followed closely behind.

Thomas's walking stick clattered to the floor. Grey steadied him while Parks bent to retrieve the stick. She waited while the men hugged without awkwardness. "They told me you were still alive—and my little Emily? Where is she?"

"I'm right here, Grandfather," she said, throwing herself into his arms. "You remember me?"

He laughed a booming laugh. "Remember you? Darling, how could I forget the girl who hung the moon in my sky? Yes. Yes, God is merciful indeed."

Chapter Thirty-Nine

Grey stifled a yawn and glanced out the window of the school room as Matthew, one of his star students, returned to his seat. Rachel stood on the library steps, hammering a Christmas wreath on the door. She glanced over and noticed him noticing her, and she blew him a kiss. How beautiful she had made their life together—no matter what they shared.

He smiled as he turned back to his class, gesturing at the next child. Poke was his troublemaker—one of his new arrivals from Cornwallis's latest stunt. Simultaneously with his surrender, the British had turned out the people they'd freed to fend for themselves in the winter's cold. At least those who survived the smallpox epidemic. Among those were more than a few starving teenagers, and many had made their way to Helentown.

He had given Poke far more attention than the rest of the class—the boy had a long road ahead to overcome his illiteracy—yet his anger and resentment were nearly insurmountable.

The boy walked to the front of the room and stood before his classmates. He startled Grey by withdrawing a fife from his pocket. Grey resisted asking him where he'd gotten it from. Their assignment had been simple: write an essay about what equality meant to them.

Anne Meredith

Poke went ramrod stiff, then brought the instrument to his mouth, and played, so softly it could barely be heard. *The British Grenadiers.* When he reached the end, he repeated it, more loudly. With each new playing, he gave the song a different attitude: sprightly, innocent, moronic; stealthy, insidious; threatening, deceptive, destructive. The progression of volume continued until it was an insane, exhausting tirade. He ended on the blast of a discordant, off-key, minor note.

He abruptly thrust the fife high overhead, his fists clenched tightly around each end of it, as if it were chains binding his wrists. He clenched it until his muscled arms trembled, and then he lowered it in front of him, lowering his head. A moment later, he raised his head and sang. Grey had learned, since returning to this time, that Camisha had taught the song years ago to the people he had once enslaved.

> Lift every voice and sing
> *Till earth and Heaven ring*
> *Ring with the harmonies of Liberty;*
> *Let our rejoicing rise ...*

One by one, the other students, unbidden, rose and joined in.

But Poke's clear, sweet tenor carried the song and might as well have slugged Grey in the solar plexus. It was as if Tate were standing there, singing the song that someday would be widely known as the Black National Anthem.

Grey was the only adult in the room, so he had no choice but to control his emotions. These children would have been alarmed if he lost it. So control them, he did.

That is, until Poke reached the last verse and began to falter over the lyrics:

> *Thou who hast by thy might*
> *Led us into the light*
> *Keep us forever ...*

There, the boy faltered, the tears freely streaming down his face, as the other students went silent, patiently waiting for his lead.

Grey crossed his arms in front of him, cradling his chin in one hand and in that motion concealing the emotion that filled him at the boy's naked confusion. He let the silence stretch out, waiting—as the other students waited.

Two of the children moved forward to stand on either side of him and took up the song, and by the end of the line he rejoined them, his naturally powerful voice soaring over theirs.

> *Keep us forever in the path, we pray.*
> *Lest our feet stray from the places, our God, where we*
> *met Thee.*
> *Lest our hearts, drunk with the wine of the world, we*
> *forget Thee.*
> *Shadowed beneath Thy hand, may we forever stand,*
> *True to our God, true to our native land.*

Grey remained silent, taking slow, steadying breaths as the students who had joined Poke returned to their seats. The boy looked around his classmates as if surprised to find himself where he was. And he spoke.

"You all know other black folks is still enslaved. Not saying anything against any of you, but you couldn't know what freedom is. Not exactly. Your parents was freed when they was little ones, littler than you. That Arnold fella, I heared tell of him, how he turned his back on the other soldiers what fought with him. He came around promising us all our freedom, to fight with them, said we'd get the same treatment as their own soldiers. So along we went. Few months later, we was dying same as the soldiers, of smallpox and starvation.

"We walked a hundred miles, same rags we had on the plantation, no shoes, no socks, in the snow, over the rough forest ground, sleeping in the mud. I learned to play the fife from a boy there in the lines, playing that same tune no matter how sick he was, no matter how scared. That boy died at Green Springs, and as he lay there bleeding to death, he gave me his fife. Said he knew I loved it. When Cornwallis turned us all out, we didn't know where to go. I'd heared—I'd *heard*—tell of you people. Black people, living free, better educated than most white men, here in the middle of plantation country. I knowed—I ... *knew*—I wasn't good enough to be one of you, get an education, but I thought, well, maybe at least they'd let me slop the hogs or do something useful, so's I could eat. Till I figure out where I can go."

He sent Grey an angry glance. "Then you come along with your sirs and your Mr. Pokes and I was sure you was mocking me, the ignorant slave boy from Westover. But then I looked again. And I saw you treated everybody like that. Reckon it told me more about who you was than who I was."

"I reckon equality means to me being smart enough to know when someone's lying to keep you in check. Arnold ain't no better than the worst slave-holder. He'd say whatever it took to beat General Washington. When it came right down to it, I reckon he was on the right side, in the end."

He gave a polite nod to Grey, then returned to his seat. After a split-second of silence, his fellow students came to their feet and applauded his presentation.

Grey joined in.

As the applause dwindled to silence, Grey spoke. "Good work, Poke. For tomorrow's assignment, I'd like everyone to write an essay ... preferably in writing ... on your own name. Write, especially, about what you'd choose as a first and last name if the choice was yours. Bearing in mind that it is."

This wasn't a random assignment. As flattering as he found it that this community had chosen his name as their own, it was impractical to say the least. He hoped to drive a conversation between the students and their parents.

It was apt that Poke, the last presenter in the class, had chosen to sing *Lift Every Voice and Sing*, as they sang it to close each school day. Camisha had also once taught their grandparents *The Star-Spangled Banner*, and they sang that each morning. Because he had little choice, Grey had decided to find amusing the number of anachronisms Camisha had sprinkled with abandon throughout the land.

He dismissed the class for the day and returned to his desk, organizing it for the next day. To think that he had imagined himself purposeless in this time, hiding in cellars like a fugitive. He was far from fearless about the world he'd returned to, but a world free of Mannings was sweet indeed.

He noticed the old newspaper article, peeking out from an attendance roll, and he withdrew it. Marley had found it in the ruins at Rosalie that same day, years ago, they'd first spied each other through the portal, and it had made its way into old Hastings' hands. Godfrey had brought it to him recently.

The article awakened in him his only regret about his move here: that he hadn't taken a few last hours to investigate those matters that had intersected with the Mannings. One noteworthy difference he'd noted right away in the headlines was that Sheppard Manning's company became overnight a decent company. The company that he had run as Max Sheppard had been plagued by lawsuits and corruption. The company now operated in the black and had been widely recognized for the innovative policies and philanthropic programs.

He placed the article before him.

Family disappears in eerie coincidence. The date of the article was August of 2016, twenty-two years later than the original.

> *"Nine people have disappeared in recent years from a remote home near Henricus Historical Park living history museum. In an eerie coincidence, this mimics a 'lantern tour ghost story' told by interpreters in Williamsburg about a family that vanished on the frontier.*
>
> *"As the legend goes, a family of settlers named Miller at the turn of the eighteenth century built the stone cottage across the James River from Henricus. When a*

brave fell in love with one of the young daughters, he kidnaped her. One by one, the family members went after the brave to bring back their daughter, until all were lost. Others in the area said the land where they built was cursed by the blood of natives who were massacred there eons ago.

"Since the new millennia, William and Mary history professor, Robert Miller, and his wife, noted historical researcher Cassandra Miller, disappeared several years ago in a case that continues to perplex Richmond police detectives.

"Their children were taken in by former Police Chief Cameron Carlyle, a personal friend of Robert Miller since they served together in the Navy. This year, all of the Miller children, as well as Chief Carlyle's daughter, have gone missing while at work or school.

"Three days ago, Carlyle and his wife, Helen, disappeared on their way home from dinner. Their car was found abandoned at Stonefield. During the original investigation of the crime scene, the Richmond police turned the investigation over to the FBI and the CIA.

"The FBI reports that no further briefings will be given until more information is available."

He was curious about the lives the children had lived. And yet—most oddly of all, to him—the three girls had ended up here, in the same timeline, married to the same men. He had ended up here, his memories unchanged. Helentown was even more efficient in its simple mission than it had been before.

He hadn't shared this article with Rachel. The prospect frightened the same old superstitious part of him that he'd had to re-educate again and again. As long as he didn't bring it up, perhaps it wasn't real. He simply thanked God, every day, for his countless undeserved joys.

Was it possible, he wondered, that because the killing of the Mannings came *after* all the other events in their lives—although it occurred *before* the events that led to the deaths of the Millers—that they would remain unaffected by it all?

Only one small detail he'd noticed was markedly different: Emily's locket was gone. The heart-shaped locket Rachel had given her as a child had vanished—and when he asked her about it, she had no idea what he was talking about. He had mentioned it to Rachel and she, too, had no memory of it.

Then, belatedly, she'd added, "My mother had a locket like that when I was a little girl, but I don't know what happened to it."

In the end, maybe it was odder that he *did* remember it. And perhaps that was his blessing and his curse—to remember everything, just as it really had happened, once upon a time.

Beyond that inexplicable mystery, two more questions remained unanswered. Where were the Millers? Still jet-setting through time?

And where was Cameron Carlyle? Perhaps now in this time, still on his way to catch up to his Helen?

Tonight he would ask Rachel her thoughts about it. Perhaps. If it meant him taking this secret to his grave to preserve their happiness, he would gladly do it. He donned his coat, folded the article, and thrust it deep into his pocket.

The evening grew cold as he left the schoolhouse. He turned up the collar of his great coat against the bitter December wind.

The family set out for Williamsburg for supper, crowded into Thomas's carriage. With Yorktown won, Thomas and Hannah had returned to their home in town. Tonight there was to be a candlelit concert at Bruton Parish, and Thomas had invited the family to attend. Everyone was coming—even Rashall, who had little use for the Anglican church since that snafu over his ordination.

Grey noticed the subtle decorations some had done to celebrate Christmas—less than three days away. Deep green pine wreathes and garlands and hollyberry and pine cones decked a hall—or an entryway—here and there.

They rolled up to the Trelawney home in festive spirits. It was little Cammie who first noticed something was amiss.

"Mom, why is their wreath black?"

Alarm flooded Grey as he craned his neck to see what she was reporting on. Indeed, a black crepe wreath hung on the front door.

Abruptly, he opened the carriage door. As he felt the collective shift of the other occupants preparing to exit, he raised his hand. "No. Bronson, come with me. Rachel, wait here for us. Rashall, keep everyone in line for now."

Grey saw the anxiety on his younger brother's face as the gate creaked and they walked through.

At the door, they exchanged a look. Grey raised his hand to knock, but as he touched the door, it was already ajar.

"Hello?" he called, pushing the door open and entered. "Father? Hannah?"

The home was silent. They quickly lit lamps and closed the door behind them, walking upstairs.

They found Thomas lying on his bed, fully dressed except for his shoes. Bronson fell at his side, grabbing his shoulders to shake him. "Father, wake up!" Only a moment later, he stopped, stricken. "He's gone. He's been gone a while."

In the corner, he heard a rustling, and a sniff.

"Hannah?"

Grey brought the lamp closer to her. Her eyes were sunken, with dark shadows beneath them. In her trembling hands she held a slip of paper and a pillbox, and she whispered. "I can't get my box open, to get to my pills. Will you help me?"

Grey easily opened the box for her, and she upturned it into her mouth.

"No!" Bronson shouted, crossing to her in a moment. He started to stick his finger in her mouth, then stopped. "Give me that shoe horn. Quickly!"

Grey handed him the shoe horn, and he shoved it into her mouth, attempting to get the pills back out. Bronson yanked her halfway across his lap. "I'll open her mouth and cover her teeth. You try to get those pills out."

They worked to get the pills out, and she collapsed beside Thomas, weeping. The slip of paper dropped to the bed: *My Thomas is gone. He lay down to take a nap—and he never woke up. I shall never survive without him. Please tell my little Marley I'm so sorry.*

He dropped the note into the fireplace. He marveled at his brother's fast thinking; somehow he'd thought she just needed to take medication. The bitterness of Thomas's death, so soon after Grey's return to his own time, was more than he could tolerate at the moment.

"That wreath," he murmured, glancing at Hannah, who was utterly unaware of them. He couldn't help comparing her to the haughty young wife he'd observed when visiting Gabriel Miller. All in all, Hannah Hastings was a pathetic figure.

"He loved Christmas. And I'm guessing it somehow made sense to her."

"How did you know to move so quickly?"

After a long moment, he said, "He made me promise to take care of her. To be kind to her."

He saw his brother's grief swell and roll over him. "I can't believe it. I just saw him two days ago, and he seemed in better health than he'd been since I was a boy."

Their father's death would hit him much harder. Thomas and Bronson had known a close, loving relationship, free of regret. Thomas and Grey had known little but that.

Grey placed a steadying hand on his brother's shoulder. "He was eighty-one years old, Bronson—nearly eighty-two. He lived a full and rich life—and thanks to you, even after I was gone, he was able to enjoy raising you. And then, loving your children as he loved my Emily. Even more freely with your children. He adored those babes," he said with a smile.

"All that time I lost to this accursed war."

Grey shook his head. "If we all knew the future, our pasts would contain no mistakes—and our lives, no joy."

"Perhaps it's punishment, for the deaths of the Mannings."

"God doesn't punish us in this life. We punish ourselves."

"You know, Grey, I wish you'd known him better. He was a much better man than the man you knew. Then again, perhaps the realization of his errors with you made him the father he was with me."

Perhaps.

Hannah was oblivious to them, stroking Thomas's cheek as she lay on the pillow next to his.

"I'll go get the others." Grey left his brother with their father.

Chapter Forty

Camisha arrived early to Thomas's funeral with Ruth, since they were singing. Ashanti had dropped them off and was finding a place for the wagon. As she'd expected, the place was packed before the service ever began.

Thomas's funeral was attended by most of the town. St. George Tucker paid his respects to Bronson and to his "cousin Bray." George Wythe eyed Grey shrewdly, certain he knew this Bray fellow. Camisha watched this exchange curiously, avoiding Wythe lest her face trigger his memory. In fact, Wythe had helped her exonerate Grey when he was on trial for the death of Letitia Trelawney, thirty-five years before. He soon abandoned his curiosity and offered condolences instead.

She noticed a curious thing: whites and blacks sitting elbow to elbow. Back home in Boston, free blacks sat in the balcony. This was purely Thomas. Those who knew Thomas knew where he stood on slavery; those who disagreed either respected his wishes today or had skipped the funeral.

When she approached Grey, she said, "Looks like most of your homeboys are here."

He smiled at her. She didn't care what Rachel said—that man would've been luscious wearing a beard of bees.

"I would've enjoyed seeing Dunraven again. Might've even outed myself to him. Maybe."

"You know, I've mostly lived in Boston the past thirty-five years, but I've not seen Donovan in all the times I visited."

"I heard he left the country years ago, at the first sight of political turmoil. He's back in London, like the dandified Englishman he was."

"Can you imagine what he'd have said if you came clean?"

"Something funny and utterly inappropriate."

She smiled. "I've been wondering--why did you guys have the funeral here?"

"It wasn't our choice. Hannah planned it. Otherwise we'd be at Rosalie, and Rashall would be the officiant."

"Then again, this makes it simpler for those in the town who'd like to come." She leaned over to hug Grey. "Anyway, I'm really sorry. I know you were looking forward to spending more time with him."

"I was able to do that, so I'll always be grateful for that."

Camisha sat with Rachel and Ruth. She and Rachel had been talking nonstop since they'd been reunited.

The rector gave a simple eulogy, one she knew Thomas would've liked. But if funerals were for the living, she hoped that his sons liked it even more.

"Today we celebrate the life of Thomas Trelawney, who was born in Wales in 1699—the year Williamsburg became the capital of Virginia. He studied law and brought his profession to Virginia. He survived the loss of three wives and a son and granddaugher, and is survived by his wife, Hannah, a son, and two grandchildren. He lived all of his life in Virginia, with occasional visits to Bermuda. Thomas served Virginia for eighty-one years, just as this old burg served the cause of independence and freedom. We recall the many things Thomas did for that cause in his work as a burgess—just as we recall the work of those who placed this village in the pantheon of liberty.

"The work of this old village is done. For a while, anyway, although we all look forward to seeing what the next chapter holds for us. Like our old village, Thomas's work here is done. Our Lord has called him home to his reward. Now we pick up the baton and we continue the race. We do it in our daily work, as Thomas did, serving our communities. But it would do us all well to humble ourselves and remember that our time here is not long. It wasn't that long ago that Thomas was a young man. He told me just the other day how he remembered walking down these streets with his wife before their son was born. We're here only a moment, he said. Your son is learning to crawl—then he's off raising his own family. In God's eyes, eighty years is like a day, and a day is like eighty years. May we remember, every day, our work here in this community—and our work for the world to come. Amen."

Camisha rose with Ruth and made their way to the front to sing. Bronson and Grey had asked them to select a hymn to close the service, and Camisha chose the most comforting hymn she knew.

Thomas was buried at the Trelawney home—beside his beloved Jennie—as he had instructed the rector, knowing, no doubt, that Hannah would otherwise have objected. Afterward, the family adjourned to a supper held at Raleigh Tavern in honor of the former member of the House of Burgesses.

"I think the joyful solemnity of this occasion would've pleased him," Grey said. "He did love order."

Bronson smiled. "I was just thinking how he disliked stuffed shirts."

Camisha leaned forward. "You each had a different father. Both were good in their own way and human in their own way. That's the best way to understand the different ways you each have of describing the elephant."

Grey went silent, sipping his rum. He reached for Rachel's hand and brought it to his mouth.

Camisha watched him, and she thought she understood his predicament. He'd learned to let his flawed, painfully brief relationship with his father go decades ago. Now, beside the son Thomas had worked so hard to love better, at least partly *because* he'd been such a poor father to Grey, it had to grate on him to have their relationships compared as if they bore comparison at all.

He looked up, saw her watching him, and gave her a short smile. "Again—no big deal. After all, how many boys have we known who've never gotten near the elephant?"

She nodded slowly. "Exactly. Sometimes all we can hope for in life from difficult relationships is the ability to let it go."

He gave a great, weary sigh, his face pained. "Yes. That's it precisely."

"Forgiveness—that's the key," Rachel said.

"Look at everything you've worked so hard to accomplish in the lives of the little girls we'll all be someday."

"I suppose you're right there, too."

"I mean think about the memories that Rachel and Marley had to endure. Juliana, too—just a little newborn, and suddenly her mommy was gone. Grey, God help the little girls and boys who know real monsters. You changed that, for these girls. And for me, too. And my daddy."

"And God knows who else," said Rashall.

As they left the Raleigh Tavern, a sudden hubbub arose far uptown, and they turned toward the noise.

"It's the Governor's Palace!" Someone called out.

Camisha gave a great cry. She shook her head, her shoulders slumping. "The Governor's Palace is on fire."

"What's happening?" Rachel asked. "Isn't anyone going to fight the fire? Get a bucket brigade going?"

Grey spoke softly. "No. It's burning down. I'd been so preoccupied with everything, I'd forgotten that was this year— the year after the capital moved to Richmond."

When they saw that all were out of the building safely, they stood in the cold before the grand old place, unable to leave.

Grey held Rachel close as they watched the flames. "Remember the governor's ball—our first kiss?"

She leaned against him. "And—oh, the fireworks!"

"You take the fireworks with us, wherever we go."

She brought his hand to her lips. "I'll miss the maze. Oh, the boxwood. What a joy to take my morning walks past that!"

He nodded. "In some ways, Williamsburg after the Restoration seemed more authentic than the real thing."

Rain began at last, putting out the flames. Aileen took the younger children home to put them to bed.

The rest stayed, saying goodbye to the old mansion as they'd said goodbye to their patriarch. Both of them, seemingly, had known that their time was past. They watched the last of the genteel old capital dying—and along with it, the days of kings and queens and royal governors ruling this land with an iron fist from four thousand miles away.

Camisha stood near her son and Juliana, and Rachel and Marley drew near her. Camisha turned and put her arm around Rachel again—finding joy, once more, in her dear friend. With so many years apart, neither of them could imagine spending much time separated.

Marley found a place next to Camisha, and Juliana, next to Rachel. Sisters all.

"I'm not going to say you can't stop progress," Marley said, her voice tight. "But this isn't progress. It's just the very first birthing pains of a country still laboring against ignorance of freedom for all."

Camisha knew the same fear and dread that Marley knew, aware of the foolishness of people as they persisted wrongheadedly in prejudice and strife.

"We're going to watch it all," Marley murmured. "The buildings being deserted, getting old, falling down, having cheap junk strung up on the ones that still stand to make them look less ... like themselves."

Camisha hugged Marley, taking a deep breath and feeling the bracing sting of the smoke lingering in the air.

"No, it's not progress," she said. "It's the cycles of life."

"You're not going to break out in song, are you?" Rachel asked dryly.

"Hakuna matata to you, too, sister."

❦

That evening, the family gathered at Rosalie to relish Marley's hot chocolate. They had grown into a family that wasn't apt to take anything for granted—not even hot chocolate.

"Why do we decorate a tree, when nobody else in town does?"

This, of course, from the ever-inquisitive Abby.

"Well," Marley said, "there actually was once a school teacher at William and Mary who had a small Christmas tree, because she was from a place where they *do* celebrate with trees, and she was homesick."

Even though the custom of decorating trees had not yet made it to their neck of the woods, they popped corn and threaded it together and wound it around the tree. They used other homemade decorations to add to the festive air.

And they sat in the warmth of their home, shoulder to shoulder, and savored simply the sight of each other.

Rachel sat on a sofa with Camisha's mother, with Grey stretched out on the floor near the hearth. It warmed her to know that they had treated Helen just as if she were their own mother. She marveled that they'd known and looked after her mother for the better part of four decades. It gave her admiration and affection for both of them a new dimension.

Ashanti walked to her and put his arm around her. "Let's go sit with your mother."

"I love this man," she whispered, kissing his neck.

They joined Mom, with Ashanti beside her on one end, and Rachel on the other. Camisha blissfully drew close to her mother.

"What do you girls think was the purpose of all this?" Helen asked.

"I think my purpose was to get Camisha into the eighteenth century, and get Grey and Emily out."

Camisha laughed. "Always about you, isn't it, honey?"

"What's that supposed to mean?"

"Maybe *my* purpose was to get *you* back there so you *could* get Grey and Emily out."

Rachel mused over that. "Hm. Sounds like the same thing."

Helen chuckled. "My little girls." She kissed Camisha, then Rachel, then turned to Ashanti, eyeing him cautiously. "I think you'll probably turn out all right, too."

"I've known her longer than you have," he said, smiling broadly. "You could *not* love this woman more than I do."

The women groaned in unison. Grey shook his head. "You were so close there."

From Marley: "Mothers *always* love us more. Always."

Ashanti exchanged a look with Grey and wisely kept his mouth shut.

Grey nodded. "There you go."

Marley was decorating the tree with Emily and the children and her husband. Juliana and Rashall sat on the couch sharing a single cup of hot chocolate.

Curious, Camisha thought, that Grey and Marley—and she—who loved this place most, were yet the most detached in speaking of the heartbreaking fire they'd seen tonight. The true end of the capital. Second only to the decision to move the capital to Richmond, this was the first and most emblematic event to usher in the Big Sleep that Williamsburg knew for nearly 150 years. Now, she knew it was up to Grey, Marley, and her, to keep alive reverence and love for this village and, especially, for the American past it brought to life for future generations.

She was just one person. So was Marley—and Grey. And John Rockefeller and Doctor Goodwin and George Washington and Lafayette and Crispus Attucks and Booker T. Washington and Rosa Parks. And Sally Hemings. One little person, each of them. But together—together, there was nothing they couldn't do.

Epilogue

The woodland countryside of Virginia—Twentieth Century
"Once upon a time in a peaceful kingdom in The Land Beyond Tomorrow, there lived three beautiful, wee princesses. They were the daughters of the wise and powerful King, and his mystical and whimsical Queen."

Three young girls watched their mother spin the tale in a lilting English accent. They clustered around her in the window seat that had seen so much love over the years, while their father tended to the fire in the ancient stone hearth. In the background, they heard the roar of thunder.

"There was the brave Princess Rachel, the eldest, with hair as black as the night, a love for truth and honor, and a smile that lit up her sisters' hearts.

"There was adventurous Princess Merrilea, with a fearless heart and laughing eyes that gave her mum and dad joy.

"And there was wise young Princess Juliana, with a mind as clever as a wizard and as quick as a fox."

With this, the youngest child, but a year old, recognized her name, laughed, and clapped her hands together in dreamy delight. Her mother clapped her own hands and resumed the story.

"Now, the King and Queen loved adventure, and many years before, they had traveled throughout the land, waging war on villains in neighboring kingdoms for many years. This made the villagers very happy, but you can imagine it made the villains quite angry. 'Who are you to say what's right and wrong? You aren't the king of us!"

"But, you see, the King and the Queen *did* know what was best, for once their very own land had been threatened by—"

"What's threaded? Like a needle, you mean?" This from Merrilea.

"No, threatened. A threat is something that can hurt you. The King and Queen knew bad men who had tried to hurt the neighboring lands. But the wise King had brave knights who helped him send the bad men far, far away."

"Where they could never hurt them?" Merrilea looked to her father for this.

"Indeed," he said. "Away from them forever. Wait—Juli dropped her dolly." He gave Merrilea the baby's rag doll, and she passed it on to her sister, patting her chubby cheek fondly as she placed it in her small hands.

"The King and the Queen knew they must find a new land for a new kingdom of their own. So, to keep the princesses safe, the King and Queen journeyed to another kingdom to pass on all the knowledge young women needed for life.

"One day, an old crone came to the village—who can tell me what a crone is?"

The eldest two girls looked at each other, laughed, raised their hands, and began yelling "Me!" in a chorus of pride. The toddler waved her hands in the air.

"All right," their mother said. "Juliana?"

The baby clapped again, her face growing serious in thought. "Bird. Black bird."

"Very good! That's what a *crow* is, that's right. Merrilea? What's a crone?"

The middle child put her arms down, grimaced, and contorted her hands into claws. "An ugly old lady," she said, through a sour expression, one hand pawing at the air before her face.

Juliana watched Merrilea somberly, wrinkling her nose and patting the air to copy her sister.

"That's my girl," Mama said, drawing Merrilea onto her lap.

Rachel drew in closer, and the youngest crawled between her sisters—all three adoring their mother and their sisters.

Merrilea's tiny fingers touched the double-heart necklace at their mother's throat. "Mama, can I have that? It's so pretty."

Their mother hugged her close, kissing her temple. "Thank you, darling. But I think I need to hang onto this. I'll get you and Rachel your own pretty little necklace."

"It wasn't for me, it was for Rachel," she said. "Her birthday's coming."

"Ah, that's quite sweet, but your daddy gave me this, and it means the world to me. See? It folds out into three sections, with portraits of my three girls. All right, now who wants to tell the next part of the story?"

"I do," Rachel said. "You never pick me, you only pick the little ones."

"Ah, my pretty girl. I pick them because I know you know the things I ask. Rachel, why don't you tell the next part of the story. You can teach the little ones how to tell a story."

Rachel's hands spread out in dramatic starbursts. "Okay. One day, the old crone came to the village. She carried an old, worn haversack. 'Who wants to see me rocks?' she cried. But what no one knew is that what she really had in her bag were *diamonds*. You see, she was testing the villagers to find out who had a pure heart. So she went to the first door and knocked—"

A brief, sturdy tap came at the front door, and the girls and their mother squealed with laughter.

Their father rose to answer the door, smiling at the silliness of his girls. At the door stood a man with laughing dark eyes and a mustache and goatee.

"Hey, Cam, come on in. They're having story time."

"Thought we'd never get here! The traffic was murder, then I got lost in a detour. And that storm's going to be here any second."

Beside the man stood a slender young girl, just Rachel's height. The girl peered around the men at the gaggle of females in the cozy window seat, her gaze alight with excitement. Nothing was more fun than Saturday morning story time.

A light of perfect love entered their mother's eyes as she rose and crossed the room to the young girl. Bending down, she met her lively eyes—a color somewhere between caramel apples and November pecans.

"I brought hot chocolate mix. It's my secret recipe. I was going to share it with Merrilea."

"Hello, Camisha! We've been waiting so very long for you."

NOTES FROM THE AUTHOR

There were no known black officers in the Continental Army. There were many brave soldiers, but, like the fictitious town of Helentown, Virginia, black officers live only in the better world that I imagined in this book.

As my readers know, historical accuracy is important to me. In this book, I made a notable departure to give Rashall Adams a military title. Although there may have been African-American officers fighting in the Revolutionary War, I found no record of it. Blacks during that time period, enslaved and free, believed in fighting for the patriot cause, and they volunteered often. The First Rhode Island was one of the few units that served throughout the Revolutionary War.

Rashall's work as a spy working with General Lafayette was inspired by the true story of James Armistead Lafayette, an enslaved man in Virginia who did serve as a spy for Lafayette.

If you aren't familiar with the story of the British prison ships of Wallabout Bay, learn more at the Prison Ship Martyrs Monument in Fort Greene, Brooklyn, New York. Depending on whose figures you go by, there were two to three times as many deaths while prisoners of war as there were in battle.

Finally, if you or a loved one are suffering from PTSD, please get help. Try starting at the National Center for PTSD.

Anne Meredith is a native Texan and the author of *Love's Timeless Hope*, *Love Across Time*, and *Tender, Immortal*, and *Forever (The Trelawneys of Williamsburg, Books One, Two*, and *Three)*. Contact her via Twitter @_AnneMeredith or at annemeredithbooks@gmail.com. Reviews of this book are welcome on Amazon and Goodreads. For more information:
www.annemeredithbooks.com
www.amazon.com/author/annemeredith
https://www.facebook.com/AMRomance
And now, enjoy an excerpt from AS TIME IS (The Trelawneys of Williamsburg, Book Four), coming soon.

Sneak Preview, AS TIME IS

Tidewater Virginia, 1986
A storm was on its way, and with the temperature dropping, he ought to be headed home—not taking harebrained joyrides down a two-lane blacktop. He had mid-terms to grade, and no time to waste in the past. George Jones was singing <u>*The Grand Tour*</u>, and he turned off the radio.

The memories had haunted him his entire life—memories his parents had dismissed with indulgent laughter until, finally, he'd just stopped talking about them.

What an imagination the lad has, his mother had said, with that musical accent of hers—a bit Brit, a bit exotic islander.

His father, the sailor—the warrior—had said nothing.

The joints of the old truck creaked as he pulled over onto the soft shoulder of the highway, second-guessing his decision to come here. After all these years of ignoring the magnetic pull of this region, he wanted almost nothing less than confirmation that they were telling the truth—or, worse, that they were lying.

Good God, man. You're forty-one years old, a decorated veteran, a tenured history professor—the son of a Navy SEAL. A man who'd loved women and been loved. And you sit here afraid of childhood daydreams.

They were not daydreams. They were as vivid as the cold draft from the driver's side window, those memories. Memories of his parents, and of the young couple they'd worked for: the man, pale but kind, as disciplined as a military drill, and the woman, an ethereal beauty as fragile as a dream.

And their daughter—only a few years younger than he, his childhood playmate, her laughter the persistent inhabitant of his heart.

Cassie.

Growing up, he knew the difference between memory and imagination. In his memory, they laughed together as children, gathering firewood, playing with the kittens born under the porch. In his imagination, through the years, she'd grown up alongside him, Cassie no more. Cassandra, his wise temptress.

Cassie lived in his memory; Cassandra, only in his dreams.

No matter how many priests or psychologists had tried to rid him of these apparitions, her memory had only grown stronger over the years.

He could not have imagined little Cassie. He *remembered* her.

I believe you, man.

Cam's voice came to him from that night he'd confessed the entire story, years before. He'd known Cameron Carlyle for years—a young man his father had taken under his wing. They'd become good friends and joined the Navy together.

Cam was easily the funniest man he knew. He could make him laugh in his gloomiest hour, without even trying. No wonder they'd become fast friends.

Just last night on the phone, Cam had urged him yet again to solve this impossible riddle, once and for all.

Drive up and see my grandma—you remember where she lives, don't you?

Granny Carlyle was the toughest old bird he'd ever known, and everything about her stood out like a brightly colored flag in his memory. Cam had been named after her. It didn't help that the woman, who he'd met as an adult, lived in the part of the country that made his unreliable memories light up like fire.

Find out the truth, and you best call me when you do.

This, Cam had insisted on out of friendship. After all—it wasn't as if all his unfounded memories were happy ones. Some were downright nightmarish.

His earliest memories, long before Cassie, were of an ocean voyage aboard a ship of misery, disease, and death. And it had been these memories that his alarmed parents had been driven to eradicate when they sent him to experts in soothing a troubled child's mind.

All had failed.

In the end, it came down to this trip, this day. He would know the truth, that it was real or a phantom of madness. And he would no longer live with the madness. Whether he would call Cam after he learned the truth, he didn't know.

He glanced over to the passenger seat, the 9mm Smith & Wesson his father had owned as a SEAL and had given to him when he joined the Navy twenty years before. He was just so tired of the memories—of his unstable certainty that they were real, when those he *knew* he could trust told him otherwise.

His jaw hardened and he reached over and put the gun away in its locked case, under the passenger seat. In all the threats his father had faced, all the oppression his mother's people—his people—had known, neither would have ever contemplated such a cowardly act.

Looking in the rearview mirror, he saw nothing but a desolate country road. A slow patter of freezing rain had begun, and he flipped on the windshield wipers, pulling back onto the road. He had no idea where the place even was—but he remembered the river and the plantations nearby. At this point, he was on an adventure.

Lord, how this place excited him. Growing up in Boston, he'd acquired a deep sense of pride in the city and its history. But this sleepy countryside was the site of the first westward expansion in America, long before it was a country. Adjacent to the oldest settlement in the original colonies, the entire area was the cradle of civilization for a student of American history.

Later he would wonder at the memories that came to him as he turned off the highway and meandered down the road until he reached an even smaller lane. *Harriman Road*, it said.

This was it. The sign was new, but the lane hadn't changed. In his mind's eye he saw the same rural trail from his vantage point in an old horse-drawn wagon, peeping over the side with Cassie giggling beside him, her eyes sparkling, her violet blue hood catching in the breeze and falling away against her woolen cape. The virgin land, its air so fresh and unspoiled by fumes and dust that a deep breath could give a person a natural buzz. The gargantuan trees, centuries old, filling the countryside.

The truck slipped on the patchy ice, and he released the accelerator, catching himself. If he was going to keep looking, he'd have to do it on foot. Sleet made the remote road treacherous.

The James River was near—he knew it before he arrived. Perhaps it was that aroma that had guided him to begin with.

At a curve where the road turned south, he noticed a smaller footpath headed toward the river, and he eased off the road and between a couple of trees, parking.

He retrieved the handgun from the case, along with his kit from his old Alice gear and his full canteen. After checking the kit for extra batteries, he stuffed that and the gun inside the roomy pockets in his ski jacket. In the glove compartment, he found his CQC-6 and slipped the knife onto his belt.

He climbed out of his old green truck, listening to the stillness of the winter woods, and shrugged into his jacket, zipping it. And he headed down the path. The layer of leaves concealed the rocky, uneven terrain beneath it.

The farther he went, the darker the storm grew. He continued on, his mind doubting his innate certainty that he knew where he was going. At this point, he was all in.

The grassy path grew clotted with rocks, then larger, smooth stones, then boulders that filled the area.

Yes! The stones. He had all but forgotten them.

The path, no longer distinguishable, had become a field of stones rising onto a hill and slick with frost. Night was falling, made more treacherous by the dropping temperatures. He pulled his coat more closely around his throat and felt the chain there—a gift from his mother on his graduation from William & Mary.

Only when lightning flashed in the distance did he see the James River—far down below, its surface mottled by the falling ice.

And only when it flashed again did he notice the house. Tucked within the primeval woods, built on a bluff overlooking the river, its chimney gently puffed white smoke. He moved forward, compelled by the hiss of sleet and the promise of shelter. Perhaps even the company of a stranger, who could explain what this place had been thirty years before.

When he drew within twenty feet of the front door, he saw the sharp descent to the riverbank below, a couple of hundred feet from the house. Another footpath followed down to that landing.

But none of that distracted him from the elation filling him as he took in the stone cottage before him.

The place was exactly as he remembered it.

It was *real.*

He walked up onto the porch and tapped gently at the door, eager to learn who lived there—to find any clue about why he was haunted by a place his parents had no memory of.

It broke his heart to consider the alternative: that they had lied to him.

He waited, stamping his feet to warm himself. It had to be down in the low twenties now.

He knocked again, harder this time, and the door opened with a creak that startled him. As the wind nudged the door open, he saw only an empty room, dark except for the roaring fire in the hearth. The outline of furniture draped with sheets told him the house was deserted—and had been for a while.

"Hello?"

No answer, no sound from inside. Only the persistent hiss of sleet and the thunder of the storm. He glanced around the porch and the immediate area beyond, but saw no footsteps in the frost at all. It was as if someone had started the fire and vanished.

He reached inside, feeling on the wall for a light switch, and flipped it on. A low-wattage bulb flickered to life from a lamp in the corner, illuminating the small room more clearly than the fire.

Excitement stole through him at what he was looking at. Yes—some aspects weren't identical. He didn't remember the details from recent decades. He remembered an ancient old house of stone.

He withdrew his gun, double-checking the safety before he tucked it in the back of his waistband. He walked inside, closing and barring the door behind him.

Emotions nearly overwhelmed him, but he set them aside and walked through the small house, making sure it was empty. He barred the back door.

And then he sank to the floor before the huge hearth. It could hold enough wood to warm a family and their servants through a cold night. It could entertain two rambunctious children for a rainy summer afternoon. As he watched the fire, the memories flooded him—he and Cassie playing in the hearth during the summer. His mother cooking dinner there, scrubbing the floor while Cassie's mother lay confined to her bed with a headache. Mr. Hastings, Cassie's grandfather, visiting his son and bringing trinkets and candies from ... he struggled to recall the name of the place where Papa had lived.

Rosalie.

Of course—the forgotten old plantation outside Williamsburg, said to have once been owned by a slave-trader, Rosalie had burned down over two hundred years before, killing both the owner and his daughter. So how could Papa have lived there?

His memories grew clearer, the longer he sat there.

He rose once more, looking around the room. This place seemed abandoned—the lamp might have been in style forty years before, just after World War II. That lamp, or its depressing dim light, he did not remember. The home itself was little changed since he had been there. But *when?*

He had grown up in Boston, of that much he was certain. He remembered its buildings, he remembered the apartment where they'd first lived, the house his father had built later.

But wait—had the apartment been in Boston? That, he wasn't sure of. And if he'd grown up in Boston, when could he possibly have lived here? Had he simply dreamed of the place—the little girl—preparing him for this hour?

Nonsense. Contrary to putting to bed any childish fantasy, each corner of this place awakened new memories in him.

He walked through the house again. Furnished but vacant, all of its bedroom furniture was covered with canvas drop cloths. The furniture in this room, even, was covered, except for the sofa before the hearth.

And the window seat.

He stopped before it, resting his hand on the solid oak frame. Who had built this home? The workmanship was fine carpentry.

The flash of a memory came to him—playing hide and seek with Cassie, and then finding her *inside* the window seat. He felt behind the back of the seat to see if he could still move it. He found the concealed latch and pressed it. The wooden frame of the seat loosened and he pulled it up. Dimly, he saw the stone stairs descending in a spiral below him into darkness.

You children, get out of there this minute!

The sound of his mother's voice rang in his memory.

He turned on his flashlight and pointed it down. Stone steps led in a tight corkscrew that, again, ultimately vanished into darkness.

He leaned in—this spiral staircase had to go down at least thirty feet. What in the world could be down there? A root cellar? His imagination ignited—a bomb shelter? Something left over from the Cold War?

He hesitated, closing the seat and turning. He walked to the front door and opened it, calling out: "Is anyone out there? Can I help?"

No one responded. At the back door, he turned his flashlight into the darkness. Only the thicket of trees, barren of greenery save for an occasional pine.

And then he called out. "Cassie! … Cassandra!"

Her name echoed in the persistent hiss of the storm.

He barred the door again and turned on the kitchen light, finding the same sense of abandonment. Cobwebs filled corners, and more than once he had to knock away a spider web.

No one lived in this home—yet the owner kept the electricity on. Had a homeless person started the fire and then abandoned the home when they saw his approach?

And had he actually called her name—without thinking, as if believing she were suddenly there with him? No; he called it as he'd done, so many times before.

All the windows were shuttered from the inside. Returning to the window seat, he opened it, then hesitated. He found a supply of candles in the kitchen and slipped them into another pocket. He had plenty of waxed matches. Any Boy Scout could build a fire without matches, but they were handy to have.

He climbed into the window seat and began descending the stairs. He pointed the flashlight below to get a perspective on what awaited him. It looked like an optical illusion.

After descending for well over a minute, he began counting the stairs. More than five hundred steps later, he arrived at a stone-paved landing. His boot nudged something off the bottom stair, and he pointed the flashlight downward.

A child's doll—a rag baby doll.

He crouched to look at it lying over his open palm, then rose. Perhaps eight inches long, the homemade doll's eyes were glass beads; a faded, tattered rosebud mouth was embroidered below. Did he remember this doll? He'd examined so many historic artifacts in Williamsburg, it was hard to say.

He slipped it into his pocket. When he got back, he'd take it to the college. It looked like quite a find. He turned away from the stairs, pointing his flashlight around. He was in a cave—its ceiling so high, he could see nothing above.

Areas of Virginia were filled with caves, and he wondered what lay here. Was this some sort of historic escape route from the house?

Perhaps the property had been a stop on the Underground Railroad, he thought, intrigued.

The *way* underground railroad.

"Over five hundred steps?" he muttered. Steeper than the Statue of Liberty.

Where the hell was he, a quarter of a mile underground?

He flashed the light around him. Stone pavement as far as he could see.

An enormous boulder overhead appeared in the flashlight beam, marking an entryway to a short passage lit with a faint light from beyond, its source unknown. Stone lined the entryway, as natural as the path beneath his feet. He continued on, into the passageway.

In another ten feet, the sky opened up above him.

The *sky?*

As he walked forward into the cool splendor of the place, his mouth fell open in awesome wonder. He studied what lay above. Not at all the sky, only sixty or eighty feet up, still well underground. But despite its vast, sparkling surface, it didn't appear to be an ordinary cavern ceiling, either. What he otherwise might have guessed to be gemstones or minerals—perhaps quartz or calcite or feldspar—flickered with dynamic life, as if they were alive.

The sparkling wasn't random. Each star had a pulse of sorts, beating in steady rhythm. Yet few beat in unison.

What he saw was impossible.

It looked like the darkest, clearest night sky he'd ever seen, filled with innumerable celestial bodies—none of them arranged in any ordinary constellation.

But it was no sky. More of a firmament, separating the world above from this world below.

What the hell was this place?

This was the source of the dim light. The stars were grouped together in breathtaking, animated asterisms—resembling family trees. Two stars at the top of each, with varying numbers of bodies below, connected with other groupings by lines that became visible only occasionally.

Some celestial patterns were fixed in almost blinding silver-whiteness, pulsing with even, slow peace. Others, in a pale, erratic flicker—still others, simply like slow, dully colored traffic lights.

Other asterisms held a tarnished copper or dull gray cast, as if dying off. In these, the heartbeat pulses were evident and weak. These constellations, he found deeply unsettling.

As his eyes grew accustomed to the darkness, he saw the entire place was an endless cavern, its eerie sky continuing on much farther than he could see, along with its high stone walls and recesses he could see built within the walls.

The unearthly experience filled him with awe and terror, and he swallowed, inching backward toward the passageway that would take him out of this place.

A sudden voice startled him, and he dropped the flashlight. It rolled out of his grasp, and he grabbed after it.

"Hello, Mr. Miller."

He grasped the cold cylinder of the flashlight and came to his feet. It was the sort of detached, friendly sound he heard when he called the bank's "637" line for time and temperature. The sound of a computer.

He found the flashlight, but it wasn't working, and he slipped it in his pocket.

His pupils grew larger, adjusting to the darkness. The dim light seemed brighter, the underground sky an inky midnight blue. He saw no one—and nothing to explain the voice. Only this subterranean labyrinth that seemed to go on forever. And then he froze.

Had someone said his name?

He walked toward the voice as he perceived the glow of a lamp in the next turn in the labyrinth. A navy cylinder rose from the floor into the underground heavens; he could not see where it vanished above. Within its face, perhaps as high as his chest, was set a small cavity the size of a shoebox. An unearthly blue paleness lit the cavity, and he drew closer.

"Good evening, Mr. Miller. Verify your identity."

The voice came from the cavity before him; dispassionate, androgynous, nonhuman.

"Who are you?"

"Verify your identity."

An area at the recessed surface of the cavity glowed purple momentarily, showing the silhouette of a human hand.

He lifted his hand and placed it vertically against the fading purple oval. The texture surprised him: light, damn near gaseous. When he would have withdrawn, a gel held him fast. He waited, tense as he heard a soft humming within the cavity.

"DNA match. Robert Juste Miller."

The surface glowed red for a split-second as it released him, then returned to its pale blue. "Born aboard the *Swallow* in the Atlantic Ocean in 1742."

"No, that has to be an ancestor," he said, as if it made perfect sense to argue with the machine. This machine that seemed to have sprung whole from stone, over a thousand feet below the ground.

And yet, its technology was so sophisticated as to seem without substance at all.

"Insert your artifact."

"My what?"

The cavity still glowed. The purple hand silhouette had morphed into a series of shifting kaleidoscope designs, leaving him no clue what it wanted.

He turned away from the machine, walking farther into the cave. It seemed an endless labyrinth, and he quickly turned back, to avoid becoming hopelessly lost underground.

As he returned, he glanced again toward the sky—noticing something new. Since that moment he'd inserted his hand as identification, one of the constellations had lit up and grown larger, blinking with heavy urgency. He paused, investigating. A grouping of dark yellow, with just five stars—as if two parents and three children. One of the parent stars, blood-red, blinked slowly, heavily—in unison with his own heartbeat.

Not far from that grouping, other constellations, large and small, above and below, in varying colors, had begun to blink in unison with the small family. Spears of fiery light flew between various stars, mutely announcing relationships between these stars.

"Insert your artifact."

The cavity spoke again, guiding him back, and he approached it.

"What's with these stars?" He didn't exactly expect a reply.

"The labyrinth firmament represents families such as your own. Insert your artifact."

He looked up again. Indeed, as he watched, he felt he understood. The darker ruddy shades represented families in turmoil. The more silvery-white the stars grew, the more in unison the pulse. Perhaps those peaceful families were those who had gone on to their reward.

"Insert your artifact."

"What artifact?"

"Why are you here, Mr. Miller?"

"I don't know."

"What brought you here?"

I can't sleep anymore. The memories keep me awake. Memories of a life I'm told I never lived.

Again, the voice repeated the same command. As if it somehow knew it would move him along.

Artifact? What did he have on him that could be considered an artifact? He thought of the Phi Beta Kappa key that he kept on his keychain with his dog tags. They weren't what he would consider artifacts.

And in one of those odd moments that happen rarely in life, he remembered the gift his mother had given him so long ago. Again, he touched the silver chain inside his collar, withdrawing it. As his fingers grazed the small, Lucite rectangle on the chain, the light in the cavity grew brighter and shifted into the exact shape of the stamp.

The jewelry was a custom piece given him by his mother— his most prized possession, a priceless artifact enclosed in Lucite and mounted on silver. His mother had taken the iconic, the meaningful, a symbol of the fight most dear to him, and made it virtually indestructible. Its timeless modernity reminded him of her.

He refused to remove the piece from his neck, and instead

leaned near the cavity, placing the artifact against the same surface where he'd placed his hand. The voice spoke again.

"You have presented a British tax stamp originating from May of 1765. Travel to this period is one-way. Accessible return is found on Rosalie Plantation and requires an artifact from your present time period."

Travel to this *period?*

He almost laughed. He was a military man, the son of a Navy commando. He was a rock.

So how could such a suggestion be real? How could the very existence of the place where he stood be real? What he saw was impossible. In all the sophisticated military training exercises he'd done, he'd never seen anything like it. It was as if an ultra-advanced supercomputer had been built into—or sprung from—ancient stones far beneath the earth.

He had read enough about DNA research to understand that what stood before him was a supercomputer that only a few within government intelligence would have access to. He was eighty miles from Langley, so that was unlikely, but what else could explain this? Perhaps when he was a child, his father had been stationed here as part of his work with the Navy? No one would have ever expected this high-tech wizardry, if they looked at the simple old cottage above.

And he thought of the house on the surface—the home where he'd imagined spending his childhood.

He had to be dreaming. There was no other explanation.

But there was. He thought of all the therapists he'd seen over the years; the clergy who had reassured him that he was simply working too hard, that the hallucinations were perfectly normal under such duress.

He took a deep breath. "What sort of artifact?"

The machine didn't reply, and he considered. The 9mm was from the late '50s. He rummaged in his pockets and found some change, his old Phi Beta Kappa key which he'd carried for ten years now, and a receipt from the store where he'd stopped that morning to buy gas and coffee.

"Answer me. Are you saying you can enable time travel?"

"The artifact enables travel to the destination. Your return must be arranged by another artifact presented at the portal on Rosalie Plantation."

"Why? Why can't I come back this way? What portal?"

"The labyrinth is inaccessible to you during the destination time period."

"Why?"

"Anomalies exist. The labyrinth is inaccessible to you. Travel cannot be arranged at this time without a return artifact. Good day."

Anomalies, he mused. What could that mean?

"Wait," he said. "What about this?"

Curious about what might happen, he produced his PBK key. No one he'd ever known displayed the key, seen as an expression of vanity and arrogance. But it broke his mother's heart that he didn't display it, so he carried it as a good luck charm. He'd been awarded membership on the 200th anniversary of the Society's inception at William & Mary.

He glanced up at the small array of stars overhead and pressed the key into the reader. The entire grouping of stars froze and began to pale. Alarmed, he drew the key away.

"Anomalies exist and the year 1976 is inaccessible to you. Travel cannot be arranged at this time without a return—"

"Will this work?" He pressed the receipt into the reader.

"Acceptable return passage. Please agree to terms of service."

"To what?"

"Please agree to terms of service."

"Come again?"

The purple hand in the reader appeared again, a signpost for the slow.

He rested his hand there, surprised at the sudden rush of a voice in his mind. The voice spoke quickly in legalese—like a car ad on the radio. Occasionally it slowed down to emphasize a point. *Live within the time. Maintain historic integrity. Leave no footprint behind.*

And, at the very conclusion, a direct command.

"Mr. Miller, under no circumstances will you attempt to change the historical events of the past into which you travel. State your full name to signify your acceptance of these terms."

His blood was pounding in his ears. *How* was he hearing all this in his own mind? No one was speaking, not even the machine before him. It was all, literally, in his own head.

"State your full name to signify your acceptance—"

"Robert Juste Miller."

In a moment, another cylinder plunged from the subterranean heavens like a bolt of lightning, then solidified and locked into the stone beside the reader. A chamber opened within it, revealing a locker of sorts. Clothing hung there, and he withdrew it, noticing a card hanging behind it.

Colonial man's cape, shirt, vest, breeches, undergarments, socks, shoes, pistol, etc., c. 1765. Haversack to neutralize return artifact.

"Neutralize how so?"

"Rendering unusable an anachronistic artifact during passage."

He withdrew the contents of the chamber and quickly changed clothes. He kept only the receipt, his chain, and the doll, which he quickly slipped into the haversack along with the rest. He wasn't sure why, but he knew that doll had shown up in his path for a reason.

He looked for a long moment at the Phi Beta Kappa key.

It didn't belong in the past.

Don't take it.

He remembered the deathly stillness of his own constellation as the machine reacted to the possibility of him traveling into his own past. And he remembered the pride beaming on his mother's face that day he'd worn the key at his graduation. He could not leave it behind and risk losing it.

He shoved it deep into the bag. The rest, including his 9mm and car keys, he placed within the chamber and closed it.

"Present the artifact to comply with terms of service."

He looked around at the place where he stood. Cool, faintly damp, like any other cave, its supercomputers operated nearly silently—unlike anything he'd ever seen.

He thought of his mother and father, in their home in Beacon Hill. He thought of Cameron—wouldn't he love to hear about this. The thought of telling Cam unexpectedly made him uneasy. Would even Cam believe this?

He thought of the other men he'd served with, and those he'd never known—mocked and spat upon, on their return from Southeast Asia. He thought of those who hadn't returned.

He owed them this much.

And he thought of his most recent therapist, ready to prescribe him the latest psychotropic drug. His nerves steeled in response.

Dreaming, dead, or insane, he was ready to move on.

"Present the artifact to comply with terms of service."

He lifted the Lucite-encased stamp to the face of the reader. A blinding brightness, a deafening crash in his head, and he remembered no more.

꙳

A snarling growl awakened him. He opened his eyes, disoriented. Where was he? And when did he get a dog?

He lay flat on his back on a rug, and his hand rested on the roughhewn plank wood floor beside the rug. Without moving and alarming the dog, he looked around the room.

He was back in the old stone home on the James River, in daylight. The shutters were closed, but light flooded the cracks.

He gave a great sigh—the whole thing *had* been a bad dream. He must've collapsed here last night, and the owners just arrived.

"Hello? Is anyone there?" he called—adding, after a moment, "Is this dog friendly?"

He lay only a few feet from the window seat—a heavy drapery was drawn around it. The room was cold, the fire on the hearth burned out.

He raised his head just slightly, to peer at the dog, who lay across the room, ready to pounce. A mutt of dubious origins, he inhaled on a growl that gave him an almost comical snort.

When he laughed despite himself, the dog bared his teeth, dripping saliva.

He inched slowly toward the window seat. If he could get behind the drapery, he stood a good chance of eluding the dog down the staircase.

The dog leapt toward him, and in that same moment he scrambled into the window seat. He shut the drapes just as the dog's jaws clamped over his thigh. He gritted his teeth against the pain, forcefully pushing the dog away. He balanced on the frame surrounding the window seat. Yanking up the seat to lower himself into the stairwell, he stopped short instead.

There was no stairwell.

Beneath the seat was a solid, immovable stone base. His breath went shallow.

Return must be arranged by another artifact presented at the portal on Rosalie Plantation. The labyrinth is inaccessible to you.

He took a slow, deep breath. True enough, if he'd dreamed the entire bizarre trip down the window seat, nothing would be here.

But how, if it were a dream, had he known the seat was movable? He knew—he *remembered*—that there was a small metal catch that, when pushed, had opened the seat into a place where Cassie had hidden when they played.

There was nothing beneath this window seat, not even storage space.

The dog growled and snapped at the drapes. He pushed at it. He grabbed his bag and used that to shove the dog away.

His *bag*? What bag?

He noted the worn brown bag around his neck and one arm—the haversack.

He looked at himself. *Colonial man's cape, shirt, vest, breeches... c. 1765. Haversack to neutralize return artifact.*

He looked into the bag, finding the pistol, the receipt, his key, a leather hat, and the makings of ammunition for the pistol. Along with a doll that was now fresh and new. Berry red lips—sewn there by a little girl's hand—curved into a smile below button eyes.

This item that he had recognized as an authentic colonial artifact was nearly new.

The dog bit his ankle.

"Damn, buddy! You're not doing much to endear yourself, here, man's best friend."

He had to try to outrun the dog.

He parted the drapes, faked throwing an item, and said, "Fetch!"

The dog looked in the other direction, and he darted toward the back door, holding the bag between him and the dog.

The dog was smart enough, though, and he quickly realized the ruse. He had only a few seconds to make it to the door. He drew back the door and went through. The dog was nipping at his heels, and he gently but firmly closed the door, using the bag to push the snarling beast back inside.

His nimbleness crossing the room surprised him; he was in tip-top shape, but he was no spring chicken. But just now, he'd moved with the agility he'd known when he first joined the Navy.

He turned, taken aback at the man who stood there, dressed as he was, in colonial clothing. Many years older, his hair was like a froth of whipped cream.

"So you're here," he said, in a faint brogue. "Welcome, and begone."

"I don't understand. Who are you? Do you know me?"

"You cannot be here. Go on to William and Mary. You know that's why you're here. The Frenchman's map."

He couldn't respond for a moment or two. The mystery of the Frenchman's map had plagued him for all of his life. Even as a child, reading about the restoration of Williamsburg, he had wondered about the unknown military man who had enabled the historic treasure that Colonial Williamsburg was.

"Yes," he said at last.

"There's a boat waiting below. It will be a hard journey, but you've spent your life preparing for this. You know you must be back within 24 hours."

"That's impossible."

"But you must—or you will remain here. You heard that in the terms of service."

"I also heard that if you have a connection to a destination, that period is extended."

The old man tilted his head shrewdly, frowning at him. At the corner of his eye was a fresh, jagged wound.

"Where did you come by that? Did someone attack you? Who are you?"

"Henderson's the name. I'll tell you how it happened, then. I disregarded the terms of service. I tried to right a wrong."

From the woods came the cry of a young girl. "Uncle Malcolm!"

The child's voice stirred something within him he'd never known, with all the years he'd learned to safeguard his men, far beyond his dutiful protection of his mother, even as a child, during the many times his father was away from home.

This visceral knotting in his gut came from pure instinct.

"Who is that child? What's your relationship to her?"

"I am her guardian. Beyond that you can know nothing. Now go."

"Wait."

"She comes even now. You must go. Your extended time here has been approved. Go straightaway to Williamsburg—do not for any reason stop at Rosalie. Not yet."

"I—I believe this may belong to her." He reached into his bag for the doll and held it out to Henderson.

The old man gazed sadly at the doll, then, finally, took it from him. "Yes. Go around the cottage, now, and take the path down to the river. You are in an anomaly."

"Is she my—"

She cannot see you—she will know you, deep in her heart."

He looked back once more at the old man.

"Just as you know her."

Her voice was close, now, and despite his every instinct to rush to the child and take her in his arms, to reassure her she was safe, he turned away from her, his chest tight with emotion. Instinctively, he knew she was all alone, in this backwoods colonial wilderness. The man he'd met had something to do with the labyrinth—he surely couldn't be much of a guardian.

But he had seemed kind, and shown concern for her.

He gritted his teeth and turned down the path toward the small boat waiting for him.

"I'm here, Juliana," said the old man, with grandfatherly kindness. "I'm here."

As is your father, he echoed silently—then deserted her.

MAJOR CHARACTERS IN THE TRELAWNEYS OF WILLIAMSBURG (SPOILER FREE)

In alphabetical order

Ashanti Adams (Series). Husband of Camisha and a leader for freedom for blacks.

George Adams (Series). Son of Rashall Adams.

Rashall Adams (*Immortal, Forever*). Ashanti's son, a sea captain.

Jim "Jimmy" Bainbridge (*Immortal*). Nan's abusive, long-term partner, the man who traumatized Marley.

Camisha Carlyle (Series). Rachel's fabulous lifelong friend and champion as well as her conscience—an attorney.

Godfrey Hastings (Series). Second in command to Grey Trelawney, Hastings manages Rosalie.

Hannah "Nan" Hastings (*Immortal, Forever*). Grandmother of Rachel, Marley, and Juliana Miller. Cassandra Miller's mother, once married to Godfrey Hastings' son, William.

Merrilea "Marley" Hastings (*Immortal, Forever*). Heroine of *Immortal*, younger sister of Rachel. An archaeologist and historian at Colonial Williamsburg.

Malcolm Henderson, Mary Van Kirk (Series). Guides for those who travel in time.

James Manning (Series). Overseer at Rosalie, later a successful sea merchant.

John "Jack" Manning (Series). A son of James Manning.

Cassandra Miller (Series). Mother of Rachel, Marley, and Juliana Miller.

Juliana Miller (Series). Rachel and Marley's sister, Hastings' great-granddaughter.

Robert Miller (Series). Father of Rachel, Marley, and Juliana Miller. A William & Mary history professor.

Max Sheppard (Series). Adopted father of Rachel, and the wealthy owner of a computer empire.

Rachel Sheppard (Series). Camisha Carlyle's best friend and the heroine of *Tender*—a marketing director.

Bronson Trelawney (Series). Thomas's son, sea captain, hero of *Immortal*.

Dan Freeman Trelawney (Series). Married to Ruth, the pastor and leader of the Trelawney extended family.

Emily Trelawney (Series). Daughter of Grey Trelawney, said to haunt the Trelawney home in modern-day Colonial Williamsburg.

Grey Trelawney (Series). The son of Thomas Trelawney, hero of *Tender*, undergoing a conscience of crisis.

Hastings "Hasty" Trelawney (*Immortal, Forever*). Youngest son of Ruth Freeman-Trelawney

Jennie Dandridge Trelawney (*Tender*). Wife of Thomas, mother of Bronson.

Ruth Freeman Trelawney (Series). Enslaved on Rosalie, a good friend to the Miller sisters, the Trelawney's schoolmistress and the chronicler of *The Trelawneys of Williamsburg*.

Thomas Trelawney (Series). Patriarch of the Trelawney clan, civic leader, and father of Grey and Bronson.

www.ingramcontent.com/pod-product-compliance
Lightning Source LLC
Chambersburg PA
CBHW031314280626
47169CB00019B/1383